Born in Newport, Monmouthshire, in 1931, Leslie Thomas is the son of a sailor who was lost at sea in 1943. His boyhood in an orphanage is evoked in *This Time Next Week*, published in 1964. At sixteen, he became a reporter before going on to do his national service. He won worldwide acclaim with his bestselling novel *The Virgin Soldiers*, which has achieved international sales of over four million copies. In 2005, Leslie Thomas recieved an OBE for services to literature.

Also by Leslie Thomas

Fiction
The Virgin Soldiers
Orange Wednesday
The Love Beach
Come to the War
His Lordship
Onward Virgin Soldiers
Arthur McCann And All his Women
The Man with the Power
Tropic of Ruislip
Stand Up Virgin Soldiers
Dangerous Davies: The Last Detective
Bare Nell
Ormerod's Landing
That Old Gang of Mine
The Adventures of Goodnight and Loving
Dangerous in Love
Orders for New York
The Loves and Journeys of Revolving Jones
Arrivals and Departures
Dangerous by Moonlight
Running Away
The Complete Dangerous Davies
Kensington Heights
Chloe's Song
Dangerous Davies and the Lonely Heart
Other Times
Waiting for the Day
Dover Beach

Non Fiction
This Time Next Week
Some Lovely Islands
The Hidden Places of Britain
My World of Islands
In My Wildest Dreams

THE DEAREST
AND THE BEST

Leslie Thomas

arrow books

Reissued by Arrow Books in 2005

3 5 7 9 10 8 6 4

First published in the United Kingdom in 1984 by Methuen
First published in paperback in 1985 by Penguin Books

Arrow Books
The Random House Group Limited
20 Vauxhall Bridge Road, London, SW1V 2SA

Random House Australia (Pty) Limited
20 Alfred Street, Milsons Point, Sydney,
New South Wales 2061, Australia

Random House New Zealand Limited
18 Poland Road, Glenfield
Auckland 10, New Zealand

Random House (Pty) Limited
Endulini, 5a Jubilee Road, Parktown 2193, South Africa

Random House Publishers India Private Limited
301 World Trade Tower, Hotel Intercontinental Grand Complex,
Barakhamba Lane, New Delhi 110 001, India

The Random House Group Limited Reg. No. 954009

www.randomhouse.co.uk

A CIP catalogue record for this book is available from the British
Library

Printed and bound in Great Britain by Clays Ltd, St Ives PLC

ISBN 9780099474227 (from Jan 2007)
ISBN 0 09 947422 0

Typeset by SX Composing DTP, Rayleigh, Essex

The Random House Group Limited supports The Forest Stewardship
Council (FSC®), the leading international forest certification organisation.
Our books carrying the FSC label are printed on FSC® certified paper.
FSC is the only forest certification scheme endorsed by the leading
environmental organisations, including Greenpeace. Our
paper procurement policy can be found at
www.randomhouse.co.uk/environment

'We have nothing to fear in the part of the inhabitants. They are a dull people who are absolutely ignorant of the use of arms.'

Intelligence report to the
French Government in 1767
on the prospects of an
invasion of England.

'I have decided to begin to prepare for, and if necessary to carry out, an invasion of England.'

Adolf Hitler, 1940.

One

After a deep and bitter winter, the worst of the century, April of 1940 was chill and rainy in the South of England, but during the first days of May the weather altered and a pale, early summer arrived.

On the morning of 3 May, at five o'clock, a grey ship was off the estuary of the Thames, passing the Nore Light, moving delicately between minefields, in fragmented mist. Windows ashore caught the first brushes of the sun, flashing the reflections back out to sea like morse lamp signals. A few of the soldiers, weary and crammed on the deck, cheered untidily.

'London,' announced one of the men to his neighbour. He pointed towards the hazy mouth of the river as he might indicate a vague and distant road. 'Just up there.' All night they had sat, propped against each other, exchanging no more than a grunt. Neither knew the other's name; they simply belonged to the same defeated army. The second man had lost three fingers in Norway, and he now stared at the bandages as though contemplating an ice-cream cone. 'Can't say I ever wanted to go to London,' he answered.

'Where you from then?' asked the first soldier, surprised. After the night of silence he seemed set now on making conversation.

'Hampshire, I'm from.' He said it as if it were a far

country. 'In the New Forest. I'm a dairyman.' He regarded his hand again. 'I'm going to find it hard milking with these.'

'How many did you lose?' asked the first soldier. He looked at the other man sharply. 'Mates, I mean, not fingers.'

'Oh, men. I don't know, rightly. Everybody got split up. Half the others, I don't even know where they got to in the end.'

In the next space along the deck, wedged between depth charges and a lifeboat, was a group of Scottish infantrymen. One of them, his rifle still on his large shoulder, began to play a small squeeze-box concertina, slowly, as if it were an effort. It was a song they had sung on the outward voyage, 'Norraway O'er the Foam'. No one sang it now. The tune idled while the destroyer slid through the dull silver water. It had become a lament. Odd ones among the crouched and khaki men began to feel the growing sun, undoing the ponderous greatcoats and the thick necks of their battledress blouses. Gratefully they squinted up at the watery warmth. There were the old soldiers, soused in experience, who had fashioned enough room on the hard plates to stretch fully out and lay like dead. The real dead were three decks below. Rifles had been religiously stacked but scattered about were other ragged mounds of equipment; packs, ammunition boxes, and strange salvage for an evacuating army, buckets, footballs and an occasional flag or banner. There were Frenchmen aboard also, Alpine soldiers of the Blue Brigade, their skis piled, and Polish infantry, sharp-cheeked with flat eyes. Purkiss, the man from the New Forest, had wondered, but only vaguely, how the Poles had got to Norway. His knowledge of geography was thin and he thought they might even have walked there when the Germans bombed and occupied their homeland.

Every man knew that things had gone badly wrong, that they had been mismanaged to the point of betrayal; fools had told them where to go and what to do and they had trusted as soldiers trust. 'Be glad to see my old woman,' said the Londoner, still eyeing the horizon as if he expected to spot her waving.

'So will I,' agreed Purkiss. 'I don't know what she'll say about coming home without these fingers. I know'd men get fingers and toes cut off in the fields, even fishing at sea, but frostbite . . . I never know'd anybody to have frostbite.'

After half an hour the wide entrance of the Thames lay shining astern, and as the morning expanded, the vessel edged along the low Kent coast and turned into the River Medway. Sly patches of mist loitered on the channel and a flight of herons moved over the ship like silent bombers. Purkiss pointed them out with his bandaged hand and smiled a mute recognition. 'Geese,' said the Londoner firmly.

An order came eerily over the ship's loudspeaker but it meant nothing to the soldiers and they cared nothing either. Rumours had spread through the naval stewards during the night that some of the army officers were almost mutinous. Angry, raised voices had been heard from the mess. Some of the young soldiers had eavesdropped like children listening to quarrelling parents. Now, almost as soon as the destroyer had eased into the middle anchorage of the river, a navy tender appeared from the Medway shore and an army officer, at the centre of a group which appeared on deck, prepared to go aboard it. Others shook his hand before he climbed down the ladder.

'That's Mr Lovatt,' said Purkiss with slow surprise. 'He lives where I live. I know'd his family well. Didn't even see he was here. There's strange, us both going to Norway.'

He and the Londoner watched the officer, an artillery captain, climb down to the launch, and then followed it as it feathered away across the sallow water. Standing amidships, James Lovatt regarded the low, slate-coloured shore ahead as he might regard hostile territory.

The leading seaman in command of the boat knew there was a lot wrong and he said nothing beyond 'Good morning, sir,' but in his turn surveyed the land ahead as if approaching it for the first time and vaguely trying to fix a seamark.

It was not far. They pulled in against a jetty, green with weed, its decrepit timbers bolstered and blocked by oddments of wood and metal, so that it might last at least through the first year of the war. The leading seaman climbed up the rusty-runged ladder first and looked about him at the vacant place; the jetty, a patch of scruffy beach, a single ghostly building.

'Did you order transport, sir?' he asked Lovatt, peering along the broken road.

'No, I didn't. I'll get a taxi. They must have a phone here.'

The leading hand was surprised. 'Yes, I see, sir. Well, there's one in the canteen. Right ahead. They're open now. I saw the old woman there a bit earlier on. Got the pennies, sir? For the phone?'

Lovatt could not help a grin. 'No. As a matter of fact I haven't,' he admitted. 'I left all my small change in Norway.'

The man grinned back in a relieved way and handed over two pennies. 'Don't worry, I'll charge it to the comforts fund, sir,' he said. He saluted and returned to his boat. James Lovatt walked above the crevices of the jetty. It creaked beneath his feet. Seaweed smell filled his nostrils. There was such an emptiness about the place, such a neglect, that he once again felt magically angry. It was as if nobody cared a damn, as if they had all gone home and forgotten about the war. He had never been there before and apart from its location on the map he knew nothing about it. He wondered what it had once been, why the rotting jetty was there at all, so far from any habitation except the single brick and wooden building towards which he was walking.

As he approached the door a woman in a flowered overall came out carrying with difficulty a wooden 'Forces Canteen' sign. She was small, almost dwarfish, and she saw him gratefully. 'Just in time,' she squeaked. 'Will you hang it up? I can't reach it without the blessed steps.' James took the board from her and lifted it so that it hooked on an outstretched iron arm. 'Have to take it in at night,' she explained. 'It's only just been done and if you leave it out around here the paint peels off in no time. It's the salt. And I reckon the paint's not much good either.' Her stockings were grotesquely wrinkled around her square legs. She gave him a second glance and then squeezed her eyes together to make out the shape of the ship in the river. 'You're nice and early,' she said.

Lovatt went in. There was an atmosphere of damp and disuse about the place, but at the same time a sense of its having once been of some importance. There was a big, ornate fireplace, empty and gaping like a theatre-mouth, with some sort of wooden shield or coat of arms at its centre, but with the embossing rubbed away. The canteen counter with its tea urn, just rousing itself to produce some steam, was carved and corniched wood, apparently part of some special décor. Lovatt did not care enough to ask. The woman said: 'Tea, is it? Coffee's not ready yet.' He said tea and looked around for the phone.

'I want to call for a taxi,' he told her.

'It's on the wall, in that funny box,' she said, pointing to a booth in the far corner. Steam from the tea urn was curiously bearding her heavy face, making her look like one of the Seven Dwarfs. He walked across to the telephone. The frosted windows of the booth were engraved with leaves and long-tailed birds. Inside he found the number of the taxi and used the leading seaman's two pennies to put into the box.

'He takes his time,' the woman called across the room. 'He's got one of those gas bags now and he makes that the excuse.'

As she spoke the call was answered and the taxi driver promised to be there as soon as he got the gas bag filled. Lovatt replaced the earpiece and walked back into the canteen. His mug of tea was waiting, a curl of vapour on its edge. She had change for a pound note although the tea was only a penny. For the first time the woman noticed his fatigue. 'Been far?' she inquired.

'Far enough,' he said.

She pursed her lips. 'Not supposed to ask, are we,' she observed. 'Not that *I'd* tell. And there's no German spies around here. Hardly anybody at all around here, let alone German spies. You can see. I don't know what use this place is, except it's my war work.'

He made no attempt to unravel the logic. 'Norway,' he said. To hell with it. Why shouldn't they be told?

'Oh yes,' she nodded vaguely. 'Yes, that Norway.' She wiped the wet ring of his tea mug from the counter. 'That's right, Norway. Saw it on the news at the pictures in Gravesend last week. Went to see *The Thief of Baghdad*, Sabu, that little Indian boy. It looked very pretty, I must say, all that snow and Christmas trees and everything.'

Why he bothered to continue he did not know. It was as if he had to tell someone. 'We were fighting there,' he informed her. And added: 'The Germans.'

'I saw,' she reassured him. 'I saw all about it.' She put her purple elbows on the counter. Behind her, above a pigmented mirror, a cardboard banner advised: 'For your throat's sake smoke CRAVEN "A".' She poured herself a cup of tea and had lit a Park Drive. She belatedly offered him one but he refused. 'They had that Magnet Line on the news, too,' she said. 'You know, those French soldiers even *sleep* there, in proper *bedrooms*. Very comfy it looked too, and they have everything they want, even a little railway to carry them and their guns and things about. I can't see Hitler blowing that up. The man what does the news, that one with the voice, you know . . . he said it was imp . . . imp . . .'

'Impregnable?' suggested Lovatt. He had finished

his tea and now backed towards the door smiling stiffly. 'That's the word they usually use about the Maginot Line. Impregnable.'

'That's the very word.' She saw he was getting out. 'Going to be a nice day,' she forecast. 'They say it's going to be a beautiful summer.'

He got out into the thin morning air with a sense of relief. There were millions like her. Millions. The beach was small and unkempt, a handful of gulls hopefully turning over specks of debris. The Medway slid, grey and quiet, up the shingle. He could see the warship and realized it would not be long before the boats would be bringing others ashore. He walked along the weedy road to see at what distance he might spot the taxi and saw to his surprise that, at one side, embedded in deeper weeds, was a section of railway line. For no reason other than that he had time to squander, he followed the rusted, half concealed track and found that it came to an intended end where the foundations and part of the uprights of a railway buffer still remained.

'Queen Victoria and Prince Albert used to come along that line,' said a voice. Lovatt turned. A spruce man in a stiff white shirt had appeared from the canteen. He looked alert and solid; he might at one time have been a sailor.

'So that's what it is,' Lovatt nodded. 'I was wondering.'

'I came to tell you that the taxi is on his way, sir,' said the man. 'He just rang up to say.' His eyes moved along the railway line. 'Called it Port Victoria,' he said. 'When Queen Victoria was going off in the royal yacht to visit the German side of the family the royal train would come down from London to here and they'd get on the boat at the jetty. It was built specially. There's all sorts of bits and pieces, like relics, in there.' He nodded towards the canteen. 'That used to be a kind of waiting-room and where all the big nobs would say goodbye or welcome her back if it was raining or the yacht was a bit delayed.'

They had begun walking back along the broken road. 'Strange bit of the country this,' said James. He wondered how a man like that could tolerate such a woman. 'All a bit mysterious, isn't it. I've never been here before.'

'Marshes and suchlike,' agreed the man. 'Miles of river bank and ponds and odd bits of beach, like this. They used to store ammunition along here in the Great War. Just up the river a bit you can see the buildings. They've got a notice warning you not to strike lucifers. Lucifers! And there are some stone gun pits built donkey's years ago when they thought Napoleon was coming.' They had reached the fringe of the beach now. 'Well, he won't be long,' the man added a little awkwardly. 'Ten minutes, probably. Do you want another cup of tea, sir? The wife said you'd been in Norway.' He looked concerned. 'Not that she'd repeat it.'

'I'll just wait here,' said Lovatt. 'The sun's coming out properly now. It will be a nice change.'

'Yes, I expect it will. For you,' agreed the man. He turned to go, then stopped on a thought. Striding to a pile of timber, the prow of a derelict boat, and some corroded machinery, all beneath a tarpaulin, he extracted an old deck chair and brushed down the faded stripes with his hand. 'Might as well have a seat while you wait,' he suggested. 'It's dry and it's not dirty.'

Lovatt grinned gratefully. 'Good idea,' he agreed. The man, like a batman, set the chair up and made sure it was safe from collapse. He turned it to face the pale but pleasant sun. Lovatt sat carefully on the chair and laughed. It seemed weeks since he had laughed. 'Just like old times,' he told the man. 'All I need now is a bucket and spade.'

The man regarded him seriously. He could see the wear in the young man's face, the dark-lined skin, the weary eyes. 'You have a bit of a rest, sir,' he said. He turned to go back towards the canteen. 'After Norway I expect you could do with it.'

It was amazing, sitting there – to be *there* in England – on that growing May morning, the fragile sun coming through the weft of clouds; seabirds calling in their wild and vacant way. Staring across the water, Lovatt realized the oddness of it, heard again the crack of guns, echoes from only days before; the cries of his men in the cries of the gulls. Then the silence and his weariness made him drop into sleep. He lay in the old deck chair, crumpled in his battledress, his officer's boots socketed into the sand. His face was still unrelaxed in sleep, his already thinning fair hair lay wispily over his white forehead. He was twenty-five years of age. Before the war he had been a junior partner in his father's dull firm of solicitors at Winchester in Hampshire. He had been married in 1937 to a girl he had known in his home village of Binford since childhood. His life, until now, had been unremarkable.

The taxi driver from Gravesend found him slumped when he arrived ten minutes later, and stood hesitating, as one might when confronted with a sleeping child. He was wearing a black, peaked cap and he pushed it back on his head in his uncertainty. He was not a decisive man and he began looking around for possible help. There was only emptiness and the canteen was too far for the trouble of walking, so he leaned forward and timidly tugged at Lovatt's sleeve. Lovatt woke up rudely, sitting abruptly upright, shouting and reaching for the flap of his revolver holster.

'No!' howled the taxi driver. 'No, sir!' Staggering back, he caught one heel in the other instep and fell into a sitting position on the sand. He remained there clownishly, his legs astride, his hands held up before his face. Lovatt stared at him, his fingers still on the butt of the revolver. 'Your taxi, sir,' trembled the man.

They walked up the short strand together, the officer apologizing, the taxi driver now, oddly, comforting him. 'Didn't realize you was back in England, eh, sir?' he said. 'Back home.' He thought of another excuse. 'And the cap, sir,' he said touching the peak. 'Looks a bit like a German cap, I expect.'

His vehicle, halted where the disused road ceased being merely rough and became impassable, was surmounted by a curious cage of metal, almost as big as the car itself, and held inside the cage, like some flabby black animal, was a gas balloon. 'Have the breeze with us going back,' observed the man, now cheerful. He sniffed at the air in a maritime manner. 'That's one thing. When you've got one of these gas bags it makes a lot of difference, you know. Sometimes along here when it gets a bit gusty it's like being on a blessed windjammer.'

They got into the car. From the rear Lovatt looked out into the flat, unused landscape and thought half idly what a classic assault place it would be for an invading force; easy landing, little high ground and a quick access to port facilities and then to London. A firm support landing on the Essex side of the Thames would secure both banks and the river to Gravesend and Tilbury.

'Been in Norway then,' said the driver. Lovatt sighed. So much for the canteen woman. He grunted.

'A side show, if you ask me,' observed the man sagely. Anxiously his eyes switched to the mirror. 'No offence meant, sir. I'm sure it don't seem like that to you. What I mean is you just watch them Jerries get through that Maginot Line. Like a piece of cheese that'll be, take it from me. Or else they'll go round. They don't have to go *through*, do they, sir? Why go *through* when you can go *round*? I ask you. Anybody can see that just by looking at the maps in the papers. Go through 'olland and round the back door. Don't tell me Adolf worries about them countries being neutral. Didn't care about Norway, did he, sir?'

'He's not particular,' agreed Lovatt.

'I was in the first lot,' said the driver. 'Somme, Ypres, all that. They didn't even think to give us tin 'ats until nineteen-sixteen, you know. Thought we had thick 'eads enough, I s'pose. Or we wouldn't 'ave been there, would we? Then when we got them, the tin 'ats, some blokes wouldn't wear 'em . . . Used them for washing and shaving. We 'ad one bloke killed while he was washing his face. Lump of shrapnel right through 'is skull.' The man laughed. 'Now they've got gas masks, the lot. All the kids, everybody. There was a bloke robbed a post office down here *wearing a gas mask*!' He snorted. 'Best one I've heard yet.'

'The war hasn't really started yet,' offered Lovatt eventually.

'That's for sure, sir. You're absolutely dead right. People don't realize there's a war on. They reckon they're "standing by", whatever that may mean. Playing at it, that's what we've been doing. Playing at it. Air-raid drills and people sitting up all night, drinking tea and eating sandwiches, and getting up to God-knows-what, and dances to help to buy bombers, all that cobblers. It's just been one big parish pump social so far, if you ask me. Good excuse for some to have a good time. Look at the ruddy fire brigade – more like the darts brigade if you ask me. There's them that reckon it will be all over by Christmas – and they'll be sorry. They'll *miss* it.'

Lovatt also thought it might be over by Christmas, although not in the way some believed, but he did not say so. They were nearing Gravesend. The masts of the ships in the Thames side docks stood up like trees behind the terraced houses. People moved about casually in the sunshine that fell in dusty bands between chimney pots and alleys. A milkman laughed with two housewives, while his horse nosed its feeding bag. One of the women was wearing trousers. An old man using a bucket marked 'For Fire Bombs Only' swilled the previous night's spilled beer from the front of a public house. They arrived at the station.

'London train in fifteen minutes, sir,' said the taxi driver, helping him out with the consideration he

13

would have awarded an invalid. 'That will be two shillings, sir.' Lovatt paid him and added sixpence tip. The man looked around at the set scene, the dull British streets that had remained unchanged for so long. Even now it was not worried, not hurried. People walked about enjoying the first morning of the new May.

'Well, sir,' shrugged the driver. 'What can you do about it, I ask you?'

Lovatt grimaced and thanked him for his kindness and conversation. He walked to the platform and bought a penny bar of chocolate from a red iron machine. What could you do about it? He went around the corner to eat the chocolate, realizing that he was in a captain's uniform. He bit into it secretly. He had not eaten breakfast. Then he went into the platform telephone box and gave the answering operator the number of the House of Commons in London..

On that same morning at the Royal Naval Dockyard, Portsmouth, James Lovatt's younger brother Harry was also disembarking from a warship, the French destroyer *Arromanches* which had berthed two hours earlier. As he went ashore, with a brief stumble down the gangway, his fellow officers, the young Frenchmen with whom he had spent three months, cheered and laughed from the deck above. The Englishman did not look so fine that morning.

'See,' he had told them on the previous riotous night in the mess. 'See, in England, see, we have to *obey* our parents still – it's called respect, see? And my mother and father, nice old dears really, wouldn't like

14

to know I'd been getting plastered with a boatload of Frogs.'

They had challenged him to stand on two chairs, one resting on the other, and then to close one eye like Nelson. His column had trembled and they had caught him as it toppled. During the voyage they had called him *Loup de Mer* – the Sea Wolf – because he was a poor sailor. Their patrol had been across the Atlantic western approaches, south over the Bay of Biscay to Bordeaux and then retracing their course to Brest, Le Havre and to Portsmouth. They had seen no action nor come upon any sign of the enemy, although one evening they found three dead men in a life-raft drifting on the sunset; seamen from a torpedoed merchant ship. They lined the rail and watched the bodies being brought aboard. One dead man was wearing blue-striped pyjamas. That had muted the junior mess a little that night, but then with shrugs, everyone bravely agreed that it was *la guerre* and to be expected. The following morning they buried the poor fellows at sea with the theatrical maritime ceremony and Harry Lovatt, as their compatriot, was entrusted with their identification discs to return to the British authorities.

He was broader, shorter and thicker-haired than his elder brother. The gap between them was more than merely three years. At Brest he had gone ashore with the French youths and after some lively drinking he had found himself, surprised and apprehensive, in a small room with a rotund prostitute. Her big, ruby mouth haunted his sleep for weeks. The toast that night, one of many raised in numerous names, was to 'The Breast of Brest'. Now he was home again from the sea.

He was certain that his mother would be waiting for him outside the dockyard gates, just as in former times she had waited for him outside his school. He felt oddly worried at the prospect of facing her but then reassured himself. For Jesus Christ's sake, he was twenty-two, and he *was* in a *war*, he could be required to die at any moment. Well, any *month*. Preoccupied with these thoughts he almost forgot to turn and wave a final salute to his French shipmates as he went ashore. At a signal, in unison, they began to chorus from the deck. 'Mama . . . Mama . . . Mama . . .' Harry felt his face warm. He flapped a dismissive hand at their taunts and went towards the dock gates with an exaggerated nautical roll. Their laughter followed him. He presented his papers at the dock-gate guard-room and saw, immediately outside, his mother sitting serenely in the little Austin seven. He felt the eyes of the naval sentry on him as she kissed him with the same warmth that she had always shown and said, looking carefully into his face: 'You've lost weight and you look tired. Was it very tiring, dear?'

'Terrible,' he laughed. She started the car and when they were on their way he kissed her cheek. 'I didn't know war could go on until such a late hour. How are you?'

'Splendid. Waiting for hostilities to start or finish, or whatever they intend doing.' He had always thought she looked like a middle-aged lovely, like a film star just touching grey. He still remembered harbouring guilty fantasies in boyhood of swopping her for Jean Harlow. 'Your father, predictably,' she said, before he asked, 'is writing to everybody, including the Prime Minister, telling them how they *should* run the war, and giving advice to people who infuriate him by apparently being too uncaring to reply.'

Mother and son laughed together. Harry said: 'He retired just in time to give his time exclusively to beating the Germans.'

Her laughter diminished to a small smile. She shook her head fondly. 'He can't understand why the war has been going on nine months and there has been no mayhem. It wasn't like that in his time, of course.' She paused and slowed the little car uncertainly. 'Aren't you supposed to report to somebody, dear? I mean you just walked out of the gate. In the films servicemen always have to *report* to someone.'

Harry pushed his arm across the back of her slim neck. 'They let me out, didn't they?' he said. 'I have to come back to report. Being on a foreign ship makes a difference. Things get a bit unofficial. I'll come back by train.'

'You'll have to, I'm afraid,' she confirmed. 'The petrol won't run to two journeys.'

'You're still getting the odd gallon, then?' he said. He put his left hand out of the celluloid window and patted the fragile door of the box Austin as he might pat an old donkey.

'A dribble. Your father gets his basic ration and some for his air-raid precautions business. On His Majesty's Service, as he says in that important way he has – OHMS. But I considered meeting you came under that heading.' They halted at some traffic lights on the edge of Portsmouth. There were two other cars, a naval lorry with some sailors in the back, several dockers on bicycles and a horse and cart piled with scrap metal. To Harry the sailors looked like new recruits, a supposition borne out when one, seeing him in the following car, attempted to salute. Elizabeth Lovatt looked at him with abrupt seriousness. 'Did you see that, Harry?' she said. 'That sailor was saluting you.'

They were moving off from the lights. 'He shouldn't have,' answered Harry, covering his pleasure. 'New intake by the look of it. They'll salute anything that moves. You can't start saluting people in cars from the back of lorries. Where would it end? Wholesale accidents.'

'You didn't experience anything . . . nothing dangerous then?' she asked cautiously. He could see how anxious she had been.

'Not a sausage, mother. Few alarms but nothing came of them.' His voice became quiet. 'All that happened was that we found some dead merchant seamen on a life-raft. Three of them. That was pretty horrible.' He put his hand into his pocket and took out an envelope. 'I've got their identity discs in here,' he said. 'I have to hand them in when I report.'

She hesitated, and he knew that she would say: wouldn't it be better to do it today? She said it. 'Perhaps people, perhaps their families, are waiting for news.'

He put the envelope away. He could feel the flat roundness of the discs inside, pieces of dead men. 'No, it's not quite like that,' he assured her. 'Their next-of-kin already know. The captain radioed all the information and their people would have been told. I just have to hand these in for confirmation, to set the record straight.'

'To finish their lives officially,' she said slowly and

strangely. Then: 'Oh, I do wish it could all be over. There's you and there's James . . .' She left the thought unfinished.

'What's James been up to?' he asked to divert her. 'Still dashing about on Salisbury Plain, blowing up dummy Germans.'

A frown creased her face. 'I don't honestly know,' she said. 'It's two weeks since anyone heard, even Millie, and that was a letter from Scotland. Not a word since.'

He laughed to reassure her. 'Well, there's no war in Scotland,' he said. 'He's probably holed up in some baronial castle, drinking malt whisky and taking pot shots at the poor old deer.'

She had taken the rural road, skirting north of Southampton, through placid fields, villages of old cottages and bright, child-faced bungalows built in the thirties, and finally to the first trees of the New Forest.

'Since rationing they've been keeping a close eye on the deer in these parts,' said Elizabeth. 'But there still seems to be the odd haunch of venison around.'

'God, I'd forgotten about rationing,' he exclaimed. 'You simply get fed in the navy. Is it terrible?'

'It's not exactly easy,' she said. 'Fancy introducing it in the middle of the worst winter for years. It seems ridiculous. The Thames frozen, everywhere iced up, trains running twenty-four hours late, people knocked down wholesale in the blackout, and you're suddenly told that you have to eat margarine.'

'Margarine! You've never bought margarine in your life.'

'I do now. I hope you've got your ration card.'

'I have. I almost didn't bother. I didn't realize it was

so bad. In France there seemed plenty of everything.'

She said: 'If there's a war we *have* to suffer. It's all part of being British. But even your father's patriotism runs low when he sees his dinner plate in the evening.'

Harry chuckled. They crossed the main London road and then drove into their home territory, an ancient part of England, a forest in the old sense of a hunting ground, established by William the Conqueror almost a thousand years before for the pursuit of his sport.

I just wish there was somebody I could ask about James, though,' she continued. 'I feel sorry for Millie being left in the dark. It was easy to find out about your time of arrival. Your father just rang his friend at Portsmouth, that vice-admiral or whatever he is, the golfer. And he told us when and where your ship would be in dock.'

'I received the message priority,' said Harry. 'It's amazing what the odd round of golf will do.'

Now they were running through the early summer trees of the New Forest, the light shimmering through the fresh green of the beeches. At the small town of Lyndhurst, they turned away from the main road, and drove, jauntily now, through cloaked copses and open moorland, over wooden bridges that arched wrinkled, brown-stoned streams, along roads where deer and donkeys wandered in the sun and beside which the ancient herds of wild ponies grazed.

'And what momentous happenings have been taking place in Binford?' asked Harry lying back in the seat. The sun was shining warm through the window.

'Nothing momentous ever occurs in Binford,' corrected his mother. 'You know that. There's not enough room. Even the war would have a job to change that. We've got an ARP post and Mr Brice has had an air-raid siren put on his roof. It looks like the head of a large hammer. They've tried it out and it makes a terrible noise. Still, it's no use having something melodic for an alarm, is it? What else . . . oh yes, there's a mystery man called Mr Stevens who has taken over the junior school.'

'Why is he a mystery man?'

'Because no one knows much about him and you know what the village is for knowing everybody's business. Even Ma Fox can't find out. He keeps very much to himself. At first she was sure he was a German spy because he went for long walks and read a book while he walked. Now she thinks he's just a figure with a tragic past.'

Harry nodded and smiled recognition. He began to feel a stir, the return of a half-forgotten excitement. His mother smiled because she sensed it in him. It was like only a few years ago, coming back from school, the reassuring road, the unchanged pattern of woodland, the fenced pond at the junction, and then threading down the lane to where the roof of the house appeared ruddily above the cloudy trees. He, Sub-Lieutenant Harry Lovatt, RN, who had sailed through dangerous waters, who had seen dead men taken from a boat, who had drunk and laughed and been with a large and lusty woman in bed, in Brest; he was home. It was a sort of triumph.

The train from Gravesend crossed the Thames bridge to Cannon Street Station, a pennant of white steam flying from its funnel. Once more James

21

Lovatt awoke sharply, in alarm, only just stifling the shout that would have thoroughly startled his three fellow passengers in the compartment. Two were men in bowler hats and proper pin-striped suits heading, at ten-thirty, for their offices in the City of London, and the third a sparse, older man with the doubled-up posture of someone with years among filing cabinets. The two city men were concerned with *The Times'* financial pages; before he had slept James had quickly noticed how they gave an identical, and cursory, glance at the leading news page within the paper before turning to the business section. They were like twins not on speaking terms, identical in their dress, in their stature and demeanour. As the train shuffled over the river they folded their papers, in unison, apparently at some secret signal, and sat gazing out of their opposite windows at the steady Thames. As the engine oozed white steam under the glass canopy of the big station, one man grunted to the other: 'The Balalaika one-thirty, then.' The other nodded. They had spent even less time looking at the fatigued young man who had been fighting in Norway than they had glancing at the news of the defeat he had witnessed. The bowed clerk smiled wanly at him, perhaps a kind of apology. Then he showed a portcullis of china teeth and said what a nice morning it was and how everyone was saying it was going to be a beautiful summer. 'Mind you,' he added with coy mischief, 'it's probably just another war rumour.'

At the station there were servicemen squatting amid encampments of equipment, kit bags, packs, suitcases. One had a cricket bat. Others squinted worriedly at the departure indicator as if it were in some sophisticated code.

But, the uniforms apart, it was difficult to imagine that this was the heart of a nation which had been at war for nine months. Posters at the station proclaimed 'Holidays in France'; ships had been sunk, there had been some air skirmishing, insignificant Denmark had been overrun in a day, but the Norwegian débâcle was the first real battle the British Army had known in this war, and cold Norway seemed so far away. Government forecasts had calculated a million dead in intensive air raids within a week of war being declared; the papier-mâché coffins and the simplified burial forms were stacked and ready; children ran around trying to frighten each other, and themselves, by wearing the hideous rubber gas masks, and air-raid shelters had been dug, filled in, and dug again in the proper locations, in public parks and gardens. Their construction eased a little the burden of a million and a half unemployed. It was not until March that the first civilian, James Ibister, was killed by enemy action, not in a crowded metropolis, but by a stray aerial bomb in the isolated Orkney Islands. The serious casualties were on the blacked-out roads during the dark and ice of the bad winter.

The anger which James had felt for days began to stiffen again as he walked through the concourse of the station. All around were the playbills for London theatres and cinemas: *The Corn is Green*, *Dear Octopus*, *Gone With the Wind*, *Snow White and the Seven Dwarfs*. His mind was still vivid with burning ships and buildings; men frozen in death, their blood pink on the snow; guns without ammunition; soldiers without rations. A

23

military policeman, standing uselessly at the station exit, noted his fierce expression and tried to please him with a banging of boots and a sharp salute. He returned it sourly and strode outside into the London sun.

Philip Benson, MP, was waiting outside the station. They shook hands and Benson studied him quickly and said: 'I'm glad you got back all right, James.' They got into a taxi and James asked: 'Where's The

Benson shook his head. 'Never heard of it,' he said. He was a thin grey man with a slight stoop which pointed his nose at the ground. He was not as old as he looked. 'Anyway, you're bound for lunch at the Commons,' he added; 'early I'm afraid, but I expect you're hungry.'

James realized he was. 'Did you get anywhere?' he asked. 'Or is everybody still asleep?'

The Member of Parliament, who was his father's friend, looked straight ahead over the taxi driver's shoulder. 'Yes, I'm afraid I did,' he replied quietly. 'It's going to be the most distasteful thing of my life, James, but it has to be done. The country can't go on in this way. Neville Chamberlain must . . .' He leaned further forward and ensured that the taxi driver's window was closed. It apparently was. He sat back. 'Chamberlain must go.' He sighed. 'I've arranged for you to see Clem Attlee as soon as we get to the House. You can imagine how *that* sticks in my throat, but you can't choose your bedfellows at a time like this.'

James's immediate and automatic thought was what would his father say. 'Attlee,' he muttered.

'And worse . . . Morrison,' added Benson. 'The

miserable midget. It was all plotted, anyway. Only the timing is to be decided. Your particular testimony will only be one more nail in this Government's coffin. Service Members have been seething about what's been going on. They are going to vote for their men, the men in their units . . .'

'Against the Conservative Government,' James finished for him.

Benson nodded: 'Exactly. They want Churchill as Prime Minister. They want Chamberlain out on his neck. And soon.'

'Churchill?' repeated James. 'Good God, Churchill was as much to blame for the mess in Norway as anyone else. Changed orders, woolly thinking, bad equipment. There were moments when I wondered if Churchill – or anyone else – had any idea where Norway actually *was*. My battery had the guns at Namsos and the damned vehicles to pull them a hundred bloody miles away. Churchill is lucky he doesn't have another Gallipoli to answer for.'

Benson seamed his lips. 'It's Churchill – Winnie – they want,' he said heavily. 'Everybody. They think he's got what I believe is called "the bullshit" to pull the country together and it's undoubtedly going to need it soon. The Germans are not going to stop now. Denmark surrendered after she had lost *thirteen* soldiers. A lot of people are beginning to wonder about the French too. Their general staff seems to think it's fighting a war a hundred years ago. They're all too damned ancient – half of them are ga-ga, I think. And the morale of the troops is suspect. There's a lot of politics in the army. Did you see their men in Norway?'

'Ski troops,' muttered James. 'Alpine regiment . . . Came with nearly everything, white battledress, goggles, skis, weapons. Unfortunately in some cases the things that fix the skis to the boots, whatever they're called, were missing, so they were not a lot of use. I came across about twenty of them keeping warm in a barn studying a book they had been issued – useful Norwegian phrases – how to order in a restaurant. Is the fish grilled or fried? Or, where can I buy _____?'

Benson nodded. 'What can you expect,' he observed, 'when one of our cabinet ministers, Kingsley Wood, tells a Member that we could not possibly bomb the German Krupp armaments factory because it's private property?'

James began to laugh, quietly, sadly, and Benson patted his arm. They were almost there, over the bridge at the Westminster side of the Thames Embankment, by the statue of Boudicca on her chariot, its wheels fitted with swords; the British queen who had fought an invader of long ago. Benson had often observed that her line of charge would take her straight on to the Members' Terrace. Big Ben was showing twelve-fifteen. Builders were working on scaffolding around the tower. It seemed they had been working up there for years. A striped awning was canopying the terrace next to the river, a target marker for a lunchtime bomber. The taxi swung into the yard, the policeman at the gate bending heavily to treat Benson to a smile of recognition and an amiable salute.

While Benson paid for the taxi, James stood on the dark polished cobbles of the courtyard of the Houses of Parliament. He looked about him. The metropolitan sun was high over the Thames now, yellow on buildings, squares and wide avenues, filtering deftly through the city dust, warming walls and roofs as it had done on summer days for a thousand years. Above the mother of parliaments the Union Jack, that incongruous banner of bits and patches, lolled in the almost windless air. Visitors were queuing to enter ancient Westminster Hall. Would the *Wehrmacht* queue to see its lofty roof and to hear the intonations of the guided tour? Would stormtroopers one morning replace the jolly policeman in this yard? Where then would be the Royal Throne of Kings? Canada?

'The Balalaika, sir,' offered the taxi driver suddenly leaning from his cab window. 'You was mentioning The Balalaika.'

Annoyance creased Benson's face. 'Yes,' he said. 'What about it?'

'One-thirty, Newmarket, sir. Four to one in this morning's paper.'

'Thank you,' said Benson brusquely. 'That's extremely kind.'

'That's all right, sir. Anything to help with the war.'

Two

Binford and its neighbouring, almost adjoining, hamlet of Binford Haven, occupied the western bank of a river which rose in the high chalk of Wiltshire and, broadened by many tributaries, flowed down through Hampshire, through the forest to a wide estuary. The Haven, as the smaller place was locally called, had been sitting modestly at the mouth since the Normans invaded, but Binford, a mile and a half upstream, although it had a few seventeenth-century houses, belonged to Nelson's age when the great, one-eyed admiral had established a shipbuilding yard at a creek halfway between the two settlements.

Some of England's bravest ships had been born there, the timbers being dragged from the forest and down the wide rutted street, still clearly to be seen through the grass of years, to the building cradles at the water's edge.

Robert Lovatt loved the past and the present of the place. As he walked along the river edge he often hummed, even sang a line or two, of 'Rule Britannia' or 'Rose of England'. He had retired on the dot of sixty from his solicitor's office and had settled himself at Binford, resolved to spend his time editing and reshaping his book, published to a certain acclaim in the late nineteen-twenties: *The Front Line: Personal*

Stories from the Trenches. The onset of another conflict had only added impetus to his work; he assessed that because so little had become of the new war, then there would be a greater interest in the old one.

He belonged to this place, loved its trees, lanes, fords and scalloped moorlands, and its issuing to the open sea. The salt flats of the estuary were the home of wintering birds; in summer the three low, pointed hills behind Binford – called the Three Sails by local mariners and fishermen, because they resembled a

Binford was a spread village, its only concentration of habitations being in the single wandering street, but at Binford Haven the intimacy of the little port, the stone quay and the solemn houses, was a contrast to the thrilling view of the English Channel from the tower of its elevated coastguard station. From there the watcher could see far down the bent coast, as far as Dorset, and to the east the cut-out haunch of the Isle of Wight with the toothy rocks called The Needles and its single finger of a lighthouse.

There were several small towns within a few miles, associated with the trades of the forest, especially the flocking holidaymakers, or with the sea. Lymington, sitting anciently by its own estuary; Lyndhurst, inland among the elms and oaks; Ringwood, where they had lodged the Duke of Monmouth captured at Sedgemoor in 1685, the last battle fought on English soil, and where there was a new picture palace. Christchurch, with its slender arched abbey, swans swimming around its feet, was twenty miles west, and beyond that spread the bathing beaches of Bournemouth. To the east were Southampton docks whence the Pilgrim Fathers had set out for America, a distinction later purloined by Plymouth where they had merely put in to hide from a storm. Beyond that, a few miles more, was Portsmouth, Nelson's home dockyard where his flagship *Victory* still lay berthed. It seemed to Robert Lovatt that half the history of England was breathing in this southern county and he loved it.

He was a tall, heavy-framed, domed man, principled and quite often pompous. His patriotism extended to sniffing the salt air of the estuary over his small oblong moustache, and thanking God he was an Englishman, not British, but *English*. He had once made a speech at a St George's Day dinner during which he had persisted in referring to the English Empire; to him – as also to Hitler – the nation was called England.

He was one of three brothers who had embarked eagerly for France at the outbreak of what he determinedly still called the Great War, and he was the only one who returned. His military connections were now few, a parade with the Old Comrades of his regiment on Remembrance Sunday, when for some reason his mild Flanders limp (a gun carriage had gone over his toe) became accentuated, and an occasional meeting with his war-time commanding officer, Major-General Sound, in his retirement, rankling in Salisbury, thirty miles away. As chairman of the Binford Parish Council Robert was also responsible for the organization of air-raid precautions in the village, a task to which he attended with as much enthusiasm as he could muster, although in his heart he did not believe the Germans were capable of air attacks on a large scale. Together with Mr Chamberlain, the Prime Minister, he believed that Hitler was bluffing or had missed the bus. Or both.

On this lucid morning in May Robert was striding beside the river, observing the ducks standing on their heads like troops taking cover, tracing the drone of a Gloucester Gladiator fighter plane across the harmless sky, the sun burnishing his pate. Regularly, three times a week, he walked from Binford towards The Haven, stopping halfway at what was still called Nelson's Yard. Only the blackened piles, standing like rotten tree stumps, now remained of the great shipbuilding cradles; the storehouses had become barns; but the home of the master shipbuilder was still intact, a lovely white house with bowed windows and a noble roof, looking down the last slopes to the water.

The ritual of visiting his friend John Lampard was always accomplished with the pleasant pretence of surprise. 'Hello, John. Thought I'd drop along and see you.' 'Hello, Robert, wondered when you'd be passing this way.'

These days Robert rarely went directly to the house but turned down an old path, now recut and reopened among the thistles and buttercups, to a landing in a half-creek of the main river, to where the fine though faded hull of an old Isle of Wight paddle steamer lay. Hammering or sawing sounds always told him when John Lampard was aboard. There was also a gramophone which sometimes played Ivor Novello songs. A retired accountant from London, Lampard had purchased the vessel the previous summer, six weeks before war was declared, and was dedicating himself to restoring it single-handed. 'It might just be finished in time for a victory sail down the Channel,' he forecast. 'If the business lasts that long.' His paddle ship was called *Sirius*.

The spicy scent of grass and weeds filling his nose, Robert made his way down the path. Glimpsed through the vegetation, the water trembled and flashed. Although the bank was steep the arched wooden housing of the starboard paddle stood above the growth like a mullioned doorway. Previously the perky funnel of the vessel had also stood up to be seen, but today it was reclined on the deck and John Lampard was contentedly painting it. 'Had to get the soot of years off that chap,' he said when Robert clambered aboard. 'Been easier to paint it black.' He straightened up, sweating. He had more hair on his chest than on his head; grey and rough hair, sprouting out of his open tartan shirt. His face was red with sunshine and exertion.

Robert had no time to reply before a breathless, slightly distressed woman's voice issued from the summit of the weedy bank. 'John, John . . . there's someone to see you. Mrs Spofforth, John . . .' The words came like a warning.

The two men exchanged groans and glances. Before they could add words, however, a stringy old woman in a bright print dress and a black straw hat came staggering over the horizon, waving a parasol and accompanied by a spotty boy wearing a bowler hat. Joan Lampard followed behind, a poor and breathless third. 'Mrs Spofforth, John . . .' she repeated in weak apology.

'Oh dear!' exclaimed Mrs Spofforth, but with a sort

of exultation. 'You've knocked the chimney down! What a pity. You'll need some help to put that straight, John Lampard.' She paused and regarded Robert with some dislike. 'Someone young,' she added pointedly. 'Like the boy here. You know Willy Cubbins, John, don't you? The last of the evacuees.'

The boy was squat and looked squatter under the bowler hat, although it took the glister away from a face that was ripe with acne. He was fifteen now and the sole survivor of the evacuated children who had come in busloads, many accompanied by moaning mothers, from threatened London on the first day of the war. Binford haphazardly took them in, gave the strangers homes, and instructed them not to stone the cows. It was the beginning of an uncomfortable period for both the town-dwellers and their reluctant hosts, but the problems had been solved by the fact that the mass air attacks on the capital had failed to happen. Mothers and children, with the exception of Willy Cubbins and a few others, who had also since returned, went home.

'That's my bowler,' pointed out John in a damaged way. 'He's wearing my hat.'

He looked from the youth towards his hapless wife who spread her hands and nodded towards the aggressive Mrs Spofforth. 'It was on your hall stand,' insisted the old lady. 'And you can hardly need it now. You never go near London.'

'But it's *my* hat.' John looked impotently towards Robert who could only nod feeble confirmation.

Mrs Spofforth prodded Willy with a finger like a jewelled lance. He grimaced and moved quickly aside. 'He needs it to keep the sun off his spots,' she announced. 'They *itch* in the sun. And if he's going to be working with you . . .'

'With *me*!' bellowed John. 'Working with me? He's not working with me.'

'You could do with a strong lad,' retorted Mrs Spofforth relentlessly, glaring over the words. 'And now he's left school he needs a job. And he's cheap at fifteen shillings a week.'

'Mrs Spofforth,' grated John, 'I *don't* want a lad,

'He wants to do some war work,' pursued the old lady, as though the matter were settled anyway. 'He's just hanging about otherwise. He was working with cows somewhere, but the cowman came home without fingers and then he was at the baker's in Lyndhurst, but they said he made the bread dirty.' She bent angularly, like a heron, and croaked confidingly: 'And he's all alone, you know, don't you. They can't find his parents in London. Vanished. Gone off and left him. Mrs Oakes looks after him, but he needs some employment.' She straightened and her tone became challenging again. 'It's the *least* you can do. He can help you put your funny old ship together.'

Defeated, John Lampard looked towards his wife and then at Robert, a pale appeal for some last help. It was not forthcoming. The boy was regarding him with smoked eyes from beneath the brim of the bowler. 'Oh, all right then,' he muttered. He looked up and fired a final shot. 'But he can get a hat of his own. He's not wearing my bowler.'

Afternoon dropped like a gauze curtain over the garden and the house. The french windows were open and the wireless was playing 'Begin the Beguine', the music muted and mixing with the mumbling of bees and other warm insects. Wadsworth, the basset hound, lolled beneath the lilac, rolling a lazy eyeball at Harry as he stepped out. The young man walked under the trees to the wooden summer house where they had kept their outdoor belongings, the bats and the racquets and the fishing tackle, when they were boys. He and James had never been close friends, usually going their separate ways and sometimes fighting briskly, even having a battle one Sunday morning in that same summer house. It had been over the possession of a landing net and they had begun to grapple inside the shaky building, in the dry, smelly dimness, and then tumbled out on to the porch, demolishing one of the door jambs as they did so. The dogs, thinking it was playful, had joined in, Benbow and Humph then, the two spaniels, both now dead; Mrs Mainprice, the daily woman, who still worked there, had finally parted them on the grass, shouting that they ought to be ashamed of themselves, and pulling them off each other with surprising ease and a pair of thick working-class arms. Harry could still taste the blood smearing his mouth, these years on. He had ended up squatting on the lawn, trying to wipe the blood and the tears from his face. 'Lousy bullying bastard,' he had shouted up at the standing James, who posed triumphantly, legs astride like some thin centurion; typical James. Mary Mainprice had screeched with shock and James, ignoring her and laughing at him, said: 'Keep your bloody landing net, pig,' and thrust it over his head while he sat there. Mrs Mainprice, hands sheltering face, had rushed back towards the house howling: 'Mrs Lovatt, Mrs L . . . these boys . . . these boys . . .'

Now Harry stepped up to the porch of the summer house. The elderly wood bowed under his shoes. He touched the door jamb and smiled as he saw it was still loose. Their father had made them repair it and they had, unspeaking, done a slipshod job which he had inspected and then had made them take out and start again. It had been a better attempt the second time, but not much. He and James had never after referred to the fight.

The house was late eighteenth century, russet brick and tiles, now half-concealed with expansive trees that had aged with it. At the back there was a lawn still edged with the final dying daffodils, the summer house and a worn wall that had, over the years, fallen down in places and been patched and rebuilt, and was now held together as much by its parasite creepers of ivy and wistaria as by its powdered mortar. That had been *his* place when he was a boy, in the sun or shade against the wall, propped up, reading through the afternoon. He could easily remember the books, indeed he still had them in his room. *The Gorilla Hunters* and *Coral Island* by R. M. Ballantyne, *Wulf the Saxon* by Henty, Percy Westerman's flying stories. Now he could still picture himself, like the ghost of another boy, trousers to the knees, socks rolled down, a grey flannel shirt. He could almost taste the apple he chewed as he read. He was like a boy from a book himself; he had played a part as he often played parts. The boy, the book, the red apple, all part of a scenario. He had taken off his uniform now and gratefully put on his grey flannels, check shirt and pullover and his old brogues; costumed for the part again, the sailor home from the sea. He walked over to the wall, touching it fondly, scraping a few puffs of dehydrated mortar away and worrying a spider from its hole.

From that place in the garden he had a view around the side of the house to the front gate. There was a rattle on the rough track outside and through the entrance came a clattering pony and trap. He grinned and went around the flank of the house as Millie, his

back. They embraced fondly.

'Amazing,' she laughed. 'You're here and James is coming home tomorrow. He's just telephoned from London. He'll be on the eleven-thirty.' She waited and her face lost its animation. 'He's been in Norway,' she said. 'I think he's had a rotten time . . . and something, I don't know what, has happened in London, so he has to stay tonight.' She looked at Harry oddly. 'He was phoning from the House of Commons,' she said.

They rode in the trap through the forest tracks, up over the May-green moorland where, knee-deep, the deer and the ponies grazed in their separate territories. At the highest point, a modest two hundred feet, of the Three Sails hills, they had a long view of the land, to where the distant trees and villages were settled in haze, to where the thin river rumbled over the steps and stones on its way to the wide tidal estuary. Up there there was a brush of wind from the English Channel.

They had always liked each other. 'No heroics, I'm

afraid,' he said when she asked him about his voyage. 'We just sailed down through the Bay of Biscay and back again. Lot of drinking and suchlike. In Brest and those places.'

'What suchlike?'

'Oh, well, just drinking, really.' He saw she was grinning frankly in his face.

'Just a pleasure cruise, to be honest,' he continued hurriedly. 'Except we found three poor devils in a life-raft, dead. From some merchant ship.' He had transferred the envelope with the identity discs to his flannels after her arrival for, typically, he wanted to show them to her. His small piece of the war. As they stopped at the height of the rise, the pony looking out over the view and snorting when he detected the wild horses grazing below, Harry took the discs out and laid them across his hand.

'Thurston G., Smith D., Wilson N.,' she recited sadly, looking closely at them and holding his hand. 'Three men in a boat.'

'I'm not sure I'd like to end up as just Thurston G.,' he admitted solemnly. 'There's not a lot of glory in it, is there? Can you imagine – Lovatt H. and that's all.'

Millie regarded him bleakly. 'Don't talk about it,' she said. Then she smiled a little mockingly. 'You'd want to have some glory, wouldn't you, Harry? You'd be the boy who stood on the burning deck.'

'Better than one of three men in a boat,' he answered bluntly.

'Sorry. I didn't mean it,' she said. 'There's nothing wrong with that, wanting some glory.' She had dark hair rolling over a pale forehead, gentle eyes and features. When they were at school she had been teased because of her roundness and she had never lost it. Her breasts lay bulky under the blouse. 'You were always the romantic,' she said. 'Even years ago you used to be the Errol Flynn.' He nodded sheepish agreement. She was a person from whom it was difficult to hide. Before he could stop himself he said, 'The French chaps used to call me *Loup de Mer* – the Sea Wolf.'

She exploded with laughter that floated away from the hill. She patted him fondly. 'Remember that time when we were playing some game at the enclosure and that gamekeeper came along, Gates or whatever his name is? He had his gun and he was livid because we were in one of his rotten sheds. James and the others all wanted to go out with their hands up and apologize, but not you. You were all for barricading us in and fighting it out with the old misery. That's you all over. Show off . . . *Loup de Mer!*'

He laughed his admission. 'Shut up, will you?' he pleaded. 'God, those days seem like a million years ago, don't they?'

'They are,' she answered.

She sharply gee-ed up the pony and they went at a brisk pace over the dipping moorland track and, turning a corner, were confronted with two donkeys lying in the road. Millie was prepared and she pulled up the pony in good distance. When you had lived in the forest all your life you knew what to expect of roaming animals. The pair were lying down on the tarmac enjoyably getting the benefit of its heat, and two more, a mother with a foal the size of a small dog, were nodding up the road towards them.

'Some things never change though,' observed Harry, jumping down and shooing the obdurate animals out of the way. He climbed back beside her.

'Perhaps they never will,' she said.

At eleven-thirty Millie was waiting at the station, the pony and trap hitched outside along with the village bicycles and a Southern Railway van. The station posters suggested Cadbury's Cocoa as a nightcap, Andrews Sparkling Salts every morning, a Burberry mackintosh, and resorts which now boasted of 'Sanctuary Hotels'. There was an invitation to a holiday camp on the Isle of Wight, and houses for sale in what was described as the 'Safe Area' of South London.

Even waiting for the train Millie began to feel the apprehension she always experienced where James was concerned, as if she were afraid of his arrival. She felt ashamed of the sensation, as she invariably was, and she always managed to conquer it in the end, as she had on her wedding day two years before.

The local train came importantly in, hooting vapour across the wooden platform, causing the calling porter, Ben Bowley, to vanish like the object of a conjuring trick. James came striding through the steam towards her. They embraced and kissed, and, arms linked about each other, went outside.

'How long?' she asked.

'A week at least,' he answered. 'Perhaps ten days. Unless things get even worse.'

Ben Bowley, whom they had both known since childhood when he regularly chased them from the line, was the second person to greet him. He told James the Germans would sue for peace by September. James did not argue.

'I always knew Horace would come in useful one day,' he laughed as they went into the station yard and climbed into the trap.. 'You're driving, I take it.'

'I certainly am,' she smiled. 'Horace is very particular who's on the other end of the reins. He wouldn't let Harry drive yesterday. Refused to budge.'

They began to trot under the cloudy elms out of the station yard. 'Harry's home, is he?' said James. 'And charging about with my wife.'

'Hardly that,' she laughed. 'I took him down to the village in this. He only got back yesterday. It sounds as if he's been on a pleasure cruise. How about you? Have you had a difficult time, James?'

'Yes,' he answered firmly. 'I think that's the word – difficult.' As they drove through Binford, people waved and called to them. They waved back. 'It's all just the same, isn't it,' he remarked.

'Just the same,' she said, unsure of his tone. 'That's how you would want it, surely.'

'I suppose so. It's just . . . well, *nobody* seems to have any idea there's a war on. It's the same everywhere.'

'Well, in Binford they try. They dash about forming ARP groups, collecting war savings and knitting for the troops and all that. There doesn't seem to be much else they *can* do. The war is out of sight here. You can hardly expect them to be digging trenches.'

She stopped abruptly because she realized with horror how easily they had begun to argue again. 'I'm sorry, darling,' she mumbled. 'I should see it from your point of view, I suppose.'

'That's the only way I can see it now,' he replied quietly. 'I can't tell you what a mess we made of the Norway business, Millie. It was bloody disgraceful. I lost six men. First time in action – they'd never seen a damned German before. If that's the way we're going to carry on we might as well say we're sorry to Hitler right now, today.'

Josh Millington, a pink old man who worked in gardens around the village, waved from his own fence. 'How are the bees today, Josh?' called Millie, half over her shoulder.

'Buzzing, Mrs Lovatt,' called the gardener. 'Buzzing.'

James and Millie drove out of the village under the newly leaved green arches of the lanes towards their house. 'I'm not particularly proud of this,' he continued quietly. 'But there's a revolt in Parliament. They're going to bring down Chamberlain. The old fool is finished. And I've provided a lot of the ammunition.' He laughed dryly. 'It made up for our lack of ammunition in Norway.'

She said: 'That's why you were with Philip Benson in London.'

'Yes. When the time comes, it might be today or tomorrow, he's going to vote against the Government – and a lot of others will too. The Birmingham undertaker has got to go. They want Churchill; at least he's belligerent. Philip took me to tell my story to Attlee and then to that puffy little Herbert Morrison.' He snorted in disgust and the pony answered him.

'Things must be very serious,' she muttered. 'And, down here, we don't realize it.'

'Nor do people in London – or not many – but

everyone will soon,' he said. 'We should be prepared, but we're not. Or aware, or even afraid. Everyone carries on as if it's no concern of theirs. I think they've got some funny idea that between us and the Germans there's a few million Frenchmen.' She released one hand from the rein and put it across his on the seat between them. 'Anyway,' he said. 'How is everybody?'

'Everybody is very well,' she answered. 'Your parents said they wouldn't come down to the station because they wanted me to do the honours, which was sweet of them. But your mother asked us to go up to supper tonight, if you're not too tired.'

'I'm all right now,' he smiled at her. 'After my cross-examination by the politicians last night I was given an excellent dinner at the Ritz and a room at the Carlton Club. It made up for the snow a bit.'

'Snow,' she repeated. 'It's difficult to think of snow now. So you'd like to go there tonight?'

'That will be fine,' he said. 'You're very pretty, you know. I'd almost forgotten.'

'Thank you,' she replied with mock formality. 'I was up at six washing my hair. After five weeks a wife can let herself go to pieces.'

'All for me.' He touched her dark hair. They were turning now on one of the dry, familiar paths from the road, running down into folds of the forest, at the end of which their small house stood. Their cat Bellows sat on the gate puffing himself out.

'It's still there,' he said. 'Our mansion.'

'Still there,' she said. 'Our little morsel of England.'

'But Morrison,' muttered Robert Lovatt at the head of the table. '*Morrison* . . . what does he know about war? He's only got one eye.' His big bare head wagged unbelievingly.

The family around the table looked at James who shrugged and said, 'I didn't choose him. It just happened that I was there to be chosen. Philip Benson didn't like it either, but there you are. There are times when you can't be too particular about your bedfellows.'

'How will Chamberlain take it?' asked his mother. 'Poor man. He never did look the part of Prime Minister. He always seemed like a rather sad parrot to me.' She was serious.

'This country can't afford too many people who come under the heading of "poor man",' chimed in Harry. They looked at him in surprise and he grimaced with pleasure. 'Whatever they say about Churchill, nobody could ever accuse him of being a "poor man". Chamberlain looks as if he should be selling matches in the street.'

They laughed. James was regarding his brother with curiosity as though his remark were the first adult observation he had ever heard from him.

Harry, encouraged by the attention, added: 'We need younger men. People like Eden. This is not going to be a war for old fogeys.' His father looked put out but he failed to notice. 'Have you seen the photographs of the French generals and so on? You should hear what the French naval officers think about them. They call them the Waxworks.'

Elizabeth and Millie rose to clear the dishes. Robert waved the wine around in his glass. 'Of course, it's all revived interest in the Great War,' he pronounced, the three words ponderously spaced out. James and

Harry caught each other's eye. They let him continue as they would have done as boys.

'Nothing of much magnitude has been happening in this one, so far.' He glanced carefully at James. 'Norway excluded, of course. But it has undoubtedly focused new attention on the Great War. Bond and Bond are very keen to publish a new edition of *The Front Line: Personal Stories from the Trenches.*' He always referred to his book title in full, never as 'the book' or 'my book', sometimes even adding without embarrassment 'By Major Robert Lovatt, MC'. The brothers were concealing grins. They had suffered hours of being taken through the bloodied pages of that volume, each eyewitness account explained and embellished by their father. Sometimes it had seemed that they themselves had campaigned through the long four years. 'How I Rang the Bells of Ypres', 'How I Shot Down Three Hun Air Aces', 'How We Tunnelled Through Flanders', and their favourite title, the intrepid story of an escaped prisoner-of-war entitled: 'My Four Years in a Frenchwoman's Cupboard'. This, for them, as boys, had become a sort of code phrase. It was difficult even now to keep sober faces when they thought of it.

Harry, with a steady, challenging eye on his brother, intoned: 'There were certainly some exciting chapters in *The Front Line: Personal Stories from the Trenches.*' His recitation of the title in full evoked an acknowledging nod from his father who found it difficult to detect humour of any kind. Prudently James shielded his mouth with his glass.

'There undoubtedly were,' admitted Robert Lovatt solemnly. 'Stirring stuff. All true. Every word authentic. Since nothing much is happening in this war, the Great War has taken on a new interest.'

James said casually: 'I liked that escaped prisoner story. Do you remember, Harry? What was it?'

They were like boys again, holding their grins. Harry pantomimed enthusiasm across the table. 'I'll say,' he agreed. 'What was it – "Four Years Under a Frenchwoman's Bed"?'

Robert Lovatt blinked disapproval. 'Nearly right, old chap,' he admonished. 'Actually it's "My Four Years in a Frenchwoman's Cupboard". Cupboard, not bed.'

Elizabeth and Millie returned. 'Let's go down to the pub,' suggested Harry. '*En masse*, just as we used to do.'

'We can't use the car,' his father pointed out. 'People don't like it. It's unpatriotic to use petrol like that.'

'We can use Horace,' said Millie before hesitating. 'But the trap will only take four at the most. Too much cargo and Horace just refuses anyway. He just stands there looking hurt.'

Elizabeth said firmly: 'The boys can go by bike. The bikes are still in the garden shed and I imagine the wheels still go round.'

'Bikes?' echoed James. He looked down at his uniform and then across at his sub-lieutenant brother. 'Bikes?'

'Well, if you want to appear more military, perhaps you could march,' said their mother. 'Nobody is going to see you in the dark.'

'I wonder where the clips are?' said Harry regarding his sharply-creased trousers.

'They're looped around the handlebars, where you left them,' said Elizabeth.

'Last one there buys first round,' said Harry suddenly. He turned and rushed for the garden. James ran after him out into the darkness and through the tree shadows. Harry was pulling the old bolts on the garden shed door; laughing like a schoolboy, he flung it open. Both young men squeezed through the door at once. James put the light on and they heard his father bellow for it to be extinguished. 'Don't you know there's a black-out?' They turned it off but it had given them time to see the two bicycles. Throwing aside accumulated family debris, they tugged the machines clear, charged them through the door, Harry just in the lead, and mounted them at a run. As they pedalled from the drive, the wheels and chains squeaking hideously, they heard their father shout again from his seat in the trap, and the women laughing as the pony began to trot.

The brothers rode noisily, bumping along the woodland paths, ducking below trees, bounding into holes and sending stones flying around sharp bends. They reached the main road far ahead of the pony and trap, and turned, only a few yards separating them, laughing and abusing each other. 'You silly bugger, Harry!' 'You daft old fart, James!'

Bert Brice, the policeman, shouted to them as they bumped through the dark, but they did not hear him. They came to a sharp bend in the road and sped around it. Lying on the tarmac were three sleepy cows. Harry could not stop. He collided with them, flying over the handlebars with a howl, landing between the second cow and the third, who, bellowing in fright, clattered to their feet, depositing him on the road. One of the animals put its hoof through the front wheel spokes of the bicycle and trying in fright to clear it, caught its horn in the wheel and charged off towards the village with the bicycle hung like a garland from its head. James avoided the collision only by swerving from the road, over some stony grass and then dipping down to a wide but shallow stream. He shouted as the bicycle bounced across the pebbled bed, sending up a bow-wave before crashing furiously against the far bank. James was flung into the gorse and grass and lay there, all the breath knocked from him. 'James!' he heard his brother call. 'James, where have you gone, for Christ's sake? I'm up to my ears in cowshit.'

They staggered towards each other in the night, laughing so much they could hardly speak. Weakly they embraced and sat down on the grass at the side, two brothers again. Two boys.

Three

Tom Purkiss, who had lost his fingers in Norway, was playing darts in the four-ale bar at the Old Crown, Binford, throwing with his left hand. His right was still bandaged. The others watched him with deference. Sid Turner, the forester, Harold Clark, a farmhand, and Hob Hobson, who kept the general stores in the village, were, with the nature of rural men, loath to make a wrong comment or ask an indiscreet question. Their faces, like their reserve and their voices, were set and slow. They had said nothing, so far, about the missing fingers. Nor had Tom mentioned it. He threw three darts.

'Don't seem to have stopped you hitting the board,' the most forward of the men, Hob, pointed out eventually. His companions looked at him sharply but with some admiration. 'Throwing with the wrong hand,' he added self-consciously.

Tom completed his throw and going to the chalk and blackboard at the side wrote up his score, again using his left hand. 'Cows don't like it,' he replied at length, returning to the end of the throwing mat. The men's forest faces were chaffed, reddened, apart from Hob who was a heavy, pale man. They had simple horizons and it was difficult for them to imagine frostbite.

'They know, I 'spect,' ventured Sid.

'Oh, cows know all right,' put in Harold, the farm labourer. 'You can't fool a cow, no matter what else. Mine, they know if I've been 'axing too much the night before. They buggers know I got a 'angover and they shove and push something terrible. They know.'

Hob frowned at him. Now he had broached the subject of the absent fingers he wanted to hear more from Tom Purkiss. It was Hob's turn to throw, but, having awkwardly taken the darts from Tom, he waited.

'They just think it's somebody else, I suppose,' said Tom, still talking about the cows. 'They're looking fine though.'

'That London kid with spots been looking to them,' said Hob.

'Oh aye, he ain't a bad boy that, 'spite all 'is face. And the cows is quite happy as long as the grass is growing. They don't care about no Hitler nor anybody.'

Hob threw his darts painstakingly, like he weighed his groceries, and they muttered as they added his scores. He went to the blackboard, parts of it thin and cracked with years of chalking. Harold said to Tom: 'All we 'eard was just rumours, like, old Ma Fox 'ere reckoned you'd been shot. We thought you was dead.' He looked around for confirmation. They nodded support. 'Then she said that you'd got no legs or no arms. You know what she's like.' He nodded heavily in the direction of the bar.

Tom grinned not at them, but almost to himself, his long-broken teeth projecting from his mouth like tattered flags.

'Bet you was disappointed then, wasn't you,' he said, and added thoughtfully, 'Can't think of me with no arms and legs.' He slowed.

Ma Fox, the huddled mother of Charlie Fox, the landlord, had appeared from the saloon bar next door. She was wiping the bar, but they guessed she had only come to tell them something. She left a puddle of beer on the wood, missing it with her cloth. 'Two Lovatt boys are in,' she whispered like someone first with a secret. 'Don't half look nice in their uniforms.'

Tom went to the bar, the handles of the pewter mugs held in the loop of his finger and thumb. 'One was in Norway,' he said. 'The older boy.'

'So they say. Did you bump into him there?' She pulled the ale handle.

The scarred door of the threadbare bar opened. A tall young gypsy came in and shyly asked for some pipe tobacco. Ma Fox sniffed and turned to get it. The gypsy half turned and nodded to the darts players. Hob Hobson ignored him but the others returned the nods. Sometimes he helped with pulling the potatoes and swedes and Harold Clark had once been private night-fishing for salmon with him, something of which few people were aware, and Harold chose to forget. The gypsy's name was Liberty Cooper, a member of a whole tribe of Coopers who lived in the forest, under strange igloos formed by the bowed branches of trees. It was called living 'under the benders'. The Coopers ate a lot of venison, wandering pork and the occasional donkey.

Ma Fox held out a surly hand for the sixpence before she parted with the tobacco. 'Like one of them

Indians in the cowboy flicks,' she sniffed when the gypsy had gone out. 'Ought to be in the army, his age. Remember that old woman, Hob? You remember, Sid, don't you?'

One of the Coopers, an old thieving grandmother, had once purloined a smouldering log from the winter fire in the bar and, putting it below her woollen pullover, had gone up the street smouldering like a funeral pyre. They all knew the story but Ma Fox told it again and laughed outrageously at it while the men smiled impatiently.

Two of the inshore fishermen from Binford Haven, brothers, with Donald Petrie, a coastguard, came into the bar, walked through and looked into the saloon and then returned. 'Too crowded,' muttered one of the fishermen. He went to the bar and got three beers.

'Not going out tonight, Lennie?' said Ma Fox. 'Not your time to come in, is it? I know your time.'

The other brother, Peter Dove, paused while the dart players began to throw a new game. 'Can't get out,' he said eventually speaking to them all. 'Something's going on. They reckon some of they Jerry Stukas was about just before dark. Looking for something to bomb.'

'Just off the Island,' said Lennie, meaning the Isle of Wight.

'There's certainly something up,' confirmed Petrie. 'We've had a coast alert since seven o'clock. Probably just the usual scare about nothing.'

'Don't reckon so,' argued Lennie. 'Too much flying about for that. Never heard so many. Anyway, we got ordered not to clutter up the Channel. So we don't go to work tonight. No fish tomorrow. No money neither.'

Petrie, the coastguard, was a short, wide-necked, firm-faced man with yellow hair. He was one of few strangers in the region; people still largely lived in one place and travelled little. He, however, had come down from the north-east of England, the ancient Viking coast. The people at Binford and The Haven had now, after two years, grown used to his remote accent.

The four-ale bar was beginning to fill. There were varnished benches around the whitewashed wall, two heavy tables and chairs, and no decoration but a stopped clock and the fixture list of the darts league.

Ben Bowley arrived from the station having ushered the last train of the day away on its evening journey to Lyndhurst, eight miles distant. John Purkiss, son of the organist of the village church, George Lavington, and Jeremiah Buck from The Haven, with the old man called Sonny who sometimes fished with the Dove brothers, came in to nods and small jokes. Henry Hadfield, the cricket captain from Radfield Compton, a village on the remote side of Ringwood, arrived to make arrangements for the annual match and was greeted as an alien with enthusiastic chaff from the Binford men. Their names went back for generations, sometimes centuries. Both the men called Purkiss, although not now directly related, knew that it was a forester of that name who had carried the body of King William Rufus from the trees after an arrow had struck him in the eye while hunting. That was on 2 August, AD 1100.

Two young Royal Air Force men came through the low door and its black-out curtain and, having taken their pints, sat on the cross bench along the wall.

Petrie and the fishermen recognized the RAF men as members of the crew of the Air Sea Rescue launch stationed at Lymington, waiting to pluck shot-down pilots from the sea. Only once so far had they been called into action and that was for a Bristol Beaufighter which had come down because of engine failure. The pilot, smothered by his own parachute, had drowned before they reached him. Petrie caught the eye of one of the airmen, a fiercely red-haired youth with freckles. 'Off duty then?' he said.

'Been a buzz on all day,' said the young man. 'But it's off now. All clear twenty minutes ago.'

Petrie turned to the Dove brothers. 'You could get out then.'

By now they would have rather stayed in the bar. But it was their living. 'Better do,' said Lennie reluctantly. 'Won't earn a wage like this.'

'I'll just make sure,' decided his brother, low-voiced so the RAF men would not hear. 'I'll go around and phone.' He went towards the door to the saloon bar. 'We've got time for another before we go, though,' he said over his shoulder.

His brother nodded and took the glasses to Ma Fox at the bar. 'Want a night out?' he said to Sonny, the old man who sometimes sailed with them.

'Aye, all right,' muttered Sonny, lifting back his beer. 'I'll go and get my bits.' He nodded around and went out.

Lennie Dove returned from the saloon bar. 'Yes,' he said. ''Tis all right. Buzz is off.' He looked at his brother and picked up his pint, then glanced around. 'We're taking the old man?' he said.

'Yes,' grinned Peter. 'He's gone to get his gun.'

*

The saloon bar of the Old Crown had chintz curtains on the inside of its black-out blinds. On the bentwood chairs were matching cushions. One of the great, but scarcely spoken, British class distinctions was here – the comfort and warmth of this room and the rude sanctuary of the public, or four-ale, bar. Each Binford inhabitant knew his place, with the prices a few pennies lower in the public bar. Some people, like Petrie the coastguard, and the Dove brothers, could acceptably cross the frontier, but not many. Charlie Fox was proud of both his little kingdoms. He provided the chalk and the blackboard for the public bar and had recently installed, in the saloon bar, a silvery, wind-up gramophone, which required no trumpet as a loudspeaker. The music issued from holes in the lid.

Above the bar the landlord had also had fitted some of the new tube fluorescent lighting, of which he was proud. If a stranger entered Charlie would turn it off and on again just to draw attention to it. It did, however, darken his blue-hued chin, enlarge the pits of his eyes and give his pale face an even deadlier pallor.

There was a stag's head just within the door. It had been killed thirty years before, cornered by hounds in the courtyard of the inn. Customers entering the bar patted it on the forehead and hung hats on its antlers. Over the years the hair had worn away to buckskin and one of the lower branches of the horns had become detached and had to be glued on again by Tom Bower, The Haven shipwright. In the winter a fire sat in the grate and in summer a jug of fresh flowers replaced it. The lamps around the room had red shades to compensate for the gauche light of the tube flooding the bar like a stage. There was no dart board on the wall here, but a notice board detailing village events, the Saturday cricket fixtures, the riding-school fees, the church services at St Michael and All Angels, and miscellaneous pieces of paper, appeals, advertisements and notices; the Young Farmers' Whitsun Supper, the Footballs for Refugees Appeal, Mrs Gloria Arbuthnot, Clairvoyant and Forecaster.

James looked about him. He could scarcely believe that he was there, safe, home in the village pub. People he had known all his life sat in their appointed, unofficial places, much as they did in church. His private anger rumbled within him again. They knew nothing, he thought, and cared nothing about the dangers, the death. They really believed no evil could harm their world. Millie and his mother occupied one of the cushioned window-seats with Joan Lampard. His father, Harry and John Lampard stood by his side at the bar. Twenty other familiar faces were in the room.

'He's not a bad lad, young Cubbins,' John Lampard was saying. 'Very willing and he can saw straight.'

Charlie Fox leaned over the bar towards James. 'Tom Purkiss is in the other bar, Mr Lovatt. Just back from Norway like you. Lost some fingers with frostbite.'

James experienced an odd relief. 'Purkiss from Harrington's Farm?' he asked.

'That's the chap,' confirmed Charlie. 'He's in there now, playing darts.'

James looked with almost a challenge at the others, as if he were about to interrupt some game they were playing. 'Excuse me,' he said, 'I think I'll just go in and have a word with him.' He moved away and Millie looked after him with a troubled expression which she converted to a smile when she turned back to the other two women. 'He's very serious about it,' she said as if needing to explain.

'I expect he's been through it,' interpolated Charlie from across the bar. 'We don't know what it's like, do we?'

James ducked through the doorway into the four-ale bar. His presence brought a brief reaction in there, as if he had stepped unexpectedly into a barrack room. Charlie followed him around the bar, beyond the partition, edging his mother away to her annoyance. 'Go in the other bar,' he prompted under his breath.

'I'm going, I'm going,' she protested. She moved to the other side of the wall, her face transforming as she did so, like a disgruntled actress walking into the lights of a stage with a smile. She hummed a snatch from 'Underneath the Spreading Chestnut Tree'.

In the other bar James waited and watched the darts players. He saw Tom's diminished hand. 'How is it?' he asked eventually when the darts were thrown and the score chalked. 'How's the war wound?'

Tom looked surprised, almost shocked, that he should know. As if it might have come from some official source. 'Oh, well, Mr Lovatt,' he stumbled, 'it ain't. If you see what I mean.'

James smiled and nodded. 'I see,' he said. 'Can I buy you a pint, Tom? Or something else?'

'We're finished now,' said Hob Hobson, although they hadn't. The players moved away towards their beer mugs.

'I've got mine, thank you, Mr Lovatt,' said Tom. The others, glancing regretfully, had theirs too, having only sipped at them through the darts game.

'I'll have a pint, Charlie, please,' said James. He put two half-a-crowns on the bar. 'And one in the kitty for these gentlemen.' They smiled acknowledgement. James said to Tom, 'Where did you get to in Norway, then?'

Tom said: 'Narvik, Mr Lovatt. I came back on HMS *Swordfish* with you. I saw you get off and go ashore.'

'You did? What a pity I didn't see you.'

'Well, there was plenty of men on board and you seemed in a bit of a hurry, if you don't mind me saying so.'

James laughed wryly. 'To get off. Yes, I was. It was an absolute mess in Norway, Tom. You know that.'

'It seemed like it from where I was,' nodded the other man reluctantly. 'Left me a bit short of fingers.' He held up his stumps.

'I lost some men from my battery,' muttered James. 'I'll never forget it. What's going to happen now?'

He had meant it in the wider sense, as if seeking some collaboration from a fellow strategist, but the dairyman misunderstood. 'Well, sir, it looks like I'll be invalided out of the army now. I'm no good like this. I'm back to milking the cows.'

James looked around. 'Nobody seems to want to wake up,' he complained, his voice lowered. 'They don't know there's a war on.'

'They soon will, if you ask me, sir,' said Tom,

keeping his voice at his normal tone. 'Just seeing what they Germans had in Norway. The tanks. Get through snow, anything. And those dive bombers, whistling as they came down on you. Frightened my bowels, sir, that did.'

'You didn't like the look of it, Tom?'

'I didn't at all,' said the dairyman simply. 'It seems to me that it won't be all that long before they're standing right in this very pub, right where you and me are standing now, sir. The soldiers in here. The officers in there.'

Charlie Fox had wound up the gramophone behind the bar. The fragile records, in their paper covers, were in a special protective case that had come with the machine. He rejected 'God Bless You, Mr Chamberlain' for the sentiment of 'Two Sleepy People' who were too much in love to say good night. The turntable trembled and then revolved and he put the smooth silvery arm with its needle on the first groove. A blonde young woman came through the door curtain and glanced about her. Harry saw her at once. 'Bess,' he said almost to himself, although his mother heard him and looked up. She frowned.

'Bess Spofforth,' said Harry.

'Yes, I'm afraid it is,' sighed his mother. 'I understood she was back.' She paused. 'It's rumoured it might be for the duration.'

Harry smiled and, walking to the window-seat, whispered: 'Jealous?'

'Not at all,' Elizabeth replied coolly. 'It's just that she was always such a . . . bother. Like her grandmother. She's a terrible old woman, you know. She hit the vicar with her walking stick. She said he was in league with the Pope and the Devil.'

'Now, now. You can't blame Bess for her granny.'

When he was fifteen the man who did the garden in those days had found him and Bess in the summer house, lying on a horse blanket on the floor. It had only been teenage tumbling, but he remembered the excitement of it now, her skirt rucked up and their legs entangled. Breathlessly they had rolled and laughed in the wooden enclosure, hot faced, frightened. Her girl's breasts were plump under her white shirt and as they tumbled he moved his cheek and then his mouth across them. She had squealed and rolled on top of him, her long hair dropped across her flushed face, her eyes bright. Then the gardener had walked in. He had seen the old summer house swaying. 'It's going to fall down,' he said, staring at the girl's naked legs. 'It'll come down over your two heads. And serve you right too.'

The story was swiftly circulating in the village and it soon reached Elizabeth, who had watched the girl closely thereafter until Bess had been sent brusquely away to boarding-school after an incident with the young man who ran the local company of the Boys' Brigade. He had also left the district and the Boys' Brigade had languished. Now she was back.

Bess saw Harry's eyes on her, and although she deftly looked away she then walked towards him. Smiling extravagantly, she kissed him on the cheek. 'You remember my mother,' said Harry nervously.

'Ah yes,' his mother said too quickly.

'Of course,' smiled Bess concisely. 'It's wonderful that so many people have actually *stayed* here. In six years I thought everybody would have escaped. But no, I seem to recognize everyone.'

'I expect you do,' said Elizabeth Lovatt. 'People don't move off very much, even now. Your parents went to London, didn't they. How are they?'

'They're very well,' Bess returned, adding: 'In their way.' She shook her fair hair. Her breasts moved a little under her dress. 'They've sent me back to grandmother. Evacuated me really, I suppose you could say. Just like one of those Cockneys. They have some idea it's going to be too dangerous for me in London.'

'Oh,' said Elizabeth. 'Well, I expect the place is crammed with servicemen now . . .' Harry glanced in annoyance at her. She recovered with a smile. 'And there's always the danger of air raids. What will you do down here, dear? Some sort of war work?'

A splinter of hardness appeared in the girl's eyes. 'I haven't thought very much about that yet,' she said coolly. 'I'll *have* to do something, I suppose. It seems to be all the rage.' She turned to Harry as if he were important to her. 'I've got a car,' she said. 'The new Flying Standard. It's very nippy. It's outside – would you like to see it? I drove all the way from London. It only took three hours.'

'Yes, I'd like to,' he said. He touched his mother's hand and said: 'Won't be long.' He and the girl went towards the door.

Elizabeth turned towards her husband and other son at the bar. Robert said: 'That's the Spofforth daughter, isn't it? She's quite a big girl now.'

'Yes, I'm afraid she is,' said his wife. Millie smiled at James.

Bess and Harry walked out into the old hollow coaching yard. It was still light enough to see the pretty, box-like Standard, with its white mudguards and running board, drawn up precociously on the cobbles. Harry whistled and she opened the door on the driving side. 'Go round,' she urged. 'Get in the other side.'

He climbed into the little car, bending in half. It still had the scent of newness. He stroked the wheel and ran his finger over the dials on the panel. 'It goes up to seventy. And it's got a self-starter. No turning handles,' said Bess.

'It's terrific,' he breathed. 'How did you get it?'

Her sudden sulk was visible in the gloom. 'I went to bed with the salesman,' she retorted. 'No one in this one-eyed bloody place ever thinks I come by anything *honestly*, your mother for one.'

'She didn't mean anything,' he said defensively. 'She still remembers about that day in the summer house.'

'Her little boy almost seduced,' Bess mocked. Her eyes stared truculently out at the dusk. 'I got the car as an inducement, if you really want to know,' she said. 'An inducement to come back to this dead-and-alive hole. My parents thought I was having too much fun in London.'

He grinned in the shadow. 'And were you?'

Her head affirmed it fiercely. 'I'll say I was. Jesus Christ, you'd think I was the only one who ever wanted to *live*.' She looked sideways at his uniform. 'How long have you been in fancy dress?' she asked.

'I've been in the navy eight months,' he bridled. 'I've just been out in the Atlantic – in a French destroyer. We picked up some dead men from the sea. From a torpedoed merchant ship.'

'Did you? That must have shocked you.'

'Two of them were naked and one was wearing pyjamas.' He felt guilty using them to impress her but it didn't stop him. He took the identification discs in their envelope from his pocket. 'Thurston, Smith, Wilson,' he recited, counting each one out separately.

'Pyjamas?' she remarked. 'You'd never think of sailors wearing pyjamas, would you?'

He looked sideways at her. Her pretty face outlined against the car window and the final shade of dusk. 'I'm sick of this war, already,' she said bitterly. 'Sick, sick, sick of it. War, war, war. That's all anybody talks about. My parents, your parents. They love it, you realize. It brings a bit of interest to their lives. They haven't *lived* since the last one. They just exist from war to war.' She mimicked a male voice: ' "How would you feel, Bess, to know Hitler was having a bath in Buckingham Palace?" That's my father. What a stupid thing to say, even for somebody like him. I don't give a damn if bloody Hitler or Musso-bloody-lini or any other bugger has a bath in Buckingham Palace!' She saw his astonished, half amused mask. 'It's all just playing at soldiers,' she went on doggedly. 'War? What war? I haven't seen any war. All this running around, pretending to be brave. Fuck the war, I say.'

Harry blinked at her language. He had never heard a woman say that before. Eventually he said: 'There's a Young Farmers' Summer Supper on tomorrow in Lyndhurst. Would you like to come?'

'All right,' she answered briskly. 'Tell your mummy

I'll pick you up in my new one-hundred-and-fifty-nine pound car.'

James and Millie, a little apart, went through the Binford churchyard, their steps sounding on the path between the yews. They had left Horace on the triangle of grass beyond the far wall and, having said their good nights at the pub, they walked through.

Beyond the lychgate there was a tombstone like a white chair in the summer night. James patted it. 'How's death treating you, grandad?' he said. 'What's it like down there?'

Millie laughed unsurely, as she so often did with him. 'Wouldn't you prefer to think of him being *up* rather than *down*?' she said.

'He's nowhere,' he said.

'All right, he's nowhere,' she agreed quietly. 'Please don't get temperamental about grandad and death in general. I'm sure we can find another excuse for an argument.'

'I'm sure we can,' he answered.

They went out of the lychgate and harnessed Horace to the trap. The horse clattered along the road towards their house. 'I'd like to do something,' said Millie. 'You said everyone should be doing something instead of sitting on their backsides.'

'What?' he asked, surprised. 'What could *you* do?'

'A good deal, I expect,' she replied. Why was it, she wondered, that their mutual anger, their ability to fashion a quarrel from nothing, erupted so quickly? 'I could join one of the women's services, for a start. There's nothing to keep me in Binford. It's not as if we have a baby.'

They were at their gate so he did not have to answer. He climbed down and opened the gate sharply, causing their cat to fall from the bar. It protested and slouched away.

Millie drove the trap to the house, without continuing their conversation, and began to unharness the pony. 'Can you manage the rest?' asked James suddenly. 'I want to hear the news.'

'I always do,' she replied. He turned and hurried into the dark house. When she had put the pony away she walked slowly to the door and went in. James was standing, hands in pockets, in the room. The news reader's level London voice came from the loudspeaker of the wireless. '. . . The voting figures were: against the Government two hundred and eighty, and for the Government two hundred. Within the next few days Mr Neville Chamberlain is expected to offer his resignation to the King.'

'God bless you, Mr Chamberlain,' said Millie quoting the song.

'Old fool,' muttered James. 'Bloody old fool.'

They went to bed and made love, but not happily. Afterwards she lay awake and, after he had slept briefly, he woke too.

'What's wrong?' he said.

'It's not one of my sleeping nights,' replied Millie.

For several minutes they were silent, James with his eyes closed, his wife with hers open.

'Aren't you glad we didn't have a child?' he said eventually.

'A baby,' she corrected. 'Yes, I suppose I am now.'

'It's no world for a child,' he said before closing his eyes again.

At seven o'clock in the morning the telephone sounded. James went sleepily downstairs. It was Philip Benson from London. 'James,' he said. 'Have you heard the news?'

'About the vote. Yes. I heard the wireless last night.'

'No, the other news. The Germans have invaded Holland and Belgium. Churchill couldn't have timed it better if he had been in cahoots with Hitler. He'll be Prime Minister tonight.'

Five minutes later James put the telephone back on its hook on the wall. Millie was stirring beneath the bedclothes. He went to the window and looked out over the early fields bright with day and beyond that to the placid sea. It was Friday, 10 May.

Four

Throughout the night the Dove brothers and the old man Sonny had fished six miles out where the long, dull waves rolled. A limp moon rose at two o'clock giving a pale illumination to The Needles at the western cape of the Isle of Wight. The rocks stood out like ghosts walking on water.

Peter and Lennie Dove had been teasing the old man Sonny about bringing the shotgun again. He had hobbled down to the jetty at midnight, encumbered with his tool bag, which he would never leave on the boat, for he had owned it since he was twelve, the solid pile of sandwiches which he had made himself in his cottage kitchen, and a bottle of Tizer, because he would never drink alcohol at sea. He also, as he had done of late, carried the shotgun, double-barrelled, as old as himself.

'Now what's that for, Sonny?' Peter had mocked as they helped him aboard. 'You got more equipment than the British Army.'

'Rabbits,' retorted the old man. 'What d'you think a shotgun's for? In case there's rabbits out there.' He went heavily down the companionway to the engine which, with the cooking galley, was his responsibility. As he pulled away the hatch a cloud of hot, oily air issued into the clean summer night. The brothers did not notice it but Sonny grumbled: 'You got to get somethin' done about this contraption down here. Time she had a proper overhaul.'

'Next winter,' promised Peter. He had climbed into the wooden box of the wheelhouse. Lennie was checking the nets, pulling at them, separating them, securing the lines.

'Be too late when she lets you down,' the voice came hollowly from the hatch.

'That shotgun,' Lennie called back. 'That makes us into an armed merchantman, you know, Sonny. Technically, that is. Geneva Convention. It makes it legal for Jerry to bomb us.'

The old man's head emerged from the hatch, the rutted face, the pale, wet eyes, the random teeth and the white hair around his ears and neck and stubbling his chin. 'They buggers would bomb us whether we got the gun or no,' he asserted. 'They don't know and they don't care, I'll bet you. Why don't you paint a red cross on the roof? See if that makes any odds.'

They had never been attacked, but fishing boats up the east and northern coasts had. German submarine commanders were honourable and often surfaced within sight of British fishing boats without showing any harmful intentions, but the Luftwaffe were not above using the small craft for machine-gun targets and bombing practice.

Fishing for the Binford Haven boat had been moderate; a long, easy sea, a warm sky and a late moon. They fished without lights but the night was pale enough to see. There was a good catch of mackerel and some pollack and cod. At five o'clock, with the grey band of day advancing from the green uplands of the Isle of Wight, they paused to eat the sausage, eggs and bread that the old man had prepared, and then turned the wheel and headed north-west towards their home port.

At six o'clock they saw a merchant convoy crouched on the horizon, going east to west, coasters carrying coal and steel from the north-east ports to the south-west, an economical sea route of long tradition.

The gathered ships did not attract more than casual curiosity from the Hampshire fishermen until Peter Dove saw that over the distant hulls there appeared small angelic puffs of cloud. The rest of the sky was blank and clear. He turned the binoculars on the horizon and the clouds. Then, like a bad rumour, the sound of the firing drifted to them on the lucid air.

'Lennie,' Peter called. 'Have a look at this.'

Lennie, hearing the gunfire, was already squinting at the horizon. He took the binoculars from his brother. 'Aye,' he said. 'I can see the planes. Little dots, see . . . They're low.' He handed the glasses back to Peter and called down to Sonny. 'Sonny, give her full speed. Everything she's got.'

'She ain't got anything!' shouted Sonny, his rumpled head appearing from the hatch. 'She ain't got full speed, that's for sure. I told you.' He became aware of the rolling echoes of the firing and his face became concerned. 'What's going on?'

'Looks like Jerry is bombing a convoy over there,' Peter told him quietly. 'About eight, ten miles out.' He was still keeping the glasses on the distant shapes. 'Let's get a move on, Sonny.'

Hurriedly, the old man vanished into the hull and

the engine laboriously picked up its note. The fishing boat struggled for more power but it scarcely managed another knot. 'That's all she's got,' grumbled the old man, calling from below. 'I told you to get the bloody old thing fixed, didn't I now.'

'Let's hope they're kept busy over there,' said Peter returning to the wheel. His brother had the glasses now. He said to him: 'I'm sorry for those poor bastards, but at least they've got something to shoot back with.'

Lennie laughed dryly. 'So have we,' he remarked. He called towards the hatch. 'Got your rabbit gun, Sonny?'

'Lot of bloody use that's going to be,' said Peter to himself. He was getting the boat as close inshore as he could, gauging the shoals and currents, alongside the steep guardian cliffs of the Island. The Needles lighthouse stood out in the strengthening light, striped and tall, like a man out for an early view of the sea. God, he thought, they were so near land. They could see sheep grazing. If they got into one of the bays then any German plane which turned off from the convoy might well miss them.

'We don't need to worry, I don't reckon,' called Lennie. 'Jerry looks like he's got plenty to do. He won't bother about the likes of us.'

The Stuka, when it arrived, descended in a screaming swoop out of the opaque sky. They heard it before they saw it, the ghostly screech as it dived towards them. Their faces turned up frantically, searching.

'Get down!' bawled Peter from the wheelhouse. His brother was already flat, flung against the side of the structure, while Peter doubled up against the wheel itself. Lennie was shouting something to Sonny which he never heard, for at that moment the dive bomber reached the pit of its descent and loosed a high explosive bomb which erupted with a numbing roar in the green sea fifty feet away. The fishing boat bucked like a stallion and heeled nervously away from the blast. Every window in the wheelhouse blew in, scattering Peter with glass. He felt the blood from the cuts on his face streaming down his cheeks like tears. His brother rolled across the deck, colliding with the rail. It was the old man who reacted first. He clawed his way from the engine room, shouting, his face rough with rage. Waving his fist upwards at the attacker who had now screamed off into the higher sky, he struggled for profanities. 'Bastards!' he bawled. 'Rotten buggers! Bombing an old man! You wait, you German bastards! You just wait!'

The wait was not long. The Stuka returned, curling gracefully far up in the lofty morning and then falling like a cormorant to a hundred feet, this time a mile away before howling in on a level run, machine guns firing, making the sea sprout and rattling along the soaking deck of the fishing boat. Peter had crawled from the wheelhouse and lay among the loaded fish barrels. They saved his life. One exploded in front of him, scattering cod over him and the deck. He scrambled back to the wheelhouse and, pulling the wheel violently to starboard, held it there with his foot while he took cover against the life-raft. The German came in for another run. Peter was aware that Sonny was lying flat out on the bow, still howling obscenities and firing both barrels of the pathetic shotgun as the attacker's grey belly showed across the masts. The plane banked, displaying its black crosses, and then headed back towards the vacant sky. This time it did not come back.

'Bloody swine,' sobbed Peter Dove towards his brother. 'I could see the bugger's face. I swear he was laughing . . . Where's Sonny?'

The excitement in their faces stilled and, both shouting his name, they rushed towards the bow. The sea slopped over the wooden prow as the small vessel, itself wounded by the machine-gun bullets that had rent its deck, lolled in the water.

'Sonny . . . For God's sake, Sonny!' It sounded like an accusation, as if they were blaming the old man.

The forepart of the boat was empty. The shotgun lay, as though carefully placed, across a coil of rope. The aroma of its powder was still in the air, mixed with the breeze and the smell of the German bullets.

'Sonny!' Peter stumbled back and thrust his head into the engine-room hatch. It was empty, the machinery croaking and choking. In the adjoining galley he could see the old man's bottle of Tizer rolling on the table. He turned back, stark faced. 'He's not . . .' he began.

He saw his brother standing still, with hunched, hopeless shoulders, looking into the sea. It was the only place old Sonny could be and there he was, floating head and legs down in the water, his back and buttocks in the air. Around him, mixing with the water, was a pink halo of blood.

Like many fishermen, neither of the brothers could swim, but there was no need for swimming. Lennie picked up the cork life-ring and made to throw it into the waves, but then he put it back on its hook, for they knew there was no reason.

Peter Dove looked up into the sky, tears running from his eyes to his mouth and chin. His brother followed his look. The sun was rising on a mocking morning, the sky like muslin, a few clouds innocent and lofty, the sea coming in long, silver tongues up the Channel. Wordlessly Peter shook his fist at the empty horizon. His brother was trembling. 'Fancy killing a poor old man,' he whispered.

As the fishing boat reached the mouth of the river, Peter Dove brought her as close inshore as he could, and his brother using the megaphone shouted at the coastguard look-out. His first shouts caused the river gulls to screech and scatter and Danny Durr, the assistant coastguard, only caught half the message as the boat slowed, wallowed, and then went on towards the harbour. 'Shot? Shot dead?' he muttered, shocked. Then he thought he realized. 'That shotgun. Sonny's gun.' He picked up the telephone and whirled the handle. Donald Petrie picked it up in the hallway of his cottage. 'What's up, Dan?'

'They Dove boys,' said Dan hurriedly. 'They just come in. Hailed me and said Sonny, the old man, got himself shot. Dead, they said, he's dead. It's that shotgun he takes out with him. Fell on it, I'll bet.'

'Call the ambulance and the police,' said Petrie firmly. 'I'll get down to the quay.' He put the phone down. 'Jesus, old Sonny,' he muttered, going out through the door. He mounted his motor cycle and drove along the shore road towards The Haven. The view of the waterway was blocked for some of the distance by trees and elevated land and then by houses, harbour buildings, and the masts of laid-up sailing craft. By the time he reached the vessels he could see the fishing boat heading towards the quay. He stopped the motor cycle and took his binoculars from the case around his neck. He waited until the boat cleared the screening rigging of the moored craft and then focused the glasses on her. He saw at once that the upper structure of the little vessel was torn into holes, there was only jagged glass in the wheelhouse, and that the wooden hull had been blown away for several feet at the bow. 'Some shotgun,' he muttered. He started the bike forward again.

When he reached the old stone quay there were already people gathering. The very calling out of the motor ambulance was a matter of excitement, but when Police Constable Brice was seen, set-faced, steel helmet on his head, pedalling his lofty bicycle furiously towards the harbour, then they knew something big had happened. By the time Petrie pulled up on the quayside, there was already a knot of people gathered to watch the Dove brothers bringing in the fishing boat. They stood, as people do when they are uncertain or afraid, in a small, compact crowd, although there was plenty of room on the quay for everyone to stand without touching. Constable Brice, who was an unpopular and officious man, saw as his first duty the clearing of spectators, as if their presence would prevent the boat docking.

'Move back,' he ordered, dismounting his angular bike. 'Disperse now, if you please. Nothing to see. Just a small accident. Nothing to see.'

'What d'you think that is then, Mr Brice?' asked

Billy Sanders, the bloodstained boy from the butcher's shop. He nodded towards the riddled boat as it sidled to the quay. On the deck was half a blanket with a mound beneath it. The butcher boy always had blood on his striped apron. He regarded it with pride, like a trade mark. The policeman looked with distaste at him: 'Go on away,' he ordered. 'Coming down here like *that*.' Billy moved back to the extent of the circumference of a cycle wheel. Bert Brice moved forward and stared at the blanket on the deck of the nearing trawler and at the bullet holes drilled along its superstructure. Petrie had moved to get the rope as the ashen Peter Dove threw it ashore. One of the old fishermen who inhabited the quay, Jeremiah Buck, said quietly: 'They look like they got a good catch too.' He peered over at the scattered silver fish that had been hurriedly pushed aside to make room for the body.

'He's dead,' called Peter Dove to Petrie before the boat had touched. 'Old Sonny.'

'Bastarding German dive bomber,' shouted his brother from the shattered wheelhouse. 'Killed an old man.'

The boat was alongside. More people came from the two shops and the houses to look. Others arrived from the direction of Binford. There were about twenty, growing to thirty, as the boat was made fast; craning forward, chattering and whispering, women in aprons and with shopping bags, a man who had been mending the road and another who had been sweeping it. Three boys and a girl stopped their bicycles and stared. Another boy, Tommy Oakes, who always wore a wolf-cub's green uniform stood, curiously, at attention. 'Go and tell the others,' whispered the girl, Kathleen Enwright, nudging the nearest boy, Gordon Giles, known as Franco. 'Go yourself,' he said, staring at the slow scene. 'I ain't ever seen nobody dead before.'

Three RAF men, from the Air Sea Rescue launch at Lymington, in their pale blue shirtsleeves, stopped their truck and walked towards the crowd. One of them was the youth with the ginger hair.

'Jerry went and done that,' nodded the man who had been tarring a square of the road. He addressed the airmen bitterly. 'Where was you, that's what I want to know? Sitting on your bums ain't no good when there's old men getting machine-gunned to death.'

'Sod off,' said the ginger youth. 'You stick to mending the bleeding holes in the road, mate. That's about all you're fit for.'

'You'd be better off doing that yourself,' answered the older man. 'You're no good for anything bloody else.'

'We 'ave to 'ave orders, don't we?' said one of the other RAF men. 'We can't just take the fucking boat out when we likes, *can* we? The officers 'ave to give orders. Blame them, not us.'

'Nobody told us,' said the ginger youth. 'Nobody knew anything about it.'

'Move back. Move back and stop arguing,' said Police Constable Brice. He regarded the RAF men astringently from beneath the rim of his steel helmet and it seemed possible he might add to the road-mender's accusations. Instead he held out his arms and eased everyone back. 'Back now, nothing to see. Give us room, please. *Give us room!*'

Four shaky ambulance men stood, a stretcher and a red blanket ready. One also carried a first-aid box, almost an afterthought. As the boat tied up, two of them moved forward with the stretcher, but Petrie, now aboard the vessel, held up his hand. 'Hang on, boys. Just a moment.'

The ambulance men stopped obediently among the crowd. Petrie leaned over and gently moved the blanket from old Sonny's face. The old man's skin was still wet from the sea. He had a composed expression, almost smug, even the trace of a smile. Petrie had a feeling that the dead man might at any moment sit up, laugh and startle them. He put the blanket back and looked up into the dumb faces of the Dove brothers.

'Tried to shoot at the plane with his shotgun,' said Peter hollowly.

Petrie turned towards the quay and beckoned to the ambulance men. PC Brice, officially and unnecessarily, cleared the way for them and then, with growing importance, stepped down on to the deck, putting his black boot on a dead mackerel. He slid and slipped backwards, falling heavily on the deck with a howl. The men around the body turned sharply and Petrie looked angrily. 'For Christ's sake,' he muttered.

'Oh . . . Oh . . . my arm!' the policeman called. His helmet had fallen. 'It's broken. I'm sure it is.' The children on the shore, who had been joined by others, began to laugh.

Petrie said to one of the ambulance men, 'See to him, will you.' The man looked hurt at being dis-possessed of his end of the stretcher. He glared at the prostrate police officer. Petrie took the handles. The

Dove brothers tenderly raised the wafer of a body, and placed it lightly on the stretcher.

They carried him ashore before the dumb crowd. Tommy Oakes, the wolf-cub, brought up three fingers in a theatrical salute. A car stopped behind him and Dr Brinton, the Lymington doctor, strode along the quay. 'I'll take a look at him,' he said briefly.

They laid the stretcher down and Brinton eased the blanket away. A tight gasp went up from the watchers. Several of the women were crying. The little girl with the bicycle suddenly rode away. Brinton glanced up at Petrie. 'Thank you,' he said. 'That's all. Not a spark there.'

Petrie nodded backwards towards the boat. 'Maybe you'd like to look at the other casualty,' he said.

The doctor looked startled. 'There's somebody else?'

'Brice, the copper,' said Petrie. 'He slipped on a fish.'

As the tranquillity of that May morning lay across the southern shores of England, as the sun gained height above beaches that were sprinkled with the first wartime holiday-makers, as the seaside shops smugly put out their striped awnings, and the coastal inns opened their doors to the bright air, so Sonny was brought dead into Binford Haven, and on the far side of the Channel, to the east and south-east, the German army was pushing heavily into Holland and Belgium.

There was news every hour on the wireless. Elizabeth Lovatt kept it on through her morning tasks in the house. Mary Mainprice did not normally come in on Friday, but she pedalled in at the gate on her bicycle, tall, curiously like an upper extension of the bicycle itself, and called breathlessly through the open window, her white spare face framed by the first roses: 'Mum, Mrs Lovatt. You there?'

The organist, Sandy Macpherson, was playing on the BBC, filling with soothing, meaningless melodies the intervals between dire war communiqués. Elizabeth turned down *Die Fledermaus* and went to the window. 'Mary, what's the trouble?' she asked. Mary was trembling with news.

'That old man, Sonny, you know he that helps the Dove boys in the boat. They just brought him dead into The Haven. Shot by they Germans, they say, mum.'

Elizabeth felt her face go stiff. 'Dead?' she repeated. 'How could he be shot by the Germans?' The Germans were on the far side of the Channel.

'Jerry plane, mum, came down and shot at the boat. Ma Fox . . . told me . . .' Her hands dabbed at her face.

Elizabeth refused to believe it. 'But . . .' she protested. 'She' probably mistaken. You know how she exaggerates, Mary. I simply don't believe it. Not the old man . . .'

Mary's expression indicated she had already spent too much time. 'Well, I'm going down to see,' she announced, as if she would be needed. 'They reckon 'ee was lying on the quay there covered with a blanket, 'is hand 'anging out of the side. I'll tell you when I come back.'

She pedalled away in a curve of small pebbles. Elizabeth returned to the close shadows of the house. No, she refused to believe it. Rumours came too quickly to life while there were people like Mary and old Mrs Fox around them. She returned to the kitchen and picked up a recipe book – *A Hundred Meals Without Meat* – she had been studying over her coffee. Robert had gone to Southampton. It irritated her that she wished he were at home.

After a moment she set the book and her cup down again and went purposefully out through the sitting-room towards the telephone in the front hall. She hesitated in the doorway. Yellow sunshine was running quietly through the windows, birds were lively in the garden, and a drift of sea-smell mingled with the scent of the May flowers. Surely not.

Making her mind up, she took the earpiece from its cradle and turned the handle. The village operator, Kathy Barratt, answered quickly, and immediately asked: 'Oh, Mrs Lovatt, have you heard?'

Now she knew. 'Old Sonny?' she asked. 'It's true is it, Kathy?'

'God rest him, yes, Mrs Lovatt. Terrible thing, isn't it? Terrible. I saw them bring him off the boat myself. He looked ever so little. Like a boy instead of an old man.'

'Thank you, Kathy,' she whispered. She had known the old man all her life.

When she had replaced the phone Elizabeth walked slowly away from it, shaking her head, into the sitting-room. Everything there was as it had always been; the home they had built up over their years of marriage. The flowered covers on the chairs and the settee, the brass pans against the walls, her chosen curtains waving briefly in the air coming in from the garden, the rug and the fire irons before the stone grate, the books and pictures on the wall. The lamp on the writing desk. Her sewing basket, the private ticking of the clock. She found herself touching these familiar things, trying to reassure her heavy heart. Then she sat down, and put her head in her hands.

She had married Robert Lovatt in 1915, on his second leave from France. It was a ghostly wedding because she had been in love with his brother Gerald who was killed during the opening weeks of that war. She still had Gerald's uniform.

Five

Within the wide anchorage at Portsmouth there lay a grey gathering of ships. Funnels and flags stood in the sun, rigging whistled thoughtfully in the breeze. Nelson's relic flagship, HMS *Victory*, sat like a wooden grandfather among the war vessels.

Harry Lovatt walked smartly from the station to the dockyard, his officer's uniform cut and clean in the dusty street air. He took a short way through a row of terraced houses, bright shoes lightly sounding. Two women were washing down the pavement immediately outside their homes, one separated from the other by three or four intervening front doors. Each worked her precise broom along the demarcation lines of her own territory, taking pains not even to splash or sprinkle the immediate neighbour's paving. As he approached, one woman shouted to the other.

'What you think about 'olland, then, Marge?'

'Poor people,' responded the second woman, laying the handle of her broom against her wide bosom and wiping both damp, crimson hands on her apron. 'Wilf says they can't even run proper in them clogs. That 'itler's a real bastard, picking on them.'

'Just give me five minutes with that swine,' responded the other ominously across the squares of paving. She swished her broom violently. They were like Amazons discussing strategy over miniature fields. 'I'd 'ave the bleeder's moustache off in no time, and the rest of what 'e's got!'

Marge hooted. 'If 'e's *got* anything!' she returned, and they both guffawed.

'Weedy little bastard,' agreed the first woman.

Smiling unsurely Harry approached and, circum-navigating the washed areas, stepped out into the road. A rag-and-bone man's cart, drawn by a spectral horse, grated down the middle of the road. The rough-skinned driver emitted his bleak cry: 'Araaaagaboners.' The women ignored the call and, leaning on their brooms rammed into the buckets, smiled like mothers at Harry. He blushed and wished them good morning.

'Goin' off to sea, lad?' asked Marge kindly.

'Might be,' he returned. 'You never know.'

'Give them one for us, love,' added the other as he went by her patch.

'I will, I promise.' He laughed and they joined in raucously. They began sloshing the pavement again and as he strode away he heard one call to the other: 'Just a kid, really. Like our Billy.'

'Terrible when they go and get theirselves killed at that age,' called the other woman loudly. 'Criminal,' agreed Marge.

Harry strode along the street and into the main thoroughfare. Naval Operations Headquarters, where he had to report, was directly ahead. There were sentries with upended bayonets on guard both inside and outside the building and the wide con-course within the main door was like a cavernous stage upon which actors were rushing to take their places moments before the curtain rose. He went to an office marked 'Officers. Movements and Postings', and stood with four midshipmen while a worn-looking petty officer and a confused clerk juggled papers behind a windowed desk. Eventually it was his turn.

'Ah, yes, the Frenchie – *Arromanches*,' said the petty officer looking at Harry's papers. 'She's putting to sea this morning, sir.' He leaned forward avuncularly: 'She's right alongside here now. Go and wave to her, if you like.'

'Oh, right,' said Harry surprised at the informality. 'Yes . . . well, I will.'

The petty officer glanced through the documents. 'You've got another seven days' leave, sir. That'll make ten days altogether. Report to HMS *Partridge* on the seventeenth, unless previously recalled.'

'When does she sail?' asked Harry. He knew HMS *Partridge* was a shore establishment, a naval barracks and gunnery school. The petty officer had heard the joke too many times.

'Just for holding, sir. They'll post you to a ship from there, I expect. Just coming back from the French Navy, like you have, you've probably got overlooked. Wish they'd overlook me.' He looked up, inclined to be friendly: 'Anyway, it looks like there's going to be more doing on the beach than on the 'oggin for a while. They been giving us rifle practice like blinding infantry.' He looked at the clock, big as a gunnery target, on the concourse wall, and once more leaned confidingly. 'If you want to see the *Arromanches* sail, young sir, I'd get moving now,' he advised. 'She's just about due to cast off. If you show your pass at the rear door you can go straight out. You'll see her. Number four berth.'

Harry thanked him and went through the criss-crossing men in the long entrance hall. He opened his pass at the door and stepped out into the oily dockside sun. There was a mine-sweeper tied up immediately before the building, her super-structure a mangle of bomb-damage. One berth down, even now easing out from the quay, was the *Arromanches*. She was going out bow first into the open water like the hand of a clock. He hurried over cables and cobbles towards her.

A group of senior French officers stood on the quay and the berth area was watched by a pair of stoic British sentries. One halted Harry, his bayonet altering its angle uncompromisingly. 'I've just come off this ship,' said Harry hurriedly, like a schoolboy explaining to an officious prefect. 'I'd . . . I'd like to give them a wave.' The man's face remained unconvinced. Harry said with a self-conscious grin, 'Wish them *bon voyage.*'

'Can't go through, sir,' said the sentry and then, without a wrinkle of change in his expression, added, 'You'll have to *bon voyage* from over there.' He nodded towards the quayside area outside the space he was guarding. Harry saluted formally as the sentry came to attention and then, like an admonished lad, he moved sideways to the edge of the dock.

The forward part of the destroyer was out in the waterway to the full extent now, and the stern, with its depth charges stacked like barrels, began to budge away from the quay. The ship's small band, half a dozen standing beneath the forward guns, began to play 'La Marseillaise' and everyone on the dock stood to attention. Harry, a figure remote from the rest, stood rigidly. The brave old martial tune floated over the morning ships, gulls looped away like pages of paper. Along the deck of the destroyer the crew were lined, the red pom-poms on their hats as vivid as poppies. By the time the final strain of the music had died the vessel was out in the mid-water of the dock. Harry watched her with real pride. She was his first ship. Then, from almost below his feet a motor launch appeared, its snout towards the grey vessel. Harry called: 'Paul! Clovis!' Briefly he turned to see if anyone else had heard. Nobody was looking. The two young Frenchmen stared up and their faces lit.

They waved and wished him well. He called: 'See you soon!' as people do even when they doubt that they will.

'*Alors!* See you soon!' the shouts came back.

'*Au revoir!* Good luck!' he called. He waved and then self-consciously stood to attention and saluted. They returned the farewell.

'Good-bye *Loup de Mer*,' Clovis called. 'Good-bye Sea Wolf!'

Their young laughter echoed across the busy water as the launch nosed noisily towards the destroyer. 'See you soon,' he said once again, this time quietly, to himself.

The afternoon was empty to the horizon, yellow shingle divided by old wooden groynes, sloping to the water; the concise touch of tide on shore the only sound apart from sudden outbreaks of shouting from the gulls. Some white washing blew outside a low line of coastguard cottages like a breezy signal of defiance.

That day, Friday, 10 May, saw the rolling armoured army of Germany make fierce inroads across the level lands of Holland and Belgium. Each news bulletin related stories of optimistic resistance but the military innuendos – confused situations, strategic withdrawals, retreats to new, prepared positions – told the true tale. Within hours the invaders were across the newly cut Albert Canal, vaunted as a formidable ditch of defence. Panic, incompetence and mean treachery were rife. The fleeing Belgians omitted to destroy vital bridges and the Panzer Divisions' tanks accepted the gift of an easy crossing.

James had listened to the news and then said he was going for a walk. 'I'll come too,' Millie had offered determinedly. 'I'll get Horace and we'll go down to the beach, if you like. Just as we used to do. We might not get many more chances.:

'Yes, all right,' he had said. 'If you like.'

They reached the coast along the familiar mottled lanes and left the pony tethered to a winch, rusty and long unused. He helped her down to the shingle and they began to walk towards the east, the white and green flank of the Isle of Wight in their view.

'I can't see any point in you joining the women's services,' he said as they walked.

'Why not? Yesterday you were saying that everyone should be *doing* something.' She paused and picking up a pebble threw it angrily into the sea.

'They're just playing games,' he said. 'Most of those women are there for the fun. They're being paid for it too.'

She threw another pebble, a short pitch that splashed only a few feet away. 'It sounds tempting,' she said. Then: 'I'll have to do something. I'm not sitting on my backside knitting.'

'There's nothing wrong with knitting,' he said. 'Who's that?' He pointed ahead. A figure was moving towards them, climbing with difficulty over each succeeding wooden groyne. 'It's old Buck, from The Haven,' he added.

'Yes,' said Millie, glad of the interruption. 'He's been putting out his lobster pots, I expect.'

They walked on, the distant figure moving towards them. 'Apparently they want people to help out at Moyles Court,' she continued. 'At the new RAF station.'

'Help out?'

'Serving drinks and suchlike.'

'If you want to be a barmaid.'

She choked back her anger, for Jeremiah Buck, the old fisherman, was now too near. Sonny had been his lifelong friend.

They arrived at one of the groynes simultaneously and stood looking over like neighbours chatting at the garden wall.

'It don't look any too good, do it, Mr Lovatt?' said the old man. He looked over his shoulder, towards the east, as if he half-expected an immediate attack.

'It certainly doesn't at the moment,' agreed James.

Millie said: 'It was a terrible thing with Sonny.' She reached up and touched the brown, pitted hand.

Jeremiah said solemnly: 'Stanley Garnet Mountford, that was his name. Nobody ever knew 'is name till he was dead. Funny, ain't it? Not me, even, and I was his old pal. Stanley Garnet Mountford, what a name to 'ave.' He wiped his eye with the back of his hand, then regarded James squarely, as if he had been meaning to ask him something for a long time, as if their meeting was not merely fortuitous.

'Mr Lovatt,' he said, 'we 'ave got some sort of *plan*, 'aven't we?'

The concern in the faded eyes turned on James. James waited. 'I would imagine so,' he answered.

'I mean, we're *bound* to 'ave. Stands to common sense,' said the fisherman, disappointed at the reply. 'We been in this war now close on a year, and God knows 'twas known it was coming, wasn't it. Our men in London must have a *plan*. I reckon they're just waiting for this Hitler to put his head in the pot – then *bang*, down comes the trap.' He looked hopefully at James.

James smiled tightly. 'They don't tell me what they have in store,' he said, 'but I imagine it's all taken care of. And there's France. We mustn't forget the French – six million men in the army.'

'Ah,' said Jeremiah sagely. 'The French. Well I always did worry a bit about they.' He took a deep breath and prepared to climb the groyne. 'We shall 'ave to see,' he said. 'Wait and see what the plan is. There must be one, else what we been doing all this time?'

He climbed over and they waved him off before mounting the groyne and continuing in the opposite direction. They turned the headland and, their own quarrels, their own doubts put aside for a moment, looked over into the serene estuary of Binford Haven, the three sail-like hills bright in the sun, hardly a movement anywhere in the landscape.

'A plan,' muttered James bitterly. 'He thinks we might have a plan.'

*

With the day settling into an evening of comfortable shadows, birds in the house eaves and the garden branches, Robert sat in his armchair near the open french window and surveyed his grass, his flowers, and observed his dog Wadsworth saunter across the sections of late sunlight. Elizabeth brought him his gin and tonic and she poured herself a small sherry and they sat waiting for the wireless news.

'It's very strange to think that possibly everything could be changed, in the space of a few weeks,' she said, breaking the silence.

'You mean, I won't be able to call my dog my own,' he smiled. He leaned forward and tapped her wrist fondly. 'They'll never get here,' he said. 'Even if they got through France, they'll find the English Channel is a bit wider than the Albert Canal.'

She patted his hand in return, a touch of thanks. 'There are great goings-on in Parliament,' she said. 'They've been talking about it all day. It looks as if Mr Chamberlain will be put firmly outside the door by tonight. He'll get all the blame, poor soul.'

Robert stood and went the one step out into the garden. May blossom was heavy by the wall. The hum of summer spiced the air. He paced around the lawn as if measuring it, pausing to push the lolling dog gently with his foot. A blackbird sang and a distinct shot sounded in the distant air.

'Clakka after rabbits,' said Robert arriving back at the french window. 'He should be saving ammunition.'

'We need the rabbits,' smiled Elizabeth. 'That's probably your Sunday lunch you heard.'

The news began at six o'clock. They sat closely together and listened intently, as if it were music. Behind the official bolstering communiqués it was clear that the Nazis were swarming through the Low Countries. The announcer with his anonymous, platonic voice read the catalogue of disaster. He ended: 'And here is tonight's sports news. Racing. Racing at Newmarket. Two-thirty. Anthony's Crown. Second, My Beauty, third, Happy Warrior. Three-fifteen. Mary Mary. Second, Downland, third, Amadeus . . .'

Irritably Robert reached up to turn the set off. It was a big brown radio, three years old, with polished knobs. 'Racing,' he grumbled. 'Racing, for God's sake, when the world's falling apart . . .' Then a hesitation in the announcer's mechanically sepulchral tone caused him to wait. The voice said: 'We interrupt the racing results for a special news bulletin. It has just been announced from Number 10, Downing Street, that Mr Neville Chamberlain has tendered his resignation as Prime Minister and that this has been accepted by His Majesty the King. His Majesty has asked Mr Winston Churchill to form a government. That is the end of the special announcement. Back now to the racing results. Newmarket, four o'clock. Gentleman Jim. Second, Trinity House, third . . .'

Bess's grandmother, Mrs Harriet Spofforth, had been wearing her gas mask for fifteen minutes, sitting in a high-back chair by the Queen Anne window of her house. She was outlined in an almost saintly fashion by evening light.

'Look – Whistler's Mother,' giggled Bess as she and

Harry approached the room. 'Don't laugh for God's sake. She gets miffed as hell if you laugh.'

They went into the tall room and Mrs Spofforth half turned. In the hideous black mask with its hanging snout she had the aspect of a thin and truncated elephant.

'My grandmother is trying out her gas mask,' said Bess loudly as they walked towards the old lady. A pair of red-rimmed, vehement ears pushed out from either side of the rubber. 'Grandma, this is Harry Lovatt. You probably remember him.'

Imprisoned eyes fixed on Harry through the celluloid oval window at the front of the rubber mutation. Grandmother tried to speak but her words were reduced to exhalations, dulled grunts, which caused the window to fog and the canister nose-piece of the mask to jog in and out in a drinking motion. Realizing she could not be heard Mrs Spofforth tugged at the straps and half eased the rubber from its tight clasp around her head. A segment of scarlet face was revealed. 'I wouldn't want to be shut in here for long,' she shouted sideways through the aperture. 'Hot as hell.'

Bess tightened her lips and then suggested that Mrs Spofforth should take the mask off. The old lady replied by letting the straps snap against her head like a dancer's garter against her thigh. She held up the fingers of one hand. 'Five more minutes,' sighed Bess. 'She's determined to keep it on for twenty minutes, which is more than I'd want to.'

'Or me,' agreed Harry. 'I think she's very brave.'

Bess moved towards the door saying to Harry: 'I won't be long, I'll be down in time for her to emerge from there. Make yourself at home. Would you like a drink?'

'Er . . . no . . . thanks.'

'Just talk to gran then, will you. Tell her where you've been. Tell her about the navy.'

Uncomfortably Harry turned back to the eyes behind the celluloid oval screen. The old lady moved the side of the mask from her face once more and hissed through the opening. '*Talk*, will you. If I start it steams up this idiotic window.'

'Yes . . . yes, of course,' hesitated Harry. He searched for something to say. The short trunk swung expectantly in his direction. 'It's . . . it's been a lovely day, hasn't it,' he began laboriously. 'They say it's going to be a nice summer. I'm taking Bess to the Young Farmers' Supper. In Lyndhurst.'

Mrs Spofforth blahed something and then in exasperation tugged the side of the rubber wide again. 'What about Chamberlain?' she called in the imprisoned voice. 'What about Churchill?'

'Oh . . . yes. I heard. It was on the news.' He felt incredibly juvenile with her. He bent closer as one would with someone deaf. 'My parents were just discussing it. They seem to think it's a good thing.'

'The Dardanelles!' she suddenly bellowed, lugging out the side of the mask again. 'Remember the Dardanelles!'

'The . . .? Oh, the Dardanelles. Yes, naturally. We mustn't forget them.' Desperately he tried to recall the Dardanelles.

'That was Churchill, remember. Bloody fool.' She abruptly pulled the gas mask away from her face. Below it her head was like a boiled beetroot. 'That's enough of that mad contraption,' she announced, gasping for air. 'They'll have to gas me, that's all. I can't wear that for hours on end. You can't hold a decent conversation.'

'They are awful,' Harry agreed. 'Cumbersome.'

'And ugly,' she shouted angrily, as if it were his fault. She pointed at her own face. 'It's bad enough having a worn-out phizog like this anyway, but that thing's even worse . . . Anyway, you can bet your life that if I was sitting there wearing it when the Nazis turned up, the buggers would bayonet me.' She turned and saw that her granddaughter had appeared in the doorway. 'Oh dear, that does look odd. Is it a barn dance?'

Harry turned towards the door. Bess was wearing a white blouse, a plaid skirt and an annoyed expression. 'No, gran.' She gathered her voice. 'It's a farmers' supper – and there's a war on.'

'Farmers!' snorted the old lady. 'Huh! They'll never starve.' She regarded Harry acutely. 'Farmers and cooks never do,' she said. 'If ever you are captured always tell them you're a cook. Cooks always survive.'

She returned to inspecting Bess. 'As long as you don't go wearing trousers,' she said. 'They're disgraceful.' She was holding the gas mask by its straps, letting it hang down like some terrible executed head. 'Girls who wear these trousers are merely taking a mean advantage of wartime conditions,' she continued fiercely. She dropped the mask metallically on the floor with a kind of disgust. 'We always went to dances, or even agricultural dinners, in a few fripperies, laces and suchlike.' She looked towards Bess again. 'Still, if that's the mode, then that's the mode. My God, Hitler must be delighted to know what he's done to society in this country. Ravaged the Hunt Ball for a start.'

Bess said firmly: 'It's not the Hunt Ball, grandma. It's a five-bob supper.'

'All this quick-stepping, fox-trotting, tangoing,' pursued the old lady villainously. 'I'm simply glad I was young in a more graceful age.' She turned in a businesslike way to Harry. Now she had rid herself of the gas mask she seemed eager to talk. 'Ah, yes, of course, I remember you now, young man. I couldn't see you properly through that dratted window. The Lovatts' boy.' She turned her cheek and eye sideways as if drawing a rifle sight on him. 'Hmm. Which one are you? The good-looking one or the other one?'

'Grandmother,' admonished Bess. She was ready to leave and began to tap her foot.

Harry laughed. 'The other one, I expect,' he said.

'No, you're not. I remember. You were the boy always into some trouble. Your brother kept his nose clean. A bit sly, I always thought.' She pointed accusingly. 'You were the one in the summer house, I recall.' She turned the finger on Bess like a gun changing target. Harry felt his face redden. Bess's mouth tightened.

'Please, grandmother. *If* you don't mind, we'll be on our way.'

The old lady regarded them steadily, individually. She moved her hands together as though washing them. 'Well, let's have no more hanky or panky,' she warned. She looked darkly at Bess. 'There's been enough trouble in London.'

The girl turned away, annoyed, and made for the

door. 'We *must* be off,' she sniffed. 'I have my key, I'll let myself in.' Harry followed her, nervously wishing Mrs Spofforth good night, bowing a little as he went.

'Give my love to your mother and regards to your father, young man,' she ordered. 'I saw him at Lampard's the other day. Heavy going as ever, isn't he? Can't think why a nice little woman like your mother ever married him. Still, down here there's not much choice, I suppose. Good night.'

'Yes . . . good night,' bowed Harry, backing towards the door. He almost fell over himself trying to get out. Bess was fuming in the hall, glaring at him as if he had abetted the old lady. She pushed past him haughtily as he opened the weighty door. They went around to the front of the house where her car was standing. Harry had arrived on his bicycle which he had rested under the garden hedge. As they passed the window they saw that Mrs Spofforth had donned the gas mask again and was outlined in profile against the pane.

'Old pig,' snorted Bess. With sudden spite she banged on the window, causing the grotesque half trunk to turn. With difficulty the mask was taken off and the crimson face appeared. 'They're coming!' shouted Bess through the glass. 'The Germans are coming! They'll get you!'

The old lady laughed uproariously and replaced the gas mask. Bess turned furiously, almost dragging the bemused Harry with her. They got into her car and she started the engine which croaked noisily as if it were an extension of her anger. 'My God,' she said bitterly, 'I ought to drive this car straight back to London and to hell with them all.' She stared accusingly at his blank expression. 'I hate this bloody place.'

Bess drove, removed and silent, through the forest, only interrupting her mood to curse and brake as some sauntering wild ponies appeared in the sliver of headlights. Harry dutifully cursed them with her. 'You don't have to agree with me,' she retorted rudely. He slumped lower in the seat.

They turned off the long street in Lyndhurst and bumped through the arch of the hotel into the former coaching yard. There were a few cars there, four buses which had brought contingents from outlying places, and a muddle of bicycles. They left the car, Bess striding a pace in front of him as they went through the wooden porch at the front of the hotel. Her backside and legs were slender beneath the plaid skirt. He remembered those legs, that dusty day in the summer house. At the door she turned to him and he was faced again with the white blouse, two straps of lace running from the shoulders over her breasts. 'Do I look passable?' she asked, more pleasantly.

'Beautiful,' he replied honestly. 'I wouldn't have wanted to come with anyone else.'

At last she smiled. 'Liar,' she said. They walked into the ante-room to the hall which was being used as a bar. He touched her on the fresh blouse, at her waist and asked her what she would like to drink.

'I'll have a gin and tonic, please, Harry,' she said. Her eyes were moving about the crowd. 'The last time you bought me a drink it must have been a bottle of pop,' she added.

Harry, pleased and conscious of his naval officer's uniform among the dusty dinner jackets and the odd patches of khaki and air-force blue, looked around the bar. They knew most of the people. Several of the girls looked at him keenly, their expressions drooping when they saw Bess. 'It's a bit like being back at school again, isn't it,' he whispered to Bess. 'Except the boys are in long trousers.'

'And two of the girls are in trouble,' giggled Bess. 'Angela Phipps and Teresa Goodridge, see? Paid-up members of the pudding club.'

'They're both married,' he pointed out primly.

'They're still in trouble,' she said. 'In my book they are, anyway. God, fancy getting in that state when you're twenty.' Harry watched her, fascinated, as she moved a couple of paces to one side and beamed at Angela Phipps, a rosy, always-round girl, now much rounder. 'Angela, how *are* you?' asked Bess. 'How wonderful, you're having a baby.'

'October,' simpered Angela. Her eyes went to the man responsible, a field-faced farmer they all called 'Dungo' at school. 'You remember William, don't you, of course?' Bess said she did. 'Hello, Harry,' Angela said, half turning away. She hung out a rosy hand which Harry shook gently before exchanging it for the flat paw of William.

Dungo had grown outwards, but not upwards. His eyes were farming blue, and seemed to be peering into the distance. 'In the navy, eh,' he said after gazing long at Harry's uniform. He let out a humphing laugh. 'Good job we've got an air force, eh?'

'What price glory?' asked another voice. A flour-skinned young man, his head trapped by his collar, stood beaming through perspiration. At school they had called him Pissington, although his name was Tissington. He was now an agricultural auctioneer.

'What price glory?' he repeated as if checking a bid. He tugged at Harry's sleeve.

'What price farm prices?' Bess put in quickly. 'You seem to be getting fat on the war. When are you going to join up?'

'I'm unfit,' said Tissington with a nervous jerk away from the attack.

'Never!' she returned, apparently amazed. '*You*, unfit?'

'Can you imagine that we ever grew up with this lot?' she demanded of Harry as they moved away. 'Christ, they're so ghastly. Just look at them – glug, glug, glug, gobble, gobble. Like a turkey house.' She turned on him sharply. Her breasts touched his jacket and he felt them give. 'And you should learn to stand up for yourself a bit. Letting that idiot make rude remarks about your being in the navy.'

'Thanks for defending me,' he said. She had remained close and his knee went out and made contact with her leg. 'I couldn't see any point in bothering.'

They moved to the table, shaking hands with their immediate neighbours and exchanging insignificant comments on days remembered, before grace was said deeply and the company sat down to soup and salmon, roast beef, trifle loaded with fruit and rum, wines and beers. Bess had always been a hearty eater. He recalled how, even at school, she had stolen pieces from his plate and the plates of others. Now she delved into the excellent repast with energy. Her mouth full of fresh salmon, she leaned towards him and mumbled: 'Grandma was right about greedy farmers, wasn't she.'

Ben Bennett and his New Forest Arcadians, an ensemble which had played at social functions in the region for as long as anyone present could recall, took up their place on the rostrum and began to perform tunes to accompany the eating, including 'Run, Rabbit, Run', with a solo on a newly purchased saxophone of which Ben, who blew it, was particularly proud. It had been made in Germany, something Ben kept private, and there were unlikely to be any further supplies available until the conclusion of hostilities. During the trifle another sound filtered through the heavy talk and the music, the air-raid siren. Ben thought he heard his Arcadians waver and his long arm went out like a derrick to urge them together.

The tune staggered to a ragged end. The clatter of cutlery could now be heard over the voices. Ben, shining with effort, reached for the microphone, and announced: 'Ladies and gentlemen, that, in case you didn't know, was "A Nightingale Sang in Berkeley Square", accompanied by the air-raid siren.' Some people laughed. 'If you wish to leave the 'all,' continued the bandleader, 'you're welcome to. But don't expect your trifle to be there when you get back. It's probably only another false alarm anyway. Adolf wouldn't dare bomb Lyndhurst. The Arcadians are carrying on, you'll be pleased to know, and our next selection is –'

Another sound was heard in the room at that moment, tuneless whistles blowing. Through the main doors at the far end rushed two air-raid wardens, the letters ARP emblazoned on their basin helmets, so dramatic and furtive that they might have been fugitives. One man's helmet had fallen forward in his hurry and only his nose and his whistle protruded. They were small men of equal size, like armoured twins. 'Stop! Stop the *orchestra*!' shouted the leading warden, tugging his whistle from his lips like a cork. He replaced it and shrieked a further cautionary blast.

The band, collectively blinking at the compliment, ceased and the eyes of the eaters were all on the intruders. The first warden pushed his helmet rim back importantly. There were some catcalls and laughter as he was recognized as an ordinary man. 'It's old Barney,' shouted a man. 'Drunk again!' Angrily he waved his finger and was about to shout something else when a shattering explosion occurred overhead. The hall windows rattled. Dust shot in clouds from the floor. 'Take cover!' howled the warden, providing an instant example by flinging himself beneath the bar. The warning was hardly issued before there was another heavy explosion and then everyone in the room was on the floor, piled on top of each other, calling, crawling towards the flimsy cover of the side tables. The men from the band scuttled below the stage, crammed there curiously like castaways on an inverted raft, Ben Bennett reappearing briefly to rescue his new German saxophone.

Two more violent bangs followed, close on each other. Harry had pulled Bess below one of the tables and was lying enjoyably close to her. The skin of their cheeks was touching. Hers felt cool.

'Let's clear out,' said Bess firmly. 'I'd rather take my chance outside. This mob will panic.'

A clattering like heavy rain sounded on the roof above them. 'Shrapnel,' said Harry. He held on to her. 'You're staying here.'

'Were those bombs?' she asked. 'Those bangs?'

'Somebody farting,' retorted a sad drunken voice nearby.

'Guns, or a gun anyway,' said Harry. 'I didn't know they had an anti-aircraft gun here.'

'Right behind the hotel,' muttered a man on the other side. 'It's only been there three days.'

As if to confirm its presence the gun exploded again, shaking the building and provoking further clouds of ancient dust from the floor. People choked on the deposits from generations of dancing pumps. Silence followed, a stretched silence, everyone on edge for another spasm. Nothing happened. Eventually Ben, the bandleader, peered out from the short curtain below the rostrum, and sneezed in the dust. Carefully he reached up and put one of the music stands on its feet. His appearance was followed by a sneaking run on the part of the senior warden, the man called Barney, scuttling like a crab across the floor to the doorway. 'Don't half smell out there,' he confided loudly to his following comrade. 'Gas, I reckon.'

'Gas!' howled a woman who overheard. 'Poison gas!'

'Grab the silly cow, Herb,' ordered Barney brusquely. His colleague slapped a hand across the woman's mouth and her husband, seizing the opportunity, reinforced the gag with his own palm. Barney looked with fearful eyes out of the door. In the distance the air-raid all-clear signal sounded, the long-tailed wail curling through the night. 'Everybody, keep calm, please,' ordered the warden. 'No rushing to the door. There's nothing to see. And there's no danger. Remain where you are until the authorities have checked.'

His colleague, Herb, stared at him with a mixture of mystery and admiration. 'The authorities?' he whispered.

'Us, you bloody fool,' answered Barney. '*Us.*'

They disappeared into the acrid street. The moon was sidling through the gunsmoke. Inside the hall everyone but the extra-nervous had straightened up and brushed themselves down. Ben had taken the saxophone to pieces and by blowing was forcing dust and spit from one of its tubes.

'I didn't hear any aircraft,' mentioned Harry.

'Nor did I,' confirmed Bess. 'Only that deafening damned gun. Can we get out of this place? I've had enough of it.'

They edged towards the door and were almost there when the ARP wardens returned and announced grandly, as if they had personally accomplished it, that everything was indeed all clear. The band re-embarked on 'Run, Rabbit, Run' and some diners returned to their abandoned food. Most went to peer cautiously out in the street.

Everywhere heads were prodding from doors and windows. Gritty smoke remained suspended above the town like a lace curtain across the modest moon.

'It's they trigger-'appy buggers on that AA gun, I reckon,' Barney said to Harry as he and Bess reached the open air. 'They been dyin' to fire the thing all this week.' His tone was confiding, one uniformed man, one warrior, to another.

'They must have been firing at *something*, they must have been given orders,' pointed out Harry.

Like a croaking spectre an upright policeman on a bicycle materialized through the fumes in the street. Around his neck he had suspended a notice board. He braked adjacent to the group outside the hall and producing a torch shone it with mute importance on the notice which said: 'All Clear. Raider Passed.'

There was scarcely time to digest this reassurance when the anti-aircraft gun behind the hotel fired again, a violent bang and a flash like white lightning. Everyone tumbled back into the hall, including the policeman who leapt smartly from his machine and let it and the false tidings of the notice fall to the ground. As if in shock he began to blow furiously on his whistle. Because of the crush in the porch he could only just get under cover and even then had to make additional room for his head by pushing backwards with his rump. He held his steel helmet forward over his forehead, whistle still shrieking below its rim, as the hot shrapnel clattered about them.

'Bloody fine all clear that was,' suggested a voice in the crush. 'Stop whistling will you!'

''T'wasn't my fault,' moaned the policeman. 'I heard the all clear and as far as I'm concerned it means all clear. It's those madmen with the gun.'

They began cautiously, though prepared for another explosion, to pick themselves up. Harry helped Bess to her feet. Her face was puffed with anger. The policeman shone his torch on them and seeing the uniform came to a fierce attention and salute. 'Good evening, sir.'

Harry's surprised response was curtailed by the howling of every dog and wailing of every cat in Lyndhurst, suddenly as if secretly arranged between themselves. The chorus issued from the gardens, alleys and backways of the town and from the overcast houses. It was joined, at once, by an echoing drubbing. The crowd in the hall doorway watched, fixed, as the cause of the sound came up the street, a flying herd of ponies, one galloping in the lead.

'A zebra,' breathed a voice in disbelief. 'It's a zebra.'

'Ponies,' corrected the policeman officially from the crowd. 'Striped.'

They were. Forest ponies painted in luminous stripes, half a dozen following the leader. The policeman embarked officially into the road, followed by the wardens with a deference indicating that the horses were outside their orbit of action. The animals wheeled and reared, neighing belligerently. One, backing on to the pavement, kicked out, viciously smashing the window of a greengrocery shop. Apples and potatoes rolled into the street. At that moment another round was fired by the anti-aircraft gun, a blinding flash and report that sent the humans stumbling back into the porch, falling on top of each other. The panicked ponies turned and snorted back the way they had come. Shrapnel again showered the street, old tiles slid from roofs, dogs and cats began to howl again. 'Barmy bastards, what do they think they're shooting at?' sobbed the policeman. When he thought it was safe he gazed up at the sky. 'There's nothing up there!' he bawled. 'Not a bloody sausage!'

A suspicious silence settled on the little town. The animal howls diminished to a few cat calls. People regained their feet. The street was occupied only by wandering smoke. 'Everybody stay under cover,' ordered the policeman. 'It's no use taking risks with these lunatics. I'll try and make my way over there.'

There was a murmur of approval at his forth-coming bravery. He stood up and squared his helmet followed by his shoulders. His foray was rendered unnecessary, however, by the casual appearance of an army car, a camouflaged Austin that groped along the street like a hedgehog and stopped sedately in front of the crowd at the hall door. A buoyant army officer pushed his moustached face from the window and called: 'Everybody hunky-dory?'

Nobody was capable of framing an adequate answer. One of the ARP wardens nudged the police-man who, after some hesitation, trudged the few paces out into the road, giving it the aspect of a considerable journey. Patently looking to the sky and once more adjusting his helmet he said: 'We was under the impression, sir, that the all clear had sounded.'

'Good deduction, officer,' grinned the young man behind the moustache. 'Operational mistake, that's all.'

'What was it you was shooting at, sir? An owl perhaps?'

'No, constable,' returned the officer, apparently seriously considering the possibility. 'Barrage balloon, we now think.'

'Barrage balloon?' asked someone in the crowd. 'I thought they were on *our* side.'

'Adrift,' smiled the officer, unruffled. 'Broke adrift. Danger to aircraft. Good night all.' He threw up a half wave, half salute, and the car rolled on.

Harry and Bess went around to the stable yard and climbed into her car. 'I think this war's driving everyone off their rockers,' she announced as the engine started. 'Striped ponies, for God's sake.'

Harry sighed. 'Unbelievable, isn't it,' he agreed. 'They painted them so they can be seen by drivers in the dark.' She drove the car swiftly under the arch and into the street. Harry said seriously: 'They only painted some. The stripes frightened the foals.'

Peevishly she accelerated down the smoky street. The inhabitants were all out of doors now, some sweeping up glass from the road and the pavement. Diners from the hall were helping the greengrocer pick up his apples and potatoes while his wife, elbows on the sill, watched from a window above the shop. 'They're all counted!' she shouted ungraciously.

At the end of the town, where the forest road turned off, they came across the anti-aircraft officer leaning against the flank of his car. He waved them down. 'Evening, sir,' he said seeing Harry. 'Everything all right?'

'In the circumstances, yes, I suppose so,' replied Harry carefully.

'Where were you when all the hullaballoo was on?' He smiled engagingly into Bess's staring eyes.

Bess answered, 'In the middle of the bombardment.'

'Don't they make a fuss?' sighed the officer. 'Don't they just. Never saw such a display. Civilians! God knows what they'll be like when this war really gets on its feet.'

The air was mild and cloudy as they drove across the night-bound forest, the thin slices of the car's masked headlights scarcely picking up the road. People there always said 'across' not 'through' the forest, for much of it was exposed moorland of gorse and flattish hills; the trees mainly clustered beside cranky streams, in ordered plantations by the side of the road, gathered unofficially about a house, or in the hoof of a valley. Both had known the road since childhood and could measure it by the wooden bridges. The ground beside the bridges was often worn, sloping ground where donkeys, pigs and horses went to drink. Bess stopped the car and looked at him mischievously. 'Want to look at the moon in the river, sailor?' she asked.

Harry saw the frank look on her face. His anticipation began to stir. She leaned over and kissed him on the cheek, then the lips, and he knew that she had not changed at all. In return he tapped her cheek with his fingers and they climbed out of the car and walked to the rail of the bridge. Below them the seams of the shallow stream glowed as they formed and reformed into noisy patterns over the stone bed. A worried night rat fell over itself to reach concealment.

Bess had walked to the bridge with her hands behind her back and now she faced him tautly, her face wry, her breasts pushed out. She remained like that, swaying a little, like a small girl who has done something bad but clever. She produced from behind her back a bottle of whisky. 'Want a drink?' she asked.

'Where . . . where did you get that?' asked Harry. The amber glowed a little even in that light. He realized. 'You didn't actually . . . ?'

'I did actually,' Bess said proudly. 'Pinched it. Pinched it from right under their noses in the bar, while all that silly fuss was going on.' She smiled. 'Technically, I suppose, that makes me a looter.'

He remained amazed. 'Yes,' he answered eventually. 'I suppose it does, technically.'

She opened the top firmly and sniffed into the neck. 'God, what a smell,' she said. She lifted the bottle with a small jerk and said: 'Cheers!' To his further amazement she took a long swig and then another. She choked and coughed violently. His hand made a shape to pat her on the back, but he couldn't bring himself to do it. Eyes watering, she held the bottle towards him. 'Now you,' she suggested. 'Take a good one. It's free. Sorry there's no glasses, but us looters don't use them.'

Slowly, feeling priggish and annoyed because of it, Harry took the bottle. Automatically he wiped the neck. 'Thanks very much,' she said. 'I hope you don't do that after you've kissed me.' She grinned and nodded towards the whisky: 'What do they say about stolen stuff always tasting better?'

Harry took a modest drink. He was not used to Scotch and it roared down his throat. He eyed Bess with some admiration. Taking the cork from her he made to push it into the neck. 'Hey, wait a minute,' she protested. 'It's my turn now.'

'Listen,' said Harry gravely. 'You've got to drive. It's hard enough to see anyway.'

'They should have striped *all* the ponies,' she suggested inconsequentially. She allowed him to replace the cork. 'All right, sir,' she said. 'I don't want to bash up my nice new car.' Abruptly she closed in on him, the Scotch bottle jammed between them, and began kissing him lasciviously. Several times she did so, on his lips, his face generally, and his neck. Her lipstick splashed all over her mouth, she withdrew to breathe and then said she had an idea. 'Let's . . . let's take it to that summer house,' she suggested, tight with mischief. 'You know, where we were that time in your garden. Let's take it there and finish it.'

'Finish the whole bottle?' Harry laughed nervously. Automatically he looked at his watch. It was still only eleven o'clock and his parents might have stayed up to hear the news.

'Finish what we never finished before,' she said archly. 'Let's have another swig and go.'

She took the bottle from his hands and lifted it for another drink. He thought she seemed quite accomplished at it. The summer house. Of course he wanted to go back to the summer house with her. If only he could keep her quiet; if only his parents had gone to bed.

Accepting the proffered bottle he took a token drink and then caught her held-out hand to go back to the car. She paused to lean dangerously over the wooden rail of the bridge, waving good night to her shadow in the stream. She insisted that he left his shadow with a similar farewell. Doing so he realized that he was going to have difficulty in keeping the situation in hand. It was a pity that his mother slept so lightly.

'Can't we go somewhere else?' he suggested lamely as they moved back to the car.

'Cowardy custard,' she retorted, staggering a little dance on the road. 'You're just frightened of mummy.'

'Not at all.'

'Yes you are, sonny. If we don't go to your summer house we're not going any-bloody-where. I told you, I want to finish it off.'

He had to help her into the car, his apprehension growing. As he went around the back to reach the far door Bess started the engine and went bumping like a kangaroo down the narrow road, leaving him staring after her. She stopped at the next bend, a hundred yards away, and leaning precariously out bellowed: 'Come on, Harry. I thought you were in. Hurry up!'

Sighing with dismay he began to lope after her, coming to a frozen halt when she suddenly put the vehicle into reverse and came charging backwards up the road to meet him. He had to leap aside into a forest ditch, fortunately dry, to get out of her path as the Standard careered by. She jarred to a stop and peered again from the window. 'Oh, there you are. Why do you keep jumping about? Come on, get in, darling.'

Heavily he climbed in beside her. She smiled extravagantly in the dark and then reaching out pressed his face into her breasts. 'Summer house, here we come,' she laughed, starting the car forward again.

The excitement of the moment when he had his nose in her bosom was soon extinguished by the car's maddened progress along the curling forest road. Harry hung on, horrified, as the small vehicle rattled crazily along the straights and skidded hideously around bends. Twice they missed the rails of bridges by inches, Bess shouting at the second escape: 'God, I thought we'd been across this one already.'

'Bess,' he told her as eventually they turned down the track towards his house. 'We've got to be quiet. If we're going to do this. We've got to be.'

'You're frightened of your mummy,' she taunted again, nevertheless slowing.

'The whole village,' he corrected. 'For God's sake, shush up.'

Two hundred yards from the house she stopped the car in a space beside a thicket. 'We'll creep in from here,' she plotted. 'Mummy won't hear us then.' A little relieved and aware of his growing sexual anticipation, Harry got out of the car and closed the door silently in answer to her exaggerated hushing and her finger on her lips. She closed her door with extravagant care, but realizing that the whisky bottle was still within the car she opened it again and slammed it heartily. Frozen-faced, Harry looked at her across the low roof. An upstairs window in the house opened with a rattle, but then closed again.

'Just having a final wee-wee, I expect,' commented Bess looking that way like a scout. She crept around to him and suddenly pulled him down beside the car, rolling on top of him. Harry felt her breasts and stomach and thighs hard against him, the pleasure only slightly diminished by the knowledge that she was grinding his uniform into the grass.

Bess, panting, eased herself off. 'There's plenty more like that,' she whispered. 'Honest. Let's get in the summer house. Come on Harry. It will be lovely.'

Their arms about each other they crept forward through the dark. Harry eased the ring of the front gate and with only a dull click it opened. He put his hand on her bottom, feeling the soft buttocks below the skirt, and pushed her forward into the garden. The summer house leaning against its supporting stays was directly ahead across the orchard grass, its miniature roof outlined. 'Our own little house,' she whispered, giggling.

They reached the squeaky porch of the wooden building and he pantomimed the need to cross it carefully because it sounded. She bent quickly and took off her shoes. Excitement was growing in his chest. He glanced over his shoulder at the house. All was solidly dark.

Now they were in the dry, sweet-smelling interior, in the blackness and standing close against each other. 'It's smaller than I remember,' she whispered. She kissed him lushly, her hands slipping down against the front of his trousers. 'The room I mean,' she added.

She had placed the whisky bottle on the floor and now she bent to pick it up, knocking her hand against it and sending it bumping across the boards. Panic-stricken he tried to find it in the dark. Bess located it first. 'We'll have a noggin,' she suggested. 'It will calm our nerves.' She pulled the cork and they each had a drink. 'Don't worry, Harry,' she whispered. 'Your old woman will be snoring by now.'

Even then he almost took issue with the affront to his mother, but Bess put his hands to the buttons of her blouse and then put hers to his navy fly. They began to unbutton each other. Bess finished first. 'God, Harry Lovatt, that's not too bad at all,' she whispered exploring him. 'I'm glad I waited until you grew up.'

Her lovely, full, pale breasts were before his stupefied gaze now, their skin like silk to his palms. From the house, Wadsworth, the basset hound, began to bark.

'Damn,' Harry muttered. 'That bloody Wadsworth.'

'Why do you call him Wadsworth?' she inquired, exposing him fully and holding him in both soft hands. She began to tug gently. Harry had difficulty in speaking. Every sensation from drunkenness to ecstasy was coursing through his blood. His trousers suddenly rippled down to his ankles.

'It was the middle name of Longfellow, you know, the poet, and he being a basset, the dog I mean, we thought it . . . Oh God, Bess, this is terrific.'

'Harry!' His father's voice sounded into the garden from an open upstairs window. 'Harry, are you there?' A torch beam wagged around the darkness.

'Oh Christ,' muttered Bess.

'Bugger it,' agreed Harry.

'Harry! There's been important news.'

He could feel her staring like a challenge at him in the gloom. 'I'll have to go and have a word with him,' he said miserably. 'He'll be coming down here otherwise. And my mother. I'll just go and come back. I'll tell them I'm going to see you home.'

'That's about *all* you're going to see,' she muttered crossly.

'We shouldn't have come here in the first place,' he returned. 'There's all the bloody forest.'

'Harry!' The shout echoed in the garden trees.

'Go on,' she said, backing away from him. 'Go to daddy.'

Sullenly he pulled his trousers up and straightened his jacket. He went out of the summer house leaving her standing in the dark with her breasts hanging out. With a half-curse, half-sob, she put them away. She went quickly out into the garden just as Harry was opening the side door of the house. She watched him go in and carefully close the door behind him. From the inside his voice came. 'Hello, dad. Were you calling?'

114

Bess swore blindly. She bent, put on her shoes and took a running kick at one of the supporting stays that had leaned against the fragile wall of the summer house for years. It fell loosely away. She cursed again and took another flying kick. 'And that's for Wadsworth,' she spat. The second stay clattered down. There came from the summer house a creaking, cracking sound and with what seemed like a relieved sigh the whole side wall fell away. The roof and the other walls groaned, shifted sideways, and leaned there crazily. Bess fled.

Within the house Robert Lovatt met his son at the top of the stairs. 'What was that?' he asked, hearing the crack and creaking of wood in the garden.

'Nothing', said Harry, pretending to listen. 'Something in the trees, I expect. A pony probably. I was just coming in.' Wadsworth appeared, red eyes revolving. Harry grimaced at him.

'Ah yes, good,' enthused his father. 'Your mother was worried. We heard the gunfire. I rang Lyndhurst and they said it was all some fool false alarm.'

'It was,' replied Harry dully.

'Anyway, I'm glad you're here, son. There's some good war news at last. Well done Churchill, I say.'

'Oh yes, what's that?'

'We're on the offensive, Harry. We've successfully invaded Iceland!'

Six

Whit Sunday, 12 May, was the traditional, if often optimistic, British beginning of summer. Across the trees, coloured moors and hills of the New Forest the sun once more shone; the sea at the forest edge was buoyant and the towns and villages of the south basked in the early weather. Church bells, called the poor man's music, tolled across the air.

On that Sunday morning James was not surprised that noticeably more people than usual were making their way towards the church of St Michael and All Angels, Binford. Rotterdam had been viciously bombed and on the English coast people said they could hear the guns in Belgium. As he and Millie alighted from the trap by the green and began to release Horace from the shafts, he saw the worshippers coming from many directions to walk below the lychgate and be greeted by the Reverend Clifford Pemberton with a smile and a clean white surplice blowing like a flag of surrender in the bright southwesterly breeze.

'Nothing like a grave crisis to improve business for the Church of England,' commented James as they walked up the slope towards the sixteenth-century door. 'Old Pemberton can hardly believe his luck.'

They saw his parents with Harry, in uniform,

walking from the village and they stood on the green, shaded by great horse chestnuts and waited for them.

Mrs Harriet Spofforth and Bess arrived in the Flying Standard. A short line of people waited to shake hands with the vicar and Harry coloured as he faced Bess. She was unworried. 'Sleep well?' she asked.

He looked about him and said: 'Yes, very well, thank you.'

'How's Longfellow?' she whispered.

'It's Wadsworth,' he muttered.

Her grandmother, lace to the neck and a velvet hat sprawled on her head, was confronting the vicar truculently. Her gas mask swung in its tubular tin container. 'You're too high, you know,' she accused, tapping on it for emphasis. 'Miles and miles too high. Incense and all that Popery. Go any higher and you'll disappear from view as far as I am concerned. You'll lose *my* custom, for a start.'

'Oh dear, dear,' said the vicar, studying her with controlled malice. 'And what a pity that would be.'

James and Millie greeted their relatives formally, shaking hands and with kisses, although they had been with them only the day before. It was the sort of ritual performed unconsciously when meeting before going into church, the unspoken comfortableness of their English lives. Harry held his mother's gloved hand as they walked into the arched coolness of the nave.

It was ten minutes before the service and there were few pews left unoccupied. Hob Hobson, the grocer, and his wife Dorcas left their seats and moved two pews further back so that the Lovatt family could sit together. Elizabeth smiled her thanks. They sank to their knees, as the people of that place had done on Sundays stretching over centuries, and prayed for God's help and protection. Robert's gas mask tin clattered on the frayed stone floor.

Mrs Gloria Arbuthnot, the clairvoyant, who sometimes called herself a soothsayer and some said was a forest aunt, a witch, crept into the church and sniffed around critically like someone walking into the premises of a rival business. The Reverend Clifford Pemberton, now within the church, eyed her with antipathy. She rarely attended, her only set and certain day being the Festival of All Souls, 31 October, the time of spirits and spells, when she wore a tiny black pointed hat. When the vicar had challenged her on this diabolical accoutrement, she turned a stiff smile on him and said it was her best Sunday bonnet.

The organ was pumped by Billy Sanders, the strong butcher's boy, who wrestled the long pump-handle up and down as if hacking meat on a block, a violence translated into the quietest of music on the far side of the screen. It had even occurred to Billy that the harder he pumped the more serene the melody. By the time the organ had sauntered through its deft and echoing variations, fingered by Mr Frank Purkiss who was also the New Forest schools' piano tuner, the church was full. Sunshine fell from the stained glass of the eastern window, seeming to Elizabeth as though it were part of the music itself and the music part of it. The housewife in her grimaced at how the same light illuminated the dust puffing from the hassocks now being tossed into their places on the choir stalls by the pimpled Willy Cubbins, the last of the evacuees.

From the edge of her eye Millie observed James,

taking in the scene, distant as a stranger, looking about him, at his family, at the heads along the pews like fairground coconuts, and then up and around at the shell of the church itself. Now there were people standing in the aisles and at the back of the church. The vicar peeped around the screen like an actor sneaking a preview of the audience. James wondered how long it was since those lettered tablets and solid memorials on the walls, those carved heads, lost for words, had looked down on a congregation of such volume. Some of those bygone faces were probably there, in life, occupying the same pews on the last occasion; the Thanksgiving for the Armistice that ended the Great War, the end of the War to End all Wars, as they called it. Or perhaps, before that, gratitude for the Reliefs of Mafeking and Ladysmith.

At eleven o'clock, the bells above, as if tired, were reduced to a single, diminishing, call. The Reverend Clifford Pemberton moved across the chancel, his surplice like a sail. A luffing movement brought him to face his congregation. 'Our first hymn on this Whit Sunday we will sing while the choir is in procession,' he intoned. 'It is not really a hymn for Whitsun, but today, I know, aware of the dangers that beset us and our beloved country, we will sing it with deep meaning and a new vigour.'

Elizabeth sensed Robert bracing himself. She knew it would be 'I Vow To Thee My Country'. Robert loved the hymn fervently, and was only slightly put out when Mr Purkiss, the organist, told him that the tune was composed by Gustav Holst. It was the words that mattered and they had been written by an Englishman, on his deathbed, and besides Holst was actually born (he discovered to his relief) in Cheltenham. The name of the tune – Thaxted – had a good English ring anyway.

Now the burnished cross held by Josiah Evritt, the vicar's churchwarden, travelled down the aisle at the van of the choir. Josiah was the loudest and flattest singer in the parish, whose voice was always first to advance on the altar.

> 'I vow to thee my country
> All earthly things above . . .'

Eyes were reverently closed as he bellowed by, followed, two by two, like cruising swans, by the men of the choir, manfully trying to retrieve the tune.

Then trod the younger choristers, scrubbed and brushed, Georgie Mainprice, Gordon Giles, whom they called Franco, Billy Hobson from the shop, Davie Burton, the apple-faced boy from Burton's Farm, and the others. Tommy Oakes, his wolf-cub green under his cassock, his yellow-braided cap rolled in one hand, tried to dig something from his ear with the other. Their young voices followed the deep tones of the men.

> 'And there's another country
> I've heard of long ago . . .'

They journeyed down the congregational valley, past the families, the friends, past the members of the parish council; some choirboys angelically rounding their lips to the words, some with scarcely controlled smirks as they passed the little girls of the village, in their fresh dresses and hair ribbons. The girls, in return, blushed, looked down at their hymn books, or stifled giggles. Millie watched and smiled as she remembered. It was as it had ever been.

Josiah was now bawling from his pew like a man imprisoned in the stocks. Frank Purkiss rolled his eyes into the mirror above the organ keyboard. He was glad when the rest of the choir had taken their places.

'That lays upon the altar
The dearest and the best.'

Elizabeth felt the church's presence more than any of her family. She was even slightly ashamed of it. Now she closed her eyes as she sang, making the hymn into a prayer.

It was not even God, for in thoughtful moments she acknowledged, if only to herself, that all this might not only be falling on deaf ears, but possibly no ears at all. Walls had ears, as the posters warning against careless talk endlessly warned, but did God have them?

No, it was the *being* of the church; it was the old, comely toughness of the wooden pew rail in front of her; it was the threadbare hymn book in her gloved hand; it was the tatty piece-of-carpet feel of the hassock when she knelt. It was the white frieze of the choir, the singing and the music wandering up and above their heads along the pale stone columns and flying beams; the truculent brass eagle carrying on its back the bulky Bible, open like spreading hands for the first lesson, which her husband was to read. It was her husband himself, stuffy old Robert, her sons and her daughter-in-law, and her neighbours in that village. It was the carved screen, the flowers clean on the altar, the embroidered banners of the Sunday School, the Mothers' Union and the Missionary Society. It was the pulpit, drilled by three bullets during a Civil War skirmish, the holes still to be seen. Once, as a girl, she had climbed into the pulpit when she thought no one was around and, crouching, looked through the bullet holes. To her astonishment she had seen her own mother come into the church and kneel and pray, and quietly cry. The memory moved her even now and she still did not know the reason for the tears.

Millie too found reassurance in the sameness of the church and the service. As they recited the familiar responses she turned her face a degree towards James and saw that his eyes were wide, scarcely blinking, and his lips silent. She wondered what would happen if the Germans arrived and conquered them. Would they still come to church in this same cosy, sure way? Were the defeated people in Belgium and Holland at church that Sunday? Were the people in Germany at church? Had Hitler or Dr Goebbels ever been to church? For some reason she thought of a song popular before the war, called 'Even Hitler Had a Mother'. It was banned then because it was said to be insulting to a foreign head of state, but now it did not matter any longer and it was on the radio again. She had heard that Dr Goebbels, the Nazi Propaganda Minister, had said in a speech that Germany's cause was God's cause. Did the commander of a Panzer division believe that Christ was at his shoulder, did the Nazi paratrooper pray before he jumped?

'Today, in our prayers . . .' The vicar's voice came

as if he were speaking through a tube. '. . . We especially remember our brother Stanley Garnet Mountford, known to all of us, whom we have lost at the hands of the enemy . . .'

Elizabeth glanced at Robert. 'Garnet,' muttered Robert from the side of his hand. 'Named after Sir Garnet Wolseley, Zululand, eighteen-seventies.'

The vicar went through the prayers like a man taking a careful meal. He prayed for the world and the village, for peace and deliverance from the arrow that flew by day and the terror by night. They sang 'For Those in Peril on the Sea' in memory of Sonny, and Peter and Lennie Dove, who until that day had only been in the church at weddings and funerals, stumbled over the words.

Robert strode out, his heavy feet bumping on the frayed stones and clanking on the memorial brasses of the aisle, to read the lesson, Psalm 23; Petrie, the coastguard, with his strange, foreign, north-eastern voice, read the second lesson from St Paul's Epistle to the Corinthians. It was when the vicar had climbed into the pulpit, announced his text and begun his sermon that he looked down and noticed that Bess's grandmother, Mrs Spofforth, was wearing her gas mask.

The good words died in his throat. She sat motionless, the black snout protruding challengingly towards him, four rows from the front. She must have only just put it on because others in the pew were only beginning to realize, staring at her from the sides. Bess, horrified, her face scarlet, put a hand out towards her grandmother, but the old lady pushed it away. Whispering and sniggering filtered through the congregation and some behind were stretching, half standing, to see the sight.

Through tight teeth Bess pleaded: 'Take it off. Get it off, please.' A muffled 'No' like an explosion of wind, came from within the mask followed by a waggle of the head which set the heavy nose of the respirator wobbling like the snout of an ant-eater.

The vicar decided to plough on, turning his eyes away from the rebellious woman and continuing to speak to the flanks of the congregation and, above her head, to those at the back. Then, he was grateful to see, the woman's granddaughter was taking positive action, prising the rubber from the old lady's face and with a strong young arm confiscating the mask, pushing the old lady from the pew and ushering her along the side of the nave. Vivid-cheeked, Bess got Mrs Spofforth through the door and out into the churchyard. The girl was in angry tears. Her grandmother was unrepentant. She sat incorrigibly on a gravestone, a stone angel peering over her shoulder, and grumbled: 'It was choking me. That bloody incense he uses was choking me.'

Bess propelled her from the churchyard and down the grass hill to where her car was parked. She bullied her into the vehicle. When the grandmother made to resist she twisted the old lady's wrist, so she squawked with pain. The car jerked angrily forward. It went down the brief hill, under the trees, and clattered through the stones and low water of the village ford.

'Incense,' muttered Mrs Spofforth again. 'Choking me.'

Bess glowered in the driving mirror. 'There was *no* incense,' she snapped. 'With all those farm people there it was probably cow shit or turnips or something.'

'Dung, if you please young lady. Dung.'

'All right. *Dung*. But dung isn't incense.'

All the Lovatt family went back to Robert and Elizabeth's house after church, a former habit that had become discontinued with James and Harry gone. Now they gladly, and naturally, assembled there again. Elizabeth had a rabbit pie in the oven. Harold Clark, Clakka as he was called, caught them and sold them at ninepence each, taking them around the village hanging from the handlebars of his bicycle like redskin scalps.

As Harry poured the drinks, so the aroma of the pie drifted in from the kitchen. Robert Lovatt had remained at the gate talking with Josh Millington about the garden. When he came in through the french windows and Elizabeth appeared from the kitchen, they all at once realized that again on a Sunday they were together as a family. The realization brought smiles and a slight embarrassment. It was James who raised his glass. 'Let's drink to ourselves,' he suggested seriously. 'We're not often together now and who knows when the next time will be.'

'Next Sunday, unless they cut our leave,' offered Harry, and they laughed with a kind of relief. 'Or we've lost the war.'

Robert raised the toast: 'The Lovatts,' he proposed. 'May we be brave.'

'And happy,' added Elizabeth hurriedly, as if she feared her husband might start to sing the National

Anthem or 'Rose of England' or 'I Vow To Thee My Country'. There were several possibilities.

'And free,' compromised Robert. 'The Lovatts.'

'The Lovatts,' they chorused.

'God bless them,' added Harry, partly to cover the embarrassment of the intimate moment. 'May they prosper.'

'May they survive,' added James. His glance took in each of them.

'Stop it, James,' warned Millie, smiling, touching his elbow. 'No messages of doom today. The news was better this morning, remember. You said so yourself.'

'*Ah*, yes,' said James formally, as if reading a communiqué. 'The front line is holding. There's even been the odd counter-attack. The British are side by side with our Dutch and Belgian allies. And to add to our conquest of Iceland we have now successfully invaded Curaçao and Aruba.'

'And where might they be?' asked Elizabeth. 'I didn't hear the news this morning. I was skinning a rabbit.'

'West Indies,' her husband told her heavily and with a defensive glance at James. 'Only Dutch colonies. Important oil refineries. We *had* to walk into Iceland to stop the Germans getting there first and sitting right above our heads.'

'One cold place and two hot places,' commented Millie curiously. 'Shall we put the news on?'

They all had been aware that it was time for the bulletin, but each had, for once, hesitated to mention it, as if they were pushing it away, not wanting it to spoil their assembly.

'Suppose we'd better,' said Robert. Harry was

nearest the set and he switched it on. The announcer was already speaking. '. . . heavy German attacks in Holland and Belgium have forced allied troops to fall back to prepared positions. Heavy casualties have been reported.'

'*Whose* heavy casualties?' asked Harry.

'When they phrase it like that, it's ours,' said James.

Their father's expression hushed them. 'Mr Churchill is to make a statement in the House of Commons tomorrow on the war situation. He is expected to offer France further British reinforcements and aircraft to the British Expeditionary Force. The French Prime Minister has described the German invasion of the Low Countries as a stab in the back but has assured Frenchmen that they have six million men under arms, ready to meet any German onslaught.'

James replenished their drinks and they sat silently through the rest of the bulletin. Outside the bright sun shone mockingly on the May garden. A bumble bee came in through the open window and busied himself with the flowers in a vase on the sill. Robert turned the set off. Millie ushered the bee out. 'Josh Millington says that he can get an extra sugar ration because he keeps bees,' said Elizabeth going towards the kitchen. She returned and picked up her drink, taking it back with her.

Each of them was aware of the dark feeling, only a shadow so far, that was moving across their safe, contented, unconsciously smug English existence. An unease was present in that traditional room in the house that they had all known throughout their lives. They had always thought that freedom and safety were theirs by right.

'I wonder what Churchill will say?' muttered Robert looking down into his drink.

'He'll think of something,' replied James sourly. 'He usually does.'

Harry said: 'At least he's pugnacious. He's got some fighting spirit.' He caught the glance of his ally, Millie; she smiled at him. He was wearing his number two uniform which he had not worn since he went back to report at Portsmouth. His mother had proudly sent his number one to the cleaners in Lymington, just as she had once sent his best school blazer there. Now, with a subconscious attempt to look pugnacious himself, he thrust his hands into his naval pockets. The left hand immediately came into contact with the three discs of the drowned sailors, Thurston G., Smith D., Wilson N. – three men in a boat, as Millie had called them. He had forgotten to hand them in.

On Monday, 13 May, after ten days of fine weather, the sun was clear again across the spotless southern counties of England. The New Forest was in its slender, first greenery, and early on that day, the Whitsun Bank Holiday Monday, visitors began to arrive at the small town stations and make their way into the trees, clutching children and picnic baskets. Reliable English kettles bubbled in many a glade and the tablecloths were spread by brown streams and under the boughs of hoary oaks. Along the coast the beaches were populated, although not with the crowds of a year before, and the striped shops were trading in teas and ice-cream. Trousers rolled and skirts held above knees, the English ventured into the chilly Channel on the distant side of which German soldiers were falling by parachute into France and heavy German tanks were cracking the pavements of the Belgian city of Liège. A great fortress, Eben Emael, which defended the city, and was said to be impregnable, was taken easily by troops who landed by glider on its flat roof. War was different now.

James was behind the hedge in his small garden at ten o'clock, phlegmatically pushing a peaceful hand-mower over the lawn. Holidaymakers in cars went by on the road, the passengers howling at donkeys which had come to graze against his borders, and Millie was putting bedding plants in the window boxes. At eleven she made some coffee and took a cup to him in the garden. The sun was climbing and his face was damp.

'This is ridiculous, Millie,' he said, thrusting the machine away. 'This is bloody ridiculous. What are we all doing? I'm mowing the lawn, there are people mooching about in cars, laughing at the donkeys, and the world's afire under our backsides. For God's sake, why aren't we *doing* something?'

From the house the telephone sounded. She went indoors and a few moments later put her head out of the cottage window. 'God must have heard you, James,' she called. 'It's Philip Benson. He's calling from London.'

James wiped the sweat from his hands and went into the house, ducking under the low lintel. The coolness of the living-room dropped over him like a hood. He picked up the telephone earpiece. 'Philip, yes, I'm here.'

'Good, I'm so glad I found you. Are you doing anything of great importance?'

'Of great *national* necessity,' emphasized James. 'I was cutting the lawn.'

'Sorry, but can you come up to London? Right now, I mean. I could send a car for you if necessary.'

'It must really be important.'

'It is. Churchill's making his statement in the House this afternoon and I want you to be there.'

'Why me?'

'You're going to work for him, James, that's why.'

Seven

Only one seat was vacant in the Chamber of the House of Commons that hot holiday afternoon. James, from his place in the elevated gallery, wedged between expectantly leaning people, could see it below. The air was tight. Whispering politicians and eager people crowded together with anxious ambassadors to see Winston Churchill, a man who had been commonplace and available for so many years, now abruptly elevated to the status of someone who could work at least one big miracle.

Churchill entered the chamber at two-thirty, an anti-climax, for he simply walked in like a person who is a little late but is not concerned by his lateness. James had never seen the real man before. He looked smaller than he had imagined. In photographs and in the cinema newsreels his visible arrogance, his width of face, heaviness of neck and shoulder had made him appear larger than life. Now he seemed to be a minor figure from which to demand so much. The talk from the benches ceased and the galleries were hushed at once, but nothing extraordinary took place, just the neatly padding feet of Britain's last hope making their way towards the front bench. It was the Labour Opposition who began cheering first, led by the clerkish Attlee and the quiffed Morrison, once the new man's enemies. The rousing sound, with its insistent echoes of a badly behaved school, rose raucously to the ancient ceiling which had looked down with equanimity on so much of the country's history. Some Conservatives joined in, but they were late and less compared with the Opposition. Having reached his seat Churchill looked about him and blinked as if surprised at the attendance.

A slight young woman with her hair in a page-boy cut under a little hat sat on James's right. She turned towards him, and he saw that her face was neat and her eyes deep. 'So much for history,' she whispered. She had an American voice.

'It's often an anti-climax, isn't it,' he returned.

They watched the scene, like bidders at a cattle auction, leaning forward on the rail. Her excellent hands were touching, as if she were thinking about praying. Appropriately there was a call for prayers below and James stood awkwardly, his head half-inclined. From the corner of his eye he could see her shoulder and slender arm. The prayers were brief and through the ensuing ritual of the opening business he returned his gaze to Churchill.

The new Prime Minister was preparing himself very concisely, an actor about to make the début he had so long awaited. He appeared to be crouched, hunched, so that his blue bow tie with the white spots was trapped under his jowl. His face swelled over his collar and set into a strangely calm frown. James could imagine him in boyhood, podgy, pink, unpopular, solitary, composing secret plays and dramas in which he was ever the hero and always had the best lines.

Churchill appeared to take no interest in what was

going on in the Chamber, or what the Speaker was intoning. He dropped a sheet of his notes on to the floor and took an age to pick it up. When he eventually straightened up he glanced about him as if to see if people were still watching. They were. Now he retreated even lower into his body, as if preparing to make his emergence all the larger. But then, when the great moment came, he merely stood up like any other man stands up. All around was tension and a thick silence.

He patted himself across the chest as if to impart comfort and encouragement. The hands then dropped to the stoutish stomach and he felt and tapped that also before transferring the hands to the outside of his trouser pockets where he patted again. The sharp chink of small change sounded throughout the Chamber.

'Mr Speaker . . .'

In only a few sentences he had them. He had thrown the spell of words like a net about them, for it was in words that his magic lay. He had no gestures of note, no charm, hardly a range of voice. It was laboured, even studied; a growl, a grunt, an elongation of syllables and phrases, and a careful lisp. But the words were everything.

'I would say to the House, as I said to those who have joined this Government, I have nothing to offer but blood, toil, tears and sweat.'

A man in the public gallery, on the far side of the American girl, was breathing heavily, as though through asthma, and it seemed to James that it could be heard everywhere. He glanced around at the man, a sallow, knife-like face, with tears running down the thin cheeks. The young woman now turned briefly towards James and he saw that her eyes were glistening. 'So much for history,' she whispered again.

Churchill had not changed. He had not grown bigger with the speech, he still peered through his thick-rimmed glasses at the paper in his hands. His brow and balding head gleamed. He had apparently made no mistakes. The nation was ready and grateful for someone who apparently made no mistakes. There had been too many.

They left the gallery and filed down the curling stone steps. James was to wait for Philip Benson outside the doors to the Chamber. He smiled at the girl who had been his neighbour. 'Goodbye,' he said. 'I hope you enjoyed the performance.'

'I certainly did. It was some show.' She smiled before turning away.

All about James the crowded voices were busy but hushed. Benson emerged eventually and took him by the arm. They said nothing until they were out in the light air of the May evening. 'It's Whit Monday,' said Benson, sniffing about him. 'The day when we all used to trek off to the seaside. Well, perhaps we will again one day.' He glanced at James with a smiling triumph. 'Bloody wonderful, didn't you think?'

James nodded. 'Where has he been all these years?'

'Waiting for this moment, I imagine,' said Benson. They were walking towards Parliament Square. 'I've never heard anything like it. Nor has anyone else. Not for a long time. Even his enemies – and he's got a few, and always will – must admit that.' He laughed briefly. 'Talk about cometh the hour, cometh the man.'

They sat on a seat in the square facing the buildings of Parliament. Big Ben moved towards six o'clock. After glancing each way James said: 'And what part have I been chosen to play in this drama?'

'A supporting role, you could call it,' smiled Benson. 'The Old Man has asked for you specially, Churchill I mean. He knows all about you and the others who kicked up such a furore over Norway and he wants you to have a position where you have the responsibility of spotting that sort of balls-up from afar. So that action can be taken before it's too late. He also has some idea of having a cadre of officers based in London who would get about the country, listening, asking questions, getting the feel of the troops, and the civvies for that matter too. He says he wants to know what people think. He wants to spot where the seams are weak before the sack bursts.'

'It sounds like a strange job. I'm a soldier. It sounds more like something for a civil servant.' He waved his hand around at the grey Whitehall walls.

'Not at all. It needs to be a serving officer. People won't talk to civil servants, not if they can help it. You'll be promoted to major.' He paused. 'Anyway, you don't have any choice. Churchill said he wants you, so he gets you. Let's go and have a drink on it.'

In the greying light James walked up the canyon of Whitehall. There was little traffic and birds sang on the buildings. Battle-dressed sentries stood outside the Horse Guards and the War Office and the Admiralty. When they stamped to attention and set off on their directed few yards of march, their boots echoed clearly among the walls. He had telephoned Millie.

She said that they had heard about Churchill's speech on the wireless and everybody felt much better now. James had smiled. There was nothing like telling people the worst possible tidings.

At the Trafalgar Square end of Whitehall there were more people. Sandbags had been solicitously stacked around Landseer's sturdy lions at the foot of Nelson's Column, so that they might be protected from bombs. The bronze nose of each lion projected from the sandbags as if sniffing the air and expecting the worst. Lovers walked in the square as they had always done in the evenings, most of the young men in uniform. Grey, puffy pigeons strutted about like small Nazis and the millions of starlings shrieked in the eves and gutters of Northumberland Avenue and the Strand.

He would need to live in London for most of the time now. Millie would stay down at Binford and he would see her whenever he could. There were numerous houses and flats to let; row upon row of them in Kensington and Belgravia, Benson had told him caustically.

James walked up the Haymarket and into the West End. A group of unemployed miners sang shiftlessly in the gutter to a cinema queue who stared stonily ahead, each one at the neck in front. They were waiting to see *Gone With the Wind*. There were a few widely dispersed coins in the flat cap the miners had placed on the pavement. Young men, idle, furtive, dead-eyed, hung around the portals to amusement arcades where others fired air rifles at cut-out German soldiers.

A group of girls, white-legged, lips like goldfish,

screamed obscenities and coughed over cigarettes as they taunted three young Norwegian sailors who stood mystified. 'You wanna learn some proper fucking English, mate!' howled one. 'Don' 'ee?' she demanded of a companion bursting flabbily from her dress. James closed his eyes and hurried his stride. The tarts, he realized, were immutable. In three months' time they might well be hanging about German stormtroopers. He went back to Trafalgar Square and through the carved tunnel of Admiralty Arch into St James's Park again. A brace of anti-aircraft guns squatted on the widest area, protecting Buckingham Palace. Their crews were sitting on the grass under the deepening sky, their steel helmets scattered about them like big mushrooms. On the lake the incongruous pelicans swam reflectively. People walked their dogs beside the flowerbeds. Somehow the British could not accept that things could change very swiftly and never again be the same.

He turned into Belgravia and saw what Benson had meant. All along the elegantly curved crescents the boards of estate agents stood out like flags. 'House for Sale', 'Apartments to Let', 'For sale . . .', 'For sale . . .', 'For sale . . .', 'Desirable property . . .', 'Safe basement flat . . .' Perhaps it had not seemed safe enough. Where were they now, these people? Residents, possibly, of the advertised Sanctuary Hotels in locations that were recommended as 'invisible from the air'. Were they among those, the rich, the writers, the rattled, who had fled, with their dogs, their valuables and cash, to America or the vast fastness of Canada? Or perhaps they were merely away, serving their country.

On the corner was a silent public house, a fashionable place once, now having the jaded air of a vault. He went in. There were only three other customers, two men in civilian clothes who emptied their glasses and went out almost as soon as he entered, and a sad-faced, elderly woman in a red coat, who sat with a glass of sipped Guinness in front of her. The landlord was leaning forward studying the *Evening News* spread over the polished wooden bar. James asked for a Scotch and soda. 'You've gained a customer and lost two others,' he observed.

The landlord, a heavy-browed and moustached man, glanced sideways as if he had not noticed. 'Off on their business, I expect, sir. *Dealing*, you know, stuff you can't get these days. They've got it cushy, believe me. The war's done them no bad turn. Get you anything, Scotch, butter, salmon, lengths of suiting, coffin handles, anything in short supply.' He handed the drink across and took the one shilling and three-pence. 'They didn't like the look of your uniform, I expect, sir, you being an officer, being connected with the proper war.'

'I thought everybody was connected with it,' observed James. 'Whether they liked it or not.' The lady in the crimson coat raised her Guinness and smiled faintly as though supporting the statement.

'Well, you wouldn't know it,' said the landlord heavily. 'Some will be *sorry* when it's all over. Making a fortune.' He tapped the evening paper in front of him. There was a photograph of Winston Churchill and the words 'Blood, Toil, Tears and Sweat' across the headline in large type. 'Blood, toil, tears and sweat he wants,' he said.

'You can't get any of them out of a stone,' sighed the grey woman. She put her glass to her mouth as if she had nothing more to add, or was embarrassed by breaking into the conversation.

'Your customers seem to have deserted you,' mentioned James.

'Gone with the wind-up, sir,' agreed the landlord, grinning over his joke. 'Scuttled off like crabs, some of them, because they reckoned London's all set to be flattened. You never saw so many furniture vans in your life. Talk about refugees.'

'And some,' said the lady stoutly, 'like Mr Perkins, went off to *fight*.' She looked flustered but determined. 'That was my employer, you see. He was one of the first to go. Naval officer. Fine man Mr Perkins and a very fair man, believe me. And Mrs Perkins is nursing somewhere in France. She went as soon as he got drowned.'

'Oh, he's dead,' said James. 'I see.'

'One of the first to go,' she confirmed. 'Off Scotland, so I understand. The water must be very cold up there.'

'Yes. I'm sorry,' said James conventionally. 'Very sad.'

The lady stifled a sniffle. 'Yes, it was,' she said. 'Mrs Perkins was ever so upset, believe me, sir.' She rubbed her hands across her eyes, reddening them, finished her Guinness with a surprising gulp and, wishing them good night, went out.

'She's a dear old dear,' sighed the landlord. 'Lost without them. She just lives in the flat, looking after the cat. It's one of those up for sale or rent. Just along the crescent here. Like to glance at the paper, sir?'

James thanked him and the man handed it across and went into the room behind the bar. James sat by the window, the daylight diminishing, and read the speech he had heard Churchill make that afternoon. The words, even flattened by print, were still resounding. 'I have nothing to offer . . .' That rumbling voice, the hunched shoulders, the belligerent jaw, the round pale hand across the chest.

Alongside the main report was an observer's view of the scene that day in the House of Commons. He read it casually but then with a sharper interest. 'An American Sees History' was the headline and below it the impressions gained that day by a woman journalist from Washington. 'I sat, not with the professional press,' she had written, 'but in the visitors' gallery. The view was very different from there.' With growing astonishment and some concern he began to read about himself, the young British officer who had listened so fiercely, leaning forward, his fists clenched on the polished wood. He was a little shocked, then relieved that there was no mention of his regiment or rank, or anything he had said. He would need to be more astute.

She was, the newspaper said, Joanne Schorner, a special correspondent of the *Washington Post*.

The landlord reappeared, came round the bar with a bucket of sand and a stirrup pump and placed them in a corner beneath a potted plant. Then he went back and returned with a bucket of water.

'Can never be too sure,' he said. 'Put them out every night, I do. During the day I keep them in the back because there's always some smart alec making

140

remarks about the water looking better than the beer and suchlike. It's just on the news that we've bombed Germany. That's put the cat among the pigeons. They're not going to take that without having a go at us.'

James had another Scotch and bought the landlord a drink. 'The old lady,' he inquired. 'Is that flat very large? I suppose it would be.'

The landlord didn't think so. 'Commander and Mrs Perkins had a place in the country somewhere, Warwickshire I think, and they only used the flat when they came to London. It's only, let me see, five doors along, towards St George's Hospital, turn left when you go out the door.'

The man went out again and returned with a steel helmet. 'Mustn't forget that,' he said, putting it on the handle of the stirrup pump.

'Not everybody takes the war seriously,' commented James.

'Well, I do,' affirmed the man. 'It's got to be serious, hasn't it? Oh, right, it's all been quiet up to now – like the Americans call it – the phoney war. Well, I've got a feeling that it won't be for much longer. The bombers will be here, mark my words, just like they've been over Rotterdam.'

'It's going to come as a hell of a shock,' predicted James. 'God, I walked through the West End this evening. Tarts and louts and singing miners.'

The landlord shrugged. 'Well, the miners can't help it. It's mad when you think of it, though. Here we are desperate, bloody *desperate*, and yet there's more than a million unemployed. It don't make sense, do it? As for the tarts and the louts, well, they'll always be there.

Even if it's all perishing rubble, they'll still be hanging around.'

James left the pub and turned left, walking along the bow of the street. He counted five and saw that the Adam building had been divided into four apartments. A board in the railed front area pronounced they were to let. He noted the name of the estate agent. There was a light in the side window of the lower flat. Obviously the lady kept to the proper servants' quarters. There was a black and white cat sitting patiently on the doorstep waiting to be let in. He stepped forward, half meaning to ring the bell. Perhaps she would let him see the number of rooms. But he decided against it and instead bent down and tickled the cat. He wondered if it went with the flat.

On the morning of Tuesday, 14 May, James waited in a ground-floor ante-room at the War Office, a place echoing like a sepulchre, with much of the windows blanked by sandbags. Sunlight came in a solid bar through the regular unbagged spaces, lighting up the millions of dust specks that floated in the room like parachutists. He stood playing a boyish game of picking them off as they fell, but there were thousands more than he could account for. They kept falling, falling. There were half a dozen bleak chairs around the walls but he was the only one waiting. The reading matter on the table consisted of some back numbers of the magazine called *War Illustrated*, its cover printed in gauche black, red and white. He picked up the top copy. Its cover was a photograph showing cheerful British soldiers with their ungainly kit disembarking from a ship, giving the eternal thumbs-up sign to the camera. The headline proclaimed: 'Tommies Land in France on Their Way to Victory.' It was dated 12 April.

He turned the pages. Nazi Germany, revealed the magazine, was a beaten enemy. 'We echo the words of Mr Chamberlain,' it went on. 'Hitler has missed the bus.' There was a picture on another page showing a long-nosed soldier wearing a fez and holding a camel. Above it the words: 'Egypt May Well be Proud of Her Camel Corps.'

Ruefully he continued leafing through the pathetically exuberant pages, studying at the end a full-page portrait, bemedalled and becrossed, of King Leopold of the Belgians, a gallant son of a gallant father, who, it forecast, would never bow to the Germans. Philip Benson came in.

'So sorry to keep you, James,' he said. He glanced at the magazine and read the words over the front cover picture. 'All our yesterdays,' he said grimly.

'A month ago,' nodded James.

'Right. Well, that's a long time in war. I've been with the Old Man.' Churchill had quite naturally and overnight become the Old Man in the same way that a captain of a ship is the Old Man. 'You'll probably be able to see him for a couple of minutes. He's trying to see all the people he's roped in. Even you and me. Christ, he's certainly a whirlwind. If a whirlwind can be *that* shape. He's got people running all over the place.'

'What is *your* new job?' asked James. 'You said you'd been roped in as well.'

'Propaganda, I suppose you could term it quite bluntly. Otherwise information. Not at the ministry, thank God, I couldn't stand that. It's buzzing around here and at Number Ten. I'm a sort of extra fielder, a bit like you really.'

James turned the magazine on to its front. 'You might start by stopping British servicemen putting up their thumbs every time they see a camera,' he suggested, tapping the photograph. 'It looks ridiculous in retrospect. A thumb to the nose would be more like it.'

'Signs and portents,' sighed Benson. 'You *have* to have something like that – something people will recognize, everybody from the simpleton to the don. Perhaps we ought to think up a replacement. I confess the British Tommy's thumb is wearing a bit thin.'

An orderly came into the room. 'Mr Benson, sir,' he said, 'Major Lovatt's office is all ready now. They've moved out all those dusty old filing cabinets.' Benson and James grinned together. 'And,' continued the man, his voice dropped a little, 'you also have clearance to show Major Lovatt the Bunker.'

Benson nodded and they went out into Horse Guards Parade, the park as bright and active as a set for a musical comedy; soldiers marching in squads and nannies shepherding children along the grass at the edge of the lake. 'The Bunker,' said Benson presently, 'is top secret. And that's not just a useful phrase. It's no funk hole. It is where the prosecution of the war will be carried on while we are under attack, either by bombers or invading forces. It will be the last thing in London to stop working. It will be operational even if the bloody Panzers are driving up The Mall.'

James glanced sideways at Benson. He saw he was smiling. 'See, somebody had some foresight after all,' his father's friend said. They strode along in the sunshine, the sound of military boots and the shouts of children mingling. Eventually Benson asked: 'All right then, major, what can you suggest to replace the soldier's thumbs-up?'

There was no immediate answer. James remembered his men again, trying to dig gun emplacements in the snow. A lot of good the thumbs-up did for them. His thoughts went to Purkiss, the man who had gone back to his home with his fingers missing. 'Why not two fingers, like this,' he held up his first and second fingers, palm of the hand forward. He had a further idea. 'Like a letter V . . . for victory, see.'

He laughed and Benson laughed also as they strode out. 'If I can't think of anything better then I'll put that in my first report,' he said. 'The only trouble is, James, it looks a bit like the Boy Scouts' salute. Remember?' He extended two fingers in the vicinity of his ear.

They had reached a building like a mound on the south-east corner of the park. Two guardsmen with fixed bayonets were stationed solidly at a door. They came to attention and a guards sergeant strutted from a side room and examined Benson's papers and then those of James.

Satisfied, he pressed three buttons and the door was opened. Inside was another NCO, and a man wearing the black coat and striped trousers of a civil servant was coming up a flight of stairs. 'Welcome to the underworld,' he smiled at Benson. 'You can go down, Mr Benson.'

It was odd descending the staircase; like going down into the belly of a large submarine. For the first time in many weeks, James suddenly felt gratified; all the tricks were, after all, not with the enemy. The air closed around them. Ahead of him Benson spoke to another guard and showed his papers. James's were examined too by a man in plain clothes who led them along a short corridor to where five other men, two civilians, an RAF officer and a jug-shaped naval captain were waiting.

Another civil servant arrived, a portly man with a wavering smile, accompanied by an angular and serious secretary, her hair pulled sternly behind her neck, her costume of blue with a stripe like that of a man. In the manner of a museum curator the portly man said: 'Good morning, gentlemen. I am Charles Beckett and it's fallen to me to show you around. I don't know whether you've all been introduced but if you haven't it's too late now, everything is being done at the double today. Under new management, you understand. Perhaps as we go around you might find a moment to whisper your names to each other. We shall have to hurry because the Prime Minister will be down here himself in a short while and we must be finished by then. The place very easily becomes cluttered.'

His smile wobbled and as though glad to be rid of it, he turned briskly, leading them along the light corridors. 'We are seventy feet below ground here, and there's a great pile of stuff on the surface, so the Luftwaffe can bomb as hard as they like and they won't touch us here. This entire area – forty separate rooms, offices and living quarters – will be used by the Prime Minister and his staff as an operations' centre.' He pointed to a notice on the wall. 'Our system of warnings,' he announced. 'Rattles sounding will announce the presence of poison gas, for example. The alarm of a klaxon will signal that German soldiers are immediately in the street over our heads.'

He strode formally on. 'I won't trouble you with all the communications details of the place,' he said. 'You will become familiar with that yourself. One thing to remember, however, is this lavatory –' he touched the door handle '– is not a lavatory but accommodates the telephone link to the President of the United States in Washington.'

He opened doors revealing basic desks, chairs and narrow beds, each with its polished wooden clothes hanger with a basket below for shoes. 'We don't run to wardrobes, you see,' said Beckett. 'This building, if you can call something underground a building – I'm not certain you can – will house more than a hundred personnel of which you, in your various capacities, will at times be a part. You will notice that armchairs are few and far between. Mr Churchill has one in his bedroom. He has to sit somewhere to think.'

Again the lolling smile. James wondered if the man really believed in Churchill. They turned a gradual bend and Beckett paused at a door. 'This is the War Cabinet room,' he said. 'You might as well have a quick peep so that you know where it is, and what it's like.'

He opened the door and ushered them in. James and Benson, who were at the front of the group, halted immediately for sitting in the chair at the centre of the great polished table sat a solitary squat figure. Beckett, from the rear of the group, called in his ushering tone: 'Go on in, if you please. We're in something of a hurry, before the Old Man gets here.'

'The Old Man is here,' announced Churchill. His white fleshy hand beckoned to them. 'But come in, by all means.'

As he came to the front, Beckett's smile opened and quickly shut. He rambled: 'Oh, Prime Minister, I'm sorry. No one informed me. You were not due until . . .'

'Well I'm here,' announced Churchill with finality. 'And I'm not going out and making another damned entrance just so you and your clerks can get the timetable in order.' A childlike, almost sweet smile eased across the large face. He stood up and came around the table towards the group. He was wearing his striped suit and spotted tie. 'I thought it would be sound planning to claim the best chair before there are any other claimants,' he said. 'Welcome, gentlemen, welcome.' The white hand waved: 'This is the place from which we intend to win the war.'

He shook hands with each of them, Beckett making ponderous introductions. James wondered whether Churchill would remember their names tomorrow, for he had heard that he did not remember people well.

As if purposely to confound the thought, Churchill, after the handshake, prodded him in the midriff and said: 'Yes, of course, you're the chap who came here so angry about Norway. There's nothing like going straight to the root of the trouble. Let us hope you can stop that sort of thing happening again. All it needs is a word in the right minister's ear. Things are going to move a trifle faster here now, indeed more than a trifle. I hear that Ernest Bevin is buckling his sword, a sight worth seeing I should have thought. He is to be my Minister of Labour. Eden is going on the wireless tonight. You should make time to listen.' He regarded them solemnly, like a headmaster with a group of senior boys. 'Anyone here got any ideas about the future conduct of the war? Anyone?' They fidgeted, half smiling. 'How about you, Benson? What about some new propaganda? It's no good just putting up posters and placards telling people there's a war in progress. My God, the Ministry of Information plastered the country with a slogan saying, "*Your* Courage, *Your* Cheerfulness, *Your* Resolution will bring US Victory."' His chin descended with displeasure. 'That sounds like a case of *them* and us. *They* do it and *we* win. What genius thought of that, I wonder?'

It seemed as though the Prime Minister were about to move on to the jug-like naval officer; his hands went behind his back and he embarked on a short, thoughtful walk, but then turned on Benson again and repeated: 'Any new idea? Anything?'

Benson looked discomfited. He glanced at James, patently desperate. 'Well, Prime Minister,' he hesitated. 'Major Lovatt and I were discussing something this morning. Just as we were walking here. It was his idea, actually.'

Churchill turned his squat face on James but immediately moved it back towards Benson. 'What is it?' he asked.

'It's rather trifling, I'm afraid, but he felt, and I agree, that it's time the thumbs-up was done away with, replaced by something new. You know, sir, the soldier . . . thumbs up .. His embarrassment made him gabble the words.

'I know, I know,' said Churchill impatiently. 'It's been going on for several wars to my knowledge. But what would replace it? Nothing too elaborate. People have got to understand it.'

'We discussed a V-sign, holding up the forefinger and middle finger, in reverse as it were. V-for-Victory, you see.'

James began to get the feeling that all this was becoming silly. To discuss fingers when people were being killed seemed futile. But clearly Churchill wanted to give it his time.

'Yes, all right. It's all very well. But that's the salute that Baden Powell thought up for his Boy Scouts. I remember his practising it in South Africa, and damned silly he looked too.'

Immediately he appeared to tire of the subject and dismissed it, or apparently so, until, having gone along the line to speak to the RAF officer, he abruptly looked back towards Benson and held up the two fingers. 'No good,' he said. 'It needs something extra. Something to go with it. We may have to persevere with the worn-out thumb.'

He confronted the RAF man, who blushed. 'You see we've started bombing Germany,' Churchill said, as if he might have missed the news. 'What do you feel about that? We're risking retaliation, you know. Right up there.' He pointed to the ceiling. 'On London.'

'Yes, sir, I'm sure it's right, sir,' responded the officer tentatively. 'According to the newspapers the bomber raid on Freiburg was very successful.'

'An error,' grumbled Churchill. 'On the part of the Germans. It wasn't *our* planes, it was the Hun, the Luftwaffe. Damned fools dropped the bombs on their own people. Broad daylight too. Navigational mistake, I understand. One hundred and forty miles off course. The bombs were meant for somewhere in France.' He had lowered his chin as if conversing with the carpet, but now he lifted it with a grim grin. 'They can make errors too.'

In a moment he appeared weary, drained, and he clearly wanted them out of the room. 'Bevin's coming,' he said, half looking towards the civil servant Beckett. 'I must be ready for him. There are also some other guests expected. Her Majesty Queen Wilhelmina and the Dutch Government. Holland, I am sad to tell you, has this morning capitulated.'

Eight

Half the nuns in the convent at Lyndhurst were, according to Ma Fox at the Old Crown, German spies, known to creep the coast by night, flashing signals to alien aircraft, and with daggers and bombs concealed beneath their black folds. For her, behind her bar like a barricade, war had so far only been exciting because of its opportunity for rumour. As with many others, in Binford and in Britain, remote communiqués and photographs of officers staring through binoculars at some unspecified horizon had failed to stir her. Stories of ten thousand cardboard coffins concealed in a forest cave, a poison gas that burned the feet off, and secret information that all dogs and cats were to be butchered when the Germans landed were the stuff she savoured. Penalties for spreading alarm and despondency she ignored as not applying to her.

Anthony Eden, War Secretary in the new Government, a slender politician with an elegant hat, had broadcast to the nation that evening and, in well-brushed tones, had called for the raising of a citizens' army, a force of Local Defence Volunteers, men previously exempt from the services. They were to have armbands and arm themselves with whatever they could, even golf clubs and pitchforks, and stand ready to meet the enemy. They were to be alert for parachutists, spies and traitors.

'Nuns,' added Ma Fox firmly. She was watching the four-ale bar fill up to an extent unknown on a Tuesday night.

Harold Clark was not sure. 'Nuns are 'aving a bad time,' he suggested doubtfully. 'Over in Belgium and 'olland, from what I hear. Jerry seems to fancy nuns.'

'Different sort of nuns,' argued Ma Fox. Charlie, her son, nudged her to get back to the pumps, for the room was filling rapidly.

Men came in from the village and from The Haven and isolated parts of the forest. Liberty Cooper and two of his brothers arrived and stood darkly against the back wall. 'Wonder 'ow they heard?' asked Gates the gamekeeper whose radio had been stolen from his cottage the previous week.

It was not the moment to voice his suspicions to Police Constable Brice who was pushing people closer together in the room. Next door the saloon bar was empty, the radio still on from Eden's broadcast and now relaying dance music.

'Mr Lovatt will be here soon,' announced Brice in his officious voice. 'It's my orders that Mr Lovatt is to take command.'

The door opened, the black-out curtain fluttered and flew back and Robert entered with Petrie. 'Make room, come on, men, make room,' called Brice.

Robert glanced around appreciatively. 'There's more arriving outside,' he said. 'We'll have to use both bars, Charlie. Can you get this partition down?'

Charlie Fox looked shocked. 'Down, Mr Lovatt?'

he said. 'Well, I expect so. Hasn't been down since the Coronation.'

Robert said sharply, 'If it came down then it will come down now. We've got to have room to move. And we need a table and a chair.'

His excitement was infused into the room. The Dove brothers took the partition down with a single screwdriver in three minutes. Charlie Fox looked on, creased with doubt. The crowd, some reluctantly, as if they were still unsure of the propriety, moved across the frontier into the saloon bar. The wireless set was playing 'We'll meet again, don't know where, don't know when'. Charlie turned it off emphatically, unwilling to extend all the privileges.

More men came through the door. Ben Bowley, wearing his railway cap set like a drill sergeant, Peter James, the estate manager, who had brought his shotgun. Others had brought rifles and shotguns also: Wilf Smith, Malcolm his brother, and George Lavington. Tom Bower, the Binford Haven shipwright, had a boathook held like a lance. Rob Noyes, the insurance agent, attempted truculence in a long raincoat, worn despite the mild evening. John Lampard came quietly in and stood at the back. With him was the spotty boy Cubbins. Robert looked doubtfully.

Charlie Fox was worried because, despite the unique crowd, he was not selling much beer. Robert, observing his anxiety, said loudly: 'Right, gentlemen, before we get down to business will anyone who wants a drink get it now.' There was an immediate shift back to the four-ale bar where beer was cheaper.

The grateful Charlie put a pint of ale on the table at which Robert had now established himself.

'That's on me, Mr Lovatt,' he said. 'It's a big night.'

As he took the first drink Robert saw Tom Purkiss come shyly through the door. He was wearing an army battledress blouse with his cowman's trousers. 'Forgot to give it back,' he said to Donald Petrie. 'When they threw me out.'

When he saw that the village men, their hands around the glasses and tankards, were ready and expectant, Robert rose behind the table. 'Right, everybody,' he announced. Seeing Purkiss in the battledress and the others with the rifles, shotguns and other weapons made him wish he had quickly looked out his old tunic. But it was too late now. 'We all know why we're here,' he continued. 'We've all heard Mr Eden tonight and the idea is that all over the country there are going to be formed units of the Local Defence Volunteers, to deal with the Germans should they be so ill-advised as to try crossing the English Channel.'

There were mumbles and smiles at his jesting boast. 'I had a telephone call from Major-General Sound, who, as it happens, was my commanding officer in the Great War, and he asked me immediately to set about forming a unit here in Binford and Binford Haven. I'm gratified that the message got around so quickly and that you've all come here.'

It was Donald Petrie who looked about and, with a sad heart, wondered what chance they would have, these village gentry, these farm men, these fishermen, these gypsies? What could they do to stop a Panzer division?

'There are many things we can do,' said Robert, 'to stop an invader. What we must remember is that he

155

has to *get* here first, over the water, or down from the sky, and that's the time to deal with him, when he is most vulnerable.' As he spoke he became aware of a small face, like that of a pixie, in a green cap, peering through the space left by two men's elbows. 'That lad,' he said. 'Off you go.'

'I can run messages,' said Tommy Oakes, the wolf-cub. 'And I've studied silent killing.'

Charlie Fox moved importantly forward. 'You're not supposed to be in the pub,' he said to the boy. 'Outside.'

'I'll start my *own*,' threatened the lad, retreating towards the door. 'Charlie Fox – got two cocks!' he piped desperately before vanishing. It was a village joke.

Charlie reddened and some of the men laughed. 'There are age limits,' pointed out Robert. 'It's no use having elderly men like old Josh Millington or Jeremiah Buck from The Haven. Nor young lads. Sixteen is the lower limit.' He glanced towards Willy Cubbins, acne gleaming in the warmth of the room.

'Sixteen next week, Mr Lovatt,' said the boy. 'I can get my birth sustificate.' He glanced up at John Lampard for confirmation. John shrugged.

Robert outlined the plans he briefly knew. Then the men lined up to give their names and addresses and details of special skills and arms they possessed. When it was all set down it did not look very much. There was, however, the secret weapon.

When the village men were going Robert and Petrie waited outside, saying good nights as they went off down the dim village street. Petrie had asked the Dove brothers and John Lampard to wait. Outside they sat quietly at one of the benches by the roadside. A donkey laughed uproariously from the forest. 'There's been a request from the Admiralty today,' said the coastguard, 'for details of all boats capable of crossing the Channel.'

The four other men looked at him oddly. 'They say that it may become necessary to use them to supply our troops in France –' his voice dropped despondently '– should they get cut off.'

'God Almighty,' breathed Lampard. 'Things must be bad.'

'Just a precaution,' Robert put in with an attempt at conviction. 'Good planning really.' He looked unsurely at Petrie.

Petrie said: 'Mr Lampard, is that paddle steamer fit for sea?'

John looked astonished. '*Sirius*? No, but she soon could be. She's very nifty, you know. Eighteen knots.'

'Good,' said Petrie. 'How about the boat, boys?' he asked the Doves. 'She's on the mud, isn't she?'

'Full of holes still,' said Lennie. 'But we can patch them up. Getting her off the mud might be harder. We've pulled her right up clear of the tide.'

'Wash her back to sea,' said Petrie. 'I've seen it done. Get the fire brigade to bring the hoses.'

Before the war they had gone on school outings to Moyles Court at the other end of the forest, for the red old manor house was full of history. It had once been the home of Dame Alicia Lisle who, in 1685, when she was seventy-one years of age, was taken to the execution block by sentence of the terrible Judge

Jeffreys, for the crime of sheltering two priests. Two gentlemen of Hampshire, outraged at the sentence, drew their swords in the court at Winchester, and also paid with their lives.

Now Millie alighted from the forest bus by the stream that tumbled over the narrow road on its way to join the Hampshire Avon. In childhood they had always picnicked there and taken off their shoes and socks to paddle in the bright and stony water.

The sunlit peace that she remembered seemed the same. Two fallow-deer grazed on the far bank of the tributary and ducks collected expectantly at the fording place. Then, from across the trees, came the violent starting of an engine, a guttural interruption that sent the deer running but did not unduly disturb the ducks.

She crossed the low ford by the stepping-stones and walked towards the gate of the big house. The engine stopped, then started again. Some rooks in the trees over the gate fidgeted and called but did not fly. At the gate was a notice saying: 'Royal Air Force. Fighter Command'. An RAF policeman came from a hut inside the gate and said, 'Yes, miss?'

Millie told him why she had come and he smirked familiarly. 'You'll cheer the place up a bit, miss,' he said. 'It could do with it, I can tell you.'

He directed her along a bare path leading to some wooden structures which had been appended to the house. 'I'll call the amenities officer on the blower,' promised the policeman. 'Such as he is.'

There was an elderly-looking biplane groaning above the airfield, making occasional slow darts at the runway and then pulling away again. Another plane with a small turret like an observatory behind the cockpit was roaring intermittently on the ground, the engine blasts she had heard from the ford.

From behind some of the wooden buildings came ragged cheers and she rounded a corner to find herself confronted by a dozen young men in baggy blue shorts who were playing netball on an area marked on the grass. Two posts sagged, one at each end of the pitch, as if they had been subject to considerable physical contact. The players were not cheering their game but the antics of the biplane which staggered across the sky. As Millie came into their view a bulky youth, white-skinned and perspiring, was preparing to pass the ball. At the sight of her he dropped it and it bounced, then rolled towards her. Adeptly she picked it up and threw it back to the player. His fair curly hair was plastered to his forehead giving him a strange Roman appearance. After their initial surprise the airmen cheered her and she felt herself flush. 'Good throw, miss,' said the fair-haired lad. 'Want a game?'

'Not just now,' she laughed. 'Perhaps another time.'

She asked to be directed to the amenities officer and there were more rough comments. The youth holding the ball pointed out the door and she walked that way, feeling the silence as they watched her go. A voice she knew was that of the fair-haired player briskly interrupted the silence. 'Right, lads,' he called. 'Let's get on with it.'

Millie smiled and reached the door. She knocked and a languorous voice invited her in. A plump man with an RAF moustache as wide as wings beamed with pleasure when he saw her. 'Hello, hello, please come in,' he enthused. 'The chap at the gate just rang. How about a cup of tea?'

She agreed before she was seated and he picked up a teapot on a side table, feeling its enamel flank like a doctor examining a patient. 'Still a bit hot,' he said. 'I've had mine.' He poured the thick tea into a mug with 'Per Ardua Ad Astra', the Air Force motto, on its side, added milk and sugar to her instructions and sat back beaming. At that moment the biplane which had been grunting in the distant sky came across the top of the building, coughing badly.

'Listen to him,' sighed the officer. 'First solo. Afraid to come down. Some of them think they can put off the evil moment by staying up there indefinitely.' He stood and held out his hand. 'I'm Conroy. Flight-Lieutenant George Conroy, that is. Amenities officer.'

She introduced herself and said why she had come. 'Jolly good of you,' he enthused. 'Jolly, jolly good. I was looking for someone to help with the sports day. And there's the library needs organizing. All sorts of things. We need plenty of activities. I mean it's pretty quiet here, and unless Jerry really starts hotting the war up then I'm afraid it's going to be a deucedly dull summer.'

The estate agent's office was one of those Dickensian enclaves that needed concentrated bombing to change it from the ways and atmosphere of a century before. It had small-paned windows and a door that whined. A tinny but discreet bell rang as James entered. The main office was hushed in dimness and the heads of the clerks behind high desks levered up hopefully, as if hoping it might be someone come to change their lives.

On the walls, in brown frames of only a slightly gloomier shade than the photographs themselves, were pictures of buildings which Messrs Henlow and Black had sold in the past, the façades of triumphs.

At the first position the elderly clerk bowed so deeply before going off to find one of the partners that he very nearly cracked his forehead on the sloped roof of his desk. He went off stiffly like clockwork and returned with Mr Henlow, another ancient, who was followed by an anxious young man in a strange suit of jagged stripes. The senior man tightened his eyes to study James's uniform, as if trying to ascertain whose side he were on, but then overcame him with fuss.

'Oh, ah, yes, of course, Major Lovatt.' He glanced over his shoulder at the worried young man. 'I *was* going to send our Mr Burton with you, but perhaps not . . .' James saw the second man's expression fade. Mr Henlow rubbed his hands thoughtfully. 'Perhaps our Mr Flowers would be more like it . . .'

'I want to rent the flat, not the man,' said James. 'What's the matter with Mr Burton? I don't have much time and I'd like to get the matter settled.'

He thought he saw a glint of gratitude in the subordinate's eyes. Mr Henlow remained doubtful. 'Mr Flowers will not be long. He knows the property very well . . .'

James said impatiently, 'It's only a flat. It's hardly Blenheim Palace.' He glanced at his watch. 'I can't hang around for Mr Flowers.'

'Right,' responded the elderly man, puffing his cheeks as if he had made his first important decision for many years. 'Right, of course. Mr Burton must conduct you.' He thought it was time for introductions. He swung on the young man almost threateningly. 'Major, this . . . is our Mr Burton.'

They shook hands. The young man began a slight, formal bow, from the waist, but then restrained himself. Mr Henlow frowned grievously. 'I will take you, sir,' said Mr Burton. 'Would it be convenient to walk? It is two minutes only.'

James said he knew and they walked out into the street. 'Why did he not want you to do this?' asked James.

The man's pale, jowly face seemed to solidify. 'Because you are a British officer. And because I am an Austrian Jew. That, to Mr Henlow, is next to being a German. Even he has given me a new name – this Burton person. Who is Burton? It is not me.'

'What is your name then?'

'Bormann,' said the man miserably. 'Michael Bormann.' He began to slow his steps as if he wanted to get it all off his chest before they reached the house. His sigh was bereft of hope. 'A Jew called Bormann,' he said.

'How long have you been in England?' asked James.

'Five years almost. They took my father to some place in 1936 and he vanished from this world. I came here with my mother. But now it is almost as bad – not quite but almost. Because we are Austrian, and of German origin, we are treated as potential enemies. I have tried to join the British Army, and I have a better reason than most to want to fight the Nazis, but they won't have me. They think I am a spy. My mother has even been interrogated by the police. And now, as the situation is, I am sure, major, it will become much worse for us.' He sighed deeply. 'I thought that we would never have to hear that knock on the door again. Nobody would ever again come to take us away. But now I am not so sure.'

The man's shoulders hunched round with despair. It began as a shrug but his shoulders remained in the crouch position as he mounted the steps to the apartment. He rang the bell doggedly and the grey woman that James had seen the previous evening answered the door. If she were surprised to see him she did not show it.

They walked in. It was as he had thought, not over-large. There was a pleasant living-room, with flowers on the sill and a tracery of sunshine on the carpet. The furniture was traditional, comfortable. There was a break-front bookcase with the shelves full, a large brown wireless set and a cabinet upon which were the framed photographs of a man in naval uniform and a round-faced woman with a small hat and a veil. He looked briefly into the bedroom, bathroom and kitchen and then returned to the living-room.

The estate agent's man appeared even more awkward than before. His suit crumbled about him. 'Mrs Beauchamp . . .' he began.

'It's *Beecham*, spelt B-E-A-U-C-H-A-M-P but said Beecham,' the lady pointed out gently. 'But you're foreign, aren't you?'

'Ah, yes, of course. Like the Beauchamp Place. I have made mistakes there also. Perhaps I should try another job.' He smiled weakly at his own small, realistic joke. 'Mrs Beauchamp,' he said correctly, 'has a small bed-sitting-room.' He hesitated. The old lady grimaced at him and said: 'What he is trying to say, sir, is when would you be wanting me to leave?'

A brief shadow of uncertainty was cast on her face. 'You don't have to leave at all,' said James. 'I was hoping you would be able to stay.' Her face cleared happily. James felt pleased. 'I'll need someone to look after the place – and me for that matter. If you'd agree, Mrs Beauchamp.'

'Well,' she replied happily, 'I do sort of come with the place.'

The young Austrian looked glad. 'Then everyone is happy?' he suggested. 'I am so happy. There is not much happiness available.'

Mrs Beauchamp looked at him as she might have regarded an actor on hard times performing at a street corner. She returned to James. 'There is just one thing, sir . . .'

'What is that, Mrs Beauchamp?'

She turned and trotted the few steps to the door which opened into her part of the flat. She closed the door behind her and the two men waited, both puzzled. It was opened again quickly and the lady returned holding a short-trousered boy by the hand. He was about six years old. His eyes went at once to James's uniform. He regarded it with wonder. 'Are you a real soldier?' he inquired.

James laughed and said: 'I hope so. Are you a real boy?'

'Yes,' replied the child stoutly. 'Look. You can pinch me if you like.'

Mrs Beauchamp said: 'His name is John Colin, sir. He's the son of Mrs Perkins.'

'That is the lady who owns the apartment,' said

Bormann decisively, glad to contribute. 'She is away, in France, I think.'

'War work. She's in a military hospital, sir, in Paris.'

'And she's left John Colin with you.'

'No, not quite, sir. He was left with his nanny in the country. In their house in Warwickshire. But nanny's not well, so he has come down to me for a few days. He often does. He likes coming here.' The house-keeper glanced at him with doubt. 'Would you mind, sir. It's only now and again. He has to go back soon, to school.'

'Worse luck,' said the boy solidly, still staring at James. 'I want to be a soldier.'

James laughed. 'I'm sure there will be plenty of room for all of us,' he said. He solemnly shook hands with the boy and with Mrs Beauchamp and went with the Austrian out into the street again. The door closed firmly behind them. James looked up at the sky between the trees and the crescent houses. 'Not a bad day for May,' he said. 'It seems I have a new home.'

'It is a good day,' smiled his companion. 'I am pleased. I am sure everything will be all right in the world. Almost sure.'

On the morning of 20 May, the day the German armies reached Abbeville and were able for the first time to stand looking out over the English Channel, Robert, driving from Binford to Salisbury, was held up by a gang of workmen unloading vicious rounds of barbed wire from the back of a lorry. One of them, standing back and letting the others manoeuvre the difficult and heavy coil over the vehicle's tail-board, strolled to Robert's car and leaned confidingly towards the window.

'Sorry to be holdin' you up,' he said. He was Irish with a grained and dark face like old stone, so heavy his eyes seemed opaque by comparison. 'Work of national importance, you'll understand.'

'Where do you come from?' asked Robert.

'Right now, sir, at this moment, from Southampton. Before that, I hail from County Sligo.' He nodded at the work gang. 'That man is from Cahirciveen in the West and that one from Dingle, County Kerry. Eire, sir, Southern Ireland, sir. We being neutrals.'

'So I believe. Standing on the touchline.'

The man nodded benign acknowledgement. 'To see fair play, maybe. But we're helping out where we can. Building and constructing defences and the like.'

'And earning good money,' suggested Robert gruntingly.

'Oh, that too, sir. The English money's not mean at all. And where do you hail from, if I may make so bold?'

'Here,' said Robert impatiently. 'Binford.'

'Oh, it's a good place this,' agreed the man. 'Not that I wouldn't like to see the shining lights of Dublin town for a while.' He watched the men shouting orders to each other as they rolled the wire coils. 'Steady, boys,' he called softly. 'Don't get them untangled.' He said to Robert. 'Jesus, wouldn't that be a terrible mess.'

Robert was becoming testy. 'Are these fellows going to be long? I have an important appointment. And it is *really* of national importance.'

The Irishman sighed in some agreement. 'But 'tis

hard to get them to move fast on a fine day like this.'
He called towards his men. 'Come along, boys, this
English gentleman wants to get through.' They all
looked up at once, almost dropping the great barbed
coil, and then hurried it to the side of the road. The
foreman saluted Robert as if he had performed some
miracle. 'There, sir,' he said, indicating the road
ahead. 'Open and clear for you. Full speed ahead.
You'll be needing to get on with the war.' Robert
ground his teeth and started the engine. 'And good
luck to you,' said the man amiably, still leaning against
the window.

'Thank you terribly,' grunted Robert. 'It's nice to
know you're right behind us.'

'Don't you worry about that, sir. We'll always be
glad to be helping.'

It was a sallow day, the forest, as Robert drove across
it, subdued to grey-green, even the flaming yellow of
the gorse diminished. A small herd of deer moved like
shadows across the middle ground. A shower
smeared the windscreen, to be replaced, as he crossed
the main Southampton road, with some dispersed
sunshine.

Just over the major road, as he again took the forest
route, Robert was forced to stop by a tree trunk on
wheels which had been placed across the way near the
entrance to a golf club. Immediately irritated, he
stopped the car. Several tentative heads emerged from
behind the tree trunk and eyes stared from below the
sheltering rims of steel helmets. 'Halt!' called a thin,
rural voice. 'Or we'll blow your tyres out.'

Robert leaned angrily from the window of the car.

'I am halted, you fathead!' he bellowed. 'What the hell is all this?'

The heads vanished all at once as though pulled down by the same string. From one side of the road a dozen donkeys viewed the scene as they chewed. He saw that men were erecting tall stakes and poles along the first fairway of the golf club. As he took in this operation a man detached himself from behind the tree trunk, an exceptionally thin and tall figure which walked with a sorrowful lurch. Robert recognized him from his solicitor's days as a man who had been a court messenger at Winchester Assizes. 'Jeffreys,' he called from the car. 'What the devil's going on?'

Jeffreys had an armband bearing the letters LDV tight as a tourniquet on his thin upper arm. He was wearing brown dungarees and carrying an air gun. His helmet was too big and wobbled as he moved his head. 'Identity card, please,' he said solemnly.

'Jeffreys, it's *me*. Robert Lovatt. God, you've known me long enough.'

The man studied him intently but with no recognition, and then intoned: 'Identity card, please. All traffic on this road is being checked.'

Angrily Robert stared at Jeffreys. No response stirred in the other's face. 'My God, what a farce!' exclaimed the older man. He produced his National Identity Card from his wallet. The guard read it minutely, turned it over and stared at the other side.

'Why don't you try smelling it, man?' demanded Robert.

'Sorry Mr Lovatt, sir,' muttered Jeffreys, returning the card with the reply: 'But that's the orders. Parachutists could be dropping any minute.'

'They could hardly be so well disguised as to look like someone you've known for thirty years,' retorted Robert. 'Now will you please ask your toy soldiers to move that ruddy tree trunk out of the way. I'm on business of national importance.'

Jeffreys appeared discomfited. 'One of the wheels 'as come off, Mr Lovatt. We can't move it. They've sent to the garage in Lyndhurst for help.'

Robert bristled. 'And am I supposed to sit here while you fix it?'

'No, sir,' said Jeffreys pointing towards the golf club. 'You can go into the golf course there and out at the far gate.' Apology festooned his face. 'You could get stopped again. Some of our unit are up there putting up the poles on the fairways.' His eyes moved towards Robert's. 'Precautions against gliders, that is.'

Robert nodded. 'Going to make the golf difficult,' he said less fiercely.

'Have to play between the poles, I s'pose,' said Jeffreys. 'I never did play myself.'

He wished Robert good afternoon and slouched back towards the tree trunk barricade. ''S all right. I know 'im,' he called towards his comrades. 'Mr Lovatt. Used to be at Winchester.'

Robert turned the car towards the golf club gate. As he did so he saw that the iron farm wheel which had been fixed to one end of the tree was leaning weakly. He remembered Jeffreys had always been a slow man, a joke among the pre-war Assize people at Winchester, where centuries before Judge Jeffreys had sent so many to the execution block. The messenger had been given many nicknames and once his friends had persuaded him to sign a joke death warrant. He

169

had gone through the years never showing a sign that he knew the significance of the jests. And now he was defending the country.

The men erecting poles and posts on the golf course did not stop Robert. Several were thick in an angry argument with the groundsman and the elderly club secretary who were apparently objecting to obstacles being thrust into the precious languid greens.

Once more he emerged into the open moorland of the forest. There were few houses there, just long slopes of wild countryside, bogs, valleys and gathered copses. Deer, ponies, cattle, donkeys and black pigs roamed freely. In the Great War, he remembered, there had been a regiment of Indian troops encamped in that place, hundreds of brown, mystified men, waiting to be fed into the trenches of Flanders. Some of the forest gypsies had tried to sell them pork.

The journey became mildly hilly and then, with a quiet delight he had always enjoyed, the point of Salisbury Cathedral stood out before and below his road, the tallest spire in England rising from the distant, dun-coloured city.

Major-General Geoffrey Sound lived in a red, mullioned house in the Cathedral Close at Salisbury. As the sun turned through the day so the shadow of the tallest spire moved like the hand of a great clock across the Close and over his house.

When Robert arrived the staunch old officer was sitting in his garden staring with a sort of dismay at a pictorial book, *Aircraft of the Fighting Powers*.

'Can't tell one damned flying machine from another,' he confessed sorrowfully. He shut the book like an explosion. 'Damned things have ruined warfare, if you ask me.'

The major-general had suffered wounds in his years of service and now, walking with a cane, he dragged his right leg like a rake across the grass. Robert told him of the forest road-block. The old man shook his head. 'What did Cromwell say to John Hampden – "Your troops are old, decayed serving men, tapsters and such kind of fellows!"'

'I'm afraid,' said Robert, 'that is what it's going to be like. My chaps are good fellows enough, but they don't have much idea.'

'Still, we must make a start. Do the best we can. It can't be any worse than getting Egyptians into shape.' He shrugged unhappily. 'Never thought I'd see the day when we had to think of troops dropping from the sky on strings,' he sighed. 'What next, I ask myself.' He put a tired hand on Robert's shoulder. 'Sit down, sit down,' he said, leading him towards a wooden seat by the garden path.

They sat. The slender veil of shade from the cathedral spire was moving over the sunny shrubs and the comforting lawn. Robert thought there was something familiar about the white stones that formed the path, so shining and regular.

'Recognize them?' asked Sound, pleased at his interest and prodding the path with his stick. 'War graves. Got them from the War Graves Commission, see. Some fool stone mason made them an inch too wide or too narrow, or some such thing, and the Commission didn't find out until it was too late and they'd paid the fellow by that time. Naturally war graves have to be of regulation size, just the same as army blankets and bits of four by two. Damned embarrassed they were, so I took them off their hands. Got them for a song. Better than wasting them, don't you think?'

Robert was unsure. He nodded vaguely. 'Useful,' he agreed, however: 'Jolly useful.'

'The War House won't be pleased with this LDV business,' said Sound. Robert was still looking at the stones in the path. 'They don't like the notion of private armies, never did. That's why Lawrence never hit it off with them.' He stood up and dragged his foot back towards the house. 'Tea?' he asked as Robert stood and followed him. 'Or a drink?'

'It's tea,' called a woman's voice from the house. 'I've just made it.'

'Tea, I'm afraid,' sighed Sound. 'There's no arguing. She's the commanding officer these days.'

'It's an idea anyway,' said Robert, still carrying on the original conversation. 'It would be mad to have able-bodied men standing hands-in-pockets at a time like this.'

The major-general paused in mid-drag: 'You've got a sharp mind, Lovatt. Always did. Never understood why you didn't stay in the army. I'm no good now. Finished. Just sitting around waiting for that damned spire to revolve once more.' Bitterness spiked his voice. They had reached the low door. Wistaria fell like a pale blue curtain over the ruddy brickwork on the wall. The major-general's wife, a tall serene woman, walked gravely towards them with a silver tea-tray.

'So nice of you to come, Major Lovatt,' she said formally. She took in her husband with a mischievous

172

smile. 'I do hope you're in time to save the country.'

'We're going to try,' put in her husband fiercely before Robert could frame a reply. 'Our damnedest, we're going to try. It's time someone took some firm action with Hitler.' He sat down heavily and arranged his cane alongside his stiff leg like a sword. 'Good God,' he sighed. 'I saw two perfectly able and fit chaps out *hiking* – hiking of all things – shorts and knapsacks and all that. At a time like this. Where's the planning, I ask you? And useless they were at hiking for that matter. I had to show them how to read a damned Ordnance Survey map.'

'They were probably spies,' said Mrs Sound, putting a cake-slice on a tassa replete with fruit-cake. She said it softly but with light malice.

Her husband reddened. 'Silly bloody spies, if you don't mind me saying so. Attracting attention like that.' He lowered his creased eyes with embarrassment. 'Anyhow, I misdirected them. Sent them in entirely the wrong direction. Just in case.'

'Jolly well done,' said his wife. She retreated unhurriedly towards the door. 'I must leave you. The butcher has promised to keep two lamb chops for me. And some beef dripping. I won't be long.'

'Two lamb chops, beef dripping,' repeated the major-general in a grumble. He turned to Robert. 'Cavalry is the answer,' he said solemnly. 'In this part of the country anyway. Plenty of open ground. I'd match cavalry against anything the Hun could put in the field.'

He was pouring the tea and he spilled it in his emphasis. The silver snout of the teapot was swivelled around like a tank turret. 'You can't fight a war with tin boxes on wheels,' he said. 'Never could. And as for these marionette blighters on their strings. A squadron of Hussars would clean them up in quick time.'

'Of course,' agreed Robert. An uneasy sensation of having gone through all this before, in childhood, came over him.

'I wager old Dodger Doddington over at Lyme Regis has already been roped in,' continued Sound. He was making a mess of pouring the tea. 'And that chap Clark, you know, in Bournemouth, remember him? He had command somewhere or other.'

'He's dead,' Robert reminded him. 'We went to the funeral.'

'Damn, so we did. He's no use then.' From somewhere within the house a clock struck softly. 'Four,' confirmed Sound. 'Let's see if the BBC has any news.'

He rose with a hint of leadership and Robert followed him as he scraped from the room. There were military pictures and mementoes on the wall; a polo team in Persia, a fancy-dress ball in India, cricket at Sandhurst, the menu card of a long-digested regimental dinner. They went into a small room, a study, with a desk and a telephone and one wall covered with a map of Europe, small flags and stickers marking the last-broadcast dispositions of the conflicting forces. Robert's eyes went to Abbeville. He remembered it well. A café and a friendly girl, long, long ago. 'I hear the Germans have reached Abbeville,' he ventured. A Union Jack and a tricolour were still pinned to the town.

'Been waiting for confirmation,' said Sound in a vexed voice. He switched on the wireless set and it began to crackle. His face had sagged when he looked up again, sadness and worry in its lines. 'I never consolidate a claim until it's announced officially, Lovatt,' he said. 'I can't bring myself to believe that it's all happening.' He looked down to adjust the pepper-pot knob of the set. 'I'm very much afraid they're going to swamp us,' he said with sudden anguish. Suddenly Robert thought the old man was going to weep. 'I don't think I could bear defeat,' he continued slowly. 'Not after winning all those years.' There was popular organ music being broadcast by Sandy Macpherson. Wrath rallied the major-general. 'That benighted bugger playing that benighted instrument again,' he complained. 'Why don't we play marches to fill the gaps like other countries do?'

An announcer, his voice as stiff as his undoubted shirt, broke into the playing and announced a special news bulletin. Sound waved Robert towards an armchair. He dropped tiredly on to the chair at the desk.

'Fierce fighting continues on the Western Front,' said the faceless man predictably. 'General Gamelin, the Allied Commander-in-Chief, in a message to French troops has said: "Any soldier who cannot advance should allow himself to be killed rather than abandon that part of our national soil which has been entrusted to him . . ." It is officially confirmed that German forces have taken Abbeville . . . Allied forces have retreated to prepared positions and to straighten the fighting line . . .'

With difficulty the major-general rose from the desk and, taking a small swastika flag, placed it resignedly into the town of Abbeville on the wall map. 'You know, old man,' he said as he turned to Robert, 'I've often thought what splendid mines could be made from milk churns. Packed with explosives they'd go off a treat, don't you think? One hell of a bang.'

The garden was coming to its best. Throughout May the weather had been exceptionally fair and the early summer flowers were bursting through under the loaded blossom of the trees. On 22 May regulations came into force which, for the first time since the signing of Magna Carta by King John in the year 1215, took away many personal freedoms from the British people. The Government voted itself power to direct any person to any occupation or place, to take over property, to make summary arrest.

Harry picked up *The Times* from the chair just within the hall as he carried his cases to the front door. His mother was coming down the stairs. 'They can send *you* out to fight now, mother,' he called. 'See, you can be directed anywhere by Winston, if he so pleases.'

Elizabeth smiled and said: 'As long as he doesn't put me down the coal mines I think I'll manage.'

He opened the door and the full colour and scent of the garden was before them. 'It's looking wonderful,' he said quietly. 'Really peaceful.'

A little tentatively his mother laughed. 'Perhaps we've spent far too much time admiring our gardens,' she added. 'Trimming the hedges, pruning the trees, mowing the grass, making sure the paths were weeded. Some of us thought that the entire blessed world was right here.'

'You mean we should have taken a peep over the

hedge,' he suggested. He put his arm around her middle-aged waist, enjoying the silk of her dress. They put his cases in the back seat of the car and climbed into the front.

He had brought the newspaper with him and he glanced at it while they drove towards the station.

'There are people in Luxemburg *paying* to get a good view of the fighting across the border,' Harry told her. 'It says here that they are sitting in deck chairs watching it all going on.'

She drove slowly as if not anxious to get to the station too early. The road, so familiar, rolled over the green moorland of the forest. There were horses in the distance drinking at a shining pool. They drove to the brow of the middle of the three modest hills and the countryside opened out around them like a coloured umbrella. From their right, from the direction of the pool, came a horse and rider. 'It's that girl,' said Elizabeth grimly.

'Bess,' he answered. 'She rides very well, doesn't she.'

'She's very accomplished,' said his mother enigmatically.

The girl encouraged the horse up the last grass incline and splashed through a low stream. 'Ah,' she said lightly. 'A sailor off to the sea. Good morning, Mrs Lovatt.'

'Good morning, dear. What a nice mount.'

Elizabeth had not stopped the car but they were progressing so slowly that Bess was able to jog easily alongside. 'I'm thinking of buying him,' said Bess. She patted the chestnut's neck. 'For my war work.'

'Are you joining the cavalry?' asked Elizabeth

177

pleasantly. Harry grimaced and nudged his mother. 'What are you doing, Bess?' he asked.

'Mounted patrols,' she announced importantly. 'Riders covering the forest to report parachutists landing. This is a big area, you know. Four hundred square miles of it.'

'And what do you do when you find a parachutist?' asked Elizabeth. 'Scream?'

The girl became tight-lipped. 'You're off to sea, then?' she said to Harry. 'Mind you don't get wet.'

'Portsmouth naval barracks, I expect,' answered Harry wryly. 'Although that's strictly a military secret.'

'I won't tell anybody, I promise,' returned the girl. She turned the horse and, waving deftly, set out again across the uneven countryside, eventually vanishing into a copse of young trees.

Harry and his mother drove on in silence for a while. 'You've never liked Bess very much, mother,' said Harry. 'Don't you think you're a bit heavy on her?'

'I always see her as such a useless person, I'm afraid,' confessed his mother stiffly. 'Amusing herself by playing games.'

They reached the station yard and he took his cases and laid them on the paving stones outside the gate. Ben, who was wearing his LDV armlet over his porter's uniform, came out and picked them up. 'Back to school again, are we, sir?' he joked wheezily.

'It is a bit like old times, isn't it, Ben?' laughed Harry. He told his mother not to get out of the car and then leaned over and embraced her.

'Take care, Harry, please,' she said, looking straight ahead. 'As far as you can.'

'Listen, lovely,' he said kissing her cheek. 'We'll *all* have to take care. You make sure you do.' He withdrew a little from her and grinned. 'What would you do if a Jerry parachutist landed in the garden? Ask him to do some weeding?'

She astonished him by saying readily: 'I have your old rook rifle. Your father says that if you hit anybody directly between the eyes with that it would account for them. I'm going to start practising as soon as you're out of the way. Here's your train now. Goodbye, darling.'

Every window of the train was latticed with strips of adhesive, each pane like a badly cut face. On this wide morning, the only other passenger in Harry's compartment had pushed down all the windows so the breeze from the sea and the country flew in unchecked.

The other man was large, made larger by festooned fishing tackle and bulky clothing. He had a plum face squashed beneath a felt hat and supported by a heavy coat and oilskin from which gaitered legs were thrust with a confidence approaching belligerence. Beside him, oddly like a pair of spare legs, were his waders, and beside them, leaning against the window, were his encased rods, with his basket and landing net on the seat beside him. 'Don't like the look of the war news,' he said to Harry. 'Not one bit.'

'Well . . . no, it doesn't seem very promising,' agreed Harry uncertainly. 'But the new regulations mean that everybody will have to pull their weight. No more dodging the war effort.'

'Not before time either,' replied the man sagely. 'Not one bit.'

Harry stared at him. It seemed pointless to ask him if he were going fishing. 'Catch much these days?' he asked eventually, giving the tackle a nod.

'Fair bit. Not so many people at it nowadays. More for the rest of us. There's quite a few salmon in the Avon. Best salmon river in the south of England, the Avon, you know.'

'Yes, I heard that.'

'Do much fishing yourself?'

'No. There's not a lot of time . . .'

'Not unless you trawl a line over the stern of the ship, eh?' The man nodded at Harry's uniform and laughed in a jolly way. 'Mind you, there's plenty in the services and in the ARP and the fire service and all the rest of the rackets who have plenty of time for fishing. I mean, there's nothing to do, is there. Nothing.'

Harry was angry but unsure. 'It looks like it will all change soon,' he ventured. 'With the Germans right on the doorstep.'

'Never,' said the man airily. 'Never in a million years. Mark my words, son, they'll sit on that side of the ruddy Channel and we'll sit here and *nothing* will happen. *Nothing*. In the end everybody will get fed up and go home. The war will be finished. We'll probably have a few air raids, just token attacks, you see, but they won't set foot here.'

He was so convinced that Harry felt that he might have some inside information. 'What do you do?' he asked diffidently. 'That's if you can tell me.'

The big man guffawed. 'Tell you? Of course I can tell you. I fish. I fish nearly every day. Retired early, see. I've had to give up the car because of the petrol, but I still fish. Nothing's going to stop that.' He looked gravely at the younger man. 'I'm a provider of food. I'm doing *my* bit in that way.'

Harry swallowed hard, but any retort he now felt compelled to make was choked back by the arrival of the train at a forest halt station and the fisherman's preparations for disembarking. He said a cheerful goodbye and Harry, abandoning the protest as too late, timidly returned the words. The man had to transport his equipment in relays to the wooden platform. Harry was almost tempted to help him. The umbrella was the last item. As the man closed the door finally he grinned quickly and half opened the umbrella to show Harry that the cover was camouflaged in green and brown whorls like a military vehicle.

'In case of air attack,' the fisherman laughed. 'Cheerio!'

Harry sat bemused as the train puffed away again. His hand went to his pocket and he fingered the three identification discs. Perhaps Thurston G., Smith D., Wilson N., had been fishermen.

At Portsmouth he handed the discs, at last, to a nonchalant leading seaman seated at an inquiry window.

'I'm a bit late with them,' said Harry apologetically.

'Don't matter, sir,' said the man taking the discs and, without a glance, throwing them on a pile of similar tags in a box with 'Ovaltine' and the picture of a country maid with a sheaf of corn on its side. He saw Harry's expression as he looked towards the pile. 'We get quite a few,' he said. 'It can't have been cleared for a bit.' As if it needed some excuse or explanation, he added: 'Sometimes people lose the discs, and sometimes the discs lose the people.'

Nine

Alan Stevens, the schoolmaster who had arrived in Binford at the start of the summer term, lived in the stone house behind the village school, beneath the same roof that had sheltered his predecessors since the small, walled school was built in the middle of the nineteenth century.

Few of the people had learned much about him. He taught single-handed at the school with music lessons being taken by John Purkiss, the church organist. There were only twenty pupils, up to the age of nine. After that the children went each day by bus to the school at Lyndhurst.

A solitary sort, the villagers decided, the type that would come out of his shell only when he was ready. Although he was only in his thirties, he had a grave, middle-aged air about him and he smoked a pipe. In the evenings he was sometimes seen walking alone by the river or gardening behind the wall of his house. The children liked him. They said he could make them laugh. Ma Fox decided that he was hiding away from the world after a tragic marriage. For once she was nearly right.

Petrie was one of the few people who had become even casually acquainted with him. They had conversed one evening near the coastguard look-out and

Stevens had said that the poet William Allingham had once been a customs officer at Lymington and had written that on his first night of duty there he had heard the nightingale four times.

'Go and see him, will you,' suggested Robert. 'Ask about the playground and see if you can find out something more about the chap. He's able-bodied as far as I can make out. He ought to be helping out, not hiding himself away.'

They were squatting in the LDV guard post, usurped from the air-raid wardens against much protest. It had once, in Victorian times, been the village schoolroom, a little stone building with a pot-bellied iron stove and a bleak ceiling. In addition to their training evening in the village hall they manned this post. It had two beds, lanterns, a trestle table and chairs, a teapot, kettle and enamel mugs, a map of the forest, and a morse tapper and receiving earphones. Tommy Oakes and some of the other village boys had politely inquired if they could use it as an outlaws' den when the LDV were not in occupation.

Petrie went to see Stevens in the evening, after his meal, leaning his motorcycle against the school wall and walking around to the cottage at the rear. It had rained that day, the sky was dull and dusk seemed early.

The coastguard was astonished as he entered the garden. It was lined with growing vegetables, minutely tended; onions, carrots, lettuces, peas and beans climbing the sticks, and potatoes in flower.

'You've certainly got this organized in a few weeks,' Petrie complimented him.

Stevens had been sitting on a wooden box, smoking

his pipe. 'Gardening,' he said, 'is the one thing that keeps you really busy, tires you out so you sleep, and, in the end, provides you with sustenance. Would you like a beer?'

Petrie thanked him. He remained in the garden while Stevens went under the low lintel of the kitchen door and returned with two dusty bottles of beer. He wiped them off with a teacloth and, having given one to Petrie, returned to the kitchen for some glasses. 'Found it tucked away in the loft,' he said. 'Somebody's secret store, I suppose. There was a whole crate. Years old, probably, but it tastes all right.'

They drank and Petrie agreed. 'You won't be able to eat all that,' he said, nodding at the garden over the rim of his glass.

'I'll give it to the kids,' said Stevens. 'Or the hospital or the donkeys or something. It's my war effort.'

'That's why I came to see you,' said Petrie. 'Robert Lovatt, you've met him, big chap, retired solicitor, parish councillor, all that. We've got a Binford unit of the Local Defence Volunteers now, you may have heard, and he asked me to ask you if we could use the playground in the evenings for drills and training.' He leaned forward with a grin. 'We could use the sports field but I think he wants to hear the boots, when we get boots, sounding on something noisier than grass. And the school wall means that it can all be done in private.'

'Why in private?'

Petrie looked embarrassed. 'Well, we're all beginners, amateurs, and we don't even have any proper weapons. One or two of the lads are worried that people will laugh at them. It looks a bit strange standing guard with a garden fork.'

Stevens shrugged. 'It's all right with me,' he said. 'I suppose the county education office ought to be asked really.'

'We didn't want to do that,' confessed Petrie. 'It would take a month of Sundays to get an answer from them.'

'Well, as I say, I don't mind.'

There was an awkward pause. 'I can't see the Belgians holding out for long,' said Petrie eventually. 'And the way the Germans are going through northern France doesn't hold out a lot of hope does it? It all looks a bit unpleasant.'

Stevens shook his head. 'Yes,' he said with care. 'I'm afraid it does.' To Petrie's surprise he picked up a packet of seed and eyed the print on the packet. 'Look at that,' he said pointing. 'Excellent, it says, for growing on air-raid shelters. Would you believe it? Old Josh Millington gave them to me. Said he wasn't going to dig an air-raid shelter just to grow these.'

They both laughed. Petrie finished the beer. 'I must be off,' he said. He grimaced. 'Weapon training tonight. We've now got two service rifles, a tommy-gun and a dozen rounds of assorted ammunition.'

Stevens said nothing but walked with him to the garden door set into the high stone wall. Petrie said as casually as he could, 'Why don't you come and join in? The LDV, I mean. We could do with some younger men.'

There was a hesitation. Then Stevens shook his head. 'No, thanks,' he said quietly. 'Tell Mr Lovatt I'm sorry but I can't.'

'Why is that?'

'I'm a conscientious objector. I don't believe in fighting.'

'A conchy!' bellowed Robert. 'A conscientious objector! Here? Teaching our children?'

Petrie restrained a grin at the wrath. 'I'm afraid so,' he said. 'He made no bones about it. Said he didn't believe in fighting.'

Robert's disbelief caused him to sit abruptly and heavily. They were on the bank of the creek above John Lampard's paddle steamer, waiting for old Jeremiah Buck and Tom Bower to bring the secret weapon, the punt gun, in from the river. It was a piebald evening and again it had rained in the day.

'I simply cannot believe it,' said Robert. 'I mean, the education authorities must have known, blithering fools.'

'He's in a reserved occupation, anyway,' Petrie pointed out. 'A teacher. He seems a nice enough chap. Perhaps he's got a reason.'

Robert regarded him as if he had uttered a treachery. 'Reason? What reason? What reason has any Englishman got for refusing to fight for his country? What's *he* doing for the war effort?'

'Well,' offered Petrie defensively, 'he's grown some wonderful vegetables. Lettuce, carrots, onions. They look a treat.'

'Onions!' exploded Robert. 'What's he going to do – throw them at the Germans? God, I've never heard anything like it.' He calmed suddenly. 'Ah, here they are now.'

Petrie had already seen them moving slowly on the

mottled water behind a bank of reeds. John Lampard came down the path from his house with the pimpled boy, Willy Cubbins. Between them they brought the punt and its two men to moor at the stern of the paddle steamer. The London boy stared at the great-mouthed gun, its ten-foot barrel occupying most of the length of the low punt. 'Christ,' he said. 'That's the biggest bleedin' gun I ever seen.'

Robert looked at him disapprovingly. 'If we are going to allow you to join the LDV,' he said severely, 'you're going to have to moderate your language. This is not some London street gang, you know.'

The boy said he was sorry, adding, 'But it is a big bugger, ain't it?'

The men looked at the odd weapon with instant affection. It had been holed up in a rotten boathouse on the far side of the river for years. Jeremiah had remembered it and he and the shipwright had recovered it and had taken it to Tom Bower's slipway for repairs.

'She was in good condition, surprising,' said Tom. 'Considering where she'd been.'

'What's the boat like?' asked Petrie, peering through the gloom. 'She doesn't look too bad.'

'Needed a few boards 'ere and there,' said Jeremiah. 'Punt 'as to be strong. Fire that thing and you could blow yourself out o' the water.' He suddenly said kindly to the still staring boy, 'Used to use that to shoot water fowl, see. Sitting and waiting for them all night, just waiting, and when they start up at daybreak – bang! You could get twenty at a time. You 'ad to because you only got the chance of one shot.'

Robert's big head nodded with satisfaction. 'Pick

off a section of Jerries with that,' he said. 'Lie in wait among the reeds and – bang!'

'But you only get the chance of one shot,' observed the boy still not taking his eyes from the gun.

The Binford LDV were grateful for the screen of the school wall as they paraded. Their initial training evenings had been held outside the cricket pavilion, which doubled as the village hall, and the muffled stampings of mixed shoes and boots on the grass had occasioned mirth and ridicule from villagers, men, women and children who were not involved but had come to watch.

They did undoubtedly appear a strange and motley formation. Some had steel helmets and some bulbous berets sent from the army depot at Winchester. Most wore dungarees although Sid Turner, the forester, wore his gaiters because he thought they looked more warlike. Weapons were equally nondescript, the odd old army rifles, the tommy-gun tucked under Petrie's arm, shotguns, air rifles, forks and pikes made from iron railings. Robert wore a khaki shirt, grey plusfours and a webbing belt to which was attached a huge, flop-eared revolver holster, which, in the absence of a revolver, was stuffed with cardboard.

Drill had been hideously embarrassing for all. Purkiss and one or two others had some notion of the movements, but there were many collisions and stumblings. Most of Binford seemed to be watching, criticizing and guffawing. The men were scarlet-faced. George Lavington said he wanted to go home. Robert fiercely refused and then, at the height of the remarks from the spectators, he had rounded on them powerfully. 'You people may laugh,' he shouted. 'Go on, get it out of your system. You'll laugh the other side of your faces when we're all that's between you and the Gestapo!'

That had sobered them for a while, but the hilarity had restarted immediately military training exercises had commenced. The sight of grown men, whom they had known for years, creeping on their stomachs through the long grass at the back of the cricket field was too much for the crowd. 'See if you can find that ball we lost last summer,' taunted a voice. Livid, Robert rounded on the caller but was at once defeated by the arrival of Tommy Oakes in his cub uniform. 'Mr Lovatt,' he said loudly, cheekily. He pointed to the perimeter of the field. 'Kathy Barratt's old dog has just cocked his leg on one of your snipers.'

In the school playground there was at least some concealment. The members of the unit had been sworn to secrecy about the new rendezvous – a promise they gladly kept – and crept into the school one by one. The effect of the drill, however, was spoiled by Purkiss, who had been promoted drill instructor, much against his wishes, having to keep his voice to a near whisper while giving the simple orders.

From outside the wall soon came signs, however, that the secret had travelled. Heads began to peer and leer over the stonework as the squad mounted an attack on the school lavatories which stood innocently in the playground. Howls of laughter were provoked by Malcolm Smith throwing a tennis ball into the cubicles and shouting 'bang'. Some watchers were so convulsed they fell from the wall.

At the end of the training Robert called his tattered squad, sweating, dusty and embarrassed, to attention. They tried their best to stand straight and serious but not even their LDV armbands were level. 'Men,' he said, 'the German Propaganda Chief, Goebbels, said on their wireless last night that the men forming our Local Defence Volunteers would be regarded by the German forces as "*franc-tireurs*" . . .' He waited. Puzzlement clouded the eyes in front of him. '*Franc-tireurs*,' he repeated. 'And if captured would be shot by firing squad.' The Adam's apples went up and down. 'In the light of that, I have orders to give an opportunity for any man who wishes – to resign now.' No one moved. Robert eyed George Lavington. 'Lavington?' he asked.

George looked shocked. 'Me, Mr Lovatt?'

'You said you wanted to go home the other night.'

'Ay, yes, Mr Lovatt, but that was because they was laughing at us. I just didn't like them laughing, that's all.'

Robert brought himself up to his powerful height. 'Squad!' he bawled. There was no point now in whispering. 'Squad. Right turn!' They turned less raggedly.

'Squad, by the right – quick march.'

'By the right, quick march!' came the juvenile echo from outside the wall.

Stevens, who had watched some of it sadly from his window, went to the garden door and saw the green-capped and jerseyed Tommy Oakes, shouting the orders to himself and marching stiffly up and down.

After the drill the men went almost shamefacedly home. George Lavington and the brothers Wilf and

Malcolm Smith trudged in their habitual silence down the road to Binford Haven. An owl sounded over the fields. Eventually George sighed. 'Never thought I'd ever be one o' they *franc-tireurs*,' he said.

Elizabeth drove from her house into the morning serenity of the village. Surely nothing would ever change it. People who had lived there two hundred years or more before would have recognized it without difficulty and would have been greeted by their descendants. Sunlight lay across tiled and thatched roofs and gathered in pools between the trees and along the single street. A handful of children paddled in the stony stream as it wandered through the ford. Three of them belonged to Mary Mainprice. She called to them to watch out as she drove the car through the water, causing a small wave, and they laughed and jumped as the water reached them.

People were working or walking. She waved to Dr Brinton from Lymington making his unhurried round and to other everyday housewives. In Hob Hobson's grocery shop there was a quietly talkative queue as women waited, ration books in hand. She joined the end of the line and chatted with the rest. The talk was, as it had always been, children, weather, ailments and husbands, but hardly a mention of the nearing war danger. Then, swiftly and suddenly, an aircraft appeared low across the village, its shadow flickering over the roofs. Its roar set the shop trembling and the dark shape loomed with fleeting menace over them. Everyone in the shop ducked, Hob behind its counter, the girl assistant beneath a pile of empty egg boxes which she brought tumbling down. Some of the customers fell on their knees, like women at prayer. The plane had gone by the time they had all reached their prone positions, swooping off towards the coast. Hob regained his feet and his proprietor's assurance. 'One of ours, ladies,' he announced, picking up the wooden pats he used to square the fats. They rose raggedly, laughing. You could never be too sure, they agreed among themselves.

Elizabeth returned to her house. The garden indeed looked full and lovely, the walls ruddy-faced, the windows open to the visiting sun, the eaves and trees cool with shade. Wadsworth was stretched on the lawn and he rolled his eyes when he saw her. She knelt and scratched his belly, something which always sent his back legs kicking like a berserk cyclist. There was a halo of bees around the herbaceous beds and a blackbird commented from a branch. As she went into the house through the french window Mary Mainprice came from the kitchen, anxiously wiping her hands on a tea towel. 'Kathy Barratt rang from the telephone exchange, Mrs Lovatt. Something about your telephone being taken over if the Germans invade.' She looked aghast, as if the danger had only just occurred to her. 'She says they've got to Boulogne, and that's only on the other side of the water, isn't it?' Somewhat to Elizabeth's surprise she began to cry, wiping her eyes on the tea towel. Her husband was a soldier in Singapore.

'It seems silly, don't it,' she said as Elizabeth comforted her. 'There's Bert's got a gun and 'ee's the other side of the world looking after Chinese, so 'ee says.' She gave her eyes, now red, a final dab with the tea towel. 'Last letter I 'ad he seems to be having a good time,' she added uncertainly. 'They go swimming and play football and there's no rationing there and no black-out or anything. And they're just a lot of Chinese.'

She returned to the kitchen and Elizabeth, smiling a little, followed her. 'I wrote to 'im and said I was thinking of taking the kids to America,' Mary said. Elizabeth was astonished.

'Oh, you can,' went on Mary before she was asked. 'You put their names down and they're going to take them over there. Anybody can go. The Government pays. You just put their names down. I'm thinking I will.'

Elizabeth made tea for both of them. Then, feeling a little foolish, she went into the loft of the house to search for the rook rifle.

Up there, the domain of martins, mildew and mice, with the daylight seeping through the old roof tiles, were all the memories of their lives. The trunks and cases, still labelled, from their one long foreign trip, to Luxor and the Nile Valley in 1934; the books from their sons' childhoods, an old rugby ball, their first radio set with its earphones hanging on a rafter nail, a lovely but impractical hat she had worn to a wedding years before. With a wry expression she took the hat and put it on. In one corner was a washstand and a mirror, a hideous Victorian assembly which Robert's mother had bequeathed to them and which went, as soon as decently practicable, into the loft. She wiped the mirror clean with a piece of newspaper, appropriately, she noted, describing the Ascot fashions for 1937. Then she placed the wide-brimmed hat on her head and posed in the dim glass. To think that when she had first worn it she had been a young wife. Up there also was the uniform that had belonged to Gerald, Robert's brother. It was in a case and she had not looked at it for years. Nor did she now.

She saw the rook rifle, propped in a corner with a gaping tennis racket. Her hand went to the latter. It had been hers also. A spider had embroidered some of the sagging holes with its web.

Elizabeth picked up the light gun and saw on the floor a tobacco tin. Opening this she found, as she remembered, it was half full of lead pellets for the gun. Carefully, still feeling odd about the whole business, she carried the rook rifle and the pellets to the aperture in the ceiling and climbed gingerly down the ladder on to the landing.

On a second thought she returned to the loft and descended again with the collapsed rugby ball and the wide, petalled hat. First looking about her, she took them out into the orchard and propped the ball on top of the log store with the wall of the garage behind it. On top of the ball she fitted the hat and then retreated to the full extent of the garden. There was one place where she had a channel of clear view through the apple trees, only a yard or so wide, and this pleased her because she felt it gave the scenario a certain authentic difficulty.

Elizabeth broke open the rifle, as she had seen her sons do, pushed the lead slug into the breech and lifted it to her shoulder. She squinted along the sights and pressed the trigger. The shot embedded itself in the first apple tree in its path. Frowning, she reloaded.

Ten minutes later, Millie, turning the corner of the house and hearing the brief crack of the rifle, found her mother-in-law wedged close to a tree, firing at the ball and the hat of long ago. 'Good God!' exclaimed the younger woman. 'How very belligerent!'

Elizabeth did not let her embarrassment prevent her firing another shot. 'There,' she said, red-faced with satisfaction. 'I got the chap right between the eyes then.'

Millie peered towards the target. 'Poor chap,' she said. 'And what a pretty hat for a German parachutist.' Laughing, they walked together through the striped trees towards the garage.

'It's the same shape as one of those German helmets,' explained Elizabeth firmly. She looked pleadingly at Millie. 'You think I've taken leave of my senses, don't you?' she said.

'As one who has been thinking about a recipe for mustard gas bombs, I can't say I'm qualified to answer that question,' returned Millie cheerfully. 'Old Granny Spofforth is telling everyone in the village to have poison ready to put in the drinking-water supplies.'

They had reached the target. 'Gran Spofforth herself ought to be enough to strike terror into the heart of any invading army,' Elizabeth said. 'Did you hear they're in Boulogne?'

'Yes, I listened to the news,' replied Millie quietly. 'And Amiens, and Arras. I've been looking in my old school atlas. They're not very far away, are they?' They examined the holes in the hat and the rugby ball.

'Not bad,' claimed Elizabeth. 'Five hits.'

'How many shots?'

'Almost the whole tin full of pellets,' admitted her

mother-in-law ruefully. 'I'll have to buy some more if you can still get them, or see if there are some lying around.'

'Can I have a go?' asked Millie.

Elizabeth handed her the light gun and they walked back to the extreme of the garden. There were only six slugs left in the tobacco tin. 'We're getting low on ammo, captain,' grinned Millie. She lifted the gun and fired. The pellet ricocheted from the guttering of the garage.

'You've got to use the sights,' protested Elizabeth. 'You wouldn't hit a tank like that. Like this, see. Watch.'

She was lining up the hat and ball and had just squeezed the trigger when Robert came around the corner into the garden. Immediately enraged he rushed towards them.

'No, no, no!' he bellowed. They turned in amazement. Almost fiercely he took the gun from Elizabeth's hand. 'Whatever do you think you're about?' he demanded. She could see he was frightened.

'Practising, Robert,' she replied firmly. 'Defending King and Country. Don't you approve, dear?'

He snorted. 'No, I damned well do not approve.' Seeing the hurt cross her face he subsided in a moment and looped his large arms around her, the gun curiously held between them. 'You *mustn't*, Elizabeth,' he said. He looked at his daughter-in-law. 'Nor you, young lady. You must never even *think* of this sort of thing. These are trained men, an army, sweeping everything before them. What . . . what good would this do?'

'I thought it might help,' said Elizabeth, subdued

but still stoutly. 'We might get one or two of them.'

'And then be very quickly eliminated,' he sighed. 'Don't you realize that you are women, and civilians. You have no right to take up arms. You must never think like that again.'

'But *you're* different,' suggested Millie.

'Yes, I am. I'm a man and I'm a military man. What I do is *entirely* different.' His voice subsided. Anxiety furrowed his face.

'The British Expeditionary Force in France is surrounded. It has its back to the sea,' he said simply. 'There's going to be an attempt to get many of those chaps out as soon as possible. By sea. Every sort of boat that can be mobilized is going to be used. I've got to organize something.'

Elizabeth looked aghast. 'You're going to *France*?' she asked slowly. *'You?'* In a boat.'

'In Lampard's paddle steamer,' he replied soberly. 'He's getting it ready now. I'm getting a crew together.'

Twilight mist lay in a cloth over the basin of the river, the final touch of the summer day added deep pits and shadows to the roundness of great trees. There were birds in Robert's garden as he left the house, a hare sat on the road outside and water fowl croaked and quacked as he reached the estuary. John Lampard was already aboard; Robert could see him moving about the deck above the mist-line that hung like a skirt around the paddle steamer.

'All shipshape, John?' he called as he reached the stubby jetty.

Lampard's head poked quickly out of a hatch. 'I'll

say,' he enthused. 'God, what a thing this is going to be. Never thought this old bucket would be going off to sea for years, let alone going off to war.'

Robert stepped clumsily aboard. Despite his love for the river and his lifetime in that place he had never been a man for boats. He always felt too big, too confined. 'What did Mrs Lampard say?' he asked carefully.

'Oh, Joan . . . well, she was all right.'

Robert nodded. 'They don't think we're up to it,' he agreed. Lampard busied himself with a strip of adhesive on the wheelhouse window. 'I didn't tell her the precise details,' he admitted. 'No point really. I merely said that they wanted the *Sirius* to do some watchkeeping work in the Channel. She wasn't all that pleased with that even; she thinks I'm too old to play at being Nelson.'

'There'll be more as old as you and I,' Robert assured him. He looked down the stokehold hatch. 'You managed some coal, then.'

'National emergency,' replied Lampard proudly. He began polishing the brass rail. 'Williams over at Marchwood *had* to give me a load. Best South Wales steam coal, too. Enough for several trips. She'll go like the Royal Yacht on that.'

'Don't you think you'd better forget the polishing,' Robert suggested with a grin. 'It's hardly going to be regatta week, you know.'

Lampard stopped guiltily. 'I'll have to rough-paint over the brasswork,' he said suddenly. 'Pity after I've spent so much time burnishing the stuff.' He paused. 'Several voyages,' he repeated. 'It's going to take all of that, don't you think? I've just made some coffee. I'll get you some. Sugar?'

'Two,' replied Robert. 'For energy, resourcefulness and courage.'

'Better have three,' suggested Lampard bringing the mug to the deck. He spooned in the sugar. 'Prewar supply that is,' he said. They sat on one of the deck benches, curled over at the back like a seat in a park, like a pair of fishing friends taking their ease between catches.

'How many men will be there, do you think?' asked Lampard.

'God only knows,' answered Robert. 'Couple of hundred thousand, at least.' He paused. 'It's an army. How did anyone allow a whole army to be trapped?'

Lampard looked around the polished wooden deck. 'Be a bit of a squeeze,' he joked wryly. 'She's never had more than thirty-five aboard, and then she rolls like hell.'

'Every seaworthy boat there is will be there,' Robert told him. 'From what I've heard anyway. It's a madness. But it looks like the only option left. Take them off the beaches.'

'It's getting close inshore is going to be the problem for most,' said Lampard. 'This old thing will be wonderful for that. She's got a very shallow draught. I bet there'll be a few like her. All the paddle steamers that use this bit of coast in the summer, and the Thames boats, let alone those further down in Devon and Cornwall and over on the coast of Kent and Sussex.' He laughed. 'The trippers called them the sixpenny sicks, you know.'

Robert drank the last of his coffee. 'You realize,' he said gravely, 'that we shall most probably be under attack. From the air if not from the land and the sea as well.'

Lampard sniffed as if testing the temperature of the river air. 'It'll be something new for me,' he said. 'I was never in the services. Too late for the first war, and I've had a bit of heart trouble, you know, that's why I quit London.' He looked abruptly at Robert. 'Not that it will make any difference to this business,' he said. 'I have to go. She's my boat. Nobody else can handle her.'

Robert laughed. 'Aye, aye, sir,' he said.

They sat in silence watching the imperturbable evening river. Ducks were becoming garrulous around the hull and two swans, exquisitely at ease, droned in flight downstream, just above the mist level.

'How's that boy with the spots?' asked Robert. 'You took him on, didn't you?'

'Willie. Yes, he's not a bad lad at all. Poor little devil has had a raw deal, if you ask me. He moved in with us last week. The people at the farm said they couldn't keep him any longer. He's all right.' He paused. 'But he sleep-walks.'

'Good heavens,' Robert said. 'Where?'

'All over the place. He says he's always done it. Joan thinks he's looking for his mother.' He shook his head with amusement. 'The people at the farm used to make him tie a cow-bell to his ankle, so they knew when he was wandering about at night.'

They laughed together. 'We'll have to remember that if we use him in the LDV,' said Robert. 'You can't have somebody on night duty who's liable to walk into the enemy while he's asleep.'

They enjoyed the idea for a while, then fell to a

comfortable silence. Darkness gathered over the estuary.

'They'll give us three hours' notice,' said Robert. Lampard had purposely not asked many questions. 'Petrie, the coastguard chap, will tell us when. He's coming with us.'

'Good,' nodded Lampard. 'With a paddler you need someone like that. Who else, the Dove boys?'

'Yes. They couldn't get their boat into the water on time. It's still full of holes. They're keen as hell. Frightened they're going to be left behind. Petrie's bringing some charts of Dunkirk and environs or whatever the naval term is.'

Lampard approved. 'That's splendid. I think I could find my way across there, although I haven't been for years, not since I was sailing.'

'But what you do when you get to the other bank is another matter. We could be stuck in the mud at the mercy of Jerry,' said Robert.

'If everyone could bring some rations,' said Lampard. 'And a bottle or two of something . . . just to keep out the cold.'

They talked for another half an hour, not of the impending adventure, but of former days, of times and characters they had known, of London, of Binford. At ten-thirty they heard voices along the riverbank and three figures came through the summer darkness. Petrie and the Dove boys came aboard and the five men sat, drinking Scotch which Lennie Dove had brought with him, while the night grew around them. They only drank one toast: to the morrow.

Elizabeth was waiting when Robert returned. 'I'm relieved,' she said, turning away quite quickly. 'I thought you'd gone off to France already.' She went into the kitchen and returned with their nightly cups of cocoa. 'You're still going, I take it?' She attempted to make the inquiry sound casual.

'Of course,' he replied gently. 'I must. Everybody must do something at a time like this. If we lose our army we'll lose the war, everything.'

'You really hate the Germans, don't you?' she said, to his surprise.

'Hate them? Of course I do. They're the most loathsome race, always have been. Look how they bombed Rotterdam the other day. Can you imagine English airmen doing that?'

They had two Dresden figures on the alcove shelf beside the fireplace. She reached from her chair and picked one up. 'And yet they made these,' she pointed out. 'And they've produced people like Luther and . . .'

He did not let her finish. '*Hitler* is the one I'm thinking about at the moment,' he said in a low voice. 'And the rest of the thugs. If we let them win they will defile us forever. I'm in no doubt about that.' He blinked at her. 'I'm surprised you even mentioned it.'

She stood up, put the figure back on the shelf. 'I wonder what it will be like in, say, thirty years' time?' she said. 'I wonder, will everybody hate them then? Or will it be different? I remember years ago, playing tennis with some German girls at Eastbourne.'

'Tennis?' he repeated. 'Elizabeth, whatever are you talking about?' He rose too. 'Are we going to bed?' he inquired.

She smiled at him. 'Sorry,' she said. 'It was all going through my mind this evening, that's all.' She waited.

'There's something I wanted to show you,' she said. 'It might be useful.'

'What's that? You're being very odd tonight, Elizabeth.'

'Yes, I suppose I am.' She went into the kitchen prepared to tell the lie. 'Mrs Mainprice found this in the loft,' she called. 'I'd forgotten all about it.'

Mystified, a little impatient, he waited. She returned holding a British Army officer's uniform on a hanger. Robert's astonishment caused him to knock his empty cup from its saucer. 'Good God,' he breathed. 'Where . . . ? Whose . . . ?'

'Gerald's,' she told him. 'He left it behind on his last leave. You said you needed a uniform for the Local Defence Volunteers. It smells a bit of mothballs but it will probably fit all right.'

He almost staggered forward and took the tunic and trousers from her. She stood helplessly. 'It's been up there all this time,' she mumbled.

Robert touched the two shoulder tabs gently with one finger. 'Wonder what rank he would have finished the war as?' he said. He looked at her and saw she was crying. Still holding the uniform he embraced and kissed her clumsily, feeling her weeping against his face.

At six o'clock the following evening the *Sirius* was ready to move out into the limp, petrol-coloured water of the estuary. Petrie and Lampard had stoked the little furnace between them and jaunty puffs of steam issued from the vessel's funnel. The unusual activity stirred waterbirds who took off with long trails along the flaccid surface, squawking in the pale air.

Robert, wearing his dead brother's tunic and trousers with his LDV armband, stood beside Lampard in the wheelhouse as, carefully, and with some small ceremony, the boat owner pushed the engine-room telegraph forward. The vessel came to life, shaking itself like a rousing animal, as the starboard paddle wheel began to revolve in the water, churning the mud and sending a further flurry of birds into the river sky.

'Slow astern, starboard,' he called down the brass trumpet next to the wheel. He turned to Robert. 'Odd smell,' he said. 'Like mothballs.'

'Slow astern, starboard, it is,' came Petrie's disembodied confirmation.

'This tunic's been packed away for a bit,' said Robert, brushing the sleeves self-consciously. He had removed the brass regimental badge and the pips from the shoulders. The *Sirius* began to pull herself awkwardly sideways from the wooden pier. Ten minutes later they were out in the estuary and making for the entrance to the sea.

They turned along the low coast, past familiar headlands and beaches. A man walked his dog peacefully along the shingle as though he knew nothing of what was happening to the world.

By eight-forty-five they were in the Solent, paddles gently waddling, duck fashion; ahead of them lay the oddly shaped naval vessel that was their rendezvous. From the wheelhouse Robert and Lampard looked out across the narrow channel and in the lemon evening light saw that the strangest flotilla was assembling in the ancient waterway. They called Petrie. He arrived, black and sweating, from the engine room where Peter Dove was helping him.

At first the coastguard breathed the evening air gratefully and then narrowed his eyes to take in the warship lying ahead. 'HMS *Avalon*,' he said. 'And . . .' He looked about him. 'My God,' he breathed. 'What a bloody collection.'

He took in each waiting vessel. '*Yarmouth*, she's the Isle of Wight ferry, and *Cowes River*, she's another. And that effort there, if I'm not mistaken, is a fire float, and that gentleman with the red sail is a barge. I hope he's got an engine as well. Those two are trawlers and that thing over there that looks like a half-finished building is a seaplane tender, *Zeus*, I think she's called. And . . . two more paddle steamers. It's like a circus.'

John Lampard laughed and nodded towards the naval vessel ahead. 'At least we've got the navy,' he said.

'She's not out of character,' Petrie grinned back. 'Fitted out for service in China, Yangtze river gunboat. She's just come home. Equipped for fighting Chinese pirates.'

They all laughed, and Peter Dove, coming on to the deck, looked around the immediate horizon also. 'Well, I'll go to sea,' he muttered. 'We're not the funniest then, not by a long chalk.'

Lampard looked his way and the fisherman understood. 'I meant, like unusual,' he said apologetically.

Petrie said: 'We can make fifteen knots, can't we, John?'

'Eighteen if we risk the paddles,' replied Lampard. 'That's more than most of those could ever raise. I bet that barge can only just get four knots in a following gale.'

Lampard patted the woodwork of the *Sirius* like a father patting a son. Fondly he remembered that it was less than a year since she had been chuffing on that same stretch of water taking the Binford children on an evening outing to see the grand yachts lying off Cowes during regatta week.

Robert lit his pipe pedantically and puffed it below his steel helmet. Lampard turned his binoculars on HMS *Avalon*. She was swinging with the tide, a curious craft, high sides, and with Browning machine guns perched on her flanks. 'Perhaps they're armed with cutlasses?' he muttered.

From the naval vessel ahead came the blare of a klaxon. Whoop . . . whoop . . . whoop, an eerie echo. They looked towards the Yangtze gunboat. A naval voice came across the coloured water. 'This is Captain Andrews of HMS *Avalon*,' the loudspeaker sounded. 'We will sail in fifteen minutes for Dunkirk. If you find you are getting left behind, carry on and you will doubtless soon find another convoy to join. There are numerous vessels sailing that way. No lights will be shown but we are promised a calm sea and a fair night. I will be taking a course due east before turning back along the coast from Ostend. This is the long way around but it does get us out of trouble with our own minefields and the German shore batteries which are now in firing positions along the French and Belgian coasts. Keep a sharp watch also for wrecks, old and recent. In the event of air attack we hope to give you some cover. Good luck to you. If you get left or lost, Dunkirk is not difficult to find. Just make your course towards the sound of the explosions and the lights in the sky.'

Petrie and the Dove brothers went below. Robert and the paddle-steamer owner remained on the miniature bridge. Robert was conscious of a tight wad of excitement in his chest and stomach. Lampard mused: 'Never thought this old relic would go to war.'

Robert laughed ponderously. 'Are you talking about the boat or yourself?'

'Both,' admitted Lampard wryly. 'You heard what he said. Set course towards the sound of the explosions.'

Lennie Dove appeared from the hatch behind them. 'Look what I found, Mr Lampard,' he said. 'We got a stowaway.' Lampard and Robert turned and saw the pimpled, worried face of the boy Willy Cubbins. Lennie held his upper arm. 'He says he wants to come,' said Lennie.

'Young sirs, I would like you to imagine, if you will, that this large and lecherous German gentleman is about to do something personal to your sister. Or, if you have no sister, then your mother or your favourite auntie. Somebody near and very dear to you.'

The marine combat instructor regarded the rank of naval sub-lieutenants with a benign malice. A line of stifled smiles faced him.

'The himplement I am about to demonstrate would be the appropriate weapon to use to defend your female loved one. It is called the British bayonet – a nasty sharp-looking chap, hisn't 'ee? On the end of the point three-ho-three rifle it makes a very 'andy prodding piece; used as a single weapon it is equally malicious, drawing blood very quick. Be careful, young sirs, how you muck about with pointed weapons. As the late King 'arold found out at the Battle of 'astings, ten-sixty-six, they can have your ruddy eye out.'

Along the parade ground at Portsmouth similar squads of naval officers and ratings were undergoing instruction in infantry combat, charging at sagging sacks with wild cries. The traditional litany for bayonet drill, 'Stick it in, twist it, pull it out', echoed over the wide concrete.

Harry Lovatt tried to imagine himself rescuing Bess Spofforth from the flesh-seeking Nazis. Khaki gaiters, webbing belts, rifles and bayonets appeared as strange appendages for sailors. 'The henemy,' announced the marine sergeant, 'will take a mean hadvantage of you, because 'ee will be able to perceive your blue uniforms much more easy than those of your comrades in arms, the brown jobs of the army. Therefore the sailor and the marine 'ave always needed to use the terrain much more hadeptly than the haforesaid brown jobs. Don't, young sirs, ever try to 'ide in a field of buttercups. You will be perceived.'

A busy-looking orderly was making his way across the square. He stopped at the sergeant and whispered tersely, meanwhile looking sideways, ominously, at the assembled squad. An almost poetic smile drifted across the rough face of the marine. His eyes were small and became bright. 'Ho, ho,' he said, poking his head forward, his neck stretched like a tortoise, his eyes narrowing towards the squad as if trying to detect minute faults. 'Ho, ho. A grand hopportunity to prove what your sergeant 'opes we 'ave been perceiving.'

Harry felt his gut flutter. His grip on the unfamiliar rifle tightened. A young officer, three down the line, dropped his with a clatter. The instructor regarded him with pained relish. 'Do not throw the weapon away, sir. You will be needing it. We don't throw our weapons away until we have decided to surrender, and that, sirs . . .' he took in the rest of the parade with beaming certainty, '. . . never, ever, hoccurs.'

The orderly had marched off, grinning; now the marine stood screwing up his eyes over a sheet of paper, as if he had difficulty in reading it or hesitated to impart its content. 'As a diversionary action calculated by the 'ighest command, no doubt, to turn the course of the present war, it has been decided to send some of you young gentlemen back on the 'oggin. The following will report immediately to Movement Control for himmediate posting to sea duty.' He read four names: Harry's was the last.

'Leave the rifles, sirs,' suggested the sergeant as they moved off. 'They belongs to the barracks.'

Six hours later, HMS *Doughty*, a naval tug, was pushing out into the calm grey Channel, making course for the French coast. Harry stood with Barraclough, Jones and Simmonds, the other sub-lieutenants called from the parade ground, in the tight wardroom. Facing them, Captain Stanley Finn, stubby, round and red, like a marking buoy, sniffed belligerently. 'There is an operation under way,' he announced, 'to evacuate the British Expeditionary Force, or some of it anyway, as much as possible, from the port of Dunkirk and the beaches adjoining. The Germans seem to have caught us with our trousers down, and this appears to be the only way out. We're going to give it a try, anyway.'

His quiet blue eyes fixed on the faces of the young

men, all of whom were taller than he. 'There's absolute chaos over there. I know because we only came back this morning. The whole damned town is on fire and Jerry has bombed the port so that it's just about impossible to use. Somehow or other, however, we have got to get the army out. Otherwise, we'll have no team when it comes to playing at home.

'Admiral Ramsay, C-in-C Dover, is in charge of naval forces and there is also the most God-amazing collection of civilian craft heading in that general direction. They've already started ramming each other. Some of the navigation leaves much to be desired. Some of these vessels may not only miss Dunkirk, they could easily miss France itself. The function of *Doughty*, and your particular job, is to put naval parties ashore and assist in an attempt to get something organized in the town. The army has its hands full, some of it keeping the Germans at bay, the rest trying to get off the beaches.

'There's no water or electricity in Dunkirk. There's gas, you can tell that because it's leaking from every hole in the streets. There are dead and dying and there are stragglers who must be organized and helped to the embarkation points. Frankly, a lot of it is a bloody shambles at the moment.

'We're going to try and sort at least some of the mess out. Each of you will have a party of a dozen ratings, plus a leading seaman and you will be under the command, once ashore, of a naval beachmaster who is already *in situ*. As I said, there are dead and dying, there are also drunks and men going mad. It's not a happy sight. You may find that your main threat, your main headaches, won't come from the

Germans but from some angry and frightened British soldiers. It's something you're going to have to sort out for yourselves. The civilian population are also at panic stations. Do any of you have good French?'

Harry said: 'Yes, sir. I last served on a French ship, the *Arromanches*.'

'Right, son. Well, you'll find that useful. One of the people who has gone missing is the Mayor of Dunkirk, regalia and all. Have a chat with him if you come across him.'

Ten

From Saint-Pol, to the west of Dunkirk, a cloak of smoke hung above a copiously burning oil refinery. It rose to ten thousand feet and spread across the town, its port and its beaches. Beneath it the buildings on the harbour blazed like footlights below a dark curtain. As the *Doughty* moved towards the shore a stick of bombs sent up distant eruptions of debris, smoke and water. On the wide beaches at La Panne to the east were dark masses like more smoke.

'They're men,' breathed Harry looking through binoculars. 'Thousands. Just waiting. Jesus Christ, what a mess.'

Spread about them, all over the cloudy sea, was a great litter of ships and boats. Chugging merchantmen, ferries, coasters, pleasure boats and trawlers. They stretched to the smoky horizon in each direction. Some were closer inshore apparently trying to embark men from the beaches. Harry looked to the sky above them. It was empty of aircraft. He turned the glasses back to the dark beaches and the burning frieze of the town.

'It smells,' said Barraclough sniffing. 'You can smell it from here.'

'Smells?' questioned Simmonds. 'It *stinks*. Like a burning rubbish dump.' He paused, then said in a hurt way: 'I thought we were going to win this war.'

The others looked at him strangely. Jones said: 'We always *win*, don't we? We *can't* lose this.'

'Looks like we're having a bloody good try, sirs.' A chief petty officer had joined them. They turned to him like boys seeking assurance from an older man. He had a face like a block of wood. 'Wait until you get inshore,' he added. 'It's a real performance, I can tell you.' He paused and sniffed the air. 'Like a bad fish and chip shop,' he commented. Then he said: 'The old man would like to give you a final few words before you go ashore. So you don't go and get into trouble or anything.'

They followed him up to the tight bridge. Captain Finn was staring at the blazing shore like a man mesmerized. 'Good morning,' he greeted them. 'As you can see, the situation does not seem to have got much better. The main town is right behind the harbour, if you can see either through the damned smoke. The beaches on our port side are being used by small draught boats to ferry men out to the bigger craft, but it's a matter of a little at a time. It will take years to get those men off at that rate and the port is just about useless.' He had spoken with the binoculars remaining at his eyes. Now he lowered them as if they were a great weight. 'The naval officer you need is located across the street from the town hall,' he said. 'That's if you can find the town hall. I think I've seen it sticking up in the smoke a couple of times, so it's probably still in existence. You can check your route by your maps, although I wouldn't be surprised if the geography has changed a little during the past couple of days.' He looked towards the great hand of smoke that covered the horizon ahead. 'On the brighter side, the smoke screen won't help the Luftwaffe. And there's no sign of their navy. So far.'

As though in answer, there was a blare on the klaxon and they threw themselves flat as a German plane screeched above them firing its machine guns. The Lewis gunner on the bow of the tug only began to fire when the plane had gone. 'He's not after us,' said Finn, picking himself up. 'He's after that destroyer.' Another screech above their heads and a second aircraft skimmed their mast. This time the Lewis gunner began firing early but the aircraft was gone in seconds, followed by a third. They curled above the destroyer, almost athwart the harbour entrance, and came in quite carefully, with precision, dropping their bombs, straddling her deck and sending a sudden curtain of sea around her. Abruptly, horrifyingly, the whole midships section of the vessel blew outwards.

On the tug the captain and the four novice officers were immobile in disbelief as explosion followed explosion, shattering the warship, filling her with smoke and flames. Another stunning eruption tore through her bow quarters and the ship, like an animal sighing in death, turned on her course and began to drift towards the harbour.

The speechlessness on the naval tug's bridge was broken by a childlike sob from Barraclough. 'That's horrible,' he whispered. 'That's just horrible.' He looked about him embarrassed.

'Right,' agreed Captain Finn softly. 'It is horrible, son.' His voice quickened. 'Christ, she's going to block the harbour mouth.' He pulled the engine-room telegraph. 'Full speed ahead,' he ordered. 'All we've got.

Give me some room, lads. Stay under cover.' They hurriedly left the bridge as he was directing the helmsman. 'Starboard two, Barnes. Let's get behind her.'

Harry, clutching his steel helmet, crouched below the overhang of the bridge with the other three young men. 'He's going to try and push it out of the way,' he said when he realized. 'Away from the harbour entrance.'

'I hope to God she doesn't blow up again,' said Jones fervently.

'There are men in the water,' realized Barraclough. 'Over there, look.'

They could see hands projecting from the oiled sea, hands waving in strange hopeless greeting. Little cries reached them. 'I can't look,' said Barraclough. 'What a horror, what a bloody horror.'

They sailed past and through the drowning men from the destroyer. Finn's eyes were only for the burning warship ahead. She was now lounging like a drunk, rolling irrevocably towards the stone piles of the harbour entrance. A series of explosions coughed through her ribs. There were still men clinging to her rails.

Captain Finn got the blunt nose of the *Doughty* between the stern of the blazing destroyer and the harbour. A trawler was moving to the front of the warship and a towline was being thrown. 'Good,' muttered Finn. 'Not a minute too soon.' He eased the burly tug off with great skill and she slowed as her bow butted the stern of the destroyer.

The klaxon of the destroyer began to whoop eerily, like someone howling their own dirge. 'Down! Everyone take cover,' Finn ordered through the bridge loudhailer.

The four sub-lieutenants lay flat behind the piled hawsers on the tug's deck. 'If she goes up now, we'll all go with her,' forecast Jones. His teeth began to chatter uncontrollably. 'Sorry,' he said. 'S . . . sorry.' Simmonds laid a hand across his back and the teeth stopped. They felt the gentle collision as the two ships met, a nudging kiss, and the padded nose of the tug began to push the larger warship away.

Everywhere there was a stench of burning, the destroyer creaking and groaning as the tug pushed her. Suddenly the four young men lying on the deck heard a screaming, high above all the other noises of the hell around them. Harry looked up and saw a man, aflame like a brand, running the deck of the destroyer. The man jumped overboard. Harry started up but Jones pulled him back. 'There won't be anything you could do for him,' he said quietly.

Then, like the rush of a mob, a dozen more men appeared on the destroyer and ran towards the stern. Two of them were being carried like battering rams by others. The deck of the tug was well below the rail of the destroyer but they began to clamber over. 'This time we've got to,' said Harry. All four clambered to their feet and hurried towards the bow. They clasped the men climbing down or being lowered. One of the men who had been carried was burned black, his eyes uncomprehending, white teeth grimacing grotesquely through charred cheeks. The other had the entire side of his head stripped to the skull.

The petty officer who had stood with them on deck as they approached Dunkirk now came forward with a stretcher party. 'Out of the way, sirs,' he ordered briskly. 'Let the dog see the rabbit . . . oh, fucking hell, sirs. What a thing.'

They got the two burned men on the stretchers and hurried them away. The others sat on the deck, stunned, staring. One suddenly put his arms around a comrade and began to cry. Harry moved forward. 'Don't cry,' he told him helplessly. 'Men don't cry. Don't cry. There's some tea coming.'

Both men, only boys less than his own age, nodded dumbly. The one who had wept wiped his eyes with the back of his hand, leaving a streak across his sooty face. All around the other men were being carried away. 'Anybody else left aboard?' asked Harry inadequately.

'Nobody, sir,' replied the man who had comforted the other. 'Not living. They're either dead or they're in the fuckin' 'oggin.' Harry helped both to their feet. They were not wounded; they trembled like babies.

'They're pushing her away, Bert,' said one strangely, staring at the tug now nudging the burning ship well clear of the harbour. 'They're going to push 'er back to Blighty! Ha, ha, ha! They're pushing her back home!' He began to laugh hysterically and his friend, trying to calm him, burst once more into tears. Harry put an arm around each and, choked with emotion himself, helped them amidships, one weeping, one chortling like a madman.

The destroyer was now out of danger of fouling the port entrance, wallowing well offshore and being carried gradually west by the current. Small boats were out picking up men from the sea. Three German planes shot across the scene without firing or dropping bombs. 'Came back to see how they'd scored,' muttered Harry. The tug was now backing off hurriedly. The captain's order was none too soon, for as the warship drifted further west, now half a mile away, she was blown out of the sea by another immense internal explosion. When the watchers picked themselves from the tug's deck they saw that she had split into three sections, like small volcanic islands, each one smouldering and steaming as it settled into the sea.

Another warship cruised in calmly on the other beam of the tug. A hollow, unhurried voice came over the intervening waves. 'Well done, *Doughty*. Proceed now according to orders. Proceed as normal.'

'Normal,' muttered the petty officer, handing mugs of tea to the survivors and then one to Harry. 'I like his idea of normal. I don't want to be here when something bloody abnormal happens, do you, sir?'

Captain Finn backed the tug off, like a pondering bull preparing for a charge, and then went forward again towards the harbour mouth. There was little space there, but she bustled her way into the port and went alongside the burned wreckage of half a dozen Dunkirk fishing boats. They were black and ragged-edged like charred paper. Harry and the other three young officers with the four sections of sailors made ready to go.

'Landing party ashore,' sounded the flat voice over the ship's loudspeaker. Harry Lovatt glanced behind him. The dozen sailors, steel-helmeted, webbed-belted and carrying rifles, returned the look expectantly. Somewhere on land a fuel tank blew up with a red and yellow tulip of flame; smoke and noise mixed in the air. With a strange realization Harry found that, after all the boyhood games, the countless imaginary parts he had played in his adolescence and his romantic disguises since, after all that, he was about to take part in something real. With the acrid noise of battle all about, he was about to become a leader of men.

Barraclough's party went first, clambering down over the side of the tug and across the burned fish-boats, picking up their gaitered boots as if they were tramping through a black morass. 'Number two party, forward.' Harry was aware of the nervous thrill as he moved ahead of them, down over the thick hull of the *Doughty*, then feeling the crackling black wood of the gutted trawlers beneath his feet. He heard the seaman behind him mutter, 'Bleeding 'ell, Nobby, we're going to get dirty.'

'You been dirty ashore plenty of times, mate,' mumbled Nobby.

'Cut the small talk, lads,' warned Harry. An obedient silence answered him. He was glad he had said it. He climbed up the broken stone of the jetty and moved a few paces forward so that the rest of the party could follow.

Having done that he stood and took in Dunkirk. For the first time he was at ground level and could see directly into the town. It was blazing all along the waterfront, the flames like skirts caught by the wind. Black smoke from the Saint-Pol refineries blotted out the summer day. A thick stench of oil, gas and cordite hung over the port. 'What d'you reckon to that, then, sir?' said a voice from slightly behind him to his right. 'Make a nice opera, don't you think?' He turned to see an army sergeant, black-faced, ragged-uniformed, pointing dramatically as if there might be some doubt of the scene to which he was referring.

'I don't think this will be so entertaining,' answered Harry solemnly. 'God, you can smell the garlic.'

The sergeant laughed. 'Very good, sir. Best one today. Just keep moving along the jetty, sir. Dunkirk is right at the end.'

Harry said: 'Very good of you,' as he might have thanked an English policeman who had given him directions. 'Party forward,' he ordered in a level voice. He felt the men move behind him as he strode out. A plane crossed above them, low, whistling, and they crouched without breaking their step, like a party of hunchbacks. They watched its bombs straddling the buildings ahead where there seemed nothing else left to destroy.

Big holes had been gnawed from the jetty. There were the masts and funnels of sunk ships protruding with an odd sadness from the harbour, as if hoping to be remembered. At the far end a line of phlegmatic soldiers was waiting to embark on a small coaster. As Harry neared he saw their faces were black and blank, they shuffled a few inches at a time, the utterly fatigued steps of chained prisoners.

The deck of the coaster was already crowded and as Harry's party approached a shout went up from someone below. 'That's enough for this trip. Any more and she'll go under.' There was no reaction from the soldiers. They stopped shuffling and merely stood. Not one of them turned to look at the fresh naval party that strode by eyeing the soldiers, but when the sailors were almost past, there was a clatter as a rifle fell on the broken cobbles and a man dropped with it. Harry hesitated but then moved on. An old infantryman at the end of the queue, a man in his forties who looked eighty, laughed, showing toothless gums, and shouted: 'Another bugger having a kip.' No one joined in.

As they reached the end of the jetty Harry saw that there were spectral groups of soldiers moving through the streets, taking no notice of the fires or the bodies of dead men which lay across the stones. A civilian bumped by on a bicycle, a man in a big cap and French blue working clothes. He took no heed of the mayhem around him, but paused at the junction of the street with the port and produced from a bag a length of bread which he began to eat reflectively.

Among the tumbled shadows of the buildings Harry saw the town hall, standing up amid the smoke, and made for it. Barraclough's party, which had gone ahead, had vanished into the debris but when Harry's section reached the rendezvous he saw that they were being formed up in proper parade order by a naval officer with a megaphone who was standing on a chair in the street. 'Come along, come along,' he called towards Harry and the other sections behind. 'At the double, sir. At the double.'

Harry gave the order and they trotted quickly into position along the littered street. A singed dog came from a doorway and sat licking its wounds. Two women, holding each other and crying out unintelligible curses, stumbled among the broken buildings.

'Welcome to Dunkirk,' said the naval officer, once all four landing parties were in position. 'By now most of you will have realized that we are here trying to get as much of the British Expeditionary Force home and dry before Jerry gets here. I'm afraid the whole damned thing is terribly difficult and it's not made easier by the fact that the brown jobs are thoroughly fed up with the entire story. There are soldiers all over this town, lost, some drunk, some half crazy. It will be your task to round them up and get them to the embarkation points. These are few and far between at the moment since most of the port is unusable, although we are managing to improvise a little. The chaps you organize you should transport to the beaches of La Panne, to the east, and sit them down quietly there until somebody can come and collect them. You may commandeer any transport you think necessary, always supposing you can find any.' His chin went up with a rugged breeziness. 'Any questions?' and immediately, 'No, I thought not. All right. Get going. And don't get lost.'

Barraclough suddenly ventured: 'Sir, there is one question.'

'What is it, sir?'

'How far away . . . ?'

'Is the Hun? Difficult to say. He's in heavy artillery range, that's for certain. Either that or the French have turned on us.' He took on an official look. 'The salient is about ten kilometres out, all around. It's being held by British and French troops and that's going to be fine until Jerry brings up his big tanks. After that it's good night Irene. Questions answered? Good. Off you go then.'

With a taut stomach and his heart clanging like a bell, Harry led his party towards the piled fires of the town. He had a terrible need to urinate and once out of sight of the town hall and its beachmaster he called a halt before some gutted shops.

'Right, chaps,' he said, in the way of a leader of a boy-scout troop on a hike, 'it's going to be some time before we can have a widdle so I suggest we all do it now.'

He saw the men grin and some look around at the rubble, reasonably wondering why the needs of nature had to be served on one particular place. They formed a line along the shop fronts, facing towards them, and thirteen silver arches played into the gaping windows like the efforts of an ineffectual fire brigade.

Harry had been afforded, by a curious acknowledgement of rank, a wider space to urinate, an interval between him and the men, and the privacy of a shop doorway. A man the other side of the broken wall began to pray vigorously as he peed. 'Our Father which art in Heaven, hallowed be Thy name . . .'

Dumbstruck, Harry finished his task and stepped back to observe the man, whose pee-ing and the prayer were timed to finish together. He buttoned his fly and saw Harry and several of his comrades regarding him. 'I am religious,' he said frankly, as though he owed everyone an explanation. 'It seemed a good time for a prayer, sir, before we venture into Sodom and Gomorrah.'

'Yes, of course,' answered Harry, taken aback. 'Don't worry. That's fine. What's your name?'

'Leading-seaman Andrews, sir.'

'Good, Andrews. Well, don't go far away. We may need you.' He looked at the grins on the faces about him. 'Come on. Let's get on with it,' he ordered. 'To Sodom.'

It was only as they went deeper into the stricken streets that Harry began to realize what a widespread and undignified defeat had been inflicted upon the British Army. The eyes of soldiers, white and sly, spied out at the fresh arrivals from holes, doors and broken windows. They remained half-hidden, like troglodytes, watching the naval party trudge by: ambushers awaiting a signal.

They discovered half a dozen military vehicles at the corner of a square, with a Royal Engineers corporal casually about to set fire to them. He was like a boy making a Guy Fawkes bonfire, building wood and straw and some bales of paper around the wheels of the vehicles. Two canisters of petrol stood waiting to be thrown on to the pile. Eighty yards away two of his comrades had righted a fallen table and two chairs of a pavement café, and sat idly, rifles thrown negligently, as if in disgust and distrust, on the ground. 'Ha!' bellowed one, 'The bloody navy's here, 'bout fucking time too.'

Harry glanced their way and saw that they had a bottle of something on the table and were taking it in turns to pour the contents into mess tins, which, at each swallow, they raised in a toast to each other.

'Here's to the Frogs,' shouted one soldier.

'The Frogs,' the other responded. 'The fucking Frogs. And the bleedin' Belgies too. And all the other poor bastards.'

'The Dutchies,' remembered the first man. 'The good ole Dutchies.'

'The Jerries,' toasted the second. He shouted to Harry who had halted his party across the littered cobbles of the square. 'Yes, mate, the Jerries. They got officers what don't run off.'

Harry's inexperience caused him to hesitate and the two soldiers laughed sourly at him. Their mockery jerked him to reality. He stepped forward towards the man who was intent on burning the trucks. 'Hold on,' he said informally. 'We're going to need one or two of those.'

'These?' the sapper said, apparently amused. 'This junk? Why? There's no-bloody-where for them to go, is there? We've run out of road, mate.'

'Where are your officers?' asked Harry firmly. 'Who is in command?'

'Command!' exclaimed the man, as if the question came from a madman. 'Command! Ha, that's a good one, a bloody good one.'

Harry took a further firm pace. 'I am a naval officer,' he said brusquely, hoping his voice did not quake. 'Stand to attention.' The man blinked and did so. Harry's relief nearly choked him.

'Officer?' trembled the man. 'Officers, sir. They went. Cleared off. Took the unit transport, they did. We just walked, legged it, thirty miles, we reckon. And . . . and when we got here we find these . . . look, these trucks. That's why I'm going to burn the bloody things, sir. That's why . . .'

The soldier shook with emotion and tears channelled his face. His inebriated comrades left the table and staggered comically, dragging their rifles by the straps, like dogs on leads. ''Ere,' said one, pointing with difficulty at Harry, 'don't you go upsetting our Alan. Look at 'im. See what you done. 'E's 'ad enough to put up with,' aven't you, mate.' He wrapped his arm around the heaving shoulders of the sapper. His expression changed to one of pleading. 'You ought to see 'is feet,' he suggested. 'They're 'orrible. All gone yellow.'

'Right,' said Harry firmly. 'Let's get one of these trucks out of this mess. Then we'll get you home.'

The trio looked at him in astonishment. 'Home?' inquired the second soldier who had been at the table. To Harry's amazement he produced a teddy bear from inside his tunic and held it by its hand. 'Home?' he repeated. ''Ow we going to get home, then?'

'By getting down to the beaches and embarking on the ships that are waiting there,' said Harry with more assurance than he felt.

'Fucking 'ell,' said the first man. 'In that case we ought to consider it, didn't we.'

'Get the truck free,' ordered Harry. He turned. 'Come on, let's get on with this.' The sailors moved forward determinedly, pulling the conflagration material away from the vehicles. Harry called to Andrews. 'Take these gentlemen back to the café,' he said, pointing to the wreckage of that establishment. 'Sit them down and have a talk to them.'

'Yes, sir,' said Andrews, patently pleased with the assignment. 'Come on, chaps,' he encouraged. 'You've done quite enough. Let the navy do a bit.'

'Good idea,' decided one of the soldiers and they turned docilely and stumbled back towards the table and its seats. They set up two more chairs and Andrews sat down with them. They explored the bottle but it was now empty. The sapper began to lick around the inside of a mess tin. Something blew up in the next street, a huge detonation sending smoke up like a tree and showering stones and tiles on to the square. The sailors all ducked, but the three soldiers sat bemused and smiling. Harry returned his attention to the vehicles. Men were getting into the cabs and testing the starters. To his amazement he heard, from behind him, the quartet singing in a hushed way at the table and then break into a blatant and enthusiastic chorus:

'A sunbeam, a sunbeam,
I'll be a sunbeam for Him.'

His men had started the engine of a fifteen-hundredweight platoon truck and then that of a one-tonner, and were backing them away from the debris into the more open part of the square, when they heard carnival sounds coming from one of the streets that led off it. Harry paused and turned. The sailors had just succeeded in getting the vehicles clear. Into the square came a fearful sight, a gang of staggering British soldiers, maddened, drunk, all pride lost, defeated in every way.

One man was dressed in women's clothes and performed a sickening dance on the cobbles to the cheers of the others. Another was wearing a woman's hat and carrying a naked dummy from a store window. Two others were wheeling a dead man in a wheelbarrow.

'Whoa!' shouted the man dressed as a woman. 'Look what we got here – it's the wanking navy. Late again!'

Harry felt paralysed by the sight, its horror, its sadness, its shame. The sailors around him stood astonished. Trembling, like a man confronting a nightmare, he stepped forward. 'Chaps –' he began.

His very tone of voice and the one word he ill-advisedly picked brought raucous reactions from the soldiers. 'Chaps?' demanded the female impersonator. 'Who are you calling "chaps"?' He advanced belligerently and produced a revolver from the ridiculous handbag he swung. 'How d'you like a flash of the knickers, then?' he screeched and lifting his skirt displayed a thick pair of thighs clad in ivory silk drawers. The audience behind howled with hilarity and the demonstrator turned to demonstrate how he had done it. Harry moved forward quickly and sensed his men move fractionally after him. But the blowsy mob leader returned in an instant and Harry found the revolver pointed directly at him from a range of four feet. He prudently stopped.

Silence fell across the torn square, an enclosed silence, with the echoes of war, the resounding explosions and the crackle of fires still coming from all around. The soldiers in the group were all armed. The man with the shop window dummy let her fall over his shoulder and levelled his rifle. The wheelbarrow was set down and the lolling corpse carefully rearranged.

Sweat was flooding Harry's face and inside his shirt, trickling down his belly and loins. 'I order you to lower those weapons,' he said, his voice emerging like a croak. 'Otherwise you can face the consequences.'

Wrath now replaced derision on the painted face of the man at the front. 'You . . . you order *us*. You ain't seen a fucking German yet! We 'ave – plenty of the bastards . . . And *you* . . .'

Harry believed he was about to shoot. He lifted his

own revolver a fraction, ready to fire directly at the green-bloused chest. He was shivering, very afraid. Then, like a walk-on in some comedy, the first soldier wandered across from the table at the side of the square. 'He's all right, mucker,' he assured the mob leader. He pointed at Harry. 'He's going to get us all home.'

'Home?' The word spread itself through the soldiers. 'Home . . .? Home . . .?' The astonishment on their faces indicated they had not even considered the possibility. 'Home?' said the man at the front, making it sound a very long word. 'And how you going to do that, then? There's no way to get in the port, I heard that already. So don't try that on 'ere, mate.'

'He promised,' said the soldier from the table. 'On 'is 'onour.' He turned to Harry. 'Didn't you?'

'We are going to the beaches of La Panne,' said Harry succinctly. 'In these vehicles. Embarkation is taking place there at this moment.' It was only half a lie and it would do for the while.

The new silence remained over the soldiers. Then the man with the tailor's dummy picked it up from the cobbles and said, 'Come on, darling, we're going 'ome.' A murmur of approval went along the mouths of the men.

The man in women's clothes let the pistol down slowly. 'You mean it?' he inquired. 'You're not bloody 'aving us on?'

Breathing with relief, Harry said carefully, 'It's either that or you stay here and wait for Jerry.' He pointed at the man's costume. 'And you wouldn't want the Germans to come and find you looking like that, would you?'

'No,' shuddered the soldier. He was trembling like a man in shock. 'No, I wouldn't either . . . sir.'

It was Andrews who finally organized the loading of the soldiers into the first truck. Cheerful and cherubic, he shepherded them aboard like a Sunday school superintendent taking children on an outing. They abandoned their strange clothes and accoutrements without fuss, suddenly sober and compliant, weariness hanging on them. The man who had been sitting at the café table with the teddy bear handed it to Andrews, who announced that together with Jesus Christ it would now be their official mascot.

He said 'Jesus Christ' in a stentorian voice, surprising when it issued from such a squat man, and with such different intonation to the usual military use of the words that some of the tired soldiers looked curiously at him. But he knew when he had a willing audience and as they drove away, through the ragged streets, east towards La Panne, he had them singing with revived spirits:

'Jesus wants me for a sunbeam,
A sunbeam, a sunbeam,
I'll be a sunbeam for Him.'

Harry allowed a moment to watch with admiration and then turned his attention to the rest of the men and the vehicles. One of the hands had got the second one-tonner started and Harry instructed him to drive it carefully through the town with the other members of the naval party in two single files, one on either side.

As they walked the whole spectre of the defeat was

there to see, and the terrible shame, the ignominy that would be deeply known and wounding to the men who were present. They had been betrayed by politicians, by fifth columnists and traitors, some by their commanders, and now like lost and laggard lemmings they were left to make their way to the sea as best they could. They came through the deranged streets and squares of the ancient port, feet burned and blistered with walking through the summer heat, faces tarnished with blood and oil, some with their rifles, some with hardly any clothing. They wandered, scores at a time, each with the same bemused, confused, shocked expression that said this could not be happening to a British army.

Men came in wriggling columns, trudging by the naval patrol and its vehicle, hardly sparing the sailors a second glance, and sometimes none at all. Harry found himself calling to deaf ears and attempting to attract the attention of glazed eyes. In the end he was merely pointing north and saying: 'That way, lads, keep going. That's the way to the sea.' As if they did not know.

The courage was chastening. Those who could still walk he allowed to continue, but then came a man pulling another on a milkman's handcart. Harry ordered him on to the lorry and they carried the borne man carefully, for he was sorely wounded. When they started again, going back in the direction from which the pair had come, the soldier who had done the wheeling began to laugh emptily. 'I've just walked all this way, miles and miles,' he complained. 'I should have sat down and waited.'

They found no more drunken or wild men, just

beaten and disillusioned warriors, tramping on until they reached the coast to fall face forward into the cooling sea, wallowing there like seaside bathers.

A soldier rode a bone-thin horse, sweat dripping down its neck like soap, and across the rump were two others, lying flat on their stomachs, one hanging one way, one another. The horse saw the lorry and, its task done, it stumbled gently and without fuss on to its knees, depositing the rider on to the cobbles and causing the other men to slide off. The horse simply rolled on its side, as if to gain a more comfortable and becoming posture for death. It half raised its head once, looking hopefully towards the sailors in the truck, and then laid it quietly, inert among the debris. The two men on its rump began crawling towards the lorry on their hands and knees and the man who had ridden it, croaked: 'Come on, will you! Help them! Help them!'

The naval men carried the soldiers on to the truck. An army orderly whom they had found in the town was using up his supply of dressings and syringes quickly. Harry could hardly look at the stony faces of the injured men, but they were scarcely less frightening than the expressions of the walking troops that walked and walked, on and on. There were thousands. How could an army of such numbers just be reduced to this awful defeated crocodile? How would they ever get them from the port and from the beaches? An officer in a mud-streaked uniform walked along, still upright, beside his men. He and Harry saluted awkwardly. The soldiers trudged on. 'Nearly there,' encouraged Harry. 'It's less than a mile now.'

'I know,' replied the officer. 'I can smell the ozone.' He looked with compassion on the soldiers. 'They've been marching like this for days. There's been nothing to eat. The people wouldn't give us anything. They spat at us for running away.' He looked pleadingly. 'I don't know what they expected.'

Harry voiced his doubts about the embarkation. 'The port is so damaged they're only getting them off slowly,' he warned reluctantly. 'And I would think that only small boats will be able to get to the beaches. I can't see how it can be done.'

The officer sniffed. 'These people,' he said sharply, 'will be glad just to bathe their feet.' He saluted stiffly and dragged himself after his troops.

Another vehicle appeared in the dust at the end of a long avenue. For a fearful moment Harry thought it might be the advancing Germans. But it materialized through the dusk as a bumping, bucking refuse cart, staggering along on a burst front tyre. It was loaded with silent soldiers.

By now the naval party had collected a full load of wounded and lame men. Harry ordered the driver to turn and drive back to the beach. He called the rest of the party to halt and they sat on the benches of a small and strangely undisturbed park, to await the return of Andrews and the first truck. Fires were burning in the streets that turned off from the little square. A burst gas main sent a brilliant fountain of flame shooting as high as the houses. To his amazement Harry saw a woman walking unhurriedly along the pavement, picking her way over rubble; a stolid woman with a shawl and a shopping basket. He watched her and saw that she went to a shop at the corner of the park where other customers were emerging with loaves of bread. Hardly able to credit it, he got up slowly and walked to the trees at the edge of the park. Not only was there a bakery doing business, but a greengrocer was trying to arrange some vegetables on a barrow, and – Harry could scarcely believe his eyes – a bistro had its doors open at a corner and through that and a shattered window he could see there were customers drinking at the bar.

As if going to view some psychic manifestation, he almost tiptoed across the street. As he reached the door his way was barred by two Frenchmen. No, he could not enter. There was no room, they said.

'*Monsieur*,' shrugged one man, 'the English are escaping. We must stay. It is we who need the drink.'

Eleven

At three in the morning Lennie Dove was at the wheel of the paddle steamer. He was only now getting used to the feel of the strange little craft, and the other vessels, with scarcely a discernible light between them, made navigation a hazard. Several times during his spell he had heard voices calling out to each other in anger or in warning. But the difficulties were compensated by the luminous quality of the calm sea, almost glowing, and the surprising speed that the *Sirius* could make. They were at the front of the convoy and twice he had needed to call his brother, in the engine room, for a reduction of knots, because he saw the large stern of HMS *Avalon* towering close ahead.

Lennie felt neither brave nor afraid. He would not have been anywhere else that night and, he knew, neither would his brother. His thoughts, however, wandered off to bright days fishing off the Isle of Wight, to nights spent having a silent smoke while they trawled the nets and waited for the mackerel to come, to clay-coloured afternoons in winter, working on the boat in harbour until it was time to go home in the four o'clock dark. It was peaceful then. He wanted those times to come again.

But if he were not afraid, he had within him, as did

his brother, a small relic of superstition, a residue of the suspicions of the sailor, particularly the fisherman, going through generations of men who had dealings with the mysterious sea. Between them this was unspoken, but it was there; no one should whistle aboard a vessel at sea, pigs and clergymen were unwelcome as passengers (an excuse, however, for a timely washing-out of the hull, after they had disembarked). Although they laughed in the crowd of the four-ale bar at sea-ghosts, crewless ships, mermaids and monsters, and liked to tell stories about them, at the expense of the gullible, alone on deck at night it was different. An odd, dark wave, a silent vessel passing close to, a nameless cry or shadows cast by the maritime moon, all held the possibility of unwelcome magic.

Thus, towards the end of his watch, Lennie became uncomfortably aware of something moving and pale in the dark on the forepart of the ship, a white shadow against the luminous sea, and a whispering that just hissed above the wave sounds. As he stared at it there came the distinct sound of a little bell.

He began to stare and sweat. There it was again, a white moving presence and a distinct tinkle. He tentatively reached out for the tube through which he could call the engine room. 'Pete,' he said, keeping his voice level. 'Come up and 'ave a look at this.'

His brother poked his head from the hatch and mounted the steps to the wheelhouse. The paddle steamer was splashing through the peaceful night scarcely lifting her bows to the waves. 'There,' said Lennie. 'For'ard. Can't make it out. It moves . . . and it's got a little bell.'

'A bell?' Peter sniffed towards Lennie's breath.

'A bell,' repeated Lennie. The tinkle sounded obediently. 'There,' said Lennie.

'Christ, what is it?' whispered Peter.

'We'll soon know – here it comes.'

The pale shape moved towards them, humped, indistinct, but with the bell now jangling with every movement. Peter's hand went to Lennie's shoulder. As they watched, so it advanced along the rail. Then a face like ash lifted itself.

''Tis that daft boy,' breathed Lennie. 'The kid from London.'

'What's he doing with a bell?'

'God knows.' Lennie leaned out of the wheelhouse and peered down. 'Sleep-walking,' he announced. 'And he's got the bell fixed on his ankle.'

'Jesus Christ. Better get him back to his berth.'

'Don't wake him,' warned Lennie. 'He might jump over the side.'

Peter climbed down and took the boy, clad in striped pyjamas, to the companionway and, bell still sounding at each step, led him down below. Lennie turned the wheel a fraction. A sliver of dawn was coming up over the far rim of the sea. He began to laugh at himself.

Willy Cubbins pushed his head cautiously from the companionway of the paddle steamer and looked out in astonishment on the amazing scene of sea and shore. The *Sirius* was lying off Dunkirk's east mole, a pier built out as a sea protection, not meant for the use of ships or men. The sky was blotched with smoke, through which, like fairytale patches of a man's

237

trousers, areas of striking blue showed, and sometimes beams of wry sunshine.

The boy looked first towards the port. Explosions rumbled from the distance, low burping explosions. He could see the fire sprinkling the harbour front, and what he first took to be fences or groynes, men lining up on the beaches. Then he gazed about him at the sea. It was like some mad regatta, ships and boats cramming the oily water. Far out, big grey war vessels waited in silhouette. Close in, busy launches moved, apparently haphazardly. Between the two were coasters and cruisers, ferries and fishers, tramp steamers and other craft to which he could not put a name. He wondered where the Germans were.

Robert Lovatt, steel-helmeted and rubber-booted, appeared around the wheelhouse. 'Like Cowes, eh, son? What a sight indeed. Like St Crispin's day. Something to tell your grandchildren.'

'I ain't got any,' said the boy.

Peter Dove and Petrie came around the deck. Lennie was on the wheel. Lampard was taking a sleep. Petrie said: 'Looks like they've decided to try and get a vessel alongside the mole, Mr Lovatt. They've got to do something.'

'Never get nothing but a trickle of men through the jetty,' put in Peter. 'You can see that from here.' He patted Willy on the shoulder. 'You all right this morning, son?'

The others looked puzzled. 'I can make some tea if you like,' said the boy and went below.

Peter said to Robert: 'He was sleep-walking last night. He had a cow-bell tied to his foot.'

'That's to stop him falling overboard,' mumbled Robert absently.

As he said the words a flight of three German fighter bombers came from nowhere, at a hundred and fifty feet, and dropped a straddle of bombs. A forest of water erupted between them and the soldiers on the mole half a mile away. The boat rocked like a cradle.

'Missed,' said Peter. No one else said anything.

'They're trying to get the *Gosport Queen* into the mole,' pointed out Petrie.

Lampard appeared, blinking, on the deck. 'Ah, that's who she is,' he said. He raised his glasses. 'Lovely old thing. Remember the evening trips she used to run to Ryde? Beer and a band on deck.'

The pleasure steamer was edging closer and closer to the mole, the wooden breadth only five feet, the water depth hardly more. They watched as, a foot at a time, the steamer eased in. At any moment she could be aground.

'If she sticks they'll never get her off,' said Peter. His brother shouted from the wheelhouse, 'They'll never get her alongside there. There's not water enough.'

Lampard, watching the manoeuvre through his glasses, said thoughtfully, '*Sirius* might do it, though. Otherwise those troops are going to be stuck there.'

Petrie said: 'We ought to have a go, didn't we?'

From the hatch behind them issued the dis-embodied sound of a gramophone record. Willy Cubbins had put it on. Robert began to smile. 'Nice touch, Elgar,' he beamed at Lampard. 'A sense of occasion.'

'I only have the Pomp and Circumstance Marches

and the Summer in the South overture,' answered Lampard. He abruptly turned and picked up a loudhailer. A naval launch was coming on a course which would take her to within calling distance. 'Ahoy there!' Lampard bellowed. 'Have you got a moment?'

The pinnace slowed to the unseamanlike question. In the midships was an officer in a huge blue jersey and thighboots. 'What is it, *Sirius*? Do you want to have a try? I was just coming to suggest it.'

'Yes, sir,' replied Lampard. 'We just might get in. We only need half a cupful.'

The man in the launch laughed. 'Right you are, *Sirius*,' he said. 'I'll go in close now. Wait for my signal. Then it's up to you. Good luck.'

'Wonderful,' breathed Lampard. 'The old tub is going to make history.' He climbed like a boy to the wheelhouse. Lennie Dove glanced at him. 'Stay on the wheel, son,' said Lampard. 'You've got the feel of her now. I might start shaking. I'll talk you in.'

They waited. It was a strange, isolated drama, as if what they were attempting was insulated from the great event that was taking place around them. The naval launch fired a green light. 'Let's have a try,' whispered Lampard. 'Slow ahead.'

'Slow ahead,' repeated the helmsman.

As they manoeuvred the ungainly craft, the paddles waddling, so they saw the multitude of soldiers waiting bravely and patiently on the shore, lining up as if expecting some huge theatre to open its doors. 'We've got to get in,' muttered Robert. 'We've got to get those chappies off.'

He turned and climbed down through the hatch. 'I think a little more music is in order,' he called behind him. In the saloon Willy was pouring tea from an enamel pot into an array of mugs. Robert took one and then said, as if he had suddenly thought it was important for the boy to be informed: 'We're trying to get alongside the mole. If we don't the entire show could be ruined.' He moved towards the portable gramophone. 'Wound up, is it, son?' he asked.

'Yes, Mr Lovatt. He's brought some rotten records though. No dance music.'

Robert picked up a record and examined the needle on the large silver pick-up arm. 'Elgar,' he announced, 'is more suited for an occasion like this.' He read the label. 'March: Pomp and Circumstance,' he recited.

'Terrible row it is,' sniffed the boy.

Robert placed the record on the velvet round of the turn-table and pushed over the switch. The quiet opening of the military march sounded through the cabin. He changed the direction of the speaker-horn so that the music would go out on to the deck. He then made for the companionway steps, singing along with the tune:

> 'Britons shall be free,
> March with me to Liberty,
> Brutes and braggarts may,
> Have their little day,
> We shall never bow the . . .'

What Britons would not bow he never uttered because a blinding explosion threw the vessel sideways, as if a massive hand had struck it. It rolled and violently righted. The aircraft noise came afterwards.

241

Then another detonation. Robert was knocked forward and gained his wind and his feet only to be knocked down again. The needle scratched all across the record and stuck in a groove which ran wildly sending out an animal screech.

Robert got to his knees and reached the deck, his steel helmet fallen forward over his forehead. When he pulled it straight he saw that a huge hole had been bitten into the wooden mole. The vessel ahead, the old pleasure steamer, was on fire and the men were scrambling down her sides. Some of them were screaming and in flames. The naval launch was broken in half and there were bodies in the water where ponds of oil flamed fiercely.

On their own vessel John Lampard was bleeding from a dozen cuts in his face. Ineffectually Robert attempted to wipe away the blood with a handkerchief, like someone half-heartedly cleaning a window. Lampard said: 'There's a first-aid box in the wheelhouse. Don't mess up your handkerchief.'

Robert brought the box out. The smoke from the burning oil filled his mouth, making him splutter and cough. As he began to wipe at the lacerations, Lampard sat slowly upright, staring unbelievingly through the blood. 'Perhaps Elgar isn't enough,' he remarked sadly.

A small drifter had materialized through the smoke and was courageously pulling aside the burning *Gosport Queen*. Petrie, in the wheelhouse of the *Sirius* now, was amazed to see the naval officer who had been in the destroyed launch standing quite jauntily on the wooden mole, calling through a loudhailer like a man coaching a boat-race crew.

242

'Right you are, *Sirius*, come on in, now. Slow ahead, if you please, *Sirius*, slowly.'

Petrie, with Peter Dove taking the wheel, edged the awkward paddle steamer inch by inch to the wooden mole. The paddles gurgled and turned, throwing up brown water and sand. The naval officer peered earnestly over the side of the wooden planks like someone looking for fish, and then got down on his stomach and looked even more closely. 'Yes, yes,' he called, lifting his head to shout through the megaphone. 'Yes, very good, *Sirius*, I think you're going to make it. Yes, splendid, very gently now . . . very gently . . .'

From the deck of the paddle steamer the crew watched the man on the mole with fascination. Fire and oily smoke were still all around. Explosions, far and near, sounded like drum-beats. Men were still being pulled, just alive or dead, from the water. But the naval man was only occupied with the calm business of getting the vessel alongside. Eventually, and with a scarcely contained joy, they felt the paddle steamer touch the piers of the mole. The naval man got to his feet in one movement like a gymnast who has finished a session of press-ups.

'Good, good, fine . . . Well done, *Sirius*.' He turned and called back down the wooden jetty. 'Right you are, army. First section first. No rushing. And don't fall down the holes.'

In tired formation the first soldiers began to appear along the walkway. They had to climb across debris and skirt around the two big apertures made by the German bombs. Engineers were already bringing up railway sleepers to fill the gaps. The evacuation was going forward.

The first soldiers reached the deck of the *Sirius*, stumbling, tumbling thankfully down, blind-eyed, black-faced, riven with despair and weariness. Robert could hardly believe it. This was the size of defeat. 'Any more for *The Skylark*?' called Petrie from the wheelhouse. The relief of getting the craft alongside had given him optimism.

Some of the men laughed in a way, but most were too numbed to react. They went passively to corners of the deck and sat down in rows like obedient infants. Soon the deck was a cobble of helmets and heads. Willy Cubbins and Robert, the boy and the elder man, went below, reappearing with cigarettes and mugs of tea which the soldiers took gratefully, but still sharing the gifts with those around them.

'Cast off, *Sirius*,' called the naval officer. 'Proceed to HMS *Benbow*. Two miles out. She'll signal you. Disembark troops and then come back for another lot. Well done.'

As the pot-bellied paddle steamer cleared the shore, the German planes came back, appearing like flattened hands in the sky. Three of them broke away from the formation and came in low with machine guns winking on their wings. There was nothing to do but to crouch.

The bullets ripped into the deck of the *Sirius*, throwing men about like bales of hay. Smoke and screams were everywhere, the soldiers desperately trying to hide under any projection of the deck or pulling down the inadequate domes of their steel helmets. 'Bastards,' grated Petrie, getting up from the floor of the wheelhouse. Then, illogically, like a man with some secret plan: 'Just wait. Just you wait.'

They began to extract the casualties from the mass of men on deck. Four were corpses, bloodied rag-bags, their faces fixed with the dismay of death. Eight more were wounded and they manhandled them below and laid them on the galley tables. A soldier stumbled out of the mass and said he was a medical orderly. They got together all the field dressings they could find and Willy Cubbins and Robert brought bowls and buckets of water. As they carried them, an odd team, Willy said, as if desperate to share a confession: 'I go sleep-walking some nights, Mr Lovatt.'

'Very dangerous thing to do,' answered Robert.

'I know. I have to wear a cow-bell on my leg.'

The wounded men remained shocked and still, as if frightened to move in case they damaged themselves further, or unconscious, or just whimpering and shivering like men lying in snow. The medical orderly said they needed more dressings. 'Lad,' said Robert. 'Go and see if any more of the chaps on deck have got field dressings. Anything will do. And we'll have to start tearing up shirts and vests.'

'All right,' mumbled the boy. The wounds and the noise had unnerved him but he went on to the open deck again. They had sailed beyond the area of smoke and were now slowly making up the distance to where the aldis lamp from the distant destroyer called them under wan sunshine. 'Anybody got any bandages?' he called loudly to the men. 'Or any vests?'

At that moment one of the planes returned, anxious to make a final run before its efforts would bring it too close to the destroyer. Other vessels were chugging to and fro across the exposed sea, but the pilot made single-mindedly for the obese paddle steamer. He fired again as he drove the length of the ship. Men scrambled and screamed. There was a separate explosion at the bow where the grenade in a man's ammunition pouch was hit and exploded, tearing the wearer almost in half and killing the man next to him. Shouting obscenities another man stood up and leaped into the sea and drowned while imploring the boat to return because he had changed his mind.

Willy, gripped by panic, stumbled across men, alive and dead, to get to the companionway. He felt himself pulled below and a stranger's voice calling: 'The lad's bleeding. Here he is. Do something for him. He's only a lad.'

'It's all right,' Willy heard himself babbling. 'It's all right. It's only my pimples. It bleeds, see. My acne . . . It's only my bleeding acne!'

When the puffing paddle steamer made its second trip to the mole, Petrie, from the wheelhouse, saw that the evacuation was working. There were now half a dozen vessels alongside the flimsy structure, all of them taking on men. The fires still smoked and the planes made further runs, but the departures went on. 'It's going to work,' said Petrie to Lampard who, patched and bandaged, had returned to the wheelhouse.

'It's time we had a share of the luck,' said Lampard. He patted the wood of the superstructure as if in superstition or encouragement to the boat.

It edged, like a plump and reluctant dancer, towards the mole once more. The queues of soldiers stretched far along it until they were diminished to dots in the distance. They waited with brave patience, each for his individual deliverance.

'Why is she called *Sirius*?' asked Petrie, eyeing the closing gap.

Lampard grinned through the plaster cradling his jaw. 'Named after the first steamship to cross the Atlantic. She was a paddler too. Got into New York a nose ahead of Brunel's *Great Britain*.'

The same naval officer was calling them alongside. 'Hello, *Sirius*,' he bawled through the hailer. 'Welcome back.' He looked up the mole. 'Something different for you this time,' he called, turning back to them. 'Very different.'

Along the mole tramped a formation of grim men in light blue uniforms and short boots. 'Bloody hell,' said Petrie as the others looked on astounded. 'They're Jerries.'

'Take these Luftwaffe chaps off, will you, *Sirius*,' called the man on the mole cheerfully. 'Get them sorted out on deck. We'll get you an escort, but we don't expect a mutiny.'

'I suppose it's nice to return with prisoners,' offered Robert Lovatt doubtfully after a long, stunned silence.

'I can't believe it,' said Peter Dove. 'All our blokes waiting and we get a cargo of Krauts.'

The Germans filled the deck space, sitting down silently and watching the amazing operation proceeding. 'Here's the escort,' called the naval man who was enjoying himself. 'Anybody speak Senegalese?'

Along the mole came a dozen immensely tall black soldiers in French uniform. 'They're not armed,' assured the naval officer. 'Their rifles went adrift somewhere.' The Africans clambered to the deck and stood regarding the Germans with a unanimous lack of expression. Their eyes were blank and white.

'Righto, *Sirius*,' called the man on the mole. 'Off you go. Have a good trip.'

At La Panne, to the east of Dunkirk, were some of the longest stretches of uninterrupted sand in Europe, dunes like waves gradually flattening as they reached the shoreline. The sea was shallow and calm. Soldiers bathed their feet in it like children at the peacetime seaside; others played football when there were no enemy aircraft above, and the sorties of the Luftwaffe were kept mercifully low because of loitering cloud, poor planning and the attendant RAF fighters. There was a church in the dunes, a makeshift cross in the sand and an amphitheatre for the congregation, many of whom had never before been to a place of religion. Others had dug foxholes in the sand, deep enough for protection, but not so deep that you could be buried alive by a random bomb. There the army, hundreds of thousands, waited to be picked up and taken home. Most of them played cards.

'God,' sighed Harry Lovatt looking out over the long scene. 'How the hell do they expect to get this lot away?' He drove down to the beaches. Great assemblies of men were leading off to thin queues imperturbably waiting to be put aboard the small boats, which could get close enough inshore, to be ferried out to the deeper water and larger ships. Men waded out to the boats, sometimes further than they could reach; some drowned without fuss at the last step, their bodies floating away to join others in the shallows.

Outside the town the salient was holding, the British and French troops dug in, bravely and bitterly holding the line so that the majority could escape. The German tanks had not materialized; Hitler, with one of the aberrations that were his great weakness, had ordered them to halt, but the town was now within range of the German medium artillery and they sent a monotonous and deadly bombardment into its already burning ruins.

Harry Lovatt's party had been ferrying men to La Panne all day. He had driven the one-tonner himself with a clutch of dead-tired Belgian soldiers in the back. The moment their king had surrendered his country to the Germans they had begun to walk resignedly west.

As he turned the vehicle in a semicircle on the firmer ground before the loose sand began, Harry saw a British army officer and two men approaching. 'Sub-Lieutenant,' the officer called breathlessly, ploughing through the sand, 'how many serviceable vehicles are there in the town? Any idea?'

The man was a Royal Engineers captain, burned by days of exposure and dark-ringed below the eyes. There was a quartermaster sergeant with him and another NCO.

'There are vehicles left all over the place, sir,' Harry replied. 'There's a whole lot, dozens, in a field waiting to be burned.'

'Right, that's what I hoped,' said the captain. 'We're going to try something. We've got to get these men off the beach quicker than this. The damned war will be over by the time we get everyone away at the rate we're going.'

Harry waited. The officer was peering backwards down to the water's edge and the waiting lines of troops. 'We've laid a bit of a track with various stuff from here to the shore, as you can see,' he said. He half-turned to the quartermaster sergeant. 'Let's just see if it works better than the steamer.' He nodded out to a pleasure boat lodged in the shallows. 'It was worth a try,' he sighed. 'But it didn't succeed.'

He seemed so weary that he had to make a conscious effort to continue. 'What I need now,' he said, 'is for this vehicle and a lot of others to be driven over the track and down to the shore – and then into the sea, which is now at low tide, as you can see. All the way, as far as she will go until she stops.'

Harry smiled with appreciation. 'We're going to make a sort of pier,' he said. 'So we can reach the bigger boats.'

'Brighton pier it is, son,' agreed the engineer with a tired sort of joviality. 'Right, let's give it a try, shall we. Will you drive?'

'Yes, sir,' replied Harry. 'It will be my first command at sea.'

'All right, let's see you shipwreck it.'

Harry coaxed the heavy lorry forward, over the strips of webbing, matting, metal and wood laid like two long carpets on the sand, and far out down to the edge of the tide. Soldiers gathered like spectators at a demonstration, cheerfully urging him on. He gritted his teeth and went into the sea, the lorry's high nose keeping well clear of the water, the wheels churning through the shallows. In first gear he forged ahead, five yards, ten yards, fifteen, twenty, until with a hurt groan and a rush of steam the vehicle stopped. He tried again but it was dead. He climbed down from the cab and dropped up to his chest into the cold water, waded back to the shore and walked up the long wet beach.

His view from there took in a wide arc of the great beach. Orders were being called across the sands and sections of the formerly idle army were moving towards the dunes and already bringing forward tail-boards and sideboards from stranded lorries, planks of wood, lengths of canvas and, from somewhere, some wooden railings were carried forward with an urgency born of new and sudden hope. Leading-seaman Andrews was already bringing the second truck towards him. He could see him singing like a choirboy behind the windscreen. He drove it hard into the light oncoming waves and stopped immediately behind the first lorry. A third vehicle was already making its way down the dunes and another parallel twin track was being laid over the sand fifty yards away by the now eager soldiers.

By dusk there were three lines of vehicles reaching from the high water mark to the low water mark and just beyond. As the tide came in Harry stood, drinking tea from an army mess tin, and grinned with the engineer as he saw that the plan had worked. Foot by foot the vehicles in front were engulfed by the surrounding water until only the canvas roofs of those at the fore remained above the surface. The tide at La Panne had one of the longest reaches in Europe and by the time it was nearing its fullness the ingenious pier was thrust far out into navigable water.

'Here come the boats,' nodded the engineer in the evening gloom. 'Now we'll see if it really works.'

Indistinct shapes chugged towards the leading submerged trucks and slowed and stopped easily. 'Sixpence round the bay,' said the captain softly as if remembering with pleasure something from long ago. 'Here they go.'

From the sands a thin line of men came from the great congregations further back as a run of wool comes from a ball, and began to move to the first trucks. Climbing on the tail-boards they moved forward, clambering over the cab roofs, and then tramping along planks of wood placed like a walkway across the stanchions of the roofs. It succeeded beautifully, the lines moving forward quickly, the outlines of the men standing up against the fading sky.

'Thank God for that,' breathed the officer. 'I do believe it's actually going to work.'

Harry watched jubilantly as the soldiers moved forward quickly now, one upon one, dropping into the large boats at the far end of the makeshift jetty. He realized that he was watching part of a miracle.

The *Sirius*, with her strange cargo of scowling Germans and grimacing black Africans, moved out into the Channel, making for HMS *Benbow* again. It was evening, a rose sky, pale violet and a touch of yellow. The wind remained subdued and the sea soft.

'Jerry will be back for a last try before dark,' forecast Petrie slowly. 'If they do give us a going-over, I think we should order all the Jerries to stand up and wave.'

'It's not a bad idea,' agreed Robert thoughtfully. 'After all, transporting prisoners, we're technically Red Cross.'

They had not long to wait. From the east came a

fleet of warplanes circling at a height, nosing out their targets. The paddle steamer was in open sea with twenty or thirty other random craft spread for half a mile either side. 'The buggers are picking us out,' muttered Peter Dove looking up into the sun. 'Can't we get this lot to wave their arms or sing or something?'

The first run of attackers came right across the small ships caught between shore and their naval vessels on the horizon. They came in threes, waggling their wings with the fun of it, firing their machine guns.

A prettily painted herring drifter, to the starboard of the *Sirius*, blew up with a vivid carbuncle of flame. The men on the paddle steamer looked away first, then ducked. A first Messerschmitt banked insolently across the top, then the second came in low and firing. She was too late and the fusillade tattered the water. 'Rotten shooting,' commented Robert. 'Let's get these Huns on their feet.'

The third fighter had peeled off and was making another run on a distant ship. One of the trawlers was firing a Lewis gun hopefully at the sky.

Robert went with Lampard across the passenger deck through the now cowering Senegalese soldiers, some moaning and incanting in their own language, until they confronted the twenty-five Luftwaffe men. Robert addressed them with gestures to indicate the diving planes and then raised his hands like a papal blessing to show that they should stand and show themselves clearly when the next attacker went overhead. The Germans heard him out sullenly and he turned back to the wheelhouse. 'Well, I told them,' he shrugged. 'Let's see how they feel about it. It's their skins as well as ours.'

They could see planes, remote above now, twenty or thirty of them, manoeuvring in the paper sky. The naval vessels were sending up puffs of anti-aircraft fire. 'Here they come again,' muttered Petrie.

Almost platonically, with the casualness of men who know they are helpless, they observed the approach of one aircraft; it was a thin view, head on, soon followed by a second, which Petrie saw first and indicated with an unspeaking nod. Everyone braced themselves, but now turned their eyes on the German prisoners. 'Get up, you bastards,' said Petrie pleadingly. 'Please.'

The Englishmen were crouching, but Robert abruptly stood and, facing the grey group of Germans in the body of the little vessel, he performed his Pope's blessing movement again, the palms of the hands held upwards and the arms raised, except that this time it was much more hurried. 'Ooops,' he ordered hopefully. 'Standen oop!'

Nothing happened, except the planes kept coming. Their machine guns grunted and the wings blinked like lamps as their pilots pressed the triggers. 'Ooop!' bellowed Robert. 'Ooop, you rotten swines! Ooop!'

The bullets tore into the hull, rattling along the length of the ship, but too low to hit anyone on deck. The second plane loosed a small bomb which exploded on the port paddle wheel, shaking the ship like a fury and sending debris and flame shooting into the sky. 'Dammit,' said Lampard, sitting up and spitting out the words with dust and splinters. 'That's torn it.'

Then, as the smoke drifted off, the Luftwaffe men in the bow all stood, their faces towards the sky, and, raising their arms in the Nazi salute, shouted as one: 'Heil Hitler!' A man in at the fore shouted in English, 'Heil to our Führer! We march against England!' They all began to sing the famous threat while the crew of the *Sirius* stood aghast. Then the tall black Senegalese soldiers, some of whom had not realized until the salute that their fellow passengers were German airmen, rose up with a tribal cry and closed angrily on the upright enemy.

The giant Africans charged among the ranks of the Luftwaffe and in a moment there was a wild battle of fists. Blacks and whites rolled and roughed about the deck.

Above the milling and the shouts Willy Cubbins piped alarmingly: 'Mr Lampard! The boat's going round in circles!'

He was right. The spokes of the crippled paddle now hung down into the water like the broken branches of an old willow. The intact paddle was still revolving, sending the vessel on a circular course. Peter Dove appeared from below like a steaming ghost and shouted: 'We're holed, sir. There's a foot of water down there.' He stopped in astonishment on seeing the pitched battle. 'What next?' he asked himself mildly. While the Germans and French negroes fought on its deck, while the sea gulped into the hold, and while an air battle still droned and exploded above them, the crew of the brave *Sirius* watched dumbly as their helpless ship described a large, lazy circle in the middle of the battle-scarred English Channel.

'My goodness,' said Robert, inadequately surveying the disastrous scene. 'Whatever do you suggest, Lampard?'

'We'll be disappearing up our own arse soon,' said Lennie Dove. 'As the saying goes, Mr Lovatt, and begging your pardon.'

The second paddle stopped then with a long sigh and the *Sirius*, a few veils of smoke wafting from her insides, began a slow drift back towards the French coast. On the deck the Senegalese had overpowered the Germans and were sitting on them or pinioning them with huge arms, grinning whitely. The final pocket of resistance was overcome at the bow when one of the prisoners was thrown discourteously over the side.

'We're listing,' put in Lampard more practically. 'We're holed below the port waterline.' He glanced towards Petrie. 'Will you go and have a look, Mr Petrie?' he asked. Petrie went. Lampard mentioned to the others: 'When a paddle steamer capsizes she does it most spectacularly.'

Petrie was back quickly to the wheelhouse. 'She's breached just at the waterline,' he said. 'It's coming in by the gallon.'

Lampard said precisely: 'Take the Dove boys down and stuff anything into the hole that might help. Mattresses are the best thing.'

'Right,' said Petrie firmly, making for the companionway. The brothers followed him. Lampard said to Robert: 'How is your French?'

'Better than my German.'

'Good, I'm pleased. Tell this rabble, all of them, white and black, that we're sinking and the only way to save themselves is, one, to stop squabbling, and, two, to get to the starboard side of the ship. Everybody over on one side. Get them into the two lifeboats as well. We want all the weight we can get. It's the only way to get the breach clear of the water.'

Laboriously Robert stepped outside the wheel-house and began to speak, sporadically, in French. The Senegalese began to grin and then laugh uproariously at his accent. Then the seriousness of the message became apparent to them and they looked with wide eyes at the listing side of the ship and made a hasty rush to the other rail. The Germans, thoroughly battered, remained prone and half-prone on the deck boards. Robert now spoke to them and indicated the starboard side. Glumly they glanced around and then, at a word from a sergeant who had begun the singing of 'We March Against England', they moved across there also, standing in a hurt group and separately from their former assailants.

'Us too,' said Lampard. 'Everyone but me. I'll stay at the wheel, not that it makes any difference now. We're not going anywhere.' He called to Robert, 'Tell them to get into the boats. We'll get them slung out so that the weight ratio is greater.'

Petrie returned anxiously to the deck. 'We've tried to plug it, but it's not much good,' he reported. 'These wooden hulls start giving all over the place once the sea gets in. I've got the Dove boys on the pump, but it's coming in faster than we're getting it out.' His eye took in the motley passengers on the starboard side. 'Good idea,' he approved. 'If we swing the boats out on the davits we'll get even more weight.'

'Get it organized, will you?' asked Lampard. 'I'm

trying to signal one of the million ships around here. They're all too busy to notice. At least Jerry's gone.'

An RAF Sunderland flying boat came low across the hapless paddle steamer. Lampard waved a tea towel which he took from Willy who had been wiping up the tea cups. 'SOS, Mayday, Mayday,' he called hollowly like a private joke.

Petrie was firmly organizing the swinging out of the two starboard lifeboats. The Germans, who appreciated organization, helped now, only to be abruptly assaulted once more by the Senegalese who thought that the whites were going to abandon ship in the boats, leaving the blacks to sink into the cold and alien sea. Petrie and Robert calmed them, although the Africans lingered, muttering suspiciously.

The list, which had become a distinct tilt, was looking dangerous. Petrie kept glancing over his shoulder at the angle. If she went another couple of degrees they would turn turtle. 'Come on, hurry up,' he called to the men trying to sling the boats out. Robert urged the Germans as they tried to get the elderly davits to work.

'I hadn't started refurbishing the davits,' apologized Lampard. He looked around at the wreck of his steamer. 'The job looks beyond me now,' he said.

With a Teutonic cheer the prisoners got the first lifeboat out and prudently stood back while the Senegalese scrambled, one over the other, into it. Then the other, more easily, was slung out and into that boat climbed the bedraggled Germans. Immediately Petrie looked behind him. He grinned. The hull was partly righted. He glanced towards Lampard who made a tentative thumbs-up sign.

Petrie then ran quickly to the companionway and went below, returning in a moment. 'I think that's done it, skipper,' he called to Lampard. 'The breach is just about clear. With the pumps going we might make it.'

'Good, good,' sighed Lampard mildly. He glanced at Robert, now back by the wheelhouse. As if confessing to a secret weakness, he said: 'I don't want to lose the old girl, now. Not if I can help it.'

'No, of course not,' replied Robert doubtfully, as he might have done in consoling someone with a terminally sick relative. He looked around. The *Sirius*, the lovely, small, placid paddle steamer, was hardly more than a hulk now, wheezing and groaning at every sough of the sea.

Petrie took two of the Germans below to relieve the tiring Dove boys on the pumps. As he did so the African soldiers began to shout and demand that their lifeboat be lowered into the sea. One of them had produced a long bayonet.

'Don't like the look of 'im,' mentioned Willy.

Lampard glanced across to the grey horizon and nodded: 'It's all right. It looks like the navy's come for us.'

A destroyer was steaming towards them and as it hove to, a few cable lengths away, the Germans began once again to sing heartily: 'We March Against England'.

'Well, I've seen some rum sights, sir,' commented a leading seaman to Lampard as they were finally helped aboard the naval vessel. 'But never one like that.'

'Yes, I suppose you could call it that. Rum,' said Lampard with deep sadness. He looked at the helplessly drifting *Sirius* now moving away from them like a castaway's raft. 'She was mine.'

The sailor nodded understandingly. 'Know how you feel, sir. Lost one or two myself. Right from under my feet.' As if to add to his statement a single shot was dispatched from one of the destroyer's forward guns. It tore through the hull of the paddle steamer. Lampard covered his eyes with his hands and when he took them away his lined face was damp with tears. Willy Cubbins stood gazing in disbelief at this sacrilege and Robert patted Lampard on the shoulder without speaking.

'Have to see she's put away properly,' mentioned the sailor. 'Danger to navigation, you understand, sir.'

Twelve

From his tall window at the War Office, James had a view across the towers, the roofs and finger spires of London, widespread under a June sky. Only the friendly silver paunches of the barrage balloons, today floating at their medium height, made it appear any different from a summer scene of the previous year. The capital city of the nation, confronted with the most dire defeat in its history, lay bathed in calmness and light.

James stood and went to the window, staring out from east to west, as if to make sure that it was really all right, that nothing untoward had happened. The telephone rang.

'Major Lovatt? Ah, good. Would you step down to the Prime Minister's office, please? Yes, right away. Thank you so much. What a pleasant day, isn't it.'

He straightened his tunic, picked up his hat and went out across the squares and along the sunlit walls to Downing Street. The sentry at the door of Number Ten came to attention and the policeman examined his papers and saluted. It was the first time he had seen an English policeman wearing a gun, a gruesome revolver, almost an artillery piece, in a huge holster. James wondered how quickly he would be able to use it.

An unhurried butler greeted him inside and took his hat, and he was passed to a smiling and equally tranquil civil servant who asked him if he would like some tea. He refused, a decision which seemed privately to please the man, and was then shown into Winston Churchill's office. The Prime Minister was standing, legs astride, facing his window, looking out intently, as if counting every brick and stone. When he turned the round face was grave, sulky.

'We have suffered a great reverse,' said Churchill eventually. He sat down, the enormous desk around him like a fortress, and motioned James to take a seat. 'It has become a most serious thing.'

James said nothing. But Churchill raised the great folded forehead and eyebrows and regarded him, awaiting an answer. 'A most serious thing,' he repeated. It was almost as if he required to be contradicted, to be told that matters were not that bad.

'Yes, sir, that is so,' agreed James. 'But not, I believe, as serious as it might have been. Three hundred and fifty thousand men brought away from Dunkirk.'

Churchill nodded ponderously but approvingly, as though he had been lent the encouragement he needed. 'I thought, at the best, it would be thirty-five thousand,' he agreed. 'The *Daily Mirror* has a blasphemous headline today, you must have noticed. Never seen a word like that in a British newspaper before.' With an almost juvenile grin he held up a copy of that morning's edition. The headline above the leader column said simply: 'Bloody Marvellous'.

'Not that I approve of bad language,' rumbled Churchill, 'but in this extraordinary instance I think it is fitting, don't you, major?'

'Very much so,' smiled James. 'My father and younger brother were there, at Dunkirk. So my mother told me last night on the telephone.'

'Good for them,' approved the premier. At once, however, he lapsed into heaviness, sitting with his pale hands over his paunch. He picked up a paper from the desk. 'Unfortunately we had to leave behind many guns, vehicles, all our tanks, and those of our gallant soldiers who, with the splendid Frenchmen, kept the perimeter secure. This morning I have given them permission to surrender their positions.' Churchill looked at him squarely. 'I have not, however, sent for you to tell you of our woes. You will know enough of them. I am preparing to tell the people the bald truth, the odds we now have to face. They won't mind. In war there are few things so bad for people as optimism.'

James smiled inwardly. He realized that the phrases were being tried out on him. 'We shall fight the Nazi everywhere,' said Churchill thoughtfully, writing on his pad. 'On the shore, the landing grounds, in the fields, in the streets, in the damned public houses, if necessary. And we will not surrender. Never.' He paused and considered his listener. 'Unfortunately,' he continued, not writing now, 'if the German comes today or tomorrow or next week, we will not be in any real position to resist him.' The fey smile fell on his lips again. 'I have a plan,' he said. 'But only the Almighty and Adolf Hitler between them can put it into operation. I plan that he doesn't try it. I plan that for some reason he funks it . . . that this time, as dear Neville Chamberlain so erroneously forecast only a few weeks ago, this time Hitler truly and literally misses the bus, or rather the boat.'

In a moment he became businesslike, staring truculently at the clock ticking loudly like a reminder on his desk. 'Yes, now let me see, major, I have a particular task for you. And I want you to report *personally* to me, in detail and, of course, in writing. The very sort of thing for which I originally brought you into these environs.'

'Yes, sir, of course.'

'In former days, commanders, the Duke of Wellington for one, used to walk about the tents on the night before a battle, listening to the soldiers.' He gave an odd, slanted grin. 'Do you know "Sam, Sam, pick up thy musket", Stanley Holloway . . .?' He began to recite. ' "It occurred on the evening before Waterloo . . ." '

James could not restrain a smile. Churchill seemed suddenly embarrassed. 'Well, this is before our battle,' he said. 'I want to know what our men coming back from Dunkirk *think*. What they think of the war, Dunkirk, the way things have happened, if they feel betrayed . . . well, let us say, let down. I want to know about their morale and their feeling for the fight. I also want to know what they think about the future and the way they expect things will go. Go and see them. Talk to them, question them, at all levels, commanding officers to cooks. Tell me how their spirit is.'

James nodded. 'Of course, Prime Minister. I will let you have my report as quickly as possible.' He stood up. To his astonishment Churchill offered him a cigar, which, although he did not smoke, he took out of sheer confusion. Then the podgy hand came across the desk and he was surprised, as they shook, at its strength and warmth. He said: 'Good morning, sir,' and turned for the door.

As he made to leave – at the door a secretary immediately hovered, waiting to alight in his place – the voice came from behind in a low boom. 'And, Major Lovatt . . .'

'Sir?'

'If the soldiers ask, as they well might, *why* you are asking these questions, there is no need to make a secret of it. Tell them you are inquiring on my behalf.' The smile unrolled across the face again. 'I would like them to know I have thought of their plight.'

Returning across Whitehall James once more became conscious of the order and serenity that had come over London. Always a sedate city, it had now become almost reposed. Everyone, it seemed, appeared determined not to move at anything more than a deliberate pace lest it should be construed as unbecoming panic. People walked in the shade of buildings as Big Ben sounded twelve-thirty. In the park there was to be a lunchtime concert, a famous pianist was to perform on a rough stage, and the people were already flocking there, sitting with their rationed sandwiches on the grass or on benches.

A man was selling the midday editions of the three evening newspapers, with photographs and words of Dunkirk all across the fronts. 'Drama tonight,' intoned the seller, as he always had, even on the most humdrum peacetime day. 'Drama tonight. *Star, News, Standard.*'

There was drama indeed. James bought an *Evening Standard*, glanced at the front page and then turned inside. Smoke and escape at Dunkirk. Pictures of weary but smiling soldiers at Dover. Another headline on the page said: 'Film-struck girl vanishes' and another: 'Body found in Epping Forest'. A third: 'Derby to be run at Newmarket'. Other things still mattered.

Returning to his office he rang for his secretary, Audrey, a clever and serious ATS sergeant who had left her husband, a brush salesman in the Midlands, to join up. James asked her to get him a sandwich and some coffee and to order his driver for two o'clock. He had some work to clear, then he would be going down to Dover.

While she was gone he carefully read again the newspaper accounts of the Dunkirk evacuation. For all the bravery, the glory, the ingenuity and the miraculous execution of it, he could see defeat staring him in the face. It was not a retreat, it was a rout. He studied the photographs of the stained and strained soldiers, ill and exhausted, and thought back only a few days to the idiotic thumbs-up of the fresh troops pictured by *War Illustrated* as they landed in France. 'On their way to Victory.' He felt aggrieved, almost as if *War Illustrated* should have some serious explaining to do. He turned a page of the *Evening Standard* and saw one soldier, black as a minstrel and still putting up that dogged, hopeless, beaten thumb.

Audrey returned. 'They're bringing in the Dunkirk men to Charing Cross Station,' she mentioned casually but knowingly in her Birmingham voice. 'There's crowds down there watching them arrive. It's like a blessed free show.'

James sighed: 'Wouldn't they just,' he said. He told

her to cancel the car. 'I'll take a walk to Charing Cross instead,' he said.

He ate his sandwich lunch and went out again, cutting through the buildings of Whitehall. People were sitting below statues and sycamores in the public gardens, feeding the pigeons, feeding themselves. At Charing Cross he saw immediately that Audrey had been right. A crowd of civilian spectators pushed against the barriers, gazing at each ambulance and bus as it left the platform. Some of them waved and clapped at the buses and sometimes the soldiers within grinned and waved back, but mostly they returned the stares of the untouched spectators.

A railway inspector came trudging to meet him. James introduced himself and said he would like to be there when the next train from Dover arrived. 'Half an hour or so, that's all, sir,' said the man. 'They're coming in all the time. Poor fellows.'

'What about this mob?' asked James caustically, thrusting his head towards the civilians. 'Can't you do something about shifting them?'

'I expect so,' said the inspector, who was tall, mildly bent forward, and had neat grey hair. 'Us or the police, or the military. But they'd only come back. Anyway, it could be a good thing for them to see the state of these boys. My lad's in France. Was, anyway, God knows where he is now, I keep thinking I'm going to see him carried off one of these trains.'

James walked with him along the avenue between the barriers. He heard voices in the crowd: 'Who's *he* anyway?' 'Who does he think *he* is, General Ironside?' 'Some high-up. They ought to go and do a bit of bloody fighting themselves.'

The inspector smiled sourly and as they walked on to the platform he said: 'Same in the First War. This station was one of the showplaces of London then. And Victoria. People coming in evening dress to see the wounded soldiers carried off the trains. And that was regular. Every night at the same time. The blokes from the trenches used to just stare at the blokes in bow ties. They couldn't believe it. It must have made them wonder what they were fighting for.'

The large waiting-room and buffet had been turned into a casualty clearing station and James strode towards it. The inspector said: 'I won't come any further, sir. It upsets me.'

James thanked him and went towards the waiting-room. The smell of ether caught him as he approached the double doors, its sickly scent issuing on to the platform. He stopped at the entrance and looked into a cavernous room. It was like a Hogarth print of primitive London. Men were lying in rows, on tables, on cots and on the floor. At one end were some ominous man-sized white boxes. He swallowed heavily. Then, to his astonishment, like some macabre puppet show, a head levered itself up from the middle box, followed by another from the next in line.

''Ere . . .' called the first head. ''Ere . . . sister. 'Ow long you going to keep me in this bleeding coffin?'

'I want to get out,' confirmed the other head loudly. 'I ain't stayin' in 'ere all day.'

A medical corps captain saw James and came quickly over. 'What are those?' James asked him. 'Those containers?'

'Unfortunately, sir,' agreed the officer impatiently, 'they do bear a resemblance to coffins, but in fact they're bed-boxes. They were put on the ships for the wounded and in a busy situation like this it's a convenient way of transporting them.'

'It can't do very much for their morale,' observed James.

The doctor rounded his lips. 'We're more concerned with physical matters at the moment. Psychiatry can come later.'

James accepted the rebuke. 'Of course. I'm sorry. I'm taking your time and you're busy.'

'Just a little, sir. I'd like to carry on.'

'Please do. Would you agree to my having a few words with some of the chaps? Perhaps one or two who are not in too bad a way. Would that be permissible?' He hesitated. 'The Prime Minister particularly wants to know how they feel.'

'Yes, I think he should,' smiled the doctor ambiguously. 'By all means. None of these fellows is in danger. We get the more serious cases away to hospital first. You could start on the two chappies in the coffins.'

James grinned his acknowledgement and thanked him. He made his way round the outside of the room, skirting a bulky tea urn from which two aproned ladies were issuing cups of tea in thick railway crockery. At first he refused their invitation to have one. One of the women said cheekily: 'Go on, sir. All uniformed personnel allowed free char.'

He took the offered cup and, feeling very strange, he went to the first bed-box and looked down at the soldier lying there. It was just like surveying a body in its coffin. The soldier opened his eyes and looked up with consternation at the face looking down.

'Blimey,' he breathed. 'It's the brass.'

He attempted to sit up, but James told him not to bother. 'How are you feeling?' he asked conventionally. The man's face had been stitched.

'Not too bad, sir. Got it in the leg and the mug. All I want is to get out of this box. I can't stand it. I woke up and I thought I'd snuffed it.'

Like some spectre from a horror story the man in the next container began slowly to rise. He looked around with curiosity and apprehension at James. 'I'd like to get out too, sir,' he pleaded. 'It gives you the willies in 'ere. 'S all right if you're dead, but all I got is a lump out of my bum and nettle rash.'

James grinned and moved to him. 'Nettle rash?' he inquired. 'That's an odd war wound.'

'I got it too, sir,' said the first soldier, determined not to lose the officer's attention. 'Lots of the blokes did. Lying down in those French fields.'

'Falling down more like it,' put in the second man. 'So dead tired we didn't know what we was doing and it was dark. We just flaked out. Woke up with this lot . . .'

'And sunburn and ants,' interpolated the first soldier.

'Copped them too. Ants as big as mice, eating us alive.'

'How far did you march to reach Dunkirk?' asked James. The first man hesitated. 'March, sir? Well, we marched at first and then we just sort of stumbled along. Thirty-five miles our lot went, more or less.'

'It seemed longer,' added the second soldier. 'We got no grub except apples and we had to go scrumping for them. The Frenchies didn't want to know us.

Wouldn't give us a drink of water. Threatened us with shotguns and dogs.'

'They were angry with you?' said James.

'Not half. But you can't blame them. We was running away, wasn't we, leaving them to Jerry.'

'You were *not* running away,' James told him firmly. 'It was a strategic retreat owing to the collapse of Holland and particularly Belgium.'

'It was no use trying to tell the Frogs that, sir,' interposed the second man. 'Even if we knew ourselves, and we didn't. We didn't know what was going on. Nothing. One minute everything was all right and the next we're just a shambollocking shambles, if you'll forgive the language, sir.'

'How about the enemy?' asked James. 'Were you faced with tanks or infantry?'

Both men peered over the edges of their boxes with comic astonishment. Each now waited for the other to speak. 'Jerry, sir?' said the first man eventually. 'Never saw no sign of him.'

'Not a hair of his 'ead,' confirmed the other. 'It wouldn't have been so bad if we had. But we never saw him at all. It was like we was just running from nothing.'

'We both got our nicks on the beach at Dunkirk,' said the second, patting his posterior. 'Playing brag and over he comes and strafes us. That's all we saw of Jerry.'

James said thoughtfully, 'You'll have a chance to see him soon, I expect.'

The first soldier frowned but quickly relaxed it when the stitches hurt. '*Here*, sir? You reckon he'll be here, in England?'

'I think he might have some thoughts in that direction.'

'Sharpish?' asked the man. 'Like in the next couple of weeks or something?' The second man was listening intently, his chin resting on the edge of the box.

'Sharpish,' repeated James. 'How do you feel about that?'

'We'll stuff him,' said the second man. 'France is France but England is England, innit, sir?'

'We'll stuff him right enough,' confirmed his comrade. 'I'm not having him lay hands on what's mine.'

'Good,' approved James gently. 'That's what I wanted to know.'

He wished them well and made to move way. The first man essayed a comical salute, levering his head and hand further from the box. James returned the compliment. As he went away the first man called after him again: 'But . . . sir . . . just make sure they don't have any more capers like Dunkirk. That ain't no way to treat a British soldier.'

An hour later the next train from Dover arrived and James stood back, among some railway trolleys loaded with civilian luggage bearing coloured stickers for south coast resorts. 'Peacehaven Grange Hotel,' he read on one label. 'Safe from the strains of modern living.' Medical corps men began to unload the stretchers from the compartments as soon as the men who were able to walk had disembarked. He was glad to see there were no further bed-boxes.

From the distant end of the platform he heard, over the steaming station sounds, the noise of tired men's voices and saw that one squad of soldiers, who could still march, were leaving singing: 'We're Going to Hang Out the Washing On the Siegfried Line', a song that only a few weeks before had been rendered with a comic swagger and assurance now gone sour. They could hardly raise their voices, their strength as hollow as the promise. The crowd of civilians at the barrier prompted a cheer.

A party of men in bandages, and on sticks and crutches, was shepherded to the roped-off station buffet and James, waiting so that he kept his distance, followed them there. He walked in through the heavy wood and frosted glass doors and at once saw the American girl, Joanne Schorner, who had sat next to him in the gallery of the House of Commons on the afternoon of Churchill's first speech. That was three weeks before and it seemed like years. She saw him at the same time and after a moment's hesitation smiled quietly. She was talking earnestly to a soldier propped up in one of the round-backed buffet chairs.

James went to the buffet where three grimy infantrymen were sitting at the bar, drinking tea and half-heartedly biting thick sandwiches. One had a bandaged head, one had strapping across his chest and the third had both his arms in slings, like a boy with two sailing boats. The others took it in turns to put his sandwich to his mouth. James approached them casually and motioned them to remain where they sat.

'No appetite?' he asked, nodding at the unenthusiastic sandwiches.

'Not much, sir. Not now,' answered the man with the dressed head. 'We got lots of grub at Dover and

273

they gave us some more at Ashford Station. All these ladies dishing out tea and Oxo and sandwiches. Even when you're starving there's only so much room inside.'

'Throwing apples and pears,' said the second, a crack of a grin showing. 'One of our platoon got wounded by somebody hitting him with a bag of Christmas nuts. Nearly took his eye out. Not a scratch at Dunkirk either.'

The man with the strapped chest lifted his cup of tea and said suddenly: 'I could have done with this a couple of days ago, sir. Walked God knows how many miles, sweating hot, trying to bring as much of my gear as I could, and when I get to the boat at Dunkirk in the end I go downstairs and there's this civvy steward, white coat, the lot, polishing glasses in the bar. The boat was rocking with the bombs. My tongue's hanging out and I ask him for a drink and he says – blimey, I can hardly believe it now – he says that he can't serve alcoholic drinks while the ship is in port!'

They all laughed and James said: 'That's what keeps us going, I expect. Not flapping, keeping things normal.'

The middle soldier soured. 'Like looking out of the windows of that train coming here. It made my blood boil, sir, it did. Everything like it was, washing on the lines, blokes doing their gardens . . .'

'But . . .' interposed James. 'Surely . . .'

'Right, surely, sir,' put in the man firmly. 'But you don't expect to come back and see playing fields full of blokes in white *playing perishing cricket*.'

James grimaced. 'No, no, you're right. I feel the

same way. But they're probably factory workers on night shift, service units or something like that.'

'Then I wish they'd go and play their games somewhere else and not next to the railway line,' argued the man. He added more softly: 'It looks bad.'

James thanked them and wished them well before moving along the tables. Some men were sitting, heads in hands, as if they feared they would topple off, others were propped asleep against the walls. He talked to another half a dozen men before accepting a cup of tea over the buffet counter. The American girl had finished talking to the soldier and she came towards him smiling slightly. 'We seem to meet in the strangest places,' he said.

'Are there any other sorts of places in this war?' she asked.

She accepted a cup of tea from the grey, bundled woman behind the bar with a smile which tightened as she tasted it.

She persevered, taking the next sip carefully.

'You're writing for your newspaper,' said James. 'I saw your article on the evening of the day we met.'

'A lot has happened since then,' she observed grimly. She looked around the big room with its ragged men. 'This is terrible,' she said. 'It makes me want to cry.'

'But we're not finished, you know,' he told her, his eyes firm, keeping his voice unhurried. 'Not by a long way. I hope you will tell your readers in America that.'

'You're not going to know what I tell my readers,' she replied, just as firmly. 'Read it in print.' Seeing his expression she added: 'If I thought you were finished, I wouldn't be here now.' Again she looked about them: 'These guys still think you're going to *win*. Not *lose*, not *draw* – *win!*' She nodded across the crowded area: 'That little guy over there says he ended up in a cellar with the Mayor of Dunkirk. He called him the buggermaster, if you'll excuse me, but he meant it well. He said the mayor was wearing his chain and all his regalia and he thought this was pretty impressive. The mayor told him that the French fleet would win the war in the end.'

James almost said: 'Yes, but on whose side?'

Two hours later they left Charing Cross Station together. As the Dunkirk men came out tiredly marching, some singing, or in buses or ambulances, so the homegoing London office workers passed them going in the other direction.

'Look at them,' said Joanne. 'It's something I can't figure. A great calm seems to have settled on everyone.'

James agreed. 'We began this war as though it were some new form of sport,' he observed. 'Everybody rushed about thinking it was very thrilling, but when not much happened they fell into a calmness that's going to take a lot of shifting.'

'That song – hanging out the washing . . .' she said.

'On the Siegfried Line?' he finished. 'It sounds pretty silly now.'

'It's a Boston two-step,' she said to his surprise. 'It's the same tune as a song called "When we are married, we'll have sausages for tea".' She smiled at his expression. 'I know because I've been writing a piece about war songs.'

James regarded her with new interest.

They walked down through the steep street to the embankment. They were both going towards Westminster so they walked by the thick river. Big Ben's tower reflected the copper evening light. Yellow smoke was streaming from Battersea Power Station. 'People seem to be *aware*, though,' she said eventually. 'Under the calm. I went to a lunchtime recital in the park the other day, I often do, and I watched the faces of the people listening to the music. It's almost as if the war, and the bad news, has given them something to live for – they're even doing things that they might never have dreamed of doing before.'

'Outdoor concerts are splendid,' he agreed wryly. 'The first thing the Germans do when they've occupied a town is to put their band in the park.' He waited, then he said: 'I understood that all American citizens were advised to leave for home two weeks ago.'

'Well, this one isn't going,' she said. 'Not yet anyway. I'm not strictly here on assignment. I'm just on a visit to my uncle and aunt. He's at the US Embassy. He's so sure *he*'s not going he's joined the American squadron, or whatever it is, of Local Defence Volunteers. He's scared the ambassador will find out – Kennedy – because Kennedy thinks you're as good as beaten.'

At Northumberland Avenue a black London taxi cruised by and she hailed it and got in. They said good-bye. 'Perhaps I'll see you in the park one lunchtime,' he said. 'Listening to the band.'

'Sure,' she smiled. 'See you in the park, major.'

Each time, it seemed to him, he telephoned Millie, she was out. He could sense that the phone was sounding in an empty house. Eventually he spoke to her late in the evening when he was alone in the flat. He realized his tone was edgy. 'At last,' he said when she picked it up. 'Where do you hide yourself all day?'

'James,' she admonished, trying to sound good-humoured,

'I'm busy. You're not the only one running a war, you know.'

'What *are* you doing? Having bayonet practice?' He eased his tone.

'Not exactly. We did try shooting at some targets, your mother and I, but your father discovered us and became incredibly upset, so we had to stop. I go over to the RAF at Moyles Court three days a week now. I was there today. You sound tired.'

He sighed. 'I suppose I do,' he agreed. 'I'm not sure I'm cut out for this job. I'm more like a rent collector than a soldier.'

'There won't *be* any soldiering now, will there?' she suggested. 'No fighting, that is, not until they come across.' She paused. 'Do you think they will?'

'If they don't they're mad,' he answered. 'They've got us down and out. We got three hundred and fifty thousand out of Dunkirk, but that's not an army, it's a rabble.'

'I know,' confirmed Millie. 'We've got hundreds of them here, under canvas. They're drained, you can see that. I saw them this afternoon, sitting among the buttercups. That's what I've been doing as well, helping your mother and the other ladies with feeding arrangements. The army hasn't got enough kitchens or something. And we've got some refugees as well. They just turned up in Christchurch harbour from

Holland and Belgium and we've been trying to sort them out, poor people. Most of them have been put in hotels in Bournemouth, although the hotels weren't too keen. They're people who've lost everything, James. Even hope. At least *we're* still all together.'

'Yes,' he hesitated. 'We're still together.'

There was a pause at both ends. Then Millie said: 'Will you be able to get home? At the weekend or something?'

'I'll try,' he promised. 'It won't be for more than a few hours, though.'

'Please try. I'd like to see you . . . again.'

He laughed dryly. 'Yes, I'd like to see you too.'

'We still love each other, don't we? I still love you.'

'That's a silly thing to say,' he told her. 'You know we're all right.'

'Yes, I do, of course. Telephone if you think you can get down. Try and come this weekend.'

'I'll try. I'll ask Winston.'

When he had replaced the receiver on the wall he poured himself a Scotch. He put out the lights in the flat and went unhappily to the windows. He opened the curtains. The stars were there, standing out finely above the lightless city. He thought that there must be people who had never noticed the night sky until the black-out. He gazed up. The barrage balloons were lurking like shadows. He could see their dark bellies. He swallowed the whisky and returned to the room, drawing the heavy curtains and switching on the light.

It was midnight. He turned on the radio for the news. The vibrations of Big Ben faded, gradually, as if reluctant to cease.

'This is the BBC Home Service. The Dunkirk

evacuation has been completed. An announcement from the War Office said tonight that a total of three hundred and fifty thousand troops had been brought back safely to Britain. Mr Churchill has spoken of "a miracle". The Prime Minister is to make a statement tomorrow in the House of Commons.'

Tiredly James listened. Within himself he felt that it was all too late.

Towards the conclusion of the bulletin there was a report from America of the reactions of American correspondents to the plight of the British. James knew, like everyone else in Whitehall, that Joseph Kennedy, the US Ambassador, was certain that the British were finished and had told President Roosevelt so. But the observers quoted were not so sure. 'The correspondent of the Columbia Broadcasting System this morning said that the spirit of Britain was like a shining light in a black world. He spoke of Dunkirk as an example of inspiration and innovation of which only England was capable. Miss Joanne Schorner, a London correspondent of the *Washington Post*, described visiting the wounded as they returned from the evacuation, and of their defiance, fortitude and good humour. They were, she said, looking forward to winning the war.'

There came a tap on the housekeeper's door and James called 'Come in.' Mrs Beauchamp entered smiling. 'Been listening, sir? I'm glad we knows where we are, at least. With our soldiers back home.'

He smiled and said he agreed with her.

'Anything else tonight, sir?' she asked. 'Before I put the cat out.'

He shook his head. 'How is young John Colin?'

280

he asked. 'When are we going to see him again?'

Her face clouded. 'Well, he should be coming down to London soon, sir, for a couple of days. His mum's still in Paris but I suppose she'll have to come home now, unless she wants the Jerries to capture her. But . . . but . . . she wrote saying that she might send John Colin to America. There's a lot of children going, you know. She thinks it might be safer there for him.' Her expression dropped to sadness and doubt and she mumbled: 'But I don't know about that.'

At noon the following day Philip Benson walked into James's office and looked around quizzically, taking in the filing cabinet, the desk and the hatstand like a tall man standing in a corner. 'It's not much,' he concluded. 'But it's better than a hole in the ground.'

'Depends where the hole in the ground is located,' smiled James. 'What's happening to our war today? Do you know any secrets?'

Benson said: 'Only that the reason the German Navy didn't bust up the Dunkirk operation was because they lost so many ships off Norway last month. Perhaps it wasn't all such a waste after all.' He sat down. 'France looks pretty groggy, I'm afraid. The whole fabric is coming to bits over there. You know what the French are like for falling out among themselves and they're doing that with a vengeance now. The Old Man is trying to persuade them to hang on, but they won't. Their army is completely *phut*. Demoralized. Trudging back with their helmets stuck on the end of their rifles.'

'Our invincible ally,' said James sourly. 'We'll be on our own soon then.'

'By the end of this month at the latest,' shrugged Benson. 'There are people who think it will be better that way. You know – good old John Bull on his island. Churchill will make a statement in the House this afternoon and I imagine he'll tell us all – or nearly all – then. Warts and everything. Will you be there?'

Rising from the desk, James said: 'Yes, I think I'd like to be. He fascinates me, you know. I can't believe he's real.'

'That's what he does to most people. That's why we've *got* to have him. There *is* no one else. You have to believe in him even if, underneath, you suspect he might be a quack. Are you going anywhere for lunch?'

James hesitated. 'Well, I usually just have a sandwich or something, and then I thought I'd take a stroll in the park and listen to the piano recital. It's not often you hear Chopin in sunshine.'

'It isn't,' Benson nodded. 'Well, I'll walk down with you.'

'Oh, don't let me stop you going to lunch or anything.'

'Not at all.' Benson glanced at his watch. 'We could have a drink and then I could go off to gorge myself and you could feed on culture.'

James was conscious of his own embarrassment. 'Come and listen if you like,' he said foolishly. 'I mean . . .'

'Don't care for the keyboard much,' confessed Benson. 'Not unless it's Charlie Kunz.'

They walked down the polished stone stairs and out into London. There was a cocktail bar opposite the Houses of Parliament and they went in there and each had a gin. The place was crowded with Members, their mouths half-hidden by drinks, as if that was the part that needed replenishing; their gossiping faces close together, sweating, creased, like Cruikshank caricatures. 'You know my father took himself off to Dunkirk?' said James.

Benson laughed. 'So I heard and I wasn't surprised. Did he enjoy it?'

'Disgusted,' grinned James. 'They took an old paddle steamer, him and some cronies, and the thing was sunk under them. Their cargo – and this is what annoyed him – was a horde of Luftwaffe prisoners and some French Africans.'

'Good heavens, fancy bringing back prisoners. I thought it was difficult enough getting our own troops out. Still, who am I to say? People do very odd things.'

James finished his gin and said: 'I must be going. There are so many people at these open-air concerts that it's difficult to get anywhere near the front. It's not like the Albert Hall.'

Benson smiled with some curiosity. 'All right, then,' he said agreeably. 'Perhaps I'll see you in the House. Enjoy yourself.'

'I'm sure I will,' promised James awkwardly. 'After all, it's Chopin . . . and it's a very nice day.'

She was standing under the park elms, outside the crowd, her face intent and content, listening to the piano in the bright light. He did not see her for some time because of the screen of people sitting on folded seats and grouped around the perimeter. The limpid music flowed over the famous park; the grass, the lake, with its cruising white pelicans, the full-leafed trees and the anti-aircraft guns.

The soloist, a man in a brown suit, played a prelude and a polonaise. There were some Polish airmen standing on the fringe of the crowd, faces still, eyes desolate to hear the sounds of their homeland. The recital was almost finished when James saw Joanne Schorner. He moved around the fringe of the audience and eventually stood beside her. She smiled, almost absently, as if she had seen him some time previously, and continued listening to the music. She was standing on a brief rise in the ground, a hump of roots from two trees, so that she could see over the heads in front of her. He saw that she had a small notebook and a gold pencil which slotted into it. She moved over on the knoll to make room for him.

They stood, elbows brushing, as the final piece was played, a popular theme, The Warsaw Concerto by Richard Addinsell. James glanced towards the Poles and saw that one small man was walking away alone across the park, as if he could bear it no more. At the final flourish the soloist stood and acknowledged the applause that floated over the grass and sent the London starlings whirling into the bland sky.

'Wonderful,' sighed Joanne as they walked back towards the buildings of Whitehall. 'Music, sunshine, open air, blue sky, and those amazing creatures.' She looked up at the barrage balloons. 'Don't you think they might be listening with those great ears?'

'They all have names,' James told her, looking up at the silver balloons. 'One is called Herbert Morrison, one is the Bishop of London, and one, naturally, is Winston Churchill. But I haven't been here long enough yet to know which is which.'

She stopped on the path, touched his sleeve, and,

asking him to wait a moment, quickly wrote something in her notebook. Once more she looked above them. 'That one must be Churchill. He looks kind of pugnacious. And that one, higher than the others, maybe that's the Bishop because he's floating nearer to God.' She looked towards Big Ben and then at her watch, cross-checking them. 'Are you going to the Commons this afternoon?' she asked.

James said he was. 'Whatever rough treatment we're getting on the battlefield,' he observed, 'we're making up for it in memorable words.'

The American regarded him unsurely. 'You sound a little caustic,' she observed.

'Not at all. People need words at times like this. Words can keep us going. And Winston's got a splendid vocabulary for emergencies.' They continued to walk by the bright flower-beds. Some of the anti-aircraft gunners were throwing a child's ball to each other.

James said: 'If we're ever overrun then you might see our exiles listening to Shakespeare in Central Park as those Poles listened to Chopin.'

They reached the road. A few cars, some military vehicles and several people on leisurely horseback passed by. Joanne smiled at the scene and shook her head. 'I'll see you this afternoon then, James,' she said. 'I have to go back to my apartment for a phone call. I have a reserved place in the gallery. It might be difficult to get in to see the show. You'd better be early.'

'I'll manage,' he assured her with a grin. 'Winston has promised he won't start without me.'

Holding out her small hand she smiled frankly. 'Same time, same place,' she said. 'See you then.'

Thirteen

Binford village hall, browed with thatch, was under the elms, a little apart from the houses, church and inn, across the cricket and football field, so that it fulfilled both the functions of sports pavilion and meeting-place. When Hob Hobson, the grocer, who was also the parish clerk, walked over the grass on the early June evening, the cricket team were practising their bowling and batting at the makeshift practice net. There had been showers that afternoon and the sky was washed and pale, with late creamy clouds in the east.

'When you've finished fooling about, are you coming to the meeting?' Hob demanded, shouting across the field. He had little patience with games. 'It's important. There'll be no playing sports if the Jerries get here.'

Cat-calls floated across the pitch, for Hob was not popular, but he guessed the men and boys would leave their bats and be there.

Almost as soon as Hob had unlocked the pavilion and, grumbling, clattered away half a dozen fold-up tables left standing from the last whist drive, people began to arrive. There had been no time to place seats in rows. Hob called to the first-comers to take a chair from the concertina pile near the door and to begin making formal rows, close together.

Across the evening green they straggled, the inhabitants of the small place, anxious, puzzled, wondering why they had been summoned so importantly. The farmers and their workmen, the foresters, those who went by bus each day to work in the shops and businesses of Lyndhurst and Lymington, the elderly who had retired to the mild south and those whose families had been there for hundreds of anonymous years.

Lennie Dove came heavily across the grass carrying a bulky wooden radio set. 'Mr Lovatt told me to bring it,' he puffed at Hob. 'So's we can hear the news and Mr Churchill at nine. Some might not get home in time.'

'Got batteries?' asked Hob typically. 'I have to account to the parish for the electricity, you know.'

'Peter's got the juice,' sighed Lennie, nodding over his shoulder to his brother coming with a crowd of others across the grass. Their laughter drifted in the evening light. The cricketers were putting away their bats and pads in a long leather bag. Peter arrived with the radio batteries.

'Soon get her fixed up, Hob,' he assured the grocer. 'Won't be using a penny of the parish money, don't you worry your brains about that.' He glanced slyly at his brother. 'Not charging us for the use of the table, I s'pose?'

Hob grunted and motioned them to put the radio set on the green-clothed table on the stage at the front of the hall. Already all the chairs were occupied, people sitting doggedly, as they always did whether it was a parish meeting or the Christmas pantomime, guarding their seats. At the rear others were standing three deep. Hob realized, with annoyance, that he had not provided for those who would be at the top table conducting the proceedings, and he fussily commandeered four chairs from a cottage family who were sitting less confidently in the back row.

Untidy Walter Beavan, the reporter of the *New Forest Gazette*, came into the hall and sniffed the air professionally. He made his way, as of right, to the side of the platform and took one of the chairs which Hob had just put in place. Pens, pencils and a pipe protruded from the pockets of his chaffed sports jacket. Taking out a grimy penknife he began to sharpen one of his pencils, letting the shavings drop on the stage. Hob frowned, then thought better of any comment. You never knew when you might need the press. He took the final chair from the downtrodden family, appropriately called Meek, that was occupied by the grandfather. The aching old man stood up.

'Nice turn-out,' mentioned Beavan, arranging his great sandwich of a notebook on the table. He waved to his friend Kathy Barratt, the telephone operator. Walter knew much that went on in Binford. 'Not seen such a crowd in here since the Irish Sweepstake draw last year.'

'The days of the Irish Sweep are gone,' said Hob, adding gloomily: 'Could be for ever.' He surveyed the room, however, with a grunt of satisfaction. 'It is a good turn-out, though. Wish they'd all come to the whist drives.' Doubtfully he regarded Beavan's notebook. 'How much of this are you going to be able to put in your paper?' he queried. 'We don't want Jerry to know what we're planning, do we now? Surely it'll all have to be hush-hush.'

Beavan regarded him with established dislike. 'I think I know what's what,' he answered. 'And if I don't somebody will soon tell me. Hitler reads the *New Forest Gazette* every week. He has it sent specially.'

Ten minutes before the meeting was due to begin Robert, in his brother's First World War uniform and wearing an LDV armband, and Elizabeth, with Millie, came into the hall. 'Make room!' shouted Hob blatantly. 'Make room for Mr Lovatt. How's he going to take the meeting if he can't get in? And Mrs Lovatt . . . yes, lots of room if you please.'

Elizabeth and Millie said they would stand at the back and, refusing seats offered by Mary Mainprice and her sister Marigold, they took their places among the faces of the cricket team. They noticed Alan Stevens, the schoolteacher, alone, even in that crowded place. Robert strode towards the platform and nodded approvingly at Lennie Dove as he saw that the big radio set had been put in position. He noticed Beavan and grimaced doubtfully. 'Would you rather I put the notebook away?' suggested Beavan seeing the expression. 'I could just sit here as an individual Englishman if you like.'

Robert nodded his large head. 'I think that would be best, Walter,' he decided. 'We don't want any of this falling into enemy hands.'

'Absolutely,' said Beavan coolly. He closed the notebook. He was a lazy man and glad of the excuse. 'I don't mind. As long as you explain to the editor.'

Robert said he would. Two other parish councillors, John Oakes and Rob Noyes, came in to take their chairs on either side of him. In the hall there was always an agreeable smell of dust. It was as if villagers from far back had left some particle as a memory. He acknowledged John Lampard and his wife as they entered. Mrs Lampard had cried when they returned from Dunkirk and, sobbing, made her husband promise that he would never do such a thing again. And to take the boy Willy, as well, was madness. Now she treated Robert to a scowl.

The vicar, the Reverend Clifford Pemberton, entered worriedly. He examined the room, surprised at the crowd, and then made his way to the platform, shaking hands with Robert, with John Oakes and Rob Noyes, who was an insurance man. Between him and the vicar it had often been a matter of professional pride and rivalry as to who arrived first at a dead man's house.

'My goodness,' the vicar whispered as he sat down, 'what a good turn-out. Perhaps we ought to take a collection.'

The hall was full now, although late-comers were still trying to get in at the back. Someone opened the windows along each side so that people could stand outside, peer in and listen. The desultory sounds of a rural evening drifted in. Rooks calling softly, noisy cows, a dog barking far off.

Robert pedantically rechecked his watch and then stood, at once provoking silence. Everyone knew he had been to Dunkirk with the Dove brothers, the coastguard and Mr Lampard. Elizabeth, standing among the cooling cricketers, saw Millie puff out her cheeks. The air was close and the cricketers were still sweating. 'I think we had better make a start,' announced Robert. 'Is everybody here who should be here?'

A woman's thin hand hovered at the front. 'My Frank can't come,' squawked the owner. ''Ee's on guard.'

'Which pub, missus?' asked a man's voice from the back. Laughter filled the room.

'Now, now,' admonished Robert mildly. 'We're not here for an entertainment. This is a matter of national importance.' He nodded towards the woman who had remained with her skinny fingers suspended. 'Yes, Mrs Root, I know all about Frank. He's guarding down at The Haven.'

'I wasn't goin' to say where, Mr Lovatt,' she told him, lowering the arm at last. She turned fiercely towards the rear of the room. 'I'm not like some, opening their big mouths all the time!'

'Splendid,' sighed Robert. 'Then let's begin . . .'

A commotion at the entrance caused him again to pause impatiently. The people at the door were being forced aside and, as they parted, the elderly Mrs Spofforth, accompanied by Bess Spofforth and a dusty stranger wearing a bereft expression and black suit, came into the room. There were murmurs of protest by those being pressed closer together or pushed sideways out of the door but the old lady was too notorious for anyone to offer real resistance.

'Hurry along, now,' said Robert but also with due caution. He was aware that the vicar, alongside him, was covering his face with his hands as if hiding behind a barricade. 'Oh God,' he heard him whisper like a prayer. 'That woman.'

'Hurry along?' exclaimed the old lady. Bess gave her a warning tug but she irritably pulled herself away. She advanced a few paces until the density of the watchers prevented even her further progress. 'Who is telling *me* to hurry along?' Her face went to the platform. 'Robert Lovatt, I'll tell you right now, and for nothing, that I've brought along someone you ought to listen to at this meeting.' Fiercely she jabbed her finger into the sad man in the shabby suit. 'Him!' she bellowed. The man's black-ringed eyes blinked unhappily. 'Him,' she reiterated. 'He knows all about Hitler.'

Robert drew a large breath. He was not going to let her take over. He remembered how, in this hall, she had wrecked the 1939 pantomime because she said the piano was out of tune. 'And who, Mrs Spofforth, is this gentleman?' he inquired gently. All around the hall people were straining to get a view of the newcomer.

'Our refugee – that's who!' exclaimed Mrs Spofforth proudly. She raised the man's arm like a prize fighter. The tight black sleeve clung to his elbow. He looked about him, clay-faced. 'Mr Van Lorn from Holland,' continued Mrs Spofforth. 'He knows what buggers the Germans are!'

Robert could see the meeting slipping out of his hands. 'Yes, yes, madam,' he said still mildly. 'We will be most interested to hear what he has to say. Any . . . tips he can give us. But first I think we must proceed with the primary purpose of the meeting. Thank you.'

Mrs Spofforth conceded, but with both hesitation and truculence, determined to have the final word of the preliminaries. 'He hasn't got any clothes,' she announced blatantly, again jabbing towards the Dutchman who moved away from her finger. 'Arrived without a rag to his back.' Her voice rose in drama: '*In the middle of the night he came and . . .'* Bess's iron grip and the Dutchman's protests, backed by Robert's exhortations, stemmed her eventually and she noisily sat on a chair swiftly evacuated by a timid woman. 'He'll tell 'em. He'll tell 'em . . .' she muttered.

'Ladies and gentlemen,' announced Robert desperately. 'The Lord-Lieutenant of Hampshire has requested, no, *ordered* this meeting as a matter of great urgency. Similar meetings are being held in communities throughout the entire country. It is simply to tell you what our present dangers are, what dangers may be upon us quite shortly, to decide what we should do as a village and – just as important – what we should *not* do. Also to put together a list of our resources – vehicles, animals, foodstuffs, weapons, all manner of items that might be useful in an emergency. Anything we can think up. All these will be entered in a book – to be called the Binford War Book – and their whereabouts noted, so that we can call on them as the need may be.'

A deeply interested excitement came over the villagers. There were some whispers but quickly silenced. Robert saw a group of forest gypsies, Liberty Cooper at their centre, standing outside the window. At the back somebody dropped a tin hat on the floor and was roundly shushed. It rocked noisily before the owner picked it up. The pale Dutchman kept looking round at the people as if they were acting out some remote play.

'First of all,' continued Robert in his solicitor's manner, *'what* to do if we are invaded. It is very obvious that any landing would put us here immediately in the front line. Binford, have no doubt, would be a scene of heavy fighting within days, perhaps hours.' Slowly hands went to the chins and mouths of people in the front. Their faces became reflective. He picked up a piece of paper from the table. 'Make sure that you give the Germans *nothing*. Don't even talk to them or tell them anything. Hide your bicycles and any food you may have, and especially petrol. If you have a car or a motor cycle it must be rendered useless.' Bess Spofforth sniffed.

A full, shocked silence filled the room. There was only a furtive fidgeting of feet and the small scrape of a chair; but outside cows still called from dusk fields and rooks from their branches.

Robert could see his wife's set face intent on him as were the others. His daughter-in-law was biting her lip. Beside him on the platform the vicar had his hands clasped together as if prepared for diving. One of the other parish councillors, John Oakes, an unruffled farmer, was puffing copious clouds from his pipe. The other, Rob Noyes, tight-faced and pale, was leaning on one thin elbow, eyes shut, wondering perhaps about insurance claims that might follow heavy fighting.

'It may occur,' continued Robert, 'that at some time you will receive orders to block the roads into the village to impede the advance of the enemy. This can be done by felling trees and wiring them together, using wheels to get them across the roads, by building barricades with farm vehicles and cars. But only under orders – we must *not* block the wrong roads.'

An elderly woman, one of the Purkiss family, stood up dramatically. Robert regarded her sternly, but she said: 'Sorry, lord, my old leg goes to sleep, see.' Tom

Purkiss, who had lost his fingers in Norway, regarded her helplessly.

Robert began reading from a printed pamphlet which had reached him in that afternoon's post. 'If you hear that the enemy have landed,' he continued after waiting for the old lady to smile her thanks and reseat herself, 'every one of you,' he gazed around the pavilion, 'each person must act like a *soldier*. Stay put and do not panic. You must trust our front-line chaps to deal with the Germans.'

Suddenly he felt hollow, helpless. Even he knew there would be no hope. What could these people do? Summoning his brisk legal voice, he went on: 'Keep your heads, that's all I can say.' He hesitated: 'If you have any doubts as to whether an officer is *British* or not . . . ask the advice of a policeman or an ARP warden . . .' His voice trailed away. He squinted hard at the pamphlet. The only words left were 'Printed in England' which he felt he would have realized, and 'Donated by the Brewers Society' which he would not.

The vicar was regarding him glassy-eyed. 'Ask a policeman?' whispered the clergyman. 'Ask an ARP warden? Jesus.'

Robert muttered: 'That's what it says here.' He tapped the pamphlet. From the back of the hall Elizabeth saw Alan Stevens shake his head in disbelief. Then Mrs Spofforth bawled: 'Rubbish! You don't know a thing about it! Let's hear the Dutchman!' She flung her arms extravagantly: 'Here he is!' The forlorn refugee in the coat composed an expression that may have been half smile, half sob, and mutely nodded.

'In one moment, Mrs Spofforth,' Robert bellowed back from the platform. 'Everything in good time.

The Prime Minister is about to broadcast to the nation. We must listen to that first.' He rolled his eyes at the wireless set.

'It's a couple of minutes yet, sir,' said Peter Dove from the lower edge of the platform.

'Get it going,' said Robert tersely. He had a horror that the meeting might get out of hand. 'Fiddle around with it, man.'

'Right you are, sir,' agreed Peter. Clambering on to the stage he began to check the various leads from the batteries to the huge set. To fill in the vacuum, to keep their attention, Robert announced: 'We must begin our war book. All our resources, everything from cars to tea kettles.' He was pleased with the phrase. It might have almost been Churchillian. 'Most gun owners have made themselves available to the Local Defence Volunteers,' he went on.

'Aye,' came a grating voice from the middle. 'And they're using them for target practice on my birds.' Gates, the gamekeeper, rose as if he had been under cover. 'If they shoots the Germans like they shoots my pheasants then we got nothing to worry about.'

The laughter that rose was severed almost before it had begun by the crackling of the wireless set. Peter was turning the waveband knob. Then chill, loud, knife-like, the voice came over the air. 'Germany calling, Germany calling. What are you trying to achieve, England? Why don't you take the friendly olive branch that Germany is offering? You are beaten. The Dutch, the Belgians and the French hate you. This war is only going on because of the money that the Jews are putting into their pockets. Are you prepared to die for the Jews?'

'Off!' hooted Robert. 'Off! Put that balderdash off! I've never –'

'Sorry, Mr Lovatt,' answered Peter Dove. He grinned. 'I thought somehow that didn't sound like old Churchill.'

The audience was again consumed with laughter. For them Lord Haw-Haw, the English traitor William Joyce, was a comedian only to be compared with Funf, the German spy in ITMA, the favourite Tommy Handley wireless programme.

John Oakes blew a great thoughtful cumulus from the bowl of his pipe towards the dusty ceiling. 'I'd like to tie that man to my bull,' he said without emphasis.

'Got it all right now, Mr Lovatt,' reported Peter, hovering beside the wireless set. 'Near damn missed it, though.'

'Mr Churchill,' announced Robert to the audience as though he expected the Prime Minister to trot from the wings. 'Quiet everybody, please.'

A stillness fell at once across the hall. Not a face moved. A fly buzzing near the door could be clearly heard at the front. Annoyed, Robert looked towards it. Surprisingly it was the Dutchman, moving with some agility, who caught it in mid-flight and squashed it in his hand. He opened his palm and regarded it with the quaint satisfaction of a victim who has just claimed a victim of his own. The faces at the windows were like a gallery of framed medieval paintings, dark skins, the round, coarse, rural expressions, puzzled, simple, trusting. Mrs Spofforth leaned to one side and brushed some dust from the shoulder of her refugee's coat.

Through the rustic room the deep, throaty,

theatrical voice of Winston Churchill sounded. Never had anyone produced such bravado with a lisp. 'We shall defend our island whatever the cost may be,' the words rolled out. 'We shall fight on the beaches, we shall fight on the landing grounds, we shall fight in the fields and in the streets, we shall fight in the hills.' Stony nods of agreement started to move about the room. Robert, still on his feet, drew himself quietly to attention. His own gaze found that of his wife and she smiled encouragement. Churchill said: 'We shall never surrender.'

When the speech was finished there was a silence that lingered through the room. There was nothing more to be said. Peter Dove glanced at Robert and turned the wireless set off. A shuffling and coughing filtered from the back. No one seemed to know what to do. Robert leaned towards the vicar. 'How about "Land of Hope and Glory"?' he suggested.

'How about "There'll Be Blue Birds Over the White Cliffs of Dover"?' suggested the vicar.

'For God's sake, vicar . . .'

The Reverend Clifford Pemberton said: 'Indeed, for God's sake . . . I don't think we ought to sing anything now, Robert. I think everybody ought to just go home.'

'Can we go 'ome now, sir?' suggested a man in the front, having overheard. 'They Jerries might be coming tonight. 'Sides which 'tis near closing time.' The man continued: 'I got to get my booby traps set.' He had no teeth and he grinned horribly at his neighbours. His wife, a red coat tied around her like a bag of blood, nodded: 'Snare wire and gunpowder, my George 'as got,' she announced loudly.

'Wait! Wait!' It was Mrs Spofforth from the rear of the room. Urgently she towed the Dutchman towards the front so that he seemed like some captive bird, shabby and black. 'You've got to give an ear to Mr Van Lorn!' Mrs Spofforth demanded. 'He's seen it all in Holland! He's suffered!'

Robert and the others on the platform knew there was no escaping this. They shuffled to make room and the spare stranger, his expression tight and white, was thrust on to the stage by the agile grandmother. He shuffled a few unhappy paces into the space left for him. Mrs Spofforth began to applaud and call: 'Bravo! Bravo!' and the Binford people sportingly joined in. While they clapped, the old lady, leaning at a sharp angle, confided to the vicar: 'He's a better class of refugee, of course.'

Eventually the acclaim stuttered and stopped. The people now waited for the Dutchman's words with almost as much anticipation as they had awaited Churchill's.

The refugee stood with a dignified uncertainty. He ignored the insistence of Mrs Spofforth who urged: 'Speak up, man. Come on . . . tell them.'

He regarded the faces from the English fields ranged before him with a kind of compassion. He turned to look at those on the platform, Robert in a stance like a statue, the vicar staring into a cloud of pipe smoke gathered like a halo above the head of Mr Oakes, Rob Noyes examining his hands as if wondering how long he could expect them to last, and the reporter Wally Beavan now licking his pencil and with his notebook expectantly open.

'My name,' said the Dutchman, 'is Johanes Van

Lorn.' The voice was surprisingly firm after the obvious nervousness of its owner. 'My home is in the town of Rotterdam. Or it was. There is nothing left now.'

A murmur of sympathy moved around the audience. Mrs Spofforth said loudly to the vicar, 'His English is as good as yours, isn't it.'

'The Germans bombed us, destroying everything. I took my family out into the fields to escape. To a place where we once used to go fishing on the canal. Then the tanks came, the Panzers, and the German soldiers. It was very bad. There was artillery shooting and I became separated from my family, from my wife, from my son, from my uncle and some other people we were hiding with. Now . . .' The tone faltered. 'Now . . . I do not know where they are. I went back to the place to look but I could not find them. I pray they are safe.'

A dumb but tangible sadness came from the hall. Someone began sniffing. Men stared with leaden faces at the upright and impressive figure on the stage. Robert coughed with English embarrassment and asked imperatively: 'Mr Van Lorn, what advice do you have . . . ? Have you any . . . er, tips . . . ?'

The Dutchman turned. 'Advice?' he said. 'If the Germans invade?'

'Yes. If they invade.'

It seemed that the white face became whiter. 'Run,' he answered. 'Run away.'

Fourteen

All night and every day now they waited, a wait of eagerness, the unskilled, unfit, unknowing amateurs, willing, *daring* the enemy to attack. To a man, the Local Defence Volunteers were desperate to shoot at a German, or some suitable substitute. Accidents and misunderstandings were not infrequent.

The professional soldiers, who knew better, were dogged with dismay by the prospect of invasion. France was tottering, the English sea was watched, the cliffs patrolled, the trenches dug, the road-blocks and concrete pillboxes planted into the ground. Sometimes defence works had to be dug up again and relocated to face the right direction. Ringlets of barbed wire were looped along the beaches and roads. The skies remained summery and mostly clear of intrusion. For a while, an uncanny, unforeseen and almost mocking peace settled across the land. Tents sat like mushrooms on the open moorland in the forest and the regular army that had returned so tattered from Dunkirk healed its wounds and rested its feet.

Soldiers sat and lay in the emerald meadows while units were being replanned, transport, supplies and weapons found. Feet, raw from the long trudge to Dunkirk, healed with the aid of vats of Valderma ointment. The men did not constitute a fighting force.

But with the odd serenity that had spread over the land, there was a certain sureness, a contrary lightness, a feeling of knowing what had to be faced and what needed to be done.

France was still fighting, so was Norway, but each with a diminishing faith. With a grim sense of relief the British had come to realize that they would soon be alone, the boundaries of war visible and unmistakable – the cliffs and beaches of their own island.

At Binford the Local Defence Volunteers brought the re-claimed punt gun up the river to cover the crossroads leading to Lymington, Lyndhurst, Southampton and Christchurch. It lay among the rushes, the fierce, elongated weapon mounted on its shallow boat, its muzzle like a baleful eye. Robert's LDV men cut away some of the reeds and willow branches to improve the field of fire. At the same junction they had a booby trap, a coil of barbed wire fixed to the garden roller which normally saw service in the cricket field. The roller was perched and pegged on a ramp and could be pushed across the road pulling behind it the opening concertina of barbed wire on the approach of an enemy vehicle.

'Excellent,' enthused Robert, crouching on a slight hill behind cover of gorse at midnight. 'Absolutely first class. Let's try it again. Bring it back and give it another shove.' Four men – Wilf Smith, his brother Malcolm, George Lavington and Tom Bower – tugged the roller back across the road and up on to its ramp. A screech owl sounded. Standing above them Robert felt younger, fitter, more essential and more important than he had for years. 'Good. Grand, chaps,' he enthused. 'Up she comes. Watch those barbs, Tom. They'll have your trousers off!' The men had steadied the roller. 'Right,' said Robert firmly. 'Let her go – now!'

The heavy roller seemed to relish its military role. Released, it performed a frisky jump, like a freed horse, and trundled blithely down the ramp, on to the road and across it, stretching out the barbed wire coil behind it.

'Car coming!' called Willy Cubbins, concealed at a bend in the road. The boy was frequently used as a look-out now because he appeared to have conquered his sleep-walking and his legs did not seize up, as did the legs of the older men, during long prone periods under cover.

'Car, Mr Lovatt!' he echoed, peeping over the top of the gorse. 'Mr Lovatt, car . . . !'

It was too late. A Morris van took the bend at a good rate just as the barbed wire was uncoiling over the road behind the roller. The vehicle wobbled briskly and charged into the wire like an elephant into a trap. A twanging, a scraping, a squealing of brakes, and finally two bangs, the first as the roller and the side of the vehicle bounced against each other, the second as a front tyre punctured on a rusty barb. Like shadows, the Local Defence Volunteers rose from their dark background.

'Halt,' ordered Robert. 'Who goes there?'

There was a scuffling, a scrambling in the dark, the car door was forced half open, but caught noisily by the wire. A face, livid in Robert's torchlight, appeared. 'Halt,' ordered Robert again.

'Halt?' returned the man vehemently, still half in, half out of the van. 'Halt? I *am* fucking halted! Look at my bleeding van. What are you stupid bastards playing at? You could have killed us.'

'You're lucky we didn't open fire,' intoned Robert. He turned his torch down to the riverbank revealing the elevated mouth of the huge punt gun. It was levelled at the vehicle. 'Identity card, please.'

Furiously the man pushed the door against the wire and managed to shift it another few inches. It was still impossible to get out. A girl's voice came from within the vehicle, attempting to calm the man. 'Bert, Bert, don't.' His arm went back and pushed her away. 'There'll only be bother, Bert.'

'Identity card, please,' repeated Robert.

'Sod off! Playing bloody soldiers at this time of night.'

'It's this time of night that spies are abroad,' answered Robert, as if quoting Shakespeare. Moving towards him he flooded the man's face with his torch. The man glared through the entangled wire.

'Spies! Do I look like a fucking spy? Do spies go around with bits of stuff in their vans?'

'Thank you *very* much,' bawled the girl from within. 'Bit of stuff am I? Just watch your mouth, mate.'

'I take it you're from London,' commented Robert mildly. 'What are you doing in this area?'

'Came down to play on the beach,' retorted the man.

'Identity card, if you please.'

'I haven't got my bloody identity card. Nor my gas mask. Nor my stirrup pump. Anything else? Blimey, don't you lot have bloody fun!'

There was a movement from the rear and Robert saw that Purkiss was peering through the window of the van with his torch pointed down. 'I'll tell you what he *has* got, Mr Lovatt,' he said. 'A dead cow.'

Almost by tradition, the day of the Binford Fête was fine. The sun warmed a blameless morning and the people of the village were about early, doing their shopping and their chores in time to go to the sports field where the event was always held.

On that same Saturday, across the English Channel, the metallic German armies were advancing towards an undefended Paris. Off the Norwegian coast the aircraft carrier *Glorious* was sunk by three German pocket battleships, the *Hipper*, the *Scharnhorst* and the *Gneisenau*. Not one of the carrier's aircraft was on patrol at the time and so no warning was given. The *Glorious* was trapped with two escorting destroyers which were also sunk by the swift German ships. Of fifteen hundred British sailors, only forty-six survived.

Hob Hobson was one of the early arrivals at the sports field. The sun fell in golden columns through the elms, and the grass, mown the day before, was pungently sweet. Some of the coloured stalls had been erected overnight but Hob, who always organized the bowling for a pig, liked to set up the canvas and skittles for his attraction first thing in the morning. Obtaining the pig this year had been impossible, Hob said, owing to the food regulations, so he was giving an IOU which could be redeemed for *two* pigs on the cessation of the war with Germany.

Other early arrivals left deep footprints in the dew; Charlie Fox who was running the beer tent appeared, rolling a barrel like a carpet across the grass. The cricketers were jealously fencing off their stretch of green wicket so that no one would set foot on the sacred twenty-two yards, while other players set up the beat-the-batsman sideshow. Flags looped around the ground, hardly a movement from their tips, and this year the flags of the Allies were hung in a brave display over the horticultural tent where some of the largest marrows, greenest beans and most tender potatoes in the South of England were displayed for judgement, surrounded by vivid flowers from country gardens. Ben Bennett's New Forest Arcadians were booked from lunchtime and there were to be races and other contests for children and grown-ups. The air-raid wardens were giving a display of gas-resuscitation, there was to be a Punch-and-Judy show and a man from the First World War who had one leg and lived in an adjoining village had promised to bring his barrel organ on the condition that he was positioned on the distant side of the field from the band. They had clashed in the past.

A family dog show had been organized and the National Savings Tent was walled with stirring war pictures; artillery-men kneeling like worshippers around their field gun, a fighter pilot laughing confidently in his cockpit, a minesweeper watch-out silhouetted against a northern sunset. There was to be a baby contest with ten jars of cod liver oil as the prize and a tug-of-war had been arranged between a village team and some of the soldiers recently evacuated from Dunkirk. These soldiers had also volunteered to act as stewards and to help with the many sideshows. They were returning to life. The vicar had expressed some misgiving about using the white tents which were normally spread over the sports field, since he feared they might catch the eye of an enemy raider. A suggestion at the Parish Council that they should be marked with the Red Cross was vetoed as it smacked of cheating. The soldiers were of the opinion that it would be worthless to attempt to camouflage the tents as that would make them a sure target. The skies had been quiet, however, and a compromise was decided, the tents being placed as far as possible beneath the swelling green of the midsummer trees, but not so far as to look to any flying German like anything but a village fête.

By ten o'clock, when the sun was well clear of the trees and the tea urns had arrived, there were busy figures scattered throughout the field, hammering tent pegs, heaving ropes, setting up coconuts, made of wood now but realistically carved by a man in the forest. The same man was giving a display of charcoal burning, an ancient art in the region, almost forgotten but now revived by the necessity of war. A suggestion that the local gypsies should be encouraged to man the lost property tent had not been taken seriously.

Robert, wearing his service revolver holster stuffed with cardboard, and three of his LDV men had arrived, manhandling the tea urns transported by Millie's horse and trap. They trotted with them as if they were trench mortars. They then set about erecting their own display, several genuine rifles, an arrangement of enamel soup plates, face down and said to have the appearance of anti-tank mines, a coil of barbed wire and their tommy-gun. This display of power was to be exhibited before a banner which proclaimed: 'The Binford Local Defence Volunteers Are Ready for Hitler.' A demonstration of making a

Molotov cocktail, the useful home-made bomb developed by the Finns in their war against the invading Russians, was abandoned on advice from PC Brice who thought local boys might use the recipe. Robert was privately relieved because no one in the unit knew, for certain, how to make one.

Children came down to the field and ran around in excitement. The little girls wore print dresses and the boys flannel shirts and flag-legged shorts with belts fastened with a snake buckle. It was rumoured that a man was bringing two donkeys from Christchurch, a rare attraction because normally at this time of year they were occupied giving rides on the beach. Now the beach was silent with barbed wire.

Noon shone over the forest and its fringe of villages and fields; serene sun lay everywhere. When Alan Stevens left his house behind the school the village was empty and dusty. He walked to the sports field. At the gate he took in the amateur scene and saw the LDV sideshow at the distant end, near the pavilion. He walked that way.

Robert saw him when he was half the field away. 'Here's our conscientious objector,' he muttered. Purkiss, who was smoothing out the creases in the warning-to-Hitler banner, turned and studied the sports-jacketed figure coming towards them. 'I hope he hasn't come to advise us to surrender,' sniffed Robert.

Stevens halted a few yards distant and looked at the meagre display of weapons and then the vain boast plastering the banner. 'Good morning,' he said to the glowering Robert. 'I wondered if you needed some help.'

'Help?' inquired Robert suspiciously. 'What sort of help?'

'Help with the stall. Help with defending the country. Anything.'

'*You* want to join the LDV?' responded Robert brusquely. 'Why don't you go off and join the army?'

'The army won't have me. I've got a hole in my lower chest. From a bullet.'

Robert swallowed his disbelief. 'A bullet? Where did *you* come across a bullet?'

'In Spain,' Stevens told him. 'In the civil war. With the International Brigade.'

Astonishment arched over Robert's large face. 'Good God, you were, were you?' Distrust caused him to pause again. 'Not a Communist as well, are you?'

'No, I can't say I am,' said Stevens firmly. 'Now, do you want some help?'

Like the leader of a gang of boys, Robert turned to Purkiss and the others. 'Shall we let him join?' he asked from the corner of his mouth. 'He might be useful.'

'Knows more than any of us, I don't doubt, sir,' suggested Purkiss. 'Ask 'im if he can make a bomb.'

Robert said: 'Can you make a bomb?'

'Up to a certain size.' Stevens smiled at their school-yard faces. Walking into the area, he lifted the Union Jack at the entrance and it draped across his shoulder. Casually he picked up the tommy-gun.

Robert blenched. 'Steady on with that,' he warned. 'It's the only one. Don't go and break it.'

Stevens snapped the weapon into its components with three sharp movements. He squinted down the barrel.

'What do you think?' asked Robert. 'Is it all right? Haven't sent us a dud, have they?'

'Better than nothing,' said Stevens unconvincingly. 'It's an improvement on peashooters. It's not going to stop the German army, though.'

Robert looked at him solidly. 'Do you want to join the Binford Local Defence Volunteers?' he inquired dramatically. 'Or are you merely here to criticize?'

Stevens nodded. 'If you'll have me.'

The big elderly man stepped forward and they shook hands. 'Right,' said Robert. 'You can help to put the banner up. I'll get you an armband as soon as I can. Elizabeth is running up a few more.' He paused, then whispered confidingly: 'It's not that tommy-gun that's going to stop the German army, Mr Stevens. It's the people.'

Major-General Sound, a great army revolver in a polished chestnut case on his shining belt, opened the fête, standing on a platform of beer crates overlaid with bunting and backed by the fluttering flags of friendly nations. Privately he thought, and not for the first time, that the Union Jack flew more bravely, with more animation even in the mildest breeze, than the banners of other nations, even those who were allies.

While the Dunkirk survivors and the combined LDV and police teams were sweating at the tug-of-war rope that afternoon, Harry went with his mother into the horticultural tent and saw Bess, her face framed by flowers, at the end of one of the long tables. His mother was intent on Kathy Barratt's tulips which she grew in window-boxes at the telephone exchange.

He touched her hand to excuse himself and moved along the blooms until he reached Bess.

He stood behind her, his chin brushing her shoulder as he looked over it. She smiled privately. 'Who can this be creeping up on me?' she whispered in her mocking manner.

'I thought how fetching you looked among the flowers,' he answered. He lightly flicked the stem of an early rose. Mary Puller, the butcher's wife, pushed his hand briskly aside.

'That's my Anthony Eden,' she said haughtily. 'Highly Commended.'

'Yes, he is,' replied Harry. He and Bess walked on. Harry was aware that his mother was noticing him through the stems and petals, from the far end of the tent. He looked briefly her way and smiled. She turned away.

'It's very close in here,' said Bess. 'And it smells like an undertaker's.'

'Do you want to take a stroll?' suggested Harry. 'I'll tell you all about Dunkirk.'

'I'll take a stroll if you promise not to,' she answered with a brief, patient smile. Beneath her flowered dress her hips and her breasts showed. 'Do you have to ask your mother?' she suggested. 'Do you want us to sneak out by different exits?'

He made a face. 'That won't be necessary,' he said unconvincingly. 'I'm a big boy now.'

'Ah, yes, you've been to Dunkirk. All right, let's go for our walk.'

He kept his eyes directly on the tent flap and moved her towards it. Ben Bennett's New Forest Arcadians were playing in the sunshine, 'Rose of England, Thou

311

Shalt Fade Not Here'. Harry saw his father standing almost to attention, listening to the lifting tune, and he felt a sharp, foolish affection for him. All around, the fête tinkled in the bright day. Everyone in the village seemed to be there and many from the surrounding forest hamlets and even as far afield as Lymington.

Laughter, calls and sunshine mixed in the meadow. The man with one leg and the hurdy-gurdy played his revolving songs, making a sly flanking movement towards the band, edging ever closer, intent on putting them off their tune. The tug-of-war teams were sitting, legs astride, on the grass, beer and lemonade bottles to their lips, sweating in their vests. One of the soldiers lay on his back, hands across his stomach, grinning at the homely sky.

Hob Hobson was arguing bitterly with George Lavington who had won a pig at bowling but refused to take his IOU for two to be redeemed after the war. George, red-cheeked, exploded: 'There might not be an after-the-war!'

Children were riding the imported seaside donkeys, the animals stopping to graze frequently and refusing all threats and cajoling, having quickly realized it was better to labour on grass than sand. The fresh green cloak of the forest stretched out and slightly up from the village and its animated field; miles of it, reaching to the horizon of the three sail-like hills and the June sky. Harry and Bess walked that way.

Strolling a little apart, they left the road and took the single thread of worn, pale path, through the deep green and blazing yellow of the gorse. The way wriggled and rose, the skyline broken oddly by bent-backed trees that seemed also to be tramping up the hill, like vagrants.

When the way narrowed Harry and Bess had to walk closer and he put her hand in his. They hardly spoke. Around them the countryside was falling away like a skirt, the village changing shape every few paces, the river showing shining patches, the farm fields between the road and the forest forming a quilt. The meadow where the fête was taking place was temporarily blocked out by a secondary rise in the ground and some high furze, but then it moved into view again and they paused, taking in the air, the sun and the view. The fête was all coloured figures among the white tents. The notes of the band wafted towards them.

'I can see your mother,' Bess mentioned maliciously. 'See her down there.' She pointed. 'She's rushing about. I think she's searching for you.'

He laughed guiltily. 'Don't, please,' he pleaded. 'She can't help it. She still thinks I'm a kid.'

She did not pursue her teasing. 'It's years since I've been up here,' she said reflectively. 'It's funny how you stop doing some things when you grow up, isn't it. I mean, we used to come up here all the time, didn't we. The whole gang of us.'

'Are you sorry you came back to Binford?' he asked. Once more they began to walk easily up the slope. Before the pause they had released hands but now she slotted hers in acquiescence into his.

'I'd rather be in London, if that's what you mean,' she said. 'It's not much fun living with my batty gran.' She glanced inquisitively at him. 'I bet you have a good time in Portsmouth, don't you? Are the streets paved with wicked women?'

'All I've been doing is marching sailors around, filling sandbags and learning the basics of the Maxim machine gun, nineteen-fourteen version,' he replied.

'You haven't answered the question,' she said but did not pursue it.

They reached the forehead of the hill. The rough gorse gave way to a plateau of comfortable grass. There was a basin in the ground which had gathered a pool, the pausing place of a forest stream, before it continued running down the flank of the mound. 'It's still here,' she laughed. 'Remember when we built a dam, all of us, and we waited at the bottom to see what happened when it burst.'

'And it flooded the road,' he finished. 'That caused a lot of bother, didn't it.'

'I got out of it,' she said slyly. 'I lied.'

'I know,' he said. 'I remember.'

They sat on the brow of the plateau, looking out over the far-reaching country. The sky and the land and sea merged in distant mist. The umphing of the band drifted to them.

'It was funny, your brother and Millie Johnson getting married, wasn't it,' she mentioned suddenly. 'I suppose it was sort of expected, but I thought they'd avoid it in the end.' She looked at him from the side of her eye. 'I always thought she'd marry you.'

'Me?' He was genuinely surprised. 'But . . . well, she's older than me, for a start.'

'Yes,' she said. 'They were the oldest ones, weren't they. Are they happy?'

'Oh yes, of course. But he's away quite a bit at the moment, that's all. Millie gets a bit lonely.'

'You should go and comfort her,' she suggested

mischievously. 'James was always a bit of a bore.'

Harry said: 'You do say some odd things.'

She was moving away and did not answer. 'Let's see if we can still drink like we used to from the stream,' she suggested. She was walking back to the cup in the land. He watched, pleasured and surprised, as she lowered herself on her knees and then gradually forward flat on her stomach with her chin over the clear revolving water. She looked around. 'Come on. *And* you. You haven't got your nice uniform on.'

His eyes were fixed on the backs of her legs. Moving to her side he lay on his stomach facing the pool. The slim, silken stream toppled over the lip of its neat fall, scarcely two feet high, into the pool sending out eddies, bubbles and low liquid sounds.

Bess began to giggle against the ground. 'You go first. Try and get a mouthful.' Harry opened his mouth and tried to position his head so that the water ran into his mouth with only his cheek getting wet. He wriggled forward and did it.

'Harry! You can still do it!' she exclaimed. 'That's marvellous. After all this time.'

'It's only ten years,' he protested, levering himself up and wiping his mouth and cheek with his hand. 'We're not ancient. Not yet.'

'But we will be one day,' she said. Her face clouded as if she were wondering how long it would take, but then she brightened. 'I bet I can still do it too. But you'll have to hold my hair back, I don't want it getting soaked. I had short hair then. And I didn't care anyway.'

She lay, face down, on the rim of the pool. He found himself almost stifled by enjoyment, her hoisted dress, the fawn skin across the backs of her thighs, her soft hair bunched in his hand. 'Harry,' she warned over her shoulder. 'You're getting fruity.'

'Can you blame me?' he asked froggily.

'I'm going now,' she announced. 'Here goes.' She stretched her neck like a bird pecking a morsel, lowering her open mouth to the sliding surface. Steadying herself and closing her eyes she let the stream run into her mouth. She swallowed once and then choked, spluttered, and laughing struggled to get up. Harry still held her hair and as her head came up he kissed her neck and then her face and then her lips. She responded with forced lightness, pushing him gently from her. 'One more go,' she said decisively. 'You try again. If you succeed . . . you will be rewarded. Like a knight in the olden days.'

Reluctantly he released her hair and, sighing, lay once more on his side on the bank and eased his mouth, sideways, a fraction at a time towards the water. He had almost touched it when she emitted a mischievous squeak and pushed his face and most of his head into the cold stream. He shouted and gasped, spitting out the water. Swiftly his hand went back and he caught her by the naked ankle as she tried to scramble up and escape.

'Don't! Don't, you beast!' she squealed like a child. 'Leave me –' She tumbled gently backwards on to the grass and he, laughing and panting, crawled after her. They fell together in a full embrace, his arms pulling her and holding her to him, his palms outstretched against the supple body below the soft dress; hers around his shirt, tugging at it. He tried to kiss her again but she bit him and they rolled together down the bank.

'You trollop!' he hooted.

'Careful!' she cried. 'We'll be in the water. Then you'll have to explain *that* to your mummy.'

'Stop it, Bess,' he said seriously. They were lying sideways, Harry gazing into her amused face. 'Stop it. Forget my mother, will you. I have.'

Her dilatory smile spread beautifully and he enabled her to roll until she was above him. She hitched her skirt hem up to her waist and bent her legs so that she was fully astride him, one egg-like knee each side of his hips. She regarded him with smug triumph. 'Got you,' she said.

'And I've got you,' he replied, almost choking. He could feel through his shirt, the skin of her legs and the bridge between them. She leaned down and put her lips over his nose. Her hands rubbed at his chest. His travelled up below her arms and cradled her perspiring breasts. Their eyes held each other, like a challenge, but then easing.

'Remember when we did this first?' he said. 'I bet you don't.'

'Yes, I do, see. It was on the cricket field. Remember, it was almost dark. Just the two of us. We must have been fourteen or fifteen. We were too scared to do it properly.'

'I'll say. But not now, are we?'

His hands fell on to her thighs, spanning the tops of her legs. 'I'm wearing pink drawers,' she mentioned. 'See.' She lifted her hem a few more inches.

'I noticed,' he said.

'You were always trying to get a look to see what colour they were. And all your pals.'

'It's one of the mysteries of boyhood,' he shrugged.

'Would you like me to take them off?' she inquired with an odd formality. 'I'll have to dismount for a minute. You can take your trousers off then. Your legs aren't all ghastly white are they?'

She was just talking for the sake of it, to fill in the moments. She rolled away, stood facing the other direction, and swiftly pulled the pink knickers away from her legs. He unbuttoned his trousers and pulled them down. 'There, see,' he muttered, staring at her revealed backside. 'No white legs. We've been wearing shorts for the sandbag filling.'

Bess said nothing more. Eyes heavy, she pulled up the front of his shirt and sat on him again. Absent-mindedly, she began to unbutton the front of her dress. The buttons went to the waist. She leaned forward and kissed his lips. 'Undo me at the back, Harry,' she said.

He released the two small hooks that held her brassière and she herself pulled it down at the front. Her pale, pink-tipped breasts framed by the silk of the dress lolled in front of his nose. 'There they are again,' she said. His hands went to them and he rubbed them tenderly. Her face hardened and she bent towards him again. 'God, I always feel so . . .' she began but did not finish. He ran his tongue over the lovely skin and then on the pale nipples. Her body stiffened like iron clothed in velvet and she made a small face, almost of annoyance, as she manoeuvred herself into a position where she could allow him into her. They went together. Harry had so many things to engage him; her body, the sight and feel of it, her face now above him, eyes clenched, framed by her flying hair and the summer sky. High up in that sky came the

A new rattle of gunfire came from the clouded combat. 'I won't bloody come again – so don't go asking!'

Angrily he stumped out of the gate, then, on a thought, partly uncovered the organ again and began brazenly to turn the handle as he hopped and stumbled along the lane. The ancient music jangled over the hedge. 'Novelties!' bellowed Henry Bunigan above his own noise. 'All they want these days, bloody novelties!'

In the field the silent people continued to watch the remote battle, as the two planes turned in the blue spaces of the sky or vanished behind a yellow cloud. Robert had his binoculars on the battle. 'Spitfire, sir,' he reported to Major-General Sound, who was now standing, unlike all the others, looking at the ground by his feet, appearing to listen rather than see. 'And an ME one-o-nine.'

'How the hell can you see its number?' demanded the old soldier irritably. 'It's damned well miles up. God, give me the time when they fought engagements within a reasonably accessible area.'

Both aircraft disappeared behind the biggest of the loitering clouds and then there came a thud, a dull echo like someone striking a carpet, before a plane appeared, curling from below the creamy clouds, spiralling and dropping towards the earth, a thoughtful wisp of smoke at its tail.

'Got him!' shouted Robert joyously, waving the field glasses. 'Got the swine! Well done, Spitfire!' Everyone in the field jumped jubilantly and cheered, especially the children. The villagers advanced, coming out of the shadows of the tents into the centre clearing to watch the distant dropping aeroplane. The Dunkirk soldiers stood smiling towards heaven, the Local Defence Volunteers stiffened. Amid it all Elizabeth and Millie now stood mutely and watched the dying machine fall to earth.

'There goes our chap!' bellowed Robert, pointing. 'Well done, Spitfire! Off you go home!'

Alan Stevens glanced at Don Petrie who watched the solitary flier turn away to the south. 'If he's going home,' he said, 'he's going a funny way about it, don't you think?'

Petrie nodded silently. He watched the plane clear some cloud and then continue. It was rolling in the sky as it went. 'Due south,' he said.

Two boys ran across the fête field towards Robert. One, in familiar green, was Tommy Oakes. 'Mr Lovatt,' he panted. 'Look. See over there.' Others were pointing also. Robert raised the glasses. 'Parachute,' he exclaimed. 'Jerry coming down.' He snapped around. 'Platoon!' he ordered. 'At the double!'

The Local Defence Volunteers all but collided with each other in their rush to reach the rifles and shotguns stacked at the back of the tent. 'Double march!' bellowed Robert. 'Come along, men!' He swung on MajorGeneral Sound. 'Permission to take action, sir?' he inquired with a snap salute.

The older soldier appeared perplexed. 'Yes . . . yes, you carry on,' he nodded eventually. 'Get the blighter.'

Robert surveyed the field worriedly. 'Bowley,' he said briskly, his eye lighting on the station porter, who wore his LDV armband over his railway uniform. 'You're used to looking after things – guard the stall.'

Ben Bowley nodded in dumb disappointment. People were beginning to stream towards the gate. 'Stop!' bellowed Robert. 'Stop at once! That Nazi is armed. He won't show any mercy.' He waved his arm like a cavalry officer and the LDV unit ran clumsily over the grass, between the sideshows and the tents, Robert still ordering the villagers aside to allow his troops to pass. Painfully, Stevens, holding his ribs, ran with the men.

In a moment the field was almost deserted. Major-General Sound sat down heavily. 'I'm not sure I like it,' he mentioned thoughtfully to Elizabeth. 'This sort of war. Women and children charging around like dragoons.' She said she would get him a cup of tea and he thanked her. Mrs Spofforth and her Dutch refugee had gone home.

The major-general, stumping over the guy ropes, followed Elizabeth to the tea tent. She was standing with a huge enamel teapot amid the deserted tables. The old soldier nodded approvingly at the pot. 'Jolly sensible size,' he commented.

Elizabeth smiled kindly at him. 'It's listed in the Binford War Book,' she said. 'You know, the list we've had to compile of all our resources. We may need it in an emergency.'

She could tell he wanted to say something to her.

He began to unbuckle his shining leather revolver holster. She watched in amazement while he handed it across to her as though in some token surrender. The butt of the service weapon was poking out. It was heavy in her hands.

'Give that to your husband,' said the major-general, avoiding her eyes. 'Hate to see a chap like that not properly armed. Damned silly if he came up on a Hun and all he had in his holster was cardboard.' He laughed gravely. 'Just for the duration,' he added. 'I'll have it back after the war. I'm too old to use it now. Properly that is.'

She thanked him sincerely. She looked about her for somewhere to put the gun. 'Only one drawback,' said Major-General Sound. 'Only one round of ammunition. Handed all the rest in.' He paused, a little shamefaced, then added: 'Kept that in case it might come in useful sometime.'

Outside Millie walked across the vacant fête, paper and a balloon blowing over the grass, towards a perambulator in which a baby had been left howling. She rocked the pram by its handle but the child still cried.

As they clambered across roadside fields and then up into the tree-line, the Local Defence Volunteers managed to pull back the agile and excited children who were leading the charge towards the fallen parachutist. 'Back! Back!' ordered Robert. 'Everyone back behind the military.'

The voices of mothers sounded. 'Come back, Betty. He's a German. Come back . . .' 'Herbie, don't you go no further. He's got a gun . . .' 'Bill, Bill . . . No showing off. You come here this minute.'

Robert, clutching his empty holster as if leaning on it for support, puffed behind his men. He had a passing hope that the LDV would never be called upon either to advance or retreat too quickly. Purkiss, Petrie and the Dove brothers were ahead, Lennie with the unit tommy-gun. As they ran up the inclining forest land, the trees replaced by high, prickly gorse, so the column languished, the children in their bright clothes and the women straggling and panting. 'I want to see 'im!' puffed a rural wife. 'I ain't never seen a German afore.'

Robert, pausing for breath and because his legs ached, looked towards the ridge and saw a swift green figure scampering far ahead of everyone. 'That boy!' he gasped. He turned, looking for someone who had more breath for shouting.

'Oakes!' called Petrie in his best coastguard hailing voice.

'Tommy Oakes.'

The wolf-cub paused and turned. He swore to himself and sat down moodily on a stone, to let the LDV men catch up. When they did he went with them to the immediate skyline. The parachute was lying like a fallen flower in a bowl of ground, a place of wild berries and brambles. As the men's heads peeped cautiously over the ridge so a breeze moved the silk and they saw it was no man but a box-like container. 'Good God, supply drop,' said Robert hoarsely. 'This could be it. This could be it. They've started the invasion.'

Stevens had just caught up. Holding his ribs he lay flat and panting alongside the others. The women and children were pressing forward up the slope behind them, eager to see. Tommy Oakes was alongside the men. So was the boy Cubbins.

Stevens took in the scene. 'Get everyone back, Mr Lovatt,' he said quickly. 'That's a land-mine.'

Robert's eyes widened. 'Are you sure?' he said. Then: 'Everybody keep down!'

The warning was none too soon. As the heads went down below the escarpment, so, with a red roar, a blast that shook the trees, and a gush of smoke, the land-mine detonated. Few of the people had ever heard an explosion like that before. Robert closed his eyes as the ground shook and his ears drummed. He was suddenly back twenty-five years and in the trenches.

Stevens, clenched-faced against the ground, felt pieces of earth dropping around him. He needed only a shorter memory. The LDV men lay stiffly, hands over ears. Behind them some of the women began to cry quietly. The children were silenced by fright.

It was Tommy Oakes who was the first to look. 'There's a great big hole, Mr Stevens,' he called towards his schoolmaster. The heads peered over the ridge again. Where the wild berries had been was a blackened crater, the whole floor of the little valley was charred, some of the brambles were burning idly. Stunned, the Binford villagers advanced to the line of the ridge and looked down at the destroyed earth.

When, minutes later, Robert led a party of men forward down the smoky slope, George Lavington found a hare, teeth showing, sitting bolt upright, stiff and dead. He showed it to Clakka, the rabbit catcher, who took its ears and held it up in wonder. 'Dead of fright,' he said wonderingly. 'Never did see that before.'

Fifteen

Sunset was late, for it was getting towards mid-summer, and as the dusk of each day drifted in so the volunteers went out from their homes to keep amateur watch on the coast, to man road-blocks fashioned from farm carts and other unlikely obstacles, and wait to spring novel booby traps under German feet. All day they had worked at their normal occupations. They slept in fitful shifts for a few hours during the night before returning to their homes for breakfast and then out to another day's work. The workers from the fields and farms were at their most occupied at that season but they unfailingly reported for duty and went trudging the nocturnal country. In Binford there were training sessions each evening with instructions for the ill-assorted troops of the Local Defence Volunteers on how best to stop an armoured division.

'I have a circulated order which I am instructed to read,' announced Robert Lovatt, standing before his group at the evening training session in the village hall. He held the paper like a shield before him.

Robert, his wife had observed wryly, had done no recent editing of his book *The Front Line: Personal Stories from the Trenches*. He was now so occupied with this war that he had no time for the last. He had, in addition, unreluctantly given up his air-raid precaution activities to concentrate on the LDV. The former organization, with its civil role, had appealed to him little. In the LDV, at least, the opportunity might occur to shoot someone.

Now, his solemn soldiers stood in three ranks, drawn up crookedly in their bits and pieces of uniform, bicycle clips, poaching jackets, shotguns, hoary rifles, and the tommy-gun. Robert wore his new revolver with a deep satisfaction. He had written a moving letter to Major-General Sound. This evening he was aware of the grip of the weapon protruding like a grey nose from the holster. His brother's uniform, still with its touch of mothballs, completed his outfit.

'This order,' he waved the square of paper, 'reads as follows: "In the event of an invasion, civilians will *not* be expected to attack large military formations." '

They glanced at each other. 'Is that us, then, Mr Lovatt, sir?' asked Purkiss. 'Are we reckoned as civilians?'

Robert squinted at the paper as if it might yield a further clue. 'I hardly think we can be,' he grunted eventually. 'Otherwise why are we armed like this? I am convinced that this order concerns women and children only. And people like air-raid wardens. They would not be expected to launch any sort of offensive against an aggressor.' He glared at them solidly for he had made up his mind: 'But that does not include this force.'

They looked generally pleased at the ruling and the ranks straightened. Firmer expressions set in, eyes hardened. 'Right,' said Robert. 'That's understood then. Platoon!' The men stiffened. 'Stand . . . easy.'

The shoulders fell away as if strings had been loosened. 'Fall out and gather round, chaps.'

They formed a half-circle about him, some squatting gratefully on the dusty floor, some with the faces of lads expecting an adventure story. He said importantly: 'Promotions: Private Alan Stevens has been promoted at once to sergeant-instructor. As you may know, he's a very experienced chap and we're lucky to have him. Fought in Spain, right through, and knows everything there is to know about mines, booby traps, ambuscades, guerrilla warfare and so on. He is going to prove invaluable to this unit and he's coming here, right away, this evening, to give a lecture and demonstration on the making of the Molotov cocktail and its effective use against tanks. He had to do something else at the school first.' He paused and took up another slip of paper.

'In the meantime, there's another bit of bumf from the War Office.' His familiarity brought careful smiles to the faces about him. 'You can bet your socks that as soon as Whitehall can start sending out a few more bits of paper, they'll be delighted to do so. The formation of the Local Defence Volunteers must have been like striking a new seam of gold to them.'

He shuffled with the paper, turning it one way then the other. 'I don't know whether this is a joke or an insult,' he said. 'Perhaps it's both. Nevertheless, I have to pass it on to you. It concerns men on road-block or ambush duty. It spells out the drill for actually shooting at a vehicle or a person who does not obey a challenge to halt. It also contains the information that any member of the LDV who shoots anyone out of a grudge must be immediately suspended.' He looked up at their wondering faces. 'So . . . no shooting out of grudges – understood?'

Petrie and Stevens walked across the evening field towards the village hall. 'Tonight,' said Stevens, 'I am going to divulge the recipe for making a Molotov cocktail – guaranteed, if you do it right, to set fire to a tank and brew up every man inside it.'

The coastguard waited, then said: 'What made you change your mind?'

'I haven't,' answered the schoolteacher. 'I still think it's all madness. I had a Spanish wife and she died in the bombing of Barcelona, you know, and that sort of thing is hard to forget, but . . .'

'But?'

'But, as has been pointed out, you can't be an island. I realized that. I watched that kid, Tommy Oakes, the eternal wolf-cub, practising drill outside the school wall one evening, and he made me realize. The bell tolls for me as well.'

Petrie laughed. They were almost at the steps of the pavilion. 'They're not going to toll for anybody now. Did you hear the news tonight?'

They reached the door and opened it to find themselves facing the assorted guns and grim faces of the Local Defence Volunteers. 'Stand easy,' ordered Robert hurriedly when he saw the two men. 'Well done, though, well done.'

Stevens almost pointed out that the Germans might consider entering through the windows, possibly with a diversionary attack through the pavilion scullery, but he decided against it. He and Petrie were scarcely in the wooden room when the door opened behind them and an anguished face appeared. It belonged to Cyril Pusey, captain of the church bell-ringers. He was aghast. 'They've . . . stopped the *bells*,' he started as he stumbled in. He looked at each face in turn. 'The bells . . .' he said advancing on Robert. 'The bells . . .'

'Out with it, man,' snapped Robert. He did not care for Cyril Pusey, who had refused to join the LDV on account of his first-aid classes.

Pusey looked injured, but said: 'It was on the news. All church bells have got to be stopped.'

'Why?'

'They're only to be rung if parachutists come. German parachutists.'

'We know they won't be New Zealanders,' answered Robert gruffly. 'Sounds like a good idea. Hear them for miles.'

Pusey looked ragged. 'But surely . . . surely,' he muttered, 'somebody would *notice* if there were thousands of parachutists falling. It would be bound to leak out, wouldn't it? Why use the bells?' He regarded the local faces around him like someone who has arrived by mistake in a strange land. 'It takes years to learn,' he said. 'Years. And practice. Hours we spend in that belfry, all day Sunday, weddings, funerals, and every Thursday practice. And now we've got to stop. Why pick on the bells?'

Robert looked at the poor man irritably. 'Orders, Pusey,' he said, 'are orders. At a time like this.'

More creases made the man's face like an old balloon. 'Church bells make people happy,' he muttered. 'They keep up the spirits.'

He was staring into the distance, his gaze going far beyond the wooden walls of the pavilion. 'And we *walk*, you know, Mr Lovatt. Our team have walked miles, ringing in churches all over the forest, through Hampshire, into Sussex, and we've been to Kent. Twice. What will we do now? It might be years.' He paused. 'People will forget how to ring,' he said huskily.

'Can't you do it with blankets, like, wrapped around the clappers,' suggested Lennie Dove.

Pusey regarded him witheringly and did not answer. 'I think it's madness.' He eyed Robert challengingly. 'I think it's showing Hitler that this country is really down.' He said it darkly. 'We're as good as beaten.'

'The Molotov cocktail,' recited Stevens steadily, watching the eager expressions, 'is an effective weapon, cheap and easy to manufacture. The Finns invented it for use against the Russians, and as a sort of joke called it after Molotov, the Soviet foreign minister. It was also used widely in Spain by both sides. Correctly assembled and correctly employed it can set a tank on fire.' The faces about him solidified.

'The recipe for making the weapon is this.' Stevens reached below the table and, like a conjuror producing a box of tricks, lifted a cardboard carton which he placed on the green baize cloth. He took a wine bottle and a beer bottle and set them on the cloth. 'Officers use wine bottles,' he said glancing up, 'other ranks beer bottles.' It was some moments before anyone saw it was a joke and laughed. 'The bottle,' continued the teacher, 'is thoroughly cleaned and then you add ingredients as follows.' Their eyes were fixed on the table.

'Petrol . . . so . . .' he said, running the liquid from a can and through a funnel. 'Paraffin . . . so . . .' He poured in the thin blue stream. 'And tar . . . ordinary, everyday tar, the stuff that's used for the roads.' He looked up. 'And that's it.' The Local Defence Volunteers, eyeing each other, began to back away. Stevens grinned. 'Don't worry. It's not primed yet. It needs one more thing which we'll have to scout around and get. I'm sure there must be some in the village – fireworks.'

'I've got some in the shop,' mentioned Hob Hobson. 'The idea was to save them for victory night.'

'I think we would be justified in commandeering them,' said Robert. He caught Hob's expression. 'Purchased at cost,' he added.

'We ought to have enough to blow up a Panzer division,' said Peter Dove, rubbing his large hands. 'I reckon we ought to set to and start making them now . . .' He looked quickly at the commanding officer. 'Don't you reckon, sir?'

'Have you ever seen a Panzer division?' Stevens regarded the fisherman.

'No . . . well, only like on the pictures.'

'They don't look so bad on the pictures,' said Stevens.

Robert stepped forward. 'We're fortunate in having Sergeant-Instructor Stevens to hand on his knowledge,' he said firmly. Stevens, until then unaware of his promotion, took it soberly. Robert continued: 'This is a good opportunity to ask questions. After all, he's been at the wars recently . . .' He looked embarrassed. 'My experience was a long time ago, more than twenty years – ancient history now.'

Petrie held up his hand. 'If the Germans should overrun this area,' he asked, 'and seeing that it is a forest, one of the wilder places in this part of the country, what do you think of the prospects of carrying out guerrilla warfare from concealed camps and suchlike?'

To their disappointment Stevens shrugged: 'Not much,' he answered. 'Not much at all. It's not exactly the Belgian Congo, is it?'

'But there are four hundred square miles of forest,' put in Robert. 'People have been lost for *days*. Riders have gone off on horses that have returned with no rider and it's taken thirty-six hours of thorough searching to find them. Surely we could hide up somewhere and strike when the time was opportune.'

'Spain,' continued Stevens, 'is a large and wild country. Mountainous, plenty of concealment, and there guerrilla warfare was possible. But not here. Any hideout would be traced in no time.'

Lennie Dove said: 'There's the gypsies, Liberty Cooper's lot. They could hide till the cows come home. They know parts of the forest that nobody's seen for years.'

Stevens answered: 'An aeroplane, a low-flying spotter, can see tracks across the most overgrown country. And we would leave tracks, even if only a handful of men used the location, and if they covered every twig behind them. After no time it would show from the air.'

Robert could not conceal his disappointment. 'What do you suggest then? We would just have to pack up and go home?'

Stevens faced him and said solemnly: 'I'm afraid

the answer is "yes". Resistance groups are all right in large conurbations or in truly wild and inaccessible country. Here they would be winkled out in no time. Small villages are also easy for revenge. Everyone knows the hostages personally – or those chosen for execution.' His eyes went around the abruptly stark faces. 'It's not a game,' he added like an apology. 'It's not the boy scouts.'

At the end of the meeting the men drifted away, over the darkening ground. Robert walked with Stevens and Petrie. At the lane they shook hands and Robert strode up the road. The two younger men remained talking. They had become friends. Stevens said: 'When I applied to be a conscientious objector some very odd things happened. There's an organization you can go to, who actually *rehearse* you in what to *say* in front of the tribunal.'

'That's what stuck in your throat,' decided Petrie. 'It would mine.'

Stevens laughed drily. 'They also said it might be a good idea to join a religious pacifist group or something like the Woodcraft Folk.'

Stevens walked towards his house behind the school. He felt the loneliness that had now become a familiar companion. It was a sorry thing when you had to use victory fireworks to make fire-bombs. And for what?

At the side of the road was one of the camps which had been established for the soldiers returned from Dunkirk. The shambles of their arrival had now been cleared and the tents were in ordered rows, some vehicles were parked on a cindered square and a sentry stood in a slope-roofed box by the gate. It had

no sides, only a roof. The guard called on him to halt
and he showed his identity card. The young, coarse-
looking soldier squinted at him from under his steel
helmet. Stevens knew what he was thinking. He
opened his jacket and lifted his shirt. 'Wounded,' he
mentioned, wondering why he was doing it.

'That's why you wasn't called up,' said the sentry.
'That looks 'orrible. Did it 'urt?'

Stevens nodded and smiled in the dark. 'Nice sentry
box,' he added. He tapped the non-existent sides.
'Very airy.'

'Bloody cold more like it,' amended the soldier. 'It'll
be murder if they don't change them before the
fucking winter. 'Ow can they make them with no
bleeding walls? What sense is there in that, I ask you?'

'Meant for India or somewhere hot. The Sudan,
somewhere like that, I expect,' Stevens told him.
Singing was coming from one of the tents, low and not
unmelodious singing. The sentry smirked. 'Fed up
and far from 'ome,' he said, 'that lot. No beer money
so they're 'aving a sing-song. They been at it all night
on and off.'

Stevens wished him good night and continued
towards the village. He passed close to the tent from
which the singing was emanating. They were
chorusing a song from the First World War.

> 'Goodbye Dolly I must leave you,
> Though it breaks my heart to go,
> Goodbye Dolly I must leave you,
> To the front to fight the foe.'

Reflectively he walked on. The Germans, the

Spanish, the Russians, the French and others had defiant, boastful marching songs, songs of triumph, or at least the promise of triumph. But the British soldier sang of making excuses to his girl before he marched off to death.

As he walked he was aware of a stiff figure standing outside the tent. Even in the dark he could see it was a sergeant-major, the very angle of the body, the cocked ear, the cane as rigid as the arm that held it.

'Listen to those squaddies,' the NCO said softly, seeing him. 'Just listen to them, sir.' He inclined further towards the tent. Then, as if ignited, he bawled: 'Stop that 'orrible noise in there! Time you was asleep in your beds. Lights out twenty minutes ago. The Germans will be 'ere in the morning.' The song was silenced.

Stevens went on. A three-quarter moon was clearing the horizon of forest trees, its light webbing the village roofs and chimneys. He was conscious of his footsteps. He remembered a rhyme he had once heard and he repeated it to himself as he walked:

'I was playing golf the day
That the Germans landed,
All our troops had run away,
All our ships were stranded;
And the thought of England's shame,
Very nearly spoilt my game.'

At what he judged to be the right moment, Mussolini, the Italian dictator, declared war on crumbling France and cornered Britain. His troops advanced to the borders at Menton where they were held up by French customs officers who only let them through on orders from their own disarrayed Government. In the first hours of the war Italian anti-aircraft guns had shot down their own greatest and most fêted airman.

The third week of June began with the Germans entering Paris, trotting their horses and drumming their men past the Arc de Triomphe. Verdun, the great bastion of the First World War, had crumbled like cake, and its old Defender Marshal Pétain, who had said at Verdun, 'They shall not pass,' made his first act on becoming France's new President the act of surrender to the foe.

When she heard the news of the French capitulation, Elizabeth left her sitting-room and walked quickly and alone across the garden and into the surrounding trees. She felt foolish, as if she were trying to hide.

She walked out into the deserted lane and turned, away from the village, and arrived, almost surprised, outside Mrs Spofforth's gate, a place like a short tunnel beneath a dark yew.

'I thought I would come to see how you are,' Elizabeth explained a little lamely when she went into the old lady's garden. Mrs Spofforth was sitting under a plum tree. She was enclosed in a barrel that had been cut into a seat. It gave her the look of a chess-set queen.

Mrs Spofforth's eyebrows arched with genuine pleasure. 'How nice of you, Elizabeth,' she said. Elizabeth was quite surprised she remembered her name. 'I'm very pleased. Pull up a barrel.'

There was another of the curiously formed seats a

few feet away and Elizabeth rolled it on its bottom coop under the plum tree and sat down. The weathered, warm wood fitted around her. 'Yes, I *am* pleased,' repeated Mrs Spofforth. 'You always were a nice little person. I've often thought we could have been great friends if you'd been a bit more ancient or me a bit less.'

Elizabeth smiled her embarrassment. 'I don't know why,' she said, 'but when I heard the news about France I just came out. I just wanted to . . . well, walk somewhere.'

'You're always welcome to walk this way,' replied Mrs Spofforth. 'We'll have some tea in a minute. So France is cooked is she? Well, I'm not surprised. Never counted on them myself. Too many men hiding behind walrus moustaches and large ornate caps. We're better off on our own, dear.' She leaned closer. 'These continentals are a funny bundle, anyway.' She nodded caustically behind her. 'Take a peep into the paddock. That Dutchman of ours in there. He just walks around there all day. It's like having a horse.'

'I can see his head,' confirmed Elizabeth, half turning.

'Looking over the hedge,' suggested Mrs Spofforth. She gurgled. 'Wants a bucket of water, I expect. I'd never have had him if I'd known.'

Elizabeth said: 'If the Germans begin bombing London we'll all be inundated with evacuees again, I imagine. Remember how they all arrived here in those buses the first time? Mothers, babies, all sorts.'

'Hah!' snorted the old lady. 'Soon scurried back

though, didn't they. Once they thought London was safe. And I, for one, wasn't sorry. Children wandering aimlessly around the countryside, stoning cows and eating deadly-nightshade.'

Elizabeth laughed. 'How is Bess settling down?' she asked carefully. 'I saw her at the fête.'

'The little madam,' sniffed Mrs Spofforth. 'Wants the bright life of London but her parents won't hear of it. So I'm having to put up with her. Fortunately she spends half the time on a horse, keeping a watch for German parachutists, she says. Lord help any poor Boche she gets her hands on.'

A bicycle bearing a woman in a flowered dress passed a gap in the hedge. 'Oh dammit,' exclaimed Mrs Spofforth. 'It's Gloria Arbuthnot. You know, the witch. I'd forgotten it was today. She's come to tell my fortune. She does every couple of weeks. Silly old fool never gets a single thing right and I lead her on something terrible, but it passes the odd hour. Time goes slowly when you get to my age. Then you look round and it's all gone.'

Elizabeth rose from the barrel with difficulty. 'Perhaps I'd better be off,' she said.

The old lady responded kindly: 'Oh no, please don't go. We haven't had any tea yet. Stay for another half an hour.' She looked sad and concerned and Elizabeth smiled and patted her hand. 'All right. Of course. I'll help you get the tea.' Mrs Spofforth thanked her happily. 'Here she comes,' she nodded towards the drive. 'Clutching her crystal ball.'

Gloria Arbuthnot, her dress like a garden, her face like puffy blossom, her streaked hair held under a wide straw hat tied up with ribbons of varying hues. 'What a sight,' sighed Mrs Spofforth. 'She's like some sort of oriental, isn't she.'

The visitor placed her bicycle up against the gate and, with a glance towards them, carefully locked it to a rail with a padlock. 'No reflection on you, Mrs Spofforth,' she bustled as she approached. 'A precaution in case an enemy agent decides to steal it. That's what they tell you to do. Good afternoon, Mrs Lovatt, how very nice to see you. What a lovely day.' She paused dramatically. 'France has fallen,' she announced.

'Your crystal ball is getting a bit worn out, Gloria,' commented Mrs Spofforth. 'I heard the news from Mrs Lovatt some time ago.'

'The crystal only tells the future,' said Mrs Arbuthnot a little huffily. 'It does not deal in events which have already taken place. That is history. Where is Mr Van Lorn? I have a message for him.'

'Good news or bad?' asked Mrs Spofforth. 'He's in a sorry enough state as it is. He'll be eating the grass next.'

'It's quite good,' claimed Gloria doubtfully. 'His aunt has escaped the Germans.'

'Where is she now?' demanded Mrs Spofforth suspiciously. 'Not coming in this direction.'

Gloria looked a shade hurt. 'She's in heaven,' she asserted. 'I had a message. Last night.'

'Tell him after we've had tea,' decided the old lady firmly. 'He'll bother us dreadfully and he'll eat all the cake. He always does.'

They had tea on an iron table on the terrace. Large clouds had gathered but the afternoon remained benign. After tea Gloria read their fortunes in the tea leaves and then revealed to them that Hitler would be dead before Christmas. That, she said, was a certainty. She produced a misty crystal ball and set it on the table. Elizabeth felt amused and tried not to smile. Mrs Spofforth said: 'It's as cracked as you are, Gloria. You ought to get a new one.'

'There's a war on, you know,' returned Gloria primly. 'You can't get them for love nor money. Nor spirit trumpets.'

'The forces have got them all, I expect,' said Mrs Spofforth briskly. 'Now, are you going to do the cards?'

Elizabeth rose. 'I must be going,' she said. As she rose she saw just over her head a spider's web, stretched beautifully across the gap between two branches of a climbing rose that bloomed pink against the house. 'See that?' she said. 'Isn't it perfect.' She looked at the other women a little shyly. 'I read the other day that the spider's web would make the perfect gunsight,' she said suddenly. 'Isn't that a sad thing?'

She left them in the garden and made her way slowly towards the gate. Mr Van Lorn was coming from the paddock and making his way towards the tea table. 'Cake?' he ventured. 'Tea?'

Mrs Spofforth and Gloria watched Elizabeth go out into the lane. 'She's a nice little person,' said the old lady. 'I went off with her father, you know. Donkeys years ago. The mother was very upset. She used to go and cry her eyes out in the church. Of course, Elizabeth never knew. We went to Bognor Regis but we soon came back.'

'Don't blame you,' said Gloria, hurrying to take

some cake as Mr Van Lorn advanced. 'Don't like Bognor myself. Why the King used to go there I can't think.' She continued looking towards the gate. 'I'm afraid though,' she said, 'that her sorrow has not all gone away. There is to be a terrible tragedy in her family, mark my words.'

Sixteen

Through the night James was driven back from Portland on the Channel coast, huddled, drifting in and out of sleep in the back of the military car while the driver went through squally rain on the road to London. At almost every village they were challenged and stopped at a road-block and the driver had to show identification. James became irritable. 'Christ,' he breathed, 'do they really think German agents are going to tear through the bloody country in an army staff car?'

'Seems like they'll believe anything, sir,' answered the driver from the front darkness. 'That last lot said they'd heard the invasion had started and that the beaches down in Devon are covered with dead Germans.'

James laughed drily. That day he had been watching a demonstration of supposed secret weapons hurriedly dreamed into existence. Bombs on carts which would, it was hoped, be rolled down hills at a conveniently exposed enemy, metal drainpipes stuffed with dynamite and aimed like the spears of ancient Britons. An amazing axle with two wheels had run amok on the shingle beach, detonating as it careered, causing the assembled military watchers to scatter ignominiously. They had also seen a grim demonstration of setting fire to the sea, with oil pumped from just below the surface and ignited; an idea, thought James, with possibilities. The rest were playthings of inventors.

The road taking them back passed only a little north of the New Forest and he was tempted to tell the driver to turn off to Binford. He could go home, to Millie, for a few hours. But he closed his eyes until they had gone beyond the region and were heading closer to London.

There were increased road-blocks and inspections as they entered the suburbs. Elderly men and boys who should long ago have been in bed were patrolling the streets like vigilantes. A boy, too young for the army, poked his face into the driver's window and demanded identification. 'It's Goering, sonny,' retorted the driver. 'Say it's Goering.'

The young head withdrew and there were whispered words outside in the dark street. Then a bald-headed man who looked as if he had never known sleep pushed his face in the window. 'Who did you say, sir? The lad is on his first night.'

The driver answered brusquely. 'This is Major Lovatt of Mr Churchill's special staff. And he's tired.'

The man chuckled. 'Ha, and he said you reckoned it was Goering,' he said. 'That's a good one, I must say.' He looked intently, poking his head closer towards James dozing in the gloom, just to make quite sure. 'Still, he's only a boy. He'll learn.' Withdrawing, he banged the side of the staff car with the flat of his hand. 'Right you are, sir. Give our regards to Winnie. Tell him we'll beat the buggers if they show their noses in South Wandsworth.'

At three o'clock they reached the flat and James let himself in. There was a light under Mrs Beauchamp's door and she opened it cautiously and appeared in a woollen dressing-gown. 'Do you want anything, sir?' she inquired. He sat down heavily and said he did not. 'Except sleep, I expect,' she said. 'You look worn out. Good night, sir.'

The curtains in the bedroom had not been drawn. Still dressed, he lay down on the bed, propped by a pillow, and slowly drank a Scotch. The sky above London was already awash with another dawn. He realized that Midsummer Day had gone by and he had not noticed.

He awoke at seven, still in his battledress, the empty glass fallen beside him on the quilt. Every limb and joint ached. He wanted to telephone Millie then but he thought he would leave it until later. He was forever putting her off and yet hoping that she might telephone him. He had a bath and shaved. Mrs Beauchamp appeared with a breakfast tray, the *Daily Telegraph* and the post.

There was a letter from Joanne Schorner, a note on a card inside an envelope. 'Have been trying to call you,' it said. 'Have two tickets for Tchaikovsky concert, Queen's Hall, Thursday 23rd. Would you like one?'

There was something inevitable about it, he knew that. He went through the newspaper as he ate his breakfast. The last ship, the Polish liner *Batory*, had escaped from France loaded with Polish soldiers. France had now completely capitulated but had refused to send its powerful unused warships into American or other neutral ports. James wondered where those ships were and how long it would be until the Germans got their hands on them.

At eight-thirty he telephoned Millie. Wearily he heard her talking about the village and its war efforts. She was going to the air-raid warden's post that day to help roll bandages. Yesterday she had cut the lawn and trimmed the hedge. Would he be able to come home for a day or a couple of days soon?

When he reached his office that morning he telephoned Joanne Schorner and said he would be delighted to go to the Tchaikovsky concert.

They sat in the circular stillness of the great cool concert hall, her shoulder touching his arm. James was full of the feeling of her presence. Joanne scarcely moved, her face intent and quiet. Romeo and Juliet, Swan Lake, Symphony Number Four, The Nutcracker Suite.

Afterwards, in the late evening, they walked through streets of tall silent houses, for a while without speaking. Eventually she said: 'When I first went to New York I used to get up early just to see the streets without people. I lived with an uncle who's a farmer in West Virginia and somehow that seemed noisier than New York.'

'Where were you born?' he asked. They knew little of each other..

'In West Virginia,' she said. 'My parents divorced and then my mother died and I went to live with my uncle and his family. He's a great man. I had a letter from him yesterday. He wants to take Hitler on single-handed.'

James laughed. 'It sounds like my father,' he said.

'Except he's too old for it. Not that anyone would tell him.'

'James,' she said, 'do you have a wife?'

'Yes,' he said. 'Her name's Millie. She lives down in Hampshire.'

'I see.' She looked about them and laughed a little sharply. 'Do you have any idea where we are?' she asked. 'We just seem to be walking.'

'It's the back of Knightsbridge,' he said. 'I'd not noticed. We seemed to be just meandering.'

'Hanson Place is quite close then, isn't it?' she said.

'Yes, I suppose so. I'm never very sure, being a mere country lad.'

'It's two blocks,' she said. 'I know where we are. That's where I live now. I've taken an apartment for a while.'

They walked on, their shoes sounding on the pavement in the darkening street. An air-raid warden approached treading with heavy carefulness like an elephant. He appeared pleased to see them and touched the rim of his steel helmet with his finger.

'All quiet, sir,' he said to James, giving the impression he had been told to make a report.

'Ah, yes,' agreed James inadequately. Joanne smothered a smile. 'Good.'

'Nothing moving but the cats,' continued the man. 'Still,' he sniffed up at the sky, 'don't suppose it will be all that long before they start on us.' He performed another salute. 'Good night, sir. Good night, miss.'

'What will he be like if they do start bombing, I wonder?' asked Joanne. She had taken his arm as they walked on.

'Frightened, but splendid, I expect,' suggested James. 'Like most people.'

They reached Hanson Place and she unlocked the outer door of a tall building and they walked into the shadowed hall. 'The elevator is out of action,' she said. 'Because of the war, naturally. It's five floors.'

'I'll try,' he said. She went up the stairs before him and he felt the excitement and, already, the guilt rising within himself. She took another key from her purse and opened the door of her apartment. It was close and dark in there. She went to the window and pulled the curtains, then turned on the lights. It was comfortably expensive. 'I've got it for three months if I need it that long,' she said. 'But maybe I'll be going home before that.'

Joanne poured two drinks and then went to the gramophone in the corner of the wide, comfortable sitting-room. 'I inherited some records with the apartment,' she said. 'See if you like this.'

She wound the handle and put the large black disc on the turntable. He stood in the centre of the room and listened. 'It's ethereal,' he said when it was almost finished. 'What is it?'

'German, I'm afraid,' she smiled. 'Franz Abt. It's called "*Uber den Sternen*" – "Above the Stars".'

He grinned at her. 'Well, you *are* neutral, after all,' he said. He paused, then asked her to play it again. She rewound the machine and put the silver arm back to the beginning of the record.

As the music began she moved to the wall and switched off the lights. 'We can listen, and see the stars,' she said. She pulled the heavy black-out curtains apart. They were on the fifth floor of the building and they looked out on the rooftops and the spread of the night sky. They stood close together and watched, before they touched, turned and exchanged their first kiss.

James had known it would be very difficult for him to tell the lies that would be necessary. He picked up the telephone only after attempting to compose himself for the ordeal. This time, after all the occasions when the call had gone unanswered, Millie took the earpiece from the hook at once. It was breakfast time.

'Sorry, darling,' she said. 'I've got a mouthful of toast.'

'That's all right.' Then defensively: 'I'm amazed to find you at home.'

'Oh, come on, James,' she replied good-humouredly. 'I'm not *always* out when you ring. But I simply can't just wait in case you call. I'm not walking hand in hand across the forest comforting lonely soldiers, you know.'

'I know, I know,' he said quietly. 'There must be lots of things to do.'

'Well, darling, there *are*. I'm working three days at the RAF station, and they've just got a new squadron arrived, and I've taken on the secretarial work for your father's LDV. You'd be astonished how much of that there is. I'm dazed by army form numbers at the moment.'

He almost said: 'It's just as well we haven't got a family,' but he didn't.

She brightened. 'Anyway you *are* coming down this weekend, aren't you? If Hitler doesn't arrive first. We can catch up on things then.'

Now was the time for lying. 'No, I'm not, Millie,' he said. It came out roughly. 'That's why I'm ringing. I'm sorry but . . .'

'Oh, I'm sorry too.' Her voice had been light even when they had come near to arguing. Now it dropped. 'Something urgent?'

'Only the bloody war,' he said wearily. 'I've got to be on duty, I'm afraid. Very few people are getting away up here. Not even for a few hours. It's understandable, I suppose.'

There seemed a long interval before she answered. 'Yes, I suppose it is.' Her voice lifted. 'Well, it can't be helped. War is hell, as they're always saying. We'll have to wait until another time.'

Miserably he said: 'I'll try and get down during the week. Just for a couple of hours. I've got visits to make to units on Salisbury Plain. I could hurry over from there.'

'Yes,' she agreed. Her voice was flat, controlled now. 'Yes, well, why don't you try? Let me know when it is.'

'I will. Goodbye, darling. I'll call you before the weekend.'

'Yes, all right, James. I hope I'll be in. If I'm not, keep trying.'

James replaced the phone. He sat with his hands cradling his forehead. Well, he'd done it now. He'd told the story. That was the difficult part. He'd never been a good liar. He picked up the earpiece again and dialled Joanne Schorner's number.

Eighty miles away his wife walked out of the cool house and into the garden. It was a grey morning, the sky blank as a sheet, the air mild. A forest pony was

351

cropping the hedge. She shooed it away brusquely. The tears in her eyes surprised her. The herbaceous blooms seemed to fuse together. Was it disappointment or was it fear? She failed to answer her own question. She did something she had never done before. She swore violently and took a flying kick at a low-hanging pink rose, smashing it and sending its fine petals flying over the lawn.

It might have been peacetime that Sunday. Londoners, as if they sensed it might be their last day off in the sun, went to the countryside, to hilly Hampstead Heath, to the trees at Epping on the city's north-east fringe, and to the towns along the River Thames to the west.

John Colin, the small boy, was staying with Mrs Beauchamp and when James was about to leave to meet Joanne he saw the child was looking out of the old lady's window, leaving the smudge of his nose on the glass as he turned round. 'Are you going out today?' asked James.

'I think we are,' answered the six-year-old. 'But Mrs Beauchamp has got things to do first.' The final sentence was blurted out: 'I want to see my mummy.'

Mrs Beauchamp came in from her small kitchen. She looked with sharp sadness at James. He appreciated the look and walked back into his own room with the housekeeper behind him. 'All the week he's been waiting for his mother, sir,' she whispered. 'He's been with the nanny. Mrs Perkins was supposed to be here by now. The nanny expected her three days ago, after the Germans getting to Paris and everything. But she hasn't turned up . . .'

The elderly woman began to poke at her eyes with her apron. 'The poor little chap's been waiting all that time. He was here all day yesterday with me. Every time he sees a woman walking along the street he thinks it's his mum and he waits for the door to ring and it doesn't.'

She gazed at him as if he might be able to help. 'It's such a shame,' she said. 'It upsets me. I don't know who to ask. You'd think she would have got a message through somehow, wouldn't you?'

James frowned. 'She was with the British Hospital in Paris, wasn't she?' He moved towards the telephone directories. 'There must be a London number or something.'

Mrs Beauchamp regarded him anxiously. 'I don't want to interfere, sir, you realize that. But it does upset me.'

'Hang on a moment,' he said. He sat with the directory at the phone. Then he closed the directory and rang a Whitehall number. Mrs Beauchamp went back to her room where the small boy still gazed from the window. James called four numbers before he had a conversation with a duty officer at the Foreign Office. He replaced the phone and opened Mrs Beauchamp's door, beckoning her to come in.

White-faced, she asked: 'What, sir? What's gone and happened?'

'Nothing to worry about, Mrs Beauchamp,' he said kindly. 'The hospital was evacuated from Paris on Thursday but by that time there was no way out to the north and the entire staff seems to have gone south-west in two buses. They either went towards Bordeaux or towards the Spanish frontier.'

'I don't rightly know what direction that would be,' she said, a little shamefaced. 'But as long as she got out.'

'The roads are crammed with refugees . . .'

'And they're bombing them, poor souls,' she said. 'I heard it on the wireless.'

'The buses are marked with big red crosses, so I was told,' he said to reassure her. 'But there has been no contact since they quit Paris. The man at the Foreign Office said he will endeavour to discover what has happened.'

'That's going to be hard to tell John Colin,' she said. 'He can't just keep staring out of the window if his mum's in Bordeaux or Spain or wherever it is. I'll have to tell him she won't be here yet.'

On an impulse which surprised him, James said: 'I'll take him out, if you like.'

Mrs Beauchamp looked taken aback. Her eyes were damp again. 'That would be very nice indeed, sir. I'm sure he'd like that.'

'I'll take him down to Hampton Court,' said James. 'I was going in that direction anyway . . . with a friend. Perhaps they still have the boats on the river.'

The sight of the old palace of Hampton Court that Sunday, with its crowded riverside, surprised James and astonished Joanne. The little boy said he did not know there were so many people in the whole world. 'The British,' remarked Joanne looking about her with a sigh, 'have no idea when they're cornered.'

They were standing on the white bridge above the thickly moving Thames. The sun was spread along the river and its grass banks, the warm brick towers of

354

the palace that Cardinal Wolsey gave to Henry the Eighth raised themselves royally above the abundant trees. People sat by the riverside spread around with picnics, children paddled and boys swam in the green water; people moved like an army along the towpath, they gazed at the old palace from without and within. The women were in bright dresses, the men in shirts, the many servicemen perspiring in uniform. Boats were on the river and from one below the bridge came a gramophone song, a South American rhythm. Carmen Miranda sang, 'I, I, I, I like you verra much.'

There were ice-cream vendors, two with newly lettered signs proclaiming: '*Not* Italian. Maltese Citizen', and another: 'British Through and Through', despite the name 'Antonio Niccovelli' about his tricycle. A crowd had gathered about a third seller and two policemen were in the act of escorting him away. A third policeman mounted the coloured tricycle and pedalled it with slow precision in the same direction. 'A Wop, that's what he is,' a man told his wife and spellbound children.

Joanne waited in a line for ice-cream while James walked with John Colin along the towpath to where a man was hiring out boats. 'Just got them back from Dunkirk, sir,' joked the vendor, a brown smile creasing his face. 'Rescued 'undreds these did.' He manoeuvred the tiny skiff to the wooden jetty and James climbed aboard, lifting the wide-eyed boy after him.

The boat man, who was elderly, was wearing an LDV armband over his striped shirt. There was a long scar on his face. 'Malay States, sir, eighteen-ninety-three,' he said mysteriously, seeing James's glance.

'You're ready to fight again, I see,' smiled James, nodding at his armband.

'As much as I can, sir,' replied the man optimistically. 'They've put me in charge of amphibious warfare.'

Joanne arrived with the ice-creams and the boatman, grinning at the little boy, called: 'Here comes mum.'

She climbed lithely over the side and James pushed the flat craft clear of the grass and rowed it carefully out into the stream. The boy shouted with delight and spread the ice-cream across his face. Joanne sat at the other end of the boat and regarded James enigmatically. 'I never thought I'd spend a day like this,' she said. 'Not now.'

'Nor me,' he responded. 'It's like something from some time that's past.'

He rowed them out into midstream, close by islets, where luxurious swans lay and willows shadowed the surface. Fingers of sunshine drifted through the branches. The little boy gazed at the swans and observed they had very big ducks on this river. For a while he seemed to have forgotten his mother.

There were many other small boats on the Thames, mostly hired punts and skiffs like their own, but one or two under sail, trying to catch the brief wind. But there were no powered boats. They had all been locked away or beached for the long winter of war. One had burned out at its moorings, its creamy bow charred.

Few people spared it a glance. They walked, even strutted, about in the sunshine, with the same enthusiasm as the many craft criss-crossed the water.

To Joanne it was like a speeded-up movie. As though people were trying to cram a whole summer into one afternoon.

After an hour they brought the skiff back to the wooden landing stage below Mr Turk's boathouse, a famous place on the Thames. The Turk family had been boatmen and swan-keepers for generations. When he had helped Joanne ashore and made sure that John Colin did not slip into the river between the low hull and the wooden jetty, James paid for the hire and made a remark about the burned-out motor cruise along the bank, lying on its side like a shot animal.

'Came back from Dunkirk she did,' said the brown boatman. 'Right as right. Not a scratch on her. First night back she caught fire. They reckon there must have been an unexploded incendiary lodged in her somewhere.' He looked at the wreck reflectively. 'First casualty we've had along here. Don't suppose it will be the last.' He studied James as if he thought he could trust his judgement. 'I don't reckon they'll invade, though, do you, sir? We've got our navy waiting for them if nothing else, and we've got a bit of an air force.'

He apparently did not expect any reassurance from what might be official sources, and he looked surprised when James asked him, 'What will you do if they do come?' Joanne was watching the conversation keenly.

'Well, sir, like I said, the LDV here will be using the boats for operations, but the minute we know we're done, when there's no way out, then I'll scuttle the lot.' His deep eyes turned sadly to the jaunty little fleet moored at his feet and then out into the boats busy on the back of the river. 'Mind,' he said, 'that'll be a terrible hard thing for me to do, because I been here since I was a bit of a kid, the eighteen-eighties, would you believe, with Queen Victoria on the throne, and some of these boats were here before me.' He rubbed the dark brown wood of a gunwale. 'And they won't be making things like this any more. They're too good to be made in the future.'

'But you'd still sink them?' asked Joanne.

He quickly picked up her accent and smiled. 'Yes, ma'am, just like you would do in your country if you was invaded any time. I'd rather have them at the bottom of the Thames than have the Gestapo going out in them on a nice Sunday afternoon.'

Mostly in silence they returned the short way to London on the train that went from Hampton Court's wayside station to Waterloo. It was a comfortable and composed silence. Even the little boy seemed to understand it. He sat against the window and looked at the suburban scenes that rolled by. The sound of the train drifted back as the line turned and the breeze came from a different quarter. John Colin moved his head from side to side, keeping childish time with the rhythm.

As they travelled they could see that the same mood as had been evident on the river was there in the gardens and houses, the streets and the parks that moved by. People were out enjoying the sun as if it might not be available again. They sat on chairs in their small, square gardens, alongside their sheds and greenhouses, having tea on little tables or upturned crates; one man sat alone by a dingy stream, fishing and eating something from a paper bag. In streets children leaped through whirling skipping ropes or played chasing games in gritty patches of sunlight. Others sailed boats on a park lake where lovers stretched blatantly on the grass paying no attention to a group of Local Defence Volunteers rehearsing unarmed combat only a few feet away. The train had paused at a station and James watched the elderly men and youths grapple with each other before a small audience composed almost entirely of uproariously laughing children. As he watched, one man detached himself from the group to chase the children away, pointing them angrily to some distant part of the park. Couples walked dogs between beds of ordinary flowers, bicycles were parked against trees, and an old woman spread out like a queen fed pigeons from a park bench. The sky was moving towards evening but clear and fine. A Salvation Army band played at a dusty junction with a few singing onlookers grouped about it. Birds sounded at stations, urchins threw stones into a murky canal, a man watered his geraniums. There was no sign of the enemy.

They reached the echoing roof of Waterloo and the scene was changed. Servicemen were everywhere, carrying kit and rifles, clinging to wet-cheeked sweethearts, looking askance at destination boards. A military policeman was giving directions to a thin soldier who looked scarcely capable of lifting his kit. His girl, in a skimpy dress, was reluctant to release her hold on his arm. Eventually the soldier moved towards the train, encouraged by the MP. The girl called after him like a wraith, 'Careful, Bertie. Don't do nothing dangerous.'

Music was coming stridently over the station loudspeakers, not martial music but the ditty called: 'Run, Rabbit, Run, Rabbit Run, Run, Run'. It was a catchy tune and a sailor with a kitbag went by whistling it like an echo.

They took a taxi back to Joanne's apartment and James went on to his with the little boy. John Colin rushed into Mrs Beauchamp's arms as soon as they had closed the front door of the flat.

'Any news?' asked James, just forming the words without sound.

Mrs Beauchamp, holding the little boy, shook her head.

'Is my mummy coming?' asked John Colin.

'We'll hear by tomorrow, I know we will,' lied the old lady. 'Come on, I've made a lovely cake.'

'We had ice-cream by the River Thames,' the boy told her. 'And we saw swans and we went in a boat that the man is going to sink when the Gestapo come. He said so.' James touched the child awkwardly on the shoulder. John Colin turned, and, at Mrs Beauchamp's prompting, shyly said thank you for the day. 'And thank you to the lady,' he said.

Mrs Beauchamp remained in the room when the boy had gone. She looked flustered. 'I hope it was all right, sir. I answered the phone about an hour ago and it was Mrs Lovatt.'

'My mother or my wife?' asked James quickly.

'Young Mrs Lovatt, sir. I said you'd gone down to Hampton Court with John Colin, but that I thought you'd be back soon . . .' Her voice faded with growing embarrassment. 'I said I'd ask you to telephone her, sir.'

'That's all right, Mrs Beauchamp,' he said attempting to sound unconcerned. He dared not ask if she had said he had gone with a friend. 'I'll give her a call now. Thank you very much.'

'Thank you, sir. For taking him out. I couldn't have stood him pressing his face to the window all day. It's taken his mind off it a bit.'

She went out. Slowly, stopping himself hurrying, James poured himself a drink and telephoned Millie. 'I thought you were on duty,' she said, her voice level. She gave him an excuse. 'Things were altered, I suppose.'

He was grateful to her. 'Yes, darling, I'm sorry. What was expected to happen just didn't. The plans were changed, and I found myself free just after lunch. I came back here intending to telephone you, but this little boy, John Colin, the one I told you about whose mother was in Paris, he was here and very upset because he was expecting his mother to come back and she hadn't.'

'That's terrible,' Millie answered genuinely. 'Poor little fellow. Where is she?'

Relieved at the tangent taken by the conversation, he said: 'God only knows. I've tried checking all over the place and all I can discover is she left Paris with the rest of the British Hospital staff on Thursday. Since then, nothing. Mrs Beauchamp is very worried, naturally.'

Millie said: 'So you took him on an outing.'

'Just down to the river. There was no time to come home, so I suddenly thought why not? It might give me some practice at being a father.' He disliked himself for that.

'You of all people,' she mused. 'Well, it was very nice of you, James.'

There was a short silence. 'When I'm moving about the south a bit this week,' he said, 'I'll get home for one night at least. About Wednesday.'

Millie said: 'All right, darling. Try and arrange it for Wednesday.' There was another break. 'Providing nothing important comes up.'

James swallowed heavily. 'Short of total war,' he said, 'I'll be there.'

When they had finished, he sat back heavily in the chair. 'Oh God,' he groaned. 'Oh God. Oh bloody dammit.'

Meals in restaurants were limited to five shillings a person, by government decree, but wine could be taken as an extra and at La Marseilles each diner was permitted two glasses. Until the previous week the narrow, candle-lit rendezvous in Kensington had for years been known as Rendezvous Vichy, but this had been hurriedly painted out because of the surrendered French Government's retreat to Vichy, where from the famous spa it now ruled with a puppet's ferocity. Few things changed so quickly in war as allegiances.

'I'm afraid,' said James, 'that the least of my talents is telling lies.'

She smiled slightly. 'You would make a bad spy, James.'

'The most miserable sort of spy. Even on the telephone I can't compose myself enough to fabricate a story.'

'Sometimes,' she said coolly, 'wives who know when their husbands are lying understand the reasons.'

He shook his head. 'Not Millie,' he said confidently. 'She has been brought up in a certain way, in one place, where we now live. I have known her since we were children.'

'I know how small towns can be,' she agreed. 'People who trust you are hell.' She confronted him with composed sadness. 'You feel like you want to call it off?'

James stared at her. 'Oh no. No, I didn't mean that.' Their hands met on the table. 'I couldn't now . . . I've never known . . . anyone like you . . . anything like this.' He knew what he was saying. 'We've only just started.'

'You're going to have to take to lying,' she told him simply. 'That's all that's left.'

As if a warning, a spectre, had appeared, James saw someone watching him. Thin as a wagging finger a man emerged from the folds of the Free French flags which engulfed the distant end of the candle-lit place. Philip Benson saw James at almost the same moment and smiled in the uncertain light. James, a piece of Crêpe de Gaulle see-sawing on his fork, whispered, 'Oh, bugger.'

Joanne's eyes widened. Benson was almost at the table and he had no option but to continue even though he had seen the girl's slight form and short hair from the back. 'Hello, James,' he said genially. 'Taking a breather?' He turned towards Joanne and smiled charmingly.

James took his time to put down his fork; the crêpe slid off it. He could feel the embarrassment burning his face. 'Oh, Phil,' he said, as if it were something which had just come to mind. 'Fancy seeing you. You must meet a friend of mine . . .'

'Yes, I must,' said Benson mischievously.

'Joanne Schorner,' faltered James. 'She is American. A writer.'

'I like to be called a journalist,' said Joanne. She and Benson shook hands.

'We've met before, I feel,' said Benson basking in the younger man's discomfiture.

'Philip is a Member of Parliament,' explained James standing unhappily. 'He's a friend of my father's . . .'

'Your *family*,' corrected Benson. 'I've known you all for years.'

Unruffled, Joanne said: 'We've probably met in the House of Commons, Mr Benson. I get there quite often. There's a lot happening there these days.'

'Yes, there seems to be,' agreed Benson. 'On and off.' He glanced at James.

'Do sit down,' invited James unconvincingly. 'We were just going to order coffee.'

'How kind,' breathed Benson. 'I don't really want to spoil your . . . evening.' He sat down with some finality. 'As a matter of fact, Pascal, the chap who runs this place, has got some brandy. I know that for a fact. Perhaps we can persuade him to part with a little.'

Joanne rose without hurry. 'I need to make a phone call,' she said. 'I'm going off to East Anglia, wherever that may be, tomorrow, and I promised to check on the details. I'll just be five minutes.'

'That,' said Benson when she had gone, 'was what is known as a diplomatic exit.' He regarded James expansively: 'She's a beautiful girl, James.'

'Oh come off it, Philip,' flustered James. 'She's just

an acquaintance. I get pretty solitary up here and it happened . . .'

Benson held up a mild hand. 'James, I have not said a word. Nor, of course, shall I.'

A half relief came to James's expression. 'Thanks . . . No, well, it's all perfectly . . .'

'Innocent? Well, of course it is. There aren't many innocent things left in this world, my boy. Having dinner with an attractive acquaintance is one that is. Up to now.' He leaned forward. 'On the other hand, *my* motives are not so innocent. I'd really like to stay a few minutes, if you don't mind terribly. I'm certain Pascal has that brandy. Do you think Miss Schorner drinks brandy? I'm not sure I could get three.'

'I doubt it,' said James, now more assured. 'What are you up to?'

Joanne returned and settled for coffee. 'East Anglia, here I come,' she said, raising the cup.

'America,' mentioned Benson, as if it followed logically, 'has been asked by Churchill to send us some of your obsolete warships. We have only sixty or so destroyers now operative.' He glanced up at her. 'I gather that some of your naval people are not being very cooperative about the suggestion. They think we're finished and they're telling President Roosevelt so.' He picked up a knife and slid it across the tablecloth like a warship travelling at speed. 'We need those ships,' he said simply. 'They must let us have them.'

To James's astonishment Joanne asked firmly in return: 'What about the French Navy? What's going to happen to that?'

'I'm glad you asked,' answered Benson, eyeing her

appreciatively. 'Your country, young lady, must use every influence it has to see that the French fleet sails to neutral, or better still, American ports. It cannot be difficult for Americans to realize that there is a threat to their own safety if the Germans get their hands on these warships. America can only be reached by sea.'

Benson rose to leave, shaking hands with Joanne and saying to James: 'My love to everyone . . . all the family. See you soon.' He turned and went towards the door. James half turned to wave briefly. Benson raised his fingers in a Churchill salute.

'It worked, see,' he called back softly.

A crouching London taxi wandered along the furtive darkness of the street, its wheels turning gratefully towards them as James hailed it, as if it had been lost and was now found.

In the back of the cab, without lights either within or outside, was like being in a burrow. Joanne felt for his hand and placed it tenderly on her breast, holding it there. They kissed while the taxi driver was seized with a fit of coughing which he finally dispelled with an audible gob from his window.

'James,' she said, her mouth moving against his lapel. 'Maybe you ought to go home later. In case your wife rings.'

'Yes,' he said unhappily. 'I think it would be wise. In the circumstances.'

'There should be a saying – when a wife calls once she'll call again.' She said it lightly. He said no more.

The taxi rumbled through streets as dark as trenches. 'Your friend, Mr Benson,' she continued, still casually. 'He's in the propaganda business, I take it.'

'He has something to do with that,' James admitted. Even though they were now lovers he found himself being cautious and was embarrassed by it.

She laughed at his worry. 'I received the message loud and clear,' she said. 'And what was all that funny business at the door when he went out. Was he just clowning? Doing that V-sign like Winston Churchill does?'

'Philip has a sort of public-school sense of humour,' said James hurriedly.

'All right, smarty,' she said without rancour. 'I'm not digging for secrets.'

He kissed her again. Her cheek was soft to his nose. The driver braked and they heard him curse the black-out.

James asked her: 'Now Italy is in the war what do you think those Italian-Americans will do if the States comes in? Will they fight against their own?'

'Sure they will,' she nodded against his neck. 'Those Italians are Americans. The lady you have your arms about at this moment has a second language and it's German. Three generations ago we came from Deutschland.'

'Jesus, I hadn't thought of that.'

'Maybe Jesus didn't either.' She pulled away in the darkness and looked at the dim shape of his face. 'Listen, this war isn't going to be won just by people called Lovatt or Benson, or even Churchill or Eden, high class as they sound. In the end it's going to be won by people called Polonie or Di Mario or Hoffmeister or Furt, and who knows, people called Omsk and Tomsk too.'

'Of course,' he said. 'But just at this moment the

war is ours, all ours. Just us and them.'

'Exclusive, British,' she laughed. 'Well, try not to keep it that way.'

The taxi left them in the vacant street. It was a dank night now, with gathering rain clouds outlined by the moon drifting aimlessly. They went up to her apartment. 'I don't want to talk any more about the war, okay?' she said. He was looking at the evening paper and she had brought him a whisky. They embraced, he with the newspaper still in his hands. 'Will you quit reading the news,' she asked softly. 'It's all bad.'

James dropped the journal on to a chair behind her. 'I was merely thinking that even official announcements have their own poetry,' he said. 'See.' He picked up the paper again. 'We don't have weather forecasts any longer, only, as it says there "the setting of the sun and the rising of the moon".'

'It sounds like "Hiawatha",' she commented bluntly. She began to undo his tie and shirt. 'I'm sorry your wife rang,' she said, closing her eyes and laying her warm forehead on his neck. 'But I really don't care about her, James. I *can't afford* to care about her. There's no time.' She kissed his face. 'This sort of thing, you understand, is not for ever.'

Seventeen

The handsome weather spread into the early days of July, the farms and gardens blooming under the sun. Elizabeth, in a light dress and straw hat, walking through the village with Wadsworth, admired the roses on Josh Millington's wall, long enough for the old man's head to appear among the pink and the white. ''S all right, Mrs Lovatt, I ain't no German parachutist,' he grinned gummily after she had started back. 'I was just down below 'ere 'aving a liddle look for that blight, or they darned flies.'

She smiled fondly. She had known him since she was first at school. His deep-roofed English cottage was called 'Babylon', after, as he was pleased to explain to the mystified, the fine willow over the beehives at the back, *Salix Babylonia*, 'Called by they Children of Israel, like in the Bible,' he said. 'When they was weeping, and 'anging their 'arps.' Elizabeth could scarcely ever remember seeing him outside his wall, except at the autumn horticultural shows. He made a point, vocally and seasonally proclaimed through the village, that he never entered the spring or the early summer shows because he was needed every moment in his garden. He believed that some disaster might strike his blooms and crops – or his beloved bees – in a moment of unguarded absence. A local joke had it that he even slept among his vegetables. Peter Dove had said, on the stage at the last village Christmas concert, that Mr Millington was found frozen to the marrow.

To the gentle countrywoman it seemed strange, yet satisfying in its way, that they could be conversing on this summer morning with danger looming, and yet so remote that it was lingering only at the back of her mind. 'I always plants out the pumpkins at the full moon, Mrs Lovatt,' he told her secretly. 'That way they grows to be like the moon hisself – big and round and a ripe colour.' He became thoughtful. 'They just coming right now. Lovely they are.' Through the fretwork of roses he studied her profoundly, as if summing up her whole character. 'I'll show you they, if you like,' he suddenly decided. 'I ain't showed no solitary soul, not yet this year. But I'll show you.'

It was an honour and Elizabeth recognized it. 'Thank you, Mr Millington,' she said, touching her throat. 'I'd love to.' She nodded downwards to where Wadsworth was sniffing like a vacuum cleaner. 'I've got the dog, I'm afraid.' The old man disappeared from among the thorns and blossoms and bobbed up beaming at his gate. He had shining stubble on his chin, like an elderly hedgehog. Opening the wooden gate – with its word 'Babylon' – with some ceremony he said: 'Dog won't hurt the pumpkins. I'll ask Mrs Millington to get you a cup of tea, if you like. She's washing the curtains and gettin' the house cleaned up in case that invasion comes along this week.'

Elizabeth blinked at the logic, but did not question it. 'No, no, thank you Mr Millington. Not if she's busy,' she said with hurried awkwardness. 'I'll just see the pumpkins and then I must be on my way.' His face screwed up like paper as he smiled. He beckoned her towards the greenhouse. Walking through the garden was like travelling through a country market, fruit and food and flowers on all sides. His glistening greenhouse stood under the morning sun. She ducked into the fetid interior. It was even more astonishing in there. Every inch was used; vegetables bright and swollen, tomatoes hanging tropically, cucumbers thick and green as serpents.

'There,' said Mr Millington with soft pride. 'There they be. Don' they look a picture?'

The pumpkins lolled fat and somnolent, like a family of overfed orientals. Elizabeth admired them diplomatically. 'If they Germans do come,' said the old man, his bristles working with emotion, 'I'm going to blow the lot up. They ain't getting they.'

Mrs Millington came from the red cottage as they returned and Elizabeth again refused a cup of tea. The old lady, bent as a crooked hairpin, was painfully hanging out her washed flowered curtains on the garden line. Wadsworth investigated her thick-stockinged ankles and she absent-mindedly lashed back at him with her heel. He moved away suspiciously. 'You never know, do you, Mrs Lovatt?' she said mysteriously. 'You just never know.'

'I wish God 'ud sent us a drop of rain,' said Josh Millington as they reached the gate and Elizabeth wished him and his garden well. 'Droughtiest summer for years, you know. 'Tis all very well the sun, but you need the water too. I reckon that 'itler will get here afore the rain.'

As she continued her way through the village

Elizabeth thought that this, of all summers she could ever recall, was indeed the most profuse. It was almost as if the brightness and the fruitfulness were some sort of local consolation for a world of death and ugliness.

The war had, it seemed, come to a temporary halt. The German guns were rimming the Channel coast, their soldiers waiting, as our soldiers waited for them. There were times when enemy planes appeared, like flights of grey pigeons, but they overflew, leaving Binford and its neighbourhood untouched.

The parish council had decided that, in view of the apparent lack of emergency, the customary summer dance would take place at the village pavilion, and Elizabeth, as she had done for several years, was making her way there to supervise the bunting and the bandstand. She did some shopping on her route for it was the day she collected her rations. Hob Hobson had the basket already packed for her. He eyed Wadsworth carefully while he handed it over; little packets of butter and cooking fat, a small wedge of cheese, a quarter of a pound of tea. He clipped the coupons from her two ration books, one for her, one for Robert, and she wondered, not for the first time, how they had managed to eat so much before the war.

When she asked Hob for the key to the pavilion, he said: 'Already open, Mrs Lovatt. The LDV are over there. They just got some uniforms. I expect the major's there too.'

Elizabeth left the shop and took the lane to the cricket field and the pavilion. Wadsworth, off the lead, loped over the grass. She walked thoughtfully; would uniforms make soldiers of the nondescript band who had pledged themselves under her husband's warrior tendencies to defend this, their corner, against a steel army? The dread in her heart was not the coming of the enemy but what would happen to the hopeless defenders of Binford. She pictured Josh Millington blowing up his pumpkins.

Dew on the grass of the cricket field blinked with sunlight. A clutch of small boys pulled the iron roller towards the clipped grass oblong at the centre, for that afternoon there was to be the match against Radfield Compton, the annual meeting, culminating in a jovial evening, the downing of beer, and the rural romance of the annual dance. The young lads were all in uniform, boy scouts, two naval cadets and one green wolf-cub, Tommy Oakes. They were pretending the roller was a field gun. Tommy shouted: 'Forward men! They've landed! They've landed!'

The door of the pavilion was open. Inside, in the warm dust and dimness, the windows dull as squares of paper, an eager group was sorting through some khaki uniforms piled haphazardly on a trestle table. 'Ha, Mrs Lovatt,' exclaimed Tom Purkiss. 'The CO is coming right down – Major Lovatt.' He said it as if she might be in doubt whom he meant. 'We got some outfits at last.'

'Least we'll look like soldiers,' added Sid Turner, 'though they look like they're a bit old.' He held up a tunic, some brass fittings still hanging to its faded fabric. Elizabeth could smell the mustiness of the consignment which had spilled out of the tin trunk. The basset sniffed at them and attempted to lift his leg. Sid moved him gently with his foot.

'First come, first served, it ought to be,' said Harold

Clark. He looked hopefully at Elizabeth. 'Don't you reckon so, Mrs Lovatt? We got 'ere first.'

'I don't know, I'm sure,' answered Elizabeth tactfully. She half lifted the open lid of the trunk. 'You'll have to ask my husband. He's in charge, not me. I've just come to see about the arrangements for the dance.'

'That's what we came for, ma'am,' said Purkiss. 'To help out. And this lot was on the doorstep. Fancy leaving them outside. Could have been stole.'

Elizabeth did not think so. She examined the damp, mouldering fabric between her fingers and then lifted the lid a fraction. The other side bore a rough painting of a military badge and the words 'Regimental Museum'. A ghostly staleness rose from the pile. She lifted a sagging khaki arm as one might lift that of a dead man. The men watched her like children, hoping not to be disappointed. 'What you think then, Mrs Lovatt?' asked Harold. 'D'you reckon they'll do us?'

Elizabeth continued sorting the tunics.

'They Germans will know we're not just beginners if we got uniforms,' Harold added after a thought. 'I reckon we ought to make the best of them. They don't look like they been unpacked for years and years.'

Dubiously Elizabeth picked up the tunic of which she had raised the arm. 'They'll need some attention,' she said.

'Airing,' suggested Purkiss, sniffing at the pile. Wadsworth sniffed also.

'Cleaning,' said Elizabeth. She suddenly, and with a dropping heart, saw that the breast of the uniform tunic she was holding was torn and burned into round holes. There was a dark, old stain, running from there to the bottom of the jacket.

'And repairing,' she added quietly.

Ben Bennett and his New Forest Arcadians had arrived in Binford for the dance with the syncopated Ben suddenly replaced by his wife.

A surprise call to war service was the official explanation of Mr Bennett's absence, although a growing number of people believed the rumour circulated by Ma Fox that he had been taken away by the police after complaints from an insurance company. His wife, Marge, wearing Ben's own sparkling jacket, carried on in his absence but her conducting was little more than a random waving of the baton. Her face was set, even hostile, compared with Ben's beaming features, she smiled only with her false teeth.

Marge also insisted on the band's punctuality (on more than one previous occasion the musicians and Ben had needed to be rooted out of some forest public house before the dancing could commence) and in the long sunshine of the evening, at seven o'clock, the musicians, carrying their instruments, trooped heavily across the cricket field. The drummer pensively bowled his drum like a hoop over the grass.

There were still people sitting on the field, at the verge, for the cricket match, which had given Binford a narrow and enthralling victory, had only finished half an hour previously. The players, still in their stained and threadbare whites, were now in the bar of the Old Crown, faces glowing, voices loud, discussing the aspects of the game and the sharp moment when victory had finally been achieved. Radfield Compton had batted first and had scored one hundred and seventeen before tea; Binford had made victory with Charlie Fox, the landlord of the pub, last man in and no cricketer, scooping the ball with the toe of his bat high over the heads of the near fielders and excitedly lumbering down the wicket for the winning run. It had been a good day.

At that time of the evening also, at the distant end of Binford, Bess Spofforth was coaxing her horse, Merlin, from the gate of her grandmother's house, turning a few yards along the road and then into the deep trees of the forest. It was her evening patrol and she had left her grandmother in outrage, for the girl had gone without doing her normal chore of pulling the old lady from her bath. Mrs Spofforth could not climb the steep sides of the old tub and it was Bess's understood duty to help her upright and steady her first frail leg over the deep side. Mrs Spofforth, in consternation, heard her granddaughter cajoling the horse through the gate and then its clip-clop on the road. She began to howl, hoping that her cries would fly through the fanlight open at the top of the window, but the hoofsounds moved away and vanished. Mrs Spofforth was left in a patriotic five inches of water (the same, so the wireless announcer had said, as that used by the King himself). She banged and bawled but to no avail. Bess had gone on patrol and would not be back for two hours.

''S all right you sayin' that Churchill is our leader,' asserted one of the Radfield Compton men, Henry Hadfield, who had worked on Southampton Docks. 'But 'ee's one of the bosses and once a boss always a boss, I say. Look at 'is bloody cigar, I say. You only have to look at *that* to know.'

Charlie Fox, still flushed with the triumph of his single victorious run, leaned across the bar. 'What d'you want then, a bloke who smokes Woodbines? Who'd follow 'im, I ask you?' He raised his fingers in the Churchillian two-digit salute. 'V-for-victory. None of your trade unionists couldn't have thought that up. It takes a big brain to think up something like that.' He leaned over darkly. 'And watch your language in this pub, Henry Hadfield. We got a swear box here, you know.'

Charlie's mother leaned gladly across to the discomfited Henry. 'They say the Germans are tunnelling under the Channel,' she announced confidently. 'They've heard banging and 'ammering from the seabed, right off Dover.'

That day a new government emergency measure had been promulgated, ordering that no one but a 'servant of His Majesty's Government might be in possession of balloons or fireworks'. It was a restriction regarded with dismay in Binford. 'What about the balloons at the dance?' asked Charlie's mother. 'I like it when all the balloons are let loose.'

'How about our Molotov cocktails?' asked Peter Dove. 'Don't say they're going to stop us making them. We've got the fireworks.'

Ron Beyton, another Radfield Compton man, leaned towards Peter. 'You got Molotov cocktails?' he inquired cagily.

Peter moved away, regarding him suspiciously from a safe distance. 'We can't talk about them, you know that, Ron Beyton,' he said.

Ron retaliated. His voice rose to take in the surrounding cricketers. 'I hear tell that Binford LDV are going to have their telephone cut off. Not paying the bill.'

A silence dropped on the local men, beer mugs were set down, eyes widened. 'Don't be daft,' said Lennie Dove, who had struck three sixes out of the ground that afternoon. ''Ow could that be? They *can't* cut off the LDV phone. What if the invasion starts? Who's going to tell us? Never heard such a load of cobblers as that, Ron Beyton.'

Beyton drank slowly from his tankard. 'All right. Just see. My brother is in the post office at Lyndhurst, and he ought to know. They're going to cut you off unless you pay up.' He smirked. 'If the Jerries invade you'd better get somebody to light a signal fire.'

Bess rode easily across the darkening moorland. The forest was wide open for miles in places, with enclaves and enclosures of woods, cosseted in vales and in remote bends in the landscape. It was a secretive place that sometimes became threatening as night came on. A single bird, lost in the dusk, piped its note.

She had ridden these paths since childhood, although even she did not know all the forest ways. The mystery, freedom and solitude of the place caught her. That night she had promised to be at the Binford Annual Dance; Harry had said that he would try to get away from Portsmouth for the evening. She scarcely cared whether he did or did not.

The sun went at ten, casting a mauve light over the gorse and making the hills black and muscular. Merlin was anxious to go home. He was frightened by a suddenly rising sparrow hawk that whirred away into the dusk. Bess caught her breath and controlled the horse. She had just decided to turn around and go back towards the main road which would take her to Binford, now three or four miles away, when she saw an aeroplane coming towards her, flying low through the gloom. It was like a spectral bat. It made no sound, but glided from the last of the daylight, its wings dipping uncertainly. It passed above her with a gush of wind, dropping lower and disappearing over the black hillocks. There was a sound, scarcely more than a heavy thud. She was left in silence, with a breeze touching her face.

'It's crashed,' she said to the horse. 'It's come down.' She turned the animal on the path, making a hundred yards or more towards the road. Then she pulled it up and with an abrupt new excitement wheeled and began, cautiously at first but with increasing pace, to ride towards the bald skyline.

'Parashots,' nodded John Lampard, at the bar in the dance. 'Much more warlike – *aggressive* – don't you think than Local Defence Volunteers?' The initials LDV, he knew, had come to mean Look, Duck and Vanish.

Robert sighed massively. 'It's about time somebody took us seriously,' he said. He looked warm in his old dinner suit and stiff collar but he had insisted on wearing it; he had always worn it to the dance. It was a mark of distinction. His voice descended. 'They've even threatened to cut off the unit telephone.'

'Yes, I heard,' said Lampard, regarding him seriously.

'Just wait until the Hun comes,' forecast Robert hopefully. 'We don't get any respect or consideration, let alone guns, and as for cutting off the phone . . . Can you see a Panzer division commander having a whip round to pay for petrol for the tanks?' He grimaced and drank moodily. 'The New Forest Arcadians haven't improved over the years, have they?' he observed.

As if the musicians had overheard they ceased playing and Mrs Ben Bennett approached the apron of the stage, her teeth clamped into a smile like a grille. 'A waltz,' she announced like someone giving an order. 'General excuse-me waltz.'

'Pigs, sir,' offered Hob Hobson approaching Robert and John Lampard as the band scraped and blew into the measured tune. 'Sally, Sally,' they played, 'pride of our alley.' 'Pigs, they reckon, sir,' continued Hob. Unusually, he had drunk several pints. 'For warning of the approach of an enemy. Pigs tethered around the village would set up such a row as we'd be bound to hear the Germans . . . or maybe geese.'

Robert regarded him kindly, as if grateful, at least, for the thought. 'I don't think we'll have any difficulty in hearing the Huns, Hob,' he observed. 'The tanks squeak.'

'Cage birds are good,' persisted Hob, happy that Robert had treated his suggestion to an answer. 'Detecting gas, they're for. They use them down the coal mines for that, don't they.' He eyed Lampard, perhaps requiring confirmation, then mumbling excuses, turned and trundled away. 'Get a few parrots,' suggested Lampard. 'They'd be able to shout.'

380

Elizabeth and Millie came and stood beside the men. The waltz revolved anti-clockwise around the floor. People sang as they danced. 'Sally, Sally . . .' It was a homely song and they now all chorused it, turning as though slowly revolving in a great vat, a turning tide of feet, sending up clouds of chalk, one, two, three . . . one, two, three . . . the voices raised; the men lustily, the women trying to sing sweetly. It touched Elizabeth deeply:

> 'When skies are blue,
> You're beguiling,
> And when they're grey,
> You're still smiling, smiling . . .'

This was the British at bay.

Mary Mainprice, partnered by a shy soldier, stopped. 'We're going, mum,' she said. She let go the soldier and began to dab her eyes. The soldier stood awkwardly. He removed the chalk from the toecaps of his boots by rubbing each one on the back of the opposite trouser leg, then reddened harshly when he saw Robert had seen him do it. 'Chalk, sir,' he mumbled. 'Gets everywhere.'

'To America,' confirmed Mary. 'The children and me. They say it will be soon.' Hurriedly her eyes went in the direction of Robert and John. Both looked away and moved, conversing, towards the bar. The woman seemed relieved they had gone. 'It's like I'm running away. But I'm only thinking about the kiddies.'

Elizabeth patted her hand. 'You are doing your best for them,' she assured.

Mary smiled gratefully. 'I won't be a minute,' she said to the soldier. She returned to Elizabeth and Millie. 'They said they'd give us a week's notice of sailing. The boys are all full of it, of course, going to America, so is the little girl, but I don't know. Going across the sea frightens me, what with their father in Singapore and not knowing what to do. He worries because nothing's happening to him out there and we're here. You'll have to get somebody else to clean, mum. My sister Marigold can do it.'

Millie said: 'They wouldn't send children if they didn't think it was safe, Mary, I'm sure of that. No wonder they're excited.'

Mary Mainprice sighed. 'I still don't rightly know,' she sniffed. She moved back towards the soldier, marching quietly on the spot. 'I'll see everybody before we go. It might be for always.'

The waltz finished and the last reluctant voice died away. Robert returned with some drinks for the ladies. They stood in a silent group then, watching the village people. 'A Nightingale Sang in Berkeley Square' was next. They joined partners and began once again the steady revolution around the room.

'Ah,' said Elizabeth with pleasure, 'Harry's here.'

Her son came in the door, and grinning, came towards them. He kissed his mother and Millie. Robert said: 'We're all safe tonight then. They wouldn't have let you out if they thought Jerry was going to try it.'

'I had a word with Hitler,' said Harry. He accepted a drink, then touched Millie's arm. 'Want to hop?' he suggested. 'It'll all be finished before long.'

Millie looked surprised. As they moved on to the

floor she said in his ear, 'You're wasting your time, sailor. I'm married.'

'I don't care,' he whispered. 'Life's too short.' He looked around the floor.

'She's not here,' said Millie.

'Bess?'

'Who else? She hasn't turned up at all.'

'You'll do,' he said, putting his cheek next to hers. 'Any port in a storm.'

They stopped talking and danced quietly together for a while, her breasts against his jacket. 'A nightingale sang in Berkeley Square,' hummed Harry. 'I wonder how many people in Binford have ever been to Berkeley Square?'

'Not many,' she said. 'I haven't been to London for years.' When she spoke her lips brushed his ear. 'At least now they've stopped playing about hanging the washing on the Siegfried line.'

'It sounds a bit silly after what's happened,' he said. He glanced towards the door for Bess.

Millie said: 'James said it comes from a song called something like: "When we are married we'll have sausages for tea."'

He laughed, surprised. 'Fancy James knowing that.'

'That's exactly what I thought.'

Elizabeth watched them with affection. Robert said: 'Some things never never change, do they?' He performed a brief bow. 'May I have the pleasure?'

Elizabeth gave a mock curtsy. 'Of course,' she said. They moved on to the floor. 'Any quickstep nonsense and we leave,' suggested Robert. She nodded. He had never been a good dancer, apparently having to think of each step. They revolved heavily around the room.

Yes, it was still the same, and yet, Elizabeth thought, there were some missing. Some would never be there again. Old Sonny, who had always worn his best blue suit, waistcoat and white silk muffler, the muffler thrown back across his shoulder like the daredevil scarf of some air ace. Mary Mainprice's husband, who had been an extravagant exponent of the South American Tango, flexing his knees, and pointing his thin wife across the floor, like a lance.

There were others, serving far away, now only known by their awkward letters home, some in ships on the oceans; some already in distant graves, far from Binford.

It was getting late. Smoke hung like a canopy in the hall, the chalk still sent up its mystic puffs, the band blared through the lit haze, and the bar was still clinking with glasses and the sound of hearty voices. At the end of the waltz, Mrs Ben Bennett advanced to the fore of the New Forest Arcadians and announced: 'Now – all form a ring for the Hokey Cokey!

'Come on, Robert,' grinned Elizabeth mis-chievously. 'Even you can do this.' Millie and Harry came to join them.

'But . . . it's . . .' Robert protested, 'ridiculous!'

'Come along,' urged Millie. 'You stand between us.'

The quartet joined the elongated chain, facing inwards, all the faces beaming in the smoke. The band bounced into the first notes.

'You put your left arm in, your left arm out, in-out, in-out, shake it all about. You do the Hokey Cokey, and you turn around, that's what it's all about. Hi!'

The carefree sound filtered through the wooden

seams of the old pavilion. The door had been opened to admit some air and the thick curtain had been tugged across it to keep the light from straying.

'Ohhhhhh, the Hokey Cokey.'
It's crazy, but it's Okeee . . .'

Out on to the moonlit cricket field the chorus drifted, where two limping, trying-to-run figures were making for the pavilion. Johanes Van Lorn tugged Mrs Spofforth along by her bony hand. The Dutchman was confused and panicky.

'Hokey Cokey,' he echoed. 'These people are mad.' He started forward again. 'Come, we must tell them the news.'

As they staggered on another messenger was pounding, heavy-booted, through the village from the LDV guard post towards the green and the pavilion. George Lavington, in his musty LDV uniform, panted as he ran carrying an envelope thrust out in front of him like a relay runner carrying a baton to the next man. He blundered into the pavilion as the villagers were crowded about Mrs Spofforth and Mr Van Lorn. 'Mr Lovatt,' he interrupted. 'Mr Lovatt, sir, there's a message.'

Robert stepped importantly forward and read the slip of paper. 'Observation post at Lymington,' he said to John Lampard, 'report a plane – probably a Hun – down in the forest.' He looked about him eagerly for his men. 'We'd better find him before somebody else does.'

The horse was nervous in the night. It gave shies and

snorts at shadowed objects and Bess had to urge him along thin paths and under the low branches of clustered trees. 'Merlin, come on now, Merlin, for Christ's sake. Nearly there. Come on, damn you.'

She was herself apprehensive. Twice she halted on the upward ride, debating whether to turn and try to regain the vanished road. Around and underfoot all was black, the sky a shade paler with a new moon on the rise.

The upland part of the forest, most of it rough moor, was saucered in places and the depressions, despite the dry summer, harboured boggy ponds through which the horse trudged uncertainly. Animal and rider stopped, startled at the cackle of a night creature.

But they went on, progressing tentatively towards the ridge that formed the skyline. It had a ragged fringe of low trees, like unkempt hair, and as Bess reached the final gradient, she caught her breath as she thought she saw a brief slip of light among the branches. She pulled the horse up and it pawed the mossy ground unhappily. There it was again, the light, certain and distinct now, moving about, reflected on the thin limbs of the copse. Bess hesitated for the final time. Biting her lip, she considered dismounting and creeping the rest of the way. But she felt safer on the horse. Whispering she urged Merlin forward. They moved from the upland grass into the scattered branches and out on to the ridge and there she halted again and saw what had happened.

The moon was small but had given a faint illumination to the shallow vale above which she stood. In the centre of the basin, flat as a butterfly pinned to a board, was the aeroplane. The torchlight was fluttering near the cockpit and she could see a figure moving and crouched. Then the beam jolted along the fuselage of the plane and with a sick start she saw the Nazi swastika on its flank. At that moment the man saw her and the beam of the flashlight picked her out, sitting white-faced upon the horse. Merlin snorted but only quivered. Bess held him. 'Please help.' The voice came through the dimness. 'I need help.'

She called back: 'I'm coming.' The firmness of her tone surprised her but she was aware of her trembling as she dismounted and, looping the rein around a branch, walked down the gradient towards the fallen aircraft. At once she saw that it had come to rest in a long, reedy mire, the sort that the basins of the forest held throughout the year. She was not familiar with this place but she had seen others like it. The wild horses and the forest donkeys drank there.

'It is good,' said the man. She could perceive the oval of his face now. 'You will help. My comrade is hurt. He will die, I think.'

Bess had reached the side of the marshy ground, and the plane's wing with its black and white cross thrust towards her like a plank. 'It is safe,' said the German. He stood up and she realized, with a kind of relief, that she was taller than he.

'What can I do?' she said. 'Where is the other man?'

'In the plane now,' replied the airman. 'There is much blood. You can step along the wing, lady. It is safe.'

Bess wondered whether he were assuring her about the metal or himself. Bravely she stepped on to the wing and walked carefully towards him. It was a curious meeting. He stood and said: 'I am Paul Heinz Teller.'

'Bess Spofforth,' she strangely heard herself answering. He was broad and young, his eyes bright in the gloom. His flying helmet, its strap and buckle hanging, framed his face like the bonnet of a baby. He was more than an inch shorter than her. She had a fleeting thought that he might want to shake hands and that she should refuse. She looked towards his waist for signs of a gun but she could see none.

'Let's do something for him,' she said decisively. 'Is he very badly hurt?'

'I think he will die,' repeated the German. 'We must get him from that place and help him.'

Bess moved towards the open cockpit. The second man was unconscious, lolled back, his head hardly seeming attached to his neck.

'The door is not good,' said the pilot. 'It is broken, see. I cannot open, so we must lift him from there. I have a bag with dressings and those things.' He climbed up on to the plane, so that he was above his comrade. 'You must also,' he beckoned to the girl.

Bess, scarcely believing what was happening, found herself clambering up the side of the aircraft. The young German held out his hand and she took it. He pulled her up, then reached down, slipped the parachute harness from his comrade and freed the seat belt. Bess could smell the blood. The man's face was like snow. The pilot made a small sound, like a sob, and reached down. He straightened up after a moment and said to her, 'He breathed a few minutes ago, lady. But now there is nothing. He has died for the Führer.'

Like massed shadows the villagers streamed from the dance, their voices babbling across the moonlit field. Robert led the way, like the leader of a sheriff's posse, striding out with his Local Defence Volunteers and the uniformed Harry a fraction behind. Mrs Spofforth, enjoying the drama, flapped along with Elizabeth and Millie, Van Lorn stern-faced beside her.

The grandmother pulled her huge woolly coat closer about her shoulders and sounded off again: 'She's probably dead by now! Serve her right, leaving me jammed in the bath!' She pointed out the Dutchman to the two women. 'He had to pull me out.'

Van Lorn raised his ragged eyes towards the new moon. 'Not a nice thing,' he muttered mildly.

'Harry,' called Elizabeth when they had reached the road, 'hadn't you better go home and put some old clothes on? You mustn't spoil your uniform on what might well be a wild goose chase.'

'Well, *I'm* going like this,' Robert put in fiercely. 'We have to move into action swiftly.'

Elizabeth regarded the evening suit. 'Well, you can't very well do much more damage to that, dear,' she observed.

'For God's sake, take it seriously, Elizabeth,' he said hoarsely, putting his big head nearer her ear. 'The girl may be in genuine danger. There's a Luftwaffe plane crashed somewhere out there, remember.'

Elizabeth said: 'I'll go home and bring two pairs of dungarees. You might need that evening suit again.'

'Bring the revolver too, will you,' he called after her. 'It's in the safe.'

She felt like calling back, 'And the bullet?' but she did not want to humiliate him.

She went up the night road with Millie. Their laughter floated back. Damned women, thought Robert. He wheeled on his men. 'All right, chaps. Everybody rendezvous at the Spofforth house in fifteen minutes. We'll need torches and sticks. And, of course, weapons. I'll bring the tommy-gun.' He looked up at the July sky. 'At least we've got a modicum of moon.'

Donald Petrie said, 'It won't be for long. There's rain on the way. What about roping in that gypsy, Cooper? He knows everywhere in the forest.'

Robert agreed at once. 'We need a tracker.' He brightened. 'Like the last of the Mohicans.' The group scattered to their homes, Robert striding with Harry towards the LDV guard post. Mrs Spofforth was escorted home by Van Lorn, the old pair quarrelling and stumbling along the narrow pavement through the village.

'Your mother thinks it's all some sort of schoolboy lark,' grumbled Robert.

'In this case she's offhand because she doesn't like Bess,' said Harry.

His father briefly stopped in his stride. 'Good God, doesn't she? And why not?'

Harry swallowed in the dark. 'Oh, nothing. She's just taken a dislike.'

The older man was striding on. 'Thinks you've been sowing the wild oats in that direction, does she?' Harry gulped with surprise. His father gave a fierce sniff and added amazingly: Well, don't blame you. Would have done myself at one time. Women never understand that sort of thing, you know.' They marched in new silence to the LDV post.

In the oil-lamp light Malcolm Smith and Sid Root sat crouched on boxes staring up at the morse key as if it were a spirit planchette board. They stood up as Robert and Harry came round the black-out blanket, their shadows giants on the whitewashed wall.

'Any news?' asked Robert.

'Not a tap,' said Malcolm looking at the morse key again.

'We been thinking we might 'ear,' said Sid Root.

'We're going to search the forest,' Robert told them decisively.

The two men looked surprised. 'All of it, Mr Lovatt?' inquired Sid.

'No, Root, not all of it. We're hoping for some leads.' He rolled his eyes towards Harry.

Millie brought two folded pairs of garden dungarees. Elizabeth, she said, would be coming shortly with coffee and sandwiches. Harry said: 'She doesn't believe it's real, does she?'

Millie said: 'She thinks it's just another bit of Spofforth family drama. So do I, for what it's worth.'

She watched him climbing into the overalls. Her hand went out and she helped him pull them up around his neck. He glanced at her and nodded in amusement towards his father struggling to pull the trousers over his evening clothes like a pantomime horse getting dressed.

'Ah, here are the rations,' said Millie. Elizabeth came through the shadows at the door carrying a haversack which she placed heavily on the table. 'Enough there for three weeks,' she announced. 'Bring back anything you don't finish. We can brighten up any left-overs for the Red Cross tea on Thursday.' Seriously she regarded Robert who was taking the tommy-gun to pieces. She handed him Major-General Sound's revolver in its holster. He growled his thanks. 'Do you really think it's worth going out there at this time of night?' she asked. 'You know how difficult it can be in the forest in the dark. If I know anything, Bess Spofforth has probably ridden over to some friend at Linley Green or somewhere and forgotten to telephone.'

'There is also a report of a crashed German plane,' Robert pointed out politely but without looking up from the tommy-gun. 'We can't ignore that.' He continued to examine the gun. Harry could see that his mother was angry. It was a long time since he had seen her like that. She turned and walked towards the door.

'I imagine,' she said narrowly, only half turning about, 'that whatever situation that young lady finds herself in, she will be more than able to adapt to it. Good night, Harry. Good night, Robert.'

'Good night, mother,' said Harry. He moved forward towards her then stopped, annoyed by the childishness of the scene. The other men were watching.

'Good night, dear,' added Robert casually, after a pause, and when she was almost gone. He still did not look up. He slammed the tommy-gun magazine home with emphasis. 'Don't worry about us.'

*

A few minutes later they left the LDV post and went, already in single file, along the village street towards the Spofforth house. Robert led the rank, his hand patting the huge and shining holster; Harry followed, self-consciously carrying the tommy-gun. The dungarees retained the smell of the garden compost heap. The moon was even less certain now, clouds were mustering, although the air remained breezeless and close.

Petrie had joined them, and Stevens, summoned from his house, with Gates the gamekeeper and Rob Noyes, his stark face shadowed by his insurance man's bowler hat. Malcolm Smith and Sid Root had been left to man the guard post. Outside the Spofforth house, the Dove brothers and a dozen others were waiting. Robert confronted the contingent. 'This is our first definite operation,' he told them grimly. 'Other units, army and LDV, will be searching by now. Let's be the first to find the girl or the Jerry, preferably the Jerry.'

He was interrupted by Mrs Spofforth bellowing from an upstairs window: 'She went up that way, Lovatt! Straight up the bloody road. Left a helpless old woman in the bath.'

Robert sighed. 'Thank you, Mrs Spofforth. Go off to bed now. You're showing a light, you know.'

'That's not all I've been showing tonight,' the brazen old woman retorted.

It was her final word of the night. Violently she slammed down the sash and Robert, making sure she had actually gone, turned to his men. 'We'll keep in single file for the time being,' he told them. 'There's no point in spreading out, not in the dark. We'll be falling down holes or getting lost ourselves. If anyone spots anything odd, he gives warning with an owl-hoot. Understood?'

They nodded uncomfortable agreement. It was difficult to believe it was real. 'What about the gypsy?' asked Petrie. 'I think he would be pretty useful up there.'

'I know where he is,' offered Gates grimly. 'The Coopers have been camping out at High Copse. Helping themselves to my pheasants.'

'He is a good horse,' nodded the German briskly. He walked round the animal and patted its haunch. Bess did not know what to do. The clouds had covered the splintered moon and the stars and they were alone in the dark countryside, with a newly sprung wind wheezing through the scraggy trees. 'I have a horse in France,' he continued. 'Every day when I am not flying I ride him.'

Bess said: 'If you rode this one you might be able to escape.' She was afraid of his calmness. She added unconvincingly: 'You might reach the coast and steal a boat. I bet you could get to France.'

The young man laughed. 'It would be a famous thing, I think. But in the Luftwaffe uniform I think maybe the soldiers would see me.' He regarded her quizzically in the darkness. Their eyes were used to it now. She could clearly see his confident smile. 'But maybe I take your clothes and ride to the sea.'

'You could try it,' she said defiantly. She knew she was the prisoner.

He grinned. 'You want me to go, I think, lady.'

Bess felt hollow. 'Well, I wouldn't be sorry,' she said.

His arm went from the horse's rump to her. She started back but he was quick to reassure. 'Please, you must not be afraid. You are with a German officer not a Russian. We will wait for the daytime to come and then you can take me to the English as prisoner.' His hand patted her sleeve. 'You will be famous for your braveness. And I will wait a little time until my comrades come to unlock the prison door. It will not be so long.'

A little reassured, Bess murmured, 'Thank you.' She looked around and said: 'It is no good trying to leave here now. This is a terrible place for wandering about in the dark.'

Casually he sat down on the rising ground and then moved over, as if on a couch, to make room for her. 'I did not know there are such places in England. I thought it was a country too small to have places where you can be lost.'

'It's not that small,' Bess retorted with sudden spirit. 'You just wait.'

He laughed jovially. 'Very good, lady,' he said. 'That is loving of your country.' He became thoughtful. 'All countries are big when you are a soldier. When you have to win them.'

'Why win them then?' she asked. Her fears were almost gone now. And – if she got through the night safely – she was going to be a heroine. And he seemed a decent man.

'We win them because in war you must win, or you lose,' he shrugged. 'Already I have my brother dead and my friend from my school. And now Alfred in the Messerschmitt.' He nodded towards the crouching plane. 'We pay a big price for our winnings.'

A skein of drizzle drifted across the clearing. He wiped it away from his head, straightening his fair hair as he did so. 'The English rain,' he murmured. 'It is true about the English rain.'

'Nonsense,' Bess replied sharply. 'It's been the most beautiful summer. Sunshine all the time. This is the first rain we've had for weeks. Actually we can do with it for the crops.'

'Yes, yes,' he pacified. 'Please, lady, I am sorry I insult the English rain. But it will make us wet.'

'Not half it won't,' she said, getting up and spreading her hands above her head.

'This is not good,' he said, trying to do the same thing. 'Is there nowhere?' As he said it the drops lessened, the rain seeming to have second thoughts. 'Maybe it is not coming,' he suggested.

'Don't count your chickens,' she said. 'It will be back. There's plenty up there. We'll get soaked. I can sit under the horse's belly. I've done that before now. He doesn't mind. I just hang on to his leg like a post to keep him still. But he might not like you doing it. In any case, there's not enough room and he is apt to pee.'

He did not understand because she spoke quickly. He said: 'There is something. I have my parachute. It will make a roof for us. Like a tent.'

'Oh, will it?' she said dubiously. The rain was beginning again. He was already hurrying to the plane. He walked surely along the wing and she saw him lean towards the open cockpit. She felt her heart sounding against her chest. He straightened and returned through the gloom carrying two bulky packs.

'One for us,' he smiled, 'and poor Alfred will give

his to the horse.' He stood in the thickening rain holding the packs, one in each hand. Seriously he continued: 'But if you want we can have different tents. One for the prisoner and one for the brave lady.'

'That's just silly,' Bess said with more conviction than she felt. 'Sitting in two tents. Ridiculous. These things don't matter in wartime. Give one to Merlin.'

'Ha, Merlin,' nodded the German. 'He will be happy.'

'I'll do it,' she said. 'He might take a bite out of you. And then you'd report me to the Red Cross.'

'Bad treatment for a prisoner,' he agreed with a smile. He began to pull the silver parachute from its bag, dragging it clear and spreading the silk on the ground. The rain was steady now. It was running down his forehead.

'I'll take it,' she said. 'You get the other one out. Otherwise we'll be soaked through.' She further unfolded the silk and dragged it like a train towards the worried-looking horse. She took off the saddle and put it on the ground. 'There,' she said, spreading it over the animal's back and head. She tied it by the cords, like a bonnet, below the horse's neck. He remained passive. 'Right-o,' she murmured when she had covered him. 'You look like a real wizard now, Merlin. Say thank you to the nice Kraut.'

She turned and saw that the German was attempting to arrange the other parachute over the low branches of the scruffy trees. Her fear had almost evaporated now and she went forward to help him. 'Merlin says thank you,' she said. 'He appreciates the thought.'

As she saw him making the tent her apprehension returned. It would be very enclosed in there. 'It's very small,' she said doubtfully.

'We have some for us,' he said patting his backside. 'For us to lie on.'

'Sit on,' she corrected firmly, hearing her voice rise embarrassingly. 'We *will* be sitting up.'

He grinned. 'It is right. But, lady, if you are not wanting this way then we must take the parachute from the horse. Then we can sit in our different houses and talk like people do over the walls.'

Bess grinned at his frankness. 'Oh, all right. I'm sorry. But you must admit this situation is very peculiar.'

He shone the torch pointing it up from below his chin. It gave his face deep shadows. 'I have told you that I am a Luftwaffe officer,' he repeated with almost comic solemnity. 'And that is I am also a gentleman. Do not be afraid.'

He lifted the hem of the parachute and with not entirely mock courtesy waved his arm for her to enter. The rain was thickening. 'You first,' she said. He bowed and crawled beneath the silk. She bit her lip, then, knowing she was getting soaked, her hair was wringing, she crawled in after him. They sat upright, awkwardly, in the torchlight. The rain clattered on the trees and onto the flapping parachute. 'I think I should sit near the door,' she said as if she owed him an explanation. She moved the material that formed the entrance through which she had just crawled.

'I am the prisoner,' the young man agreed amiably. He lifted up the hem at his end of the tent. 'But there is a door this way also.'

She laughed. 'This whole thing is mad,' she said.

'There is much madness in the world,' he agreed. He fumbled beneath his flying jacket and she watched nervously but he only produced a bottle. 'Schnapps,' he said. 'The best. We have it in the plane for times like now.'

'Oh,' she said tentatively. 'I've never tasted that.'

'It is good,' he assured her. 'Schnapps is good for warmth.'

'You're going to drink it now?' she asked nervously. 'Why don't you keep it for later.' She knew she was sounding desperate. 'For the prison camp.'

He laughed and patted her arm, a touch without threat. 'I think we drink some now, for the coldness.' He poured a measure into the cap of the bottle and offered it to her. She made to sip it but he said: 'It is better to take at once. It is bad for the lips.' He made a swigging motion with his hand.

She took the cap and bravely did as he said. The liquid blazed down her throat, searing the inside of her chest and landing in her stomach. 'Jesus Christ,' she spluttered. She coughed and after a hesitation he patted her back in a cordial manner.

'It is good,' he repeated practically, 'for keeping warm.' He poured and took a gulp himself, smiling afterwards. 'Another?' he suggested. They both drank again. Then he put the cap on the bottle.

'You're going to stop now?' she inquired.

His fair eyebrows went up. 'You would like?'

'Well, just a sip, well, a swallow, if it's all right with you.'

'Of course.' He poured the liquid into the cap. 'Perhaps only half?' he asked.

'Yes, you'd better make it half. I wouldn't want to rob you.'

They each had another drink. He recapped the bottle and they sat there in the torchlight, the rain vibrating on the silk. An odd delayed embarrassment came over them, a retarded shyness. Eventually Bess said: 'In circumstances like this the English always sing.'

'Germans also are singers,' he claimed. 'We have songs for every happy thing and every unhappy thing. Would you want to sing now?'

Before she could comment he began to hum and then, drifting into the words, to sing strongly but not loudly: *'Deutschland, Deutschland über Alles . . .'*

'That's a hymn tune,' she said. 'Praise the Lord for He is Glorious.'

'It is *our* national anthem.'

'Bloody hell, you're *not* singing that, mate! All right . . .' She broke lustily into song herself:

> 'There'll always be an England,
> Where there's a country lane' . . .

He laughed and chimed in, singing against her.

> *'Deutschland, Deutschland über Alles . . .'*

At the outrageous climax of their chorus a distant thunder roll sounded and a wan light touched the tent for an instant, the rain increasing on the silk around them, like fingers drumming.

'Donner and Blitzen,' said Bess. 'And that's all the German I know apart from Hansel and Gretel.'

'It is good,' he enthused solemnly.

'Donner and Blitzen are two of Santa Claus's reindeer,' she answered. 'Donner and Blitzen, Bellman and True. Could I have some more Schnapps, please?'

'There is some,' he said without emphasis, picking up the bottle. 'For you and for me.' They each drank another capful. She attempted to swallow and choked again. Once more he patted her on the back.

When she had recovered Bess told him: 'You're not bad for a German.'

'*Danke*,' he answered with polite gravity. 'I am only a man dressed up. Like the Santa Claus.'

'Your English is very good. Have you been in England before?'

'Doncaster, Swindon, Crewe Junction,' he recited. 'My English is from school in Germany but my father, you understand, was a railway engineer. I was in all those places for some time with him, with the locomotives. Swindon is very nice.'

'Never been there,' she said. 'I must try it.'

'And the English will be good for me to speak during the coming time.'

'In the prison camp?'

Silently he handed the bottle to her and without waiting she took another drink. So did he. 'No, when the occupation is here,' he said.

Bess felt her face flush. 'I wouldn't count on that!' she replied hotly. Her eyes lolled heavily. He was leaning back on the ground. His face was exhausted. Lightning, swift as a wing beat, illuminated the tent. Thunder exploded above them. The end of the parachute flew up in the gusty rain. 'Poor Merlin,' she said. She crawled towards the opening and looked out into the streaming wet. Another burst of lightning lit the surroundings. The crashed plane showed up vividly. She looked around wildly. There was no horse.

'Oh God,' she muttered, slowly moving back into the cover. 'He's buggered off.' She saw that the young German was deep asleep. 'Gone,' she added, her voice dropping.

The initial rain had begun by the time Robert led the LDV men as far as High Copse. He had tramped just ahead of the contingent, even now straggling because of the difficult narrowness of the terrain and the unfitness of most of the members. Gates, the gamekeeper, puffed alongside him and Harry was just a few paces behind. He watched Gates's back heaving as he stumbled along the track and wondered how he managed to do his job. Twice the party had to be halted so the gamekeeper could recover his breath. ''Tis walking at night does it,' Gates said, glaring a challenge at the village men held up behind him. 'In the daylight I'm all right, see, but 'tis different *sort* of walking at night.'

As the clouds thickened, darkness multiplied and the first rain touched their foreheads, they reached the gypsy encampment, a clearing in a wooded place. 'Watch out for they dogs, sir,' warned Gates. 'Nasty as hell they are.'

The camp was dark except for the eye of a smouldering fire now being finally deadened by the wet. Dogs began to bark as they reached the clearing but they seemed to be enclosed somewhere at the rear of the ragged, low tents and the strange habitations, the benders, made like igloos from the bowed branches of low trees, patched and thatched with twigs, cardboard, canvas and pieces of corrugated iron. Robert shone his torch around but there was no movement.

'Not very wide awake,' grumbled Robert. 'Fine lot of gypsies they are, I must say.' He peered at the entrance of one of the houses. 'Gates,' he said, 'give them a shout, old chap. You know their lingo, I suppose. You can't very well knock on the door, can you.'

Gates strutted to the fore. 'Hey, come on out!' he shouted unequivocally. 'Come on, out you come!'

The response came from behind. A polite clearing of a number of throats and some children's giggles. The LDV men turned and saw in their torchlight that the trees were full of gypsies, their brown faces, bright eyes, at all levels, staring out. There were men and women, old crones and ancient fathers, children close to the ground, looking around the tree trunks and lodged in the branches.

'Oh, there you are,' said Robert.

An old man stepped from the trunk shadows. He wore a long, aromatic overcoat. 'At last we're getting some rain,' he mentioned politely.

Robert wiped the wet from his domed forehead and agreed. 'Is Mr Cooper here?' he asked.

Every man stepped from the trees. They stood in a half-circle with the LDV men in the middle. 'Every man is Mr Cooper,' said the elder. 'That's my name. And his . . . and his . . . and his . . .' He pointed at random men. 'Even his,' he added indicating a skinny youth who half hid behind another, 'though we don't know right if he is one. We never know where he came from.'

'*Liberty* Cooper,' said Gates with impatient gruffness. He looked apologetically at Robert. 'Sorry, Mr Lovatt, but you can't get anywhere with this lot unless you pin them down. I know too well. We'll be here all night.'

'We got several Liberty Coopers,' pointed out the chief happily. 'It's a popular name with us.'

Gates snorted and strode forward. He pointed to Liberty Cooper, known in the village and the farms. 'This Liberty Cooper,' he said testily.

'What you want?' asked the young man.

Robert stepped forward. 'I'll take over,' he said to Gates. The gamekeeper grimaced and stepped back with the other men. 'We wondered,' Robert said with deference, 'if you would spare some time to guide us up through the forest?'

'You looking for the girl?' asked Liberty at once. 'She went up to the top of Pine Place. She was on that nifty horse.'

'What time?' put in Harry. His father frowned at him and he retreated. 'Any idea?' the son added lamely.

'Getting dark time.'

'Didn't see a plane, did you?' asked Robert. 'A Hun.'

'It went over. No engines,' said Liberty. 'Plenty of scrap metal lying around somewhere.'

'Didn't you see the markings?' insisted Harry.

His father scowled again but said: 'Didn't you see the marking?'

'It was good as dark,' shrugged Liberty. 'We can't see a thing at night.'

Apologetically Robert brushed the drizzle from his eyes. 'No, of course, sorry, old chap. But you know your way through the forest, don't you?'

'Sometimes,' shrugged Liberty. 'You want to go an' look?'

'That was the plan. If you can spare a few minutes.'

Liberty nodded. 'All right,' he said. 'I don't know how. Sometimes I fall in the ponds too.' He pulled an old coat about his shoulders. The gypsies, seeing the confrontation was over, began to crawl under the bent branches and into the tents. A child began to cry.

'They thought it was Germans coming,' said Liberty nodding towards the encampment. He looked at the curious patrol. 'Stay in one line,' he suggested.

'Good chap,' said Robert. 'Let's get a move on, shall we?'

Liberty nodded, but then abruptly turned back towards the encampment. He went into one of the benders and returned to hand Robert his service revolver. Robert's hand went to the empty holster. 'You have to watch out,' Liberty explained casually. 'Somebody thought it was nobody's.'

Liberty Cooper led the way, then came Robert, puffing gamely and glad it was so dark; he tried to hush his breath but Harry close behind could hear it. Petrie was next, at a strong and steady gait, then Stevens, and behind him the long, motley tail of the company, spread over two hundred yards of rough track. The rain had eased for a while but now, towards the sea, thunder sounded and lightning flickered. 'We could do with this,' murmured Harold Clark, the farm hand, trudging at the end of the column. 'So my guv'nor says.'

Sid Turner, the forester, grunted a few feet in front. 'Stops fires,' he said. The insurance man, Rob Noyes, took off his bowler hat and fingered it, feeling for damage by the rain. Silently he replaced it on his ashen head. Because of his profession and his bowler Rob considered himself a little aloof.

'*I* ought to be up in front,' grumbled Sid as he trudged. 'I work in the forest, don't I? I knows my way around as well as that gypsy bloke. And a sight better than old Gates. Gamekeeper! Sits on 'is arse all day having a smoke behind some 'edge.'

Rob stopped and turned carefully. The rain had begun streaming again. 'Why don't you go up the front and take charge then?' he inquired. The water was dropping in a cascade from the rim of the bowler. One outfall struck the top of Rob's nose, long and white like a parsnip. 'Go ahead. You show them.'

Sid glowered at him in the dark. 'I don't push myself forward like some,' he argued grimly. 'I don't know what it's got to do with you anyway, Rob Noyes. What do you know about the forest? You sells insurance round the doors.'

'When it comes to street fighting,' sniffed Rob, 'I'll know my way around.' He turned and trooped on. The figures ahead, dipping and stumbling through the rain, were scarcely discernible. Surface water was making the narrow path slippery. Harold fell over and cursed as he picked himself up. Gorse and brambles pulled at their trousers and patches of low dank trees smote them as they struggled on.

406

At the head of the odd column Robert called a halt, raising his arm like an old-time cavalry officer. Those immediately behind stopped but there were those further back who did not see the signal and, bent against the rain, collided with the men in front. Oaths sounded. Eventually the entire group of eighteen men caught up. They were on a stony forest track running at right angles to the single path they had travelled.

'Right,' whispered Robert, 'gather round, chaps.'

'What's he whispering for?' Harold asked Sid.

'Case the Germans 'ear, you daft,' replied the forester.

''Ow we goin' to find that young tart if we goes about shushing?' pursued Harold.

'Chaps . . . men,' intoned Robert, 'Mr Cooper has suggested we can spread out a bit here, along the track. Split up, half go each way. I'll take the right-hand side and Stevens and Petrie the left. Sub-Lieutenant Lovatt had better come with his father.'

He got his intended grins, the oddments of rural teeth showing like small windows. 'Sir?' asked Harold Clark. 'Can we call out for this young lady? Or do we still think they Jerries are about?'

'Good question,' acknowledged Robert. Harold beamed in the rain. Robert continued: 'I think it would be as wise if we kept quiet. That plane may have come down anywhere. So we'll have to look for Miss Spofforth silently. Just . . . look.' He glanced around. Thunder began to lumber nearer. Lightning fluttered across the low hills, a momentary vision of bright green and yellow gorse.

'We might see 'er by the lightning,' suggested Harold in a low voice.

'Spofforth,' ruminated Rob Noyes as they turned away and began to walk left on the stony path. The rain was running down it like a stream over a pebble bed. He shook the rain from his hat with a twist of his head. 'Not a family I know well. They're not Co-op insurance people.'

'Spofforth was a bowler,' said Sid dragging his legs over the stones. 'Cricketer. Years ago.'

As if reminded, Rob took his hat off and shook it fiercely. He eyed the bowl as if seeking leaks. 'My father's, that was,' he said. 'That bowler's been miles and miles. You couldn't get one like that now.'

Harold was straying behind them, with the rest of the contingent spread out for two hundred yards ahead along the gritty track. Harold had been studying the rain rivering darkly between his boots as he tramped and wondering if he would ever get a rifle, when a sound in a clearing to his left made him turn. A big flash of lightning illuminated the area and in it Harold saw a silvery-caped steed madly paw the air before plunging into the trees.

Stark-faced, the farm labourer stumbled forward, mouth open, and caught Sid's arm. Rob Noyes, in front, stopped and looked.

'Sid, Rob,' trembled Harold. 'I just seen a fucking ghost!'

It was daylight at four-thirty, a soaked dawn, grey to the horizon, birds muttering. Bess awoke stiff and cold and saw that the German pilot's head had moved to lie against her breast in the night. He opened his eyes.

'Sleep well?' she asked.

'I must tell you that I have not been sleeping for one

hour,' confessed the young man. 'But I was liking that place so I stayed there. I will remember this night when I am in the prison camp.'

Bess did not reply. She crawled to the opening of the parachute and out into the damp day. She shivered. 'I remember it being like this when I went camping with the girl guides.'

'What is that?' he inquired following her out. He handed her the Schnapps bottle and she was surprised that it was almost empty. She took a drink and felt it warm her inside. He drank the rest and carefully put the bottle under the parachute. 'What is this girl guides, please?'

She was looking around for the horse. 'Well, it's like . . . well, weren't you ever in the boy scouts? Camping and parades and all that?'

He nodded. 'Also I was in the Hitler Youth,' he replied soberly. 'It is the same.'

Bess had reached the top of the rise so that she could look out down the hill. 'Ah,' she called without turning, 'there he is. He's coming this way. Good old Merlin. He's still wearing his parachute.'

The young airman was looking at his watch. 'It is near to five o'clock,' he said. He held up his wrist. 'I have a Swiss watch, see.'

Surprised at the boast, she said: 'So have I. There.' She showed him.

'The Swiss make things for others who are enemies,' he observed.

She had come down and stood by him now.

There was silence between them with only a few piping birds sounding. 'I'm sorry,' she said. 'I'm not even sure what I'm sorry about, but I am.'

'It is okay,' he shrugged. 'That is how everything is now. I think I must give you my gun.'

'God! You've got a gun? Where is it?'

'In the plane,' he smiled. 'I did not want you to shoot me. I will get it. Then we must go.'

'Yes, I'm afraid so.' She turned as Merlin appeared at the top of the bank. 'Ah, there you are,' she said. 'Poor old thing.'

The horse trotted gratefully to her. The parachute was sagging to one side though still secured around the animal's neck and under its belly. She could not release the knots. The German walked along the wing from the plane. He handed her a pistol. 'For you,' he said.

'I can't undo the knots,' she said, taking it nervously. It was heavy.

'Also, I have a knife,' he said. 'I have brought that too.'

He cut the knots in the parachute cords and quietly handed her the knife. 'Now you must take me to the soldiers,' he said.

'I suppose so,' she replied without looking at him. 'Let me saddle Merlin and you can climb up behind.'

The young German half frowned. 'It would be better if I was walking at the side,' he said. 'As a prisoner.'

'You're riding pillion,' she said firmly. She turned away from him and began to saddle the horse. He walked back to the edge of the mire and studied the plane. She saw his shoulders drop for a moment before he turned to her.

'Merlin's ready,' she said. 'I'll get up.'

'Please.' He made to help her but she gently pushed

him aside. When she mounted he climbed easily behind her and slipped his arms about her waist. His chin was just touching her neck. 'I hope this is right,' he said.

'Yes, it's all right. Come on, let's go now.'

The horse carried them in the grey, damp dawn, over the irregular land, through gorse-covered dips and shoddy copses, and eventually on to a ridge from which they could look down to the distant road. 'England,' the German said moving his mouth to her ear. 'I did not think I would see it so close. Not yet.'

On the road she saw a line of figures, shabby and slow. 'There they are,' she said. 'I thought they'd be out searching.' She moved the horse forward. 'Here goes.'

The LDV men saw them as they descended and stood in a dumbstruck group, staring at the girl and her captive. 'Jesus,' muttered Harry, mouth sagging, seeing the grey uniform. 'She's got a Jerry.'

Bess slowed the horse to a trot and then a walk, moving slowly towards the astounded men. Only Liberty Cooper was expressionless. Robert forced himself to move forward. 'Miss Spofforth,' he called, 'are you all right?'

'Fine, absolutely fine,' Bess called back. 'This is Paul Heinz Teller,' she shouted proudly. 'He's a German.'

At ten in the morning, with the night rain diminished to a drizzle, Robert and his son trudged tiredly towards home. Millie was standing at the gate of her cottage, a coat over her head. 'There's been a call for you, Harry,' she called as they approached.

'Your mother just rang. There's a message from Portsmouth. You've got to report back right away. They're sending a car for you at eleven.'

Robert grunted in agreeable surprise. 'I didn't know you were so important.'

Harry shrugged. 'Neither did I. Sending a car.' He halted wearily at the gate. 'Thirty-six-hour pass,' he grumbled. 'All I get is twelve hours and I spend that hiking around the forest in the dark.'

Millie opened the gate. 'I've got your uniform jacket here,' she reminded him. 'There's some coffee ready. I want to hear about the German. Is it true that Bess Spofforth caught him?' She looked narrowly at Harry.

'It's true,' he sighed. 'She would, wouldn't she.' He smiled meagrely. 'As Harold Clark pointed out, he wasn't a very big German anyway.'

They went into the kitchen and she poured the coffee. Robert moved Bellows the cat from the rocking chair and sat down heavily, grumbling. 'We put in all the effort and she'll get all the glory,' he said. 'That newspaper chap, what's-his-name, Beavan, was talking to her as we left. It's disgraceful when you think about it. Organizing the search, getting wet . . . all that, and she rides down with the blighter hanging on like fury behind her. Then, just to add insult to injury, he's finally taken off by the *police*. The police! I mean, that dim-wit Brice. Put him in a car and whisked him off to Southampton.'

Thoughtfully Harry sipped at his mug. 'I can't imagine what the flap is from Portsmouth,' he said. 'God, why send for me? All I've done for the past six weeks is organize the filling of sandbags.'

His father sniffed. 'Maybe they want some more filled in a hurry,' he offered moodily. He rose. 'Well, I'm going. We also serve who only stand and wait.'

Millie said to Harry: 'Do you want to get tidy here? I'll give you some breakfast. There's some fresh eggs today.'

'Thanks, Millie,' said Harry. 'I don't have to go back home then.' He turned to his father who was just plodding from the door. 'I'll give mother a call,' he promised. 'I'll ask her to get the navy to pick me up here. They might turn up before you get back.'

Robert nodded heavily. 'All right, son. Let us know what it's all about – if you can. *When* you can, anyway.' Oddly he turned and shook hands with Harry. The younger man stood up with surprise. 'Thanks for turning out last night,' said his father. 'Sorry it ruined your bit of leave.'

Abruptly he went out across the wet garden and turned down the road behind the border hedge. 'Poor old devil,' said Harry. 'He's flaked out.'

'I've never seen his shoulders so bowed,' agreed Millie. 'It's all a bit too much for him.'

'If *we'd* nabbed the German instead of Bess, he would have been full of fun,' said Harry. 'The glory would have kept him going until the end of the war.'

She went to the stove and put an egg in a saucepan. 'I'll go and have a wash and shave,' said Harry. 'Damn. My shaving stuff's at home.'

'James's razor is in the bathroom,' mentioned Millie over her shoulder. 'He keeps a spare here.' She paused. 'It hasn't been used for some time. And there's a spare toothbrush. Pre-war. Brand new.'

He could see by her stance at the stove, her back

still to him, how unhappy she was. 'Any chance of James coming home this week?' he asked awkwardly.

'He might,' she answered levelly. 'He says he might.' She turned and he could see the sadness in her eyes. 'But I don't know. He's just very busy, that's all. You'd think he was running the war by himself . . .' She looked flustered. 'Sorry, I shouldn't go on like that.'

'It must be rotten,' he mumbled. 'I think I'd better get shaved.'

'There are plenty of husbands overseas,' she continued. 'It's just that he's only in London.'

He turned and went up the enclosed stairs with the sharp bend at the top. Rain was smearing the window on the landing. She had arranged a line of books on the window sill. He glanced at them. They were from her childhood: *Little Women*, *The Girls from St Teresa's*, *Swallows and Amazons*. 'I'll bring you another cup of coffee, shall I?' Millie called from below.

'Fine,' he responded. 'I may have to rush.'

'I've given your tunic a brush,' she added. 'Would you like me to run an iron over it?'

'Would you? Thanks, Millie. Perhaps they're going to parade me before the King or Winston Churchill or somebody. Perhaps I've done something gallant or wonderful that I didn't realize at the time. But I doubt it.'

'Now who's after glory?' she laughed. He was relieved to hear her laugh. He stripped to the waist and gratefully washed in the hot water. He cleaned his teeth and then lathered his face. As he began to use the razor she knocked on the door, called 'Coming in' and entered.

'Thanks, love,' he said familiarly through the lather as she laid the coffee down. He wiped the soap from his lips and chin and leaning towards her kissed her on the cheek. Small blobs of shaving soap adhered to her skin. 'Now *you'll* need to shave,' he said.

She remained smiling at him and then, turning quickly, said: 'I'll get the iron ready. You'll want to have a decent tunic for your Victoria Cross, won't you.'

'Some bloody hope of that,' he called after her. He heard her going down the cottage stairs and turned to the mirror again, shaving over the lump that had suddenly appeared in his throat.

Eighteen

As June became July London remained in a kind of tranquillity with only a scattering of small raids from wandering enemy bombers. The guns were prepared, squatting in the parks, their long noses sniffing at the sky; unlit searchlights stared upwards like blind men. Air-raid shelters were scrubbed and stocked, emergency water and power supplies had been planned, and all the snakes and other poisonous creatures at the Regent's Park Zoo had been put to death. What incidents might follow the bombing needed deep consideration, whether they concerned escaped rattlesnakes or panicked civilians. Churchill had long feared that one night of saturation bombing by the Germans might result in the headlong flight of four million or more people from London. Its control, he said bluntly, might unduly absorb the efforts of the armed services.

The deep bunker at the edge of St James's Park was now brought fully into use as an operations centre for the conduct of the war, and it was there, far below the ground, that the War Cabinet met every day under the Prime Minister who had taken to wearing a chubby blue battledress, like a boiler suit. He smoked endless large cigars, slept for half an hour after lunch, sat late into the night with his drowsy subordinates, and showed the everyday people the Victory V-sign with his fingers when he came to the surface of the capital. They cheered and shouted: 'Good old Winnie!'

James Lovatt continued to work in his room at the War Office, travelling the country in his function as one of Churchill's unofficial ears and eyes, arriving at defence positions, garrisons, beaches and other ready places and compiling a weekly report which he himself delivered to the Prime Minister.

The rounded old man liked him and often took time to go through his reports and to question him on the things he had heard and seen. He encouraged James to talk about his own New Forest village and how the people were faring there, how their spirit was. 'They are directly behind the front line,' he announced. He even rose heavily from his chair to detect the hamlet on the widespread map of the United Kingdom on the wall of his office. 'Binford, Binford,' he squinted. 'Ah, yes, there it is.' He sat down smiling, as if pleased with his discovery, leaning back in his encompassing chair. 'A proposed German landing would extend probably from Ramsgate in the east . . .' He remained seated but picked up a wooden pointer and pushing it over his head touched Ramsgate. '. . . to the Isle of Wight in the west.' James could not suppress a smile and the old man grunted and apologized. 'Yes, well, I imagine you are well versed in the whereabouts of both Ramsgate and the Isle of Wight,' he intoned. He regarded James as if considering whether to tell him every secret he knew. 'Herr Hitler,' he said, 'has called his plan Operation Sea Lion. We must wait and see if the sea lion actually takes to the water.' He gave a cynical sniff. Then he smiled, not a large smile for he rarely used one, but a minute grin more in the eyes than around the mouth, boyish and mischievous. 'And how is your father's private army?'

'Eager as ever, sir,' responded James.

Churchill said: 'I'm going to change the name to the Home Guard. It sounds better. Every soldier must be proud of the name of his regiment. They would fight all the better for it.'

'They'd fight as best they could, Prime Minister, whatever they're called,' suggested James. 'My wife told me last night that my father's chaps had been out all night trying to capture a Luftwaffe pilot whose plane came down in the forest. But a girl on horseback found him and brought him in – much to their annoyance.'

Churchill beamed recognition: 'Of course she did! I read it in Beaverbrook's paper. Pretty young woman too. What else? Tell me what else?'

He leaned forward, genuinely eager to know, like a distant, elderly relative, anxious for any scraps of information about his family. It was clear to James that he enjoyed these few minutes fitted in between the serious and momentous moments of the day.

James ventured: 'Well, my father's unit are anxious to get their hands on the American rifles they hear are about to arrive.'

'I hope this week,' grunted Churchill without hesitation. 'They'll have some task getting them out of the grease, I should think. And they're outmoded, even ancient, I'm afraid. Stonewall Jackson would doubtless be familiar with the mechanism. But better than nothing. A good deal better.' He puffed at the cigar. 'And we want those fifty old warships,' he mused. 'Obsolete destroyers. I asked President Roosevelt if we would need to train sailmakers.'

James laughed. Churchill seemed in no hurry to dismiss him. 'What other intelligence have you gleaned?' he inquired. He lifted James's latest written report from the desk. 'This is most valuable, you know, major. It gives me an ear to the ground. Whose notion was it in the first place? Was it Philip Benson or was it me?' Not giving James time to say it was Benson, he continued, 'It was one of my ideas, I expect. What about the military on our coast?' Even in conversation he was theatrical. 'Watching the seas. How is their morale?'

'It's pretty good,' replied James, 'in the circumstances.'

'Waiting is a difficult part of war,' mumbled Churchill. 'Or anything else for that matter. I remember that.'

'They feel it's real enough,' said James. 'The danger. I suppose the difficult part, sir, is keeping on your toes when not much is happening.'

Churchill frowned. 'Let us hope to God it goes on *not* happening,' he said. Suddenly he asked: 'How do they feel about the King?'

James had thought he had ceased to be surprised, but now he hesitated. Churchill helped him. The Prime Minister leaned forward confidingly. 'Their Majesties, their noble Majesties,' he said solemnly, 'have indicated to me that under no circumstances will they leave *London*, let alone leave this country. There have been suggestions here and from the

Empire that they, or at least Princess Elizabeth and Princess Margaret Rose, should be transported to safety in Canada. But the King will not hear of it.'

'Regard for the Royal Family has never been higher,' James said truthfully. 'You only have to see the way people in cinemas applaud spontaneously when their Majesties are shown on the newsreels.'

Churchill nodded. 'Yes, I've heard that also. I must go to a picture house again when I have a moment. I'm very fond of the Marx Brothers, you know.' He paused, again impishly. 'I understand the people applaud my appearances on the screens, do they not?'

Keeping a straight expression, James said: 'Yes, sir, that is true.'

'Excellent,' said Churchill. He apparently saw something below the desk and blew cigar smoke at it like a discharging gun. He mused mysteriously: 'When you think what might have been.' He looked James in the eye, as if it were essential to impress him. 'We have a noble King,' he said.

James knew the interview was at an end. He had learned the nuances by now. As if by some signal a secretary opened the door with an anxious expression and a sheaf of papers. James rose and took his leave. 'Goodbye, major,' said Churchill. 'Come and see me again soon.' His big shoulders seemed to contract in the chair as the official advanced with the papers. 'And now,' he said, 'for the dire business of the day.'

It was just beyond noon when the naval staff car arrived at the Portsmouth headquarters. Harry went into the main busy concourse and was at once directed to an office on the ground floor. In an ante-room were a dozen young naval officers. Barraclough, who had been one of the contingent at Dunkirk, was among them. 'I wonder what mess they want us to settle this time?' he grinned at Harry. 'There's not many places left which we can evacuate.'

'Perhaps it's England,' grimaced Harry.

They were silenced by the arrival of a chief petty officer who came from the inner door and said amiably: 'Ah, all here now are we, sirs? Will you be so kind as to follow me.' He strode noisily along a corridor with rooms on either side, compartments full of the stutter of typewriters and teleprinters. A dark Wren, her tunic buttons tight over her bust, handed the petty officer a sheet of paper as he passed. 'Thanks, lovely,' he said and led the junior officers on. They paused outside a double door. 'Commodore Howlett lives in here, sirs,' he announced like a butler. 'He wants to have a chat with you.'

They trooped into the office and arranged themselves along the back wall, while the commodore, after glancing up, returned to frown through rimless spectacles over a sheaf of papers. An attentive captain waited seated at his side. It was the captain who eventually looked up and said: 'Ah, so you're all here,' as if he had not noticed them file in. He stood back and the senior officer at the desk said: 'I'm sorry there is nowhere to park yourselves, gentlemen. In this department at present we don't have a lot of time to sit down.'

Tentative smiles went along the line of youthful officers. He regarded the young men grimly. 'Each of you gentlemen has, during the past year or so, served with ships of the French Navy.' He checked down a list next to his elbow. 'Roberts,' he said, 'the *Dunquerque* . . . Sanders, the *Richelieu* . . . Lovatt, the *Arromanches* . . . and so on.' He glanced up. 'Barraclough . . .'

'Yes, sir.'

'You were seconded to the *Surcouf*, I see. What was she like?'

'Tremendous, sir,' replied the youth eagerly. 'Biggest submarine in the world, sir . . .' He paused and said awkwardly, 'I expect you know, sir.'

Howlett smiled at the eagerness. 'Yes, I had heard,' he said. 'She even carries a seaplane, doesn't she?'

'I'll say she does, sir. In a hangar by the conning tower.'

'You enjoyed serving with her? You got on well with your shipmates?'

'Rather, sir. They were –'

'Right,' interrupted the commodore sharply, uncomfortably. 'That's fine.' He looked very grey, thought Harry, almost haggard. 'We have an unpleasant task before us,' he announced. 'Without embroidering the facts, it is to be our job to take over a number of French ships to see that they do not fall into German hands. When France threw in the towel they promised that Hitler would not get his fingers on their fleet, but, needless to add, it seems very likely that Hitler *will* get his fingers on it. Most of the larger vessels, the *Dunquerque* and the *Richelieu*, for example, are overseas, but others are in British ports. Here in Portsmouth, at Sheerness and in Plymouth. The *Surcouf*, for example,' he glanced, almost a challenge, towards Barraclough, 'is at Plymouth. So is the *Arromanches*.' His eyes went to Harry. 'It will be necessary to take charge of them. We sincerely hope

422

with the cooperation of their captains and their crews. Otherwise it will have to be . . . well, otherwise.'

A cold place formed in Harry's stomach. He could hardly credit what was being said. He heard Barraclough draw in a distressed breath.

'I can't take any questions,' said the commodore. 'This is not a matter for discussion. But I thought it was my duty to tell you myself rather than let you find out the other way. Captain Verry here will give you further instructions and detail you to the various operation groups. Detailed briefing will be carried out before twenty-two hundred hours today. Gentlemen, thank you. That is all.'

They marched deliberately from the room like men made prisoners, back along the corridor, raising hardly a glance from the busy rooms on either side. The captain remained behind and the chief petty officer led the single file across the main concourse to another elongated room, like a station waiting-room, with heavy polished benches down each side. Above the gaping marble fireplace was a photograph of the King in naval uniform. A spiritless-looking plant stood in an urn in one corner. The windows looked out on the dockside, ships and water, shades of grey in the wet day.

The chief petty officer said nothing more but left them to sit like children on the brown benches and closed the door behind him with a firmness that suggested he feared they might abscond. For a minute or more the young men remained silent, some staring straight ahead, some studying the regal portrait, others finding something of interest in the listless plant. Eventually it was Harry who stood and walked the two paces to the window. Looking across the anchorage, through the low day, he could see a clutch of small craft, minesweepers, minelayers and two torpedo boats, with a large motherly vessel alongside. It was clearly flying the tricolour.

'What d'you think they're going to do?' The words came from Barraclough.

Harry turned. All at once he saw how idiotically juvenile they all looked. One was trying to grow a nautical beard. He said: 'Take over the French ships. By fair means or foul.'

'By peaceful or otherwise,' corrected Barraclough. He turned on Harry. 'You were on the *Arromanches*?'

'Right,' nodded Harry. 'Two months ago.' He waited cautiously, but then said: 'I can't believe it. If they're right here – God, there's some of them right outside this window . . . if they're in British ports then you'd have thought that they'd just come over to us as a matter of course. It never occurred to me . . .'

'Things *don't* occur to you,' the one trying to grow the beard said, 'do they?' He looked at the door as if he might be overheard. 'I thought the French were on our side . . .'

'They *were* on our side,' grunted Barraclough. 'But they've surrendered lock, stock, barrel – and ships. Politicians give the orders, remember, not captains. Captains don't matter.'

Harry turned savagely back to the window. 'They'll *have* to come on our side,' he said. 'Christ, they've *got* to. What about this de Gaulle man? I thought he was in command now. I can't believe they'd turn around and fight *us*.'

Violently the door banged open and the junior

officers stood hurriedly. It was Captain Verry. He was alone and he closed the door, quietly, behind him. He had heard the last words spoken by Harry and he looked heavily at him. 'I hope they don't put up a fight, sub-lieutenant,' he echoed. 'I hope to God they don't.' He looked around. He was a fierce-looking man with a soft voice. 'All right, chaps, sit down. Let me tell you what this is all about.'

The two lines of uniforms sat on the benches. The captain went to the top of the room where he stood under the chin of the King. 'Everyone is aware of how you're feeling, and how you're *going* to feel if this business backfires,' he said. 'And everyone is very sorry about it, particularly me because I've also served in French vessels and I have friends too. But having said that, we are now going to forget that aspect of it. We're not here to make decisions, only to carry them out.'

He produced a big blue handkerchief and twice blew his nose violently. 'What is important is that the ships of the French Navy are sailing with us at the end of this week and not with the Germans or the Italians. It's a straightforward matter. They are getting their orders from their new Government in Vichy and those gentlemen are under the thumb of Hitler. We have issued an ultimatum to their ships, wherever they are in the world. Those in foreign ports have been told to sail for America, other neutral countries, or French overseas territories, like those in the West Indies, so we can keep an eye on them. Either that, or throw their lot in with us and sail for Gibraltar or Alexandria. This is no secret now. They know and we know, and, of course, the Germans know. That is outside your concern, however. Your concern is with vessels in British ports, like those craft outside this window in the harbour. We require those ships *intact*. We hope their crews will volunteer to remain with us, with the Free French forces, and will hand over the ships on demand. If they resist, or if there is any attempt to scuttle the ships, then we must use force against them.' He looked around grimly. 'That,' he said, 'is it in a nutshell.'

He paced the length of the long room, like the commander of a submarine, brushing along the knees of the young men. 'I'm not taking questions,' he told them. 'Your individual, *operational* questions will be dealt with at your final briefing tonight. The CPO will be back to direct you to your operational area. Some will remain here in Pompey, another group will be transported to Plymouth and a smaller number to Sheerness.' He had reached the door. The chief petty officer was waiting outside. 'Right, chief,' said Captain Verry, 'tell these young men what to do next.'

The chief, brisk and businesslike, strode into the room and said: 'The officers for Plymouth and Sheerness will be picked up by transport at fifteen hundred hours, which will give you time to get into battle order, draw arms and ammunition, and get something to eat. The mess has been alerted and they're expecting you in half an hour. The Portsmouth group will remain in their quarters until called upon.' He lifted a list attached to a board. 'First, the Plymouth contingent, sirs.' He lifted it closer as if his eyes were not good. 'Sub-lieutenant Barraclough, Sub-lieutenant Lovatt . . .'

*

Seven of the junior officers left for Plymouth. They went in a small naval bus, oddly like a sports team going to an away fixture. There was sufficient room for each man to have a seat to himself and they chose to sit like that. No one said very much during the four-hour drive along the coastal road. Harry sat on the left-hand side of the bus and watched the dull sea, framed with barbed wire, with gun emplacements and watching places. Sentries stood at junctions and near concrete emplacements, expectantly facing the Channel.

The coast towns, in peacetime so full and lively at that time of the year, were desolate, empty but for a few people walking, heads down as they would in winter. Hotels piled with sandbags stood along the seafront like elderly men in mufflers. The stormy wind rocked a line of sad, obsolete coloured lights; the sands were flat and bleak. Offshore merchant and naval vessels moved cautiously, noses to the waves.

They reached Plymouth in the early evening, Drake's redoubtable old city, the passage place of the Pilgrim Fathers; its dockyards and streets full of the stuff of the navy. It was a place of legends and brave men, where battles had been refought in taverns since the days of the first Elizabeth. As they reached the Hoe and the little bus went close to the sea, Harry looked out over the great anchorage to see if he could detect the shape of the *Arromanches*. Barraclough, who had been on the other side of the bus, moved across to stare out into the harbour also. Neither said anything until they stopped outside the naval barracks – a terrace of former hotels – and were leaving the bus. Then Barraclough said: 'Right then. Into bloody battle.'

A spray of rain fell across his face as, standing on the pavement after the bus had driven away, he looked out to the famous dockyard. His expression creased bitterly, as though it were the rain that distressed him. 'God,' he said to Harry. 'There she is. Look, you can't mistake her.'

Following the direction of his finger Harry saw the submarine *Surcouf* lying quite close inshore, wallowing low and long in the grey Plymouth water. 'She's a hell of a size,' he said.

'Biggest in the whole world,' muttered Barraclough again with some pride. 'The spotter plane is housed under the gun in the conning tower.'

Abruptly he turned and went up the steps into the requisitioned hotel. Harry paused and looked up. The front of the heavy-jowled Victorian building had been daubed in camouflage grey, even to white-topped waves between the first and second floors.

The name 'Hoe View' was still in chipped but bright golden letters across the front of the building and, true to the idiosyncrasies of wartime planning, the letters glowed even on the dull day, as if they had been polished. Perhaps that was an item of double-disguise as well. Harry walked up the outside steps and into the gloomy hall. The reception desk was still in its place and was occupied by two WRNS, one thin, tight-haired, the other round as a balloon; like Laurel and Hardy. Peacetime posters had been left on the walls, attractions for the holiday-maker of the final peace-time summer, all that long year ago, perhaps the last holidaymaker of all. A boat trip navigating the River Dart, a bus tour of Exmoor, joy trips in a biplane.

'This way, sir,' boomed the big girl. Her small

companion waved at him as if he might not realize whence the words were emanating. He smiled conventionally and went towards them. The little one was already holding out a piece of paper. 'Sub-lieutenant Lovatt,' she recited. 'Must be.'

'Yes, that's correct.'

'You're the only one left,' she pointed out, giggling. 'If it wasn't you – then you shouldn't be here at all!'

He almost said that he wished he were not, but he merely took the paper. It said he had been assigned to room 22, which he could make use of until the following day. Dinner would be at eight and all arriving officers were expected to be in the briefing room at twenty-two hundred hours.

'In the ballroom, the briefing is,' announced the fat girl seeing that he had read the instruction through. 'The ballroom,' she repeated, looking as if she expected an invitation to dance. She made a little cradle with her arms as she would have done with a partner and he laughed obligingly. 'I wish that's what it was for,' he said.

'Oh, it is,' joked the little one. 'We're having a band in, aren't we, Cheryl?'

'Save me the last waltz,' said Harry. He went up to room 22, took his shoes off and lay on the bed. The walls looked chill. There were no bedclothes, apart from a coverless pillow and a holed eiderdown on the bed. The holes had been made by a cigarette, each one round and brown, done neatly, done purposely so they looked as if bullets had passed through. There was a flowered jug and washing bowl in one corner, with only a dead spider in the jug. The curtains sagged, looking as though they had been forced apart at some time. He tried to draw them but they began to tear at the top. Rain was smearing the four big panes of the window. He thought he would be glad when it was dark.

The French, he told himself, would not make trouble. He lay back on the burned counterpane and remembered again his days on the *Arromanches*. How could they? Not those jolly-hearted young men, René, Clovis and the rest. Never. After all they were in it with us; we were their allies; the Germans were the enemies, worse, their invaders, their conquerors. Surely every Frenchman would want to fight them. It stood to reason . . . didn't it?

Unusually for him, he dozed. He awoke almost an hour later and stared about the room like a prisoner aroused in a cell. Sometimes, as a boy, he had frightened himself by the imagination of how terrible it would be to wake up on the morning they were going to hang you. He got up stiffly and went to the lavatory in the corridor. There was a corroded bath in there. When he turned the tap the water came out like thin tea. He let it run and went back to his room for the flowered jug, hoping that when he returned it would be clearer. It was not but it was steaming hot so he filled the jug anyway. He washed and shaved in the brown water and then went downstairs. It was just before eight and naval officers were appearing in the foyer and making their way to the dining-room. He was surprised there were so many. They talked as they went, filling the lofty stairwell with a buzz. He saw Barraclough with three of the other young officers who had come with them from Portsmouth and he joined them.

In the dining-room there was a table reserved for them. The others were all obviously familiar with both the surroundings and each other and took no notice of the newcomers. There was good-natured talk and some laughter during the meal, although at Harry's table the young men ate for the most part in silence.

One of the youths, sitting opposite Harry and finding it embarrassing not to converse, began talking about butterflies. Some of the others stared at him with expressions of disbelief, but he chatted determinedly on. Politely Harry agreed that they were fascinating and added that he lived in the New Forest and had spent some hours catching butterflies when he was a schoolboy. 'The Marsh Fritillary,' said the youth staring accusingly across the table, 'is to be found in that part of the country but it's becoming rarer.'

'Oh,' said Harry flatly. 'I didn't realize that. Probably I had something to do with it, then. Catching them.'

'Men will be getting scarce at some time,' put in Barraclough from the lepidopterist's right arm. 'They're in danger of being wiped out too.'

His neighbour was not deterred. 'If we looked after the Grayling and the Clouded Yellow,' he enunciated, 'then perhaps humans might also have more chance of survival.' He dug doggedly into his sultana pudding and custard.

When the moment for the loyal toast arrived, a lieutenant-commander at the distant end of the room rose, a man as thin as a rope. 'Gentlemen,' he announced, 'Admiral Jackson is unable to be here this evening. Some sort of minor flap. Probably the German invasion or something.'

'A Red Admiral,' said the butterfly boy, 'is really a Red *Admirable*, you know.'

There was laughter from around the tables at the joke about the invasion. The lieutenant-commander said: 'Anyway, he's asked me to apologize. He hopes to be back in occupation of this chair tomorrow. It therefore falls to me to propose the toast of His Majesty the King.'

In the old naval tradition, the toast was taken sitting down. The braided sleeves raised their glasses. 'The King,' they echoed.

The senior officer then immediately rose. 'Our second toast,' he intoned. 'Gentlemen, be upstanding. The toast is Our Allies.'

Harry watched Barraclough's face tighten. 'Our Allies,' came the echo about the room.

'God bless them,' said someone close by.

'God help them,' corrected Barraclough quietly.

At midnight they moved into positions among the jetties and buildings of the dockyard. There were contingents of marines and armed sailors moving through the shadows, shuffling, so that their boots did not sound on the ancient cobbles and stones of the dockside, so that no echoes were set up. Harry watched the dark figures moving. Out in the anchorage the French ships lay still, apparently asleep. The marine officer who had given them the final briefing had made a sour joke about it being the first time the British had known the opportunity to fight the French since the days of Napoleon. He had told them that they must regard the operation as action against an enemy. While he was talking in the hushed and crowded room, Harry wondered where his own youth, his days of innocence, his days of catching the Marsh Fritillary had gone.

Harry was with a group of twenty-five sailors under the charge of a captain. The orders were recited to him and embedded in his mind. 'Sub-Lieutenant Lovatt will act separately, individually, from the squad as a whole, unless ordered to do otherwise by the officer-in-command. Your function, as one familiar with the ship we are to board, is to act as guide, interpreter, and, if necessary, intermediary. Should the officer-in-command be put out of action then you will take charge. The officer-in-command has sole discretion in the minute-to-minute running of the operation, *including the decision to open fire*. The priority, on boarding the vessel, must be to prevent any attempt by its crew at scuttling the ship. It is probable that charges may have already been prepared with this in mind, or they may attempt it by opening the sea-cocks. On the other hand every matelot may come forward and shake hands. Welcome them to our side for the rest of the war. Let's hope they do. But don't count on it.'

They had been taken in trucks to points in the dockyard, behind naval stores and other buildings. The main road was blocked to all but naval traffic prosaically by two Devon constables, with white gloves so that their upraised hands could be seen in the dark.

The rain had eased now and the moon had appeared between large ragged clouds spread like a map across the western sky. There remained a sulky wind pushing across the blacked-out harbour. Once they had left the trucks the sailors and marines advanced to their positions in long, shuffling single files. By midnight all was ready.

Harry stood, face blackened, waiting in the shadow of a harbour office, the men stretched along the wall like loiterers, their features smeared, their eyes moving visibly like those of negroes. He felt himself become rigid with apprehension. To his left was the set, oily face of the senior officer, Captain Furness. His own face felt sticky under its smeared mask. Furness looked at his watch. 'Right,' he muttered. 'Let's get on with the business. Good luck. Let's hope we're in for a quiet night.'

The operation was staggered, a few minutes elapsing between the action against each of the five French ships in the port. As they moved forward Harry was astonished to see French sailors, many in their underwear, some wearing pyjamas, already being trooped down the gangway of a vessel tied to the jetty. They came, like a silent farce, down the sloping chute and lined up obediently but ignominiously on the quayside, while British marines, with fixed bayonets, herded them with the efficiency of sheepdogs.

Harry's unit were to embark in two naval launches, for the *Arromanches* was anchored offshore. As they went down the chaffed old steps to board them a thin pink firework sizzled into the dark night above the harbour. It exploded in a fairy-like shower.

'Wonder what that means?' droned Captain Furness. 'It's not one of ours. French, I expect, being pink.'

434

The two deep-throated boats turned out into the choppy harbour. Harry, standing in the bow alongside the helmsman, saw the familiar shape of *Arromanches* fill out ahead of them. His throat was like lead. She was black and hushed. 'She's shut the door,' mentioned Furness quietly. There was no ladder down the flank of the destroyer. The boats bumped alongside and from each one a sailor threw a hooked line on to the destroyer's rail and like a man in a circus clambered up the flank. Quickly there were four rope ladders thrown down to the boats and the sailors and marines began to climb. Furness and Harry reached the deck first and were briskly joined by the marine sergeant from the second boat. 'All aboard, sir,' reported the sergeant, saluting.

'So far so good,' said Furness quietly. 'Get your chaps into position, sergeant. We'll go and see who is at home.' He moved towards the bridge with Harry close behind him and after him four sailors with rifles. He saw Furness check that his revolver was loose in its holster and he made the same nervous movement. He was conscious of the breathing of the men close behind.

They went swiftly to the bridge, where the door was opened courteously, as though by a butler, and standing there was a young Frenchman. Harry recognized him at once, Clovis. Harry knew what he had to do. He stepped forward. *'Loup de Mer,'* smiled Clovis before the Englishman had a chance to frame his words. 'So you have come back.'

'Please take us to the captain,' said Harry forcing his voice to steadiness.

'Of course,' said the young Frenchman. He leaned

briefly and confidingly forward for a moment and touched his upper lip. 'You will see I have grown a moustache, a little piece of dog, you would say.'

'Yes, Clovis,' said Harry. It was almost a plea for reason. 'Captain Furness would like to see your commander.'

The young Frenchman saluted like an actor. 'He is expecting you.'

'Thanks, Clovis,' said Harry. Relief began seeping through him. It was going to be all right. Clovis turned smartly and went with short, precise steps along the deck and through the companionway. He stopped at what Harry remembered as the captain's door and tapped smartly, then opened without waiting for an answer.

'Sir,' said Clovis in English, 'the British have come.'

Captain Furness moved forward firmly and saluted. The French commander, pale-faced, responded. Harry did not recognize him. 'Sir,' said Furness at almost a whisper, 'I have orders to take over this ship. I hope that there will be no resistance. Our hope is that we can go on fighting together against the Germans who have occupied your homeland.'

It was a succinct, prepared speech. The Frenchman smile wanly. 'I wish, captain,' he said in slow English, 'that our life was so simple. Unfortunately it is not. My orders are to scuttle this ship. The charges are about to be exploded.'

Furness whirled about. 'Stay here!' he ordered two of the sailors. 'Lovatt come with me!' Followed by the other two sailors they rushed down the companionway and along the steel deck. Astonished, they saw that the French crew were lined up on the far side of

436

the ship, at their lifeboat stations, silent company, staring straight ahead towards the sea, and beyond that France. A group of marines stood guarding the with embarrassed expressions. 'Sergeant!' shouted Furness. 'Sergeant! Where are you?'

Two marines appeared from a door. 'He's below, sir,' said one. 'I think he's just nabbed the Frog in time.'

They almost fell down the ladder and then down another until they clattered on to the engine-room deck. Marines were flattened like shadows along the walls of the companionway. Furness pushed by and Harry followed closely. They stepped through the hatch into the engine room and saw, at the distant end, the marine sergeant and two men crouched against the machinery. The officers slipped forward. The sergeant scarcely looked up. 'We've accounted for two officers, sir,' he said. 'They gave up without firing the charges. But there's another one, hiding behind the bulkhead down there, and he says he's not coming out. He's going to blow his hole in the side of the ship. I can't understand half what he's saying, but that's the gist of it.'

'The next bulkhead?' asked Furness.

'That's right, sir. If he'd only poke his head out I could get a shot at him. He's still got to get to the firing pin. That's down there on the right, sir, behind that winch. It's out of his reach just now. He took cover when we turned up. He'd get to it, easy, though, just a quick dash or even on his hands and knees. It's no distance. Only a few yards.'

Furness said: 'We've got to get him into the open.' He glanced at Harry. 'This is where you do your stuff, sub-lieutenant. You talk to him.'

Harry felt his face twitch under the black coating. 'Yes, sir,' he muttered. The words sounded idiotic as he called them. ''Allo, 'allo. This is Sub-lieutenant Lovatt. I was with this ship. Who is that?'

'Lovatt?' returned the voice echoing through the metal room. 'It is you? This is René le Carré.'

Harry pictured him as he had been once, pink-faced, rounded, joking. 'René,' he called, 'you must come out. You are our friend. *My* friend.'

'I have orders to explode these charges.' A pause. 'How are you, *Loup de Mer*?'

'René, come on out, will you? Please, for God's sake. We are British and you are French. We are allies. You will be doing this for the Germans.'

'My orders are first,' the voice called back flatly. 'Your country has betrayed France. You left us. You will not have this ship.'

'René –' began Harry again.

Furness nudged him. 'Go and get him,' he whispered tersely. 'We'll cover you. Just *get* him.'

Harry caught his breath. 'Jesus,' he breathed. 'Yes . . . all right, sir.' He rose from his cover and moved a pace forward. Immediately the voice sounded eerily ahead. 'Stay, *Loup de Mer*. I see you and I can kill you. I do not want to do this. Stay there.'

Trembling, Harry edged to one side but took another pace. He was almost surprised to find that his revolver was cocked in his hand. 'Still, I see you,' called René. There was a sob in his voice. 'Still I can kill you, my friend.'

Sweat was running channels down Harry's blackened face. He could feel his tongue shaking as he licked his lips. 'René,' he said. It sounded in the steel compartment like a descant. 'You are a Frenchman – you must not help the Nazis.' He lied desperately. 'The others have surrendered. The captain of this ship has surrendered. You must come out and be with us.' In his own ears his diligent footsteps sounded like hammer blows. He had gone four paces now, a third of the way across the space to the Frenchman's hiding-place. 'René . . .' he said, grotesquely conversational, 'René . . . would your father let you do this . . . for the bloody Boche?'

When the young Frenchman came into the open it was almost casually. His hands went above his head and he edged halfway into the exposed space. Relief flooded through Harry. '*Loup de Mer*,' smiled René, 'it is good to see you.'

'He has a weapon,' came the sergeant's voice from behind Harry. 'Tell him to throw it into the open.'

There was no time to deliver the order, for René, now upright and two slow paces from his hiding-place, abruptly made a dive forward to where the trigger of the charge was hidden. The marine sergeant was a second quicker. He fired a burst from his tommy-gun, the deafening shots resounding in the chamber. Harry threw himself flat but not before he saw René flung back against the bulkhead with the force of the bullets that hit him in the neck. He lay still, hung across the winch, like a prisoner on the execution block. 'Good shooting, sergeant,' Harry heard Furness say quietly. Harry began to cry. He could not stop himself.

Twenty-four hours later the naval bus taking Harry and the other junior officers back to Portsmouth stopped at the Binford crossroads and he got off and started to walk in the deep darkness towards his home. Barraclough had also died. So had three others, French and British. Barraclough had been struck by a stray British bullet during a fracas at the quayside. The other three deaths, two British, an officer and an able seaman, and one French, occurred aboard the great submarine *Surcouf*.

It was a lonely walk for Harry. The commonplace war deaths haunted him. The trees at the roadside seemed lurking with shadows. An edgy wind moved them to whisper and once an alarmed rabbit sprang from the hedge, leaving the man just as startled. He stood white-eyed and shaking. It was like it had been when he was a boy walking at night, crowded with the unadmitted fears of concealed fiends. Once, when he was in the boy scouts, he had run terrified for two miles and slammed the kitchen door of his father's house, because a drowsy tramp had clattered from the trees at the side of the void road.

In the returning bus they had silently passed round a bottle of rum and it had done little to warm or cheer them. But he was glad of it now. He had taken a deep drink from the bottle before leaving the bus and he could feel it working within him. A weariness had settled in his body which added to his lack of courage. He wanted to go home and get into his own bed.

He had walked another hundred yards and had turned a bend in the road when something tumbled out of the hedge to his left. He was so startled he jumped away. A short figure righted itself in the road and stared towards him. For a moment Harry thought it might be a German parachutist. Then a voice said in the dimness: "'S all right. It's me.' It was Willy Cubbins. 'Hello, Mr Lovatt,' said the boy. 'Fancy you being out this time of night.'

Harry recovered. 'What are *you* doing out is more like it?' he asked. 'It's two in the morning.'

They began to walk along together. Had they met by daylight there would have been no more than a nod and a greeting between them. Now, at night, they naturally became companions, trudging towards the village. They had never had a conversation before.

'I been for a bit of a walk,' said Willy. 'Where you been, Mr Lovatt?'

Harry felt momentarily tempted to tell him. Instead he said, 'Just to Plymouth.'

'Plymouth?' echoed the boy as if it were Samarkand. 'Is it nice?'

'Not very,' said Harry. They were pacing step to step, incongruous figures from different lives, each now with his hands in his pockets. 'It's a bit late for going for a walk, isn't it?'

Willy grunted. 'I do sometimes, to tire myself out, see.' He looked sideways in the dark. 'I sleep-walk, see. Did your dad tell you?'

'No,' answered Harry, surprised. 'He didn't mention it.'

"Ee's a good bloke,' said Willy. 'But I do. I used to wear a cow-bell on my leg. But now I go for walks 'cos you feel bloody silly with a cow-bell. I go for miles sometimes at night. I look out for Germans, so I reckon I'm sort of on patrol.'

They walked along the road, the great-legged trees along its flanks standing in the dark. Eventually Harry

441

said: 'You're the last of the London evacuees left, aren't you?'

'Last one,' confirmed Willy. 'They even took Eva back now. She was my sister, or we made out she was.'

Harry said: 'How do you mean, you *made out* she was?'

The boy gave a half-grunt, half-laugh. 'Well, when we was coming 'ere in the buses from London, the day after the war started off, Eva was sitting next to me and we changed her label, you know they put a label on you like a parcel, and made out she was my sister.'

Slowly Harry said: 'And nobody found out?'

'No. We never told nobody, never. It don't matter now she's gone away. We just 'tended we was brother and sister and when we got to Binford they kept us together.'

'You just liked each other,' said Harry. 'How old was Eva?'

'Eleven. She was twelve when she was 'ere. We used to sleep in the same room at the farm and if she was scared she used to come into my bed. I'm sorry she's gone back.'

They were nearing the village now. Willy Cubbins paused because he was taking the turning to the Lampards' house.

'Your parents haven't come for you, have they?' asked Harry. He knew that they had not.

The boy sniffed. 'My old man came back a few weeks ago,' he said. 'Not for me, just to nick some meat for the black market. 'Ee was the bloke with the tart what your father and the others caught in the road-block, in the barbed wire. I saw 'is mug in the torchlight, so I 'id. I don't know who the tart was. She weren't my mum.'

The boy said good night and began to walk down the lane, dark as a tunnel, towards John Lampard's house.

'Good night, Willy,' Harry called after him.

'Good night, Mr Lovatt,' came back the whisper.

Harry continued towards the village.

It was still half a mile when he saw a cat sitting on a gate, watching the ground for field mice. It was Millie and James's cat, Bellows, so called for its habit of puffing out its chest. Harry turned off the road and approached it.

'Bellows,' he said. 'It's me, Harry.'

The tabby glanced up, gave a single purr of recognition and continued to peruse the ground. Harry, all at once, wondered if he dared to disturb Millie. Perhaps she would give him a cup of tea. As much as he wanted to be home, the remaining walk seemed a fair way and he knew that there would be nothing, nobody awake there; he would, after all that had happened to him, just go silently to his single bed.

Hesitating, he opened the gate and the cat swung with it, balancing calmly until he closed it again: 'I wish I could do things as easily as that,' said Harry. The house was outlined ahead, the low, frowning roof topped with a chimney like a jaunty hat. He walked across the dim and dewy lawn to the kitchen door. After another pause he knocked. There was no response. He told himself he would permit himself another firmer knock before going away. He did so, three times. As he waited he suddenly wondered what would happen if James were there. It was ridiculous to worry like that. After all, they were all one family. Millie was his sister-in-law, more like a sister for they had known each other since childhood.

He heard her voice through the door: 'Who is it? Who's there?'

'Millie, it's all right. It's me, Harry.'

'Harry?'

'Yes, me. Harry.'

The bolts were pulled on the far side of the old wood and the door swung open. She stood there in a dark dressing-gown, her face and neck showing white. In her hand was a hammer. 'Please don't use that,' nodded Harry. 'I've had enough bloody battering for one week.'

They sat on either side of the empty fireplace, in the two aged armchairs that had originally been in his parents' house. Her deep blue dressing-gown was folded about her, her hair was pinned up, something he had never seen before.

He had told her the story now. He said: 'I couldn't believe it was happening. I've been stuck in a damned room all day, waiting for the so-called debriefing, and every time I've even dozed off it's given me night-mares . . . René, someone who was my friend a couple of months ago, and they had to go and kill him. It's just all so . . . so . . . bloody.' He had a Scotch now. He finished the tumbler.

Millie asked quietly: 'Did you hear the news tonight?'

'No, nothing. What's happened now?'

'It said that we've destroyed the rest of the French fleet. Somewhere in the Mediterranean. In port.'

'Jesus Christ, what next?' His voice was like dust.

'Goodness knows what next,' she sighed. 'They said that casualties were kept to a minimum and they had given the French time to surrender.'

He looked up at her. Her head was inclined a little, as though staring into the fireless grate. 'I must be off to bed,' she said rising.

'And I must get home. I'm sorry I woke you.'

'I was awake,' she answered. 'I have a lot on my mind just now.'

'James?'

'Yes, James.'

'I'm sorry. I haven't liked to ask.'

'It's all right. Neither have your parents. I'm sure your mother has noticed even if Robert hasn't.' She stood, the velvet dressing-gown folding into pleats about her. He picked up his cap and began to button his tunic.

'You know that boy Cubbins,' said Harry. 'The boy with the spots.'

She nodded, surprised.

'He was walking along the road just now. He wanders about at night because he thinks it stops him sleep-walking.'

'John Lampard told me,' she said.

'He said that when he came here with the rest of the kids from London he and a girl made out they were brother and sister. They altered her label.'

She smiled faintly. 'I heard about it,' she said. 'Nobody realized until the girl's mother eventually turned up to visit her. Then there was hell to pay.'

'What a strange thing to do,' he said. They began to move towards the kitchen door.

'There was no harm,' said Millie. 'They were only children.'

She paused and added quietly, 'They simply needed somebody.'

They had almost reached the door. Millie said: 'You could sleep on the sofa, if you want to, Harry. It's a pity to make you walk up there at this time of the night. When are you due back to Portsmouth?'

'I'll have to report tomorrow. This is slightly unofficial.'

'French leave,' she said.

He laughed drily. 'French leave.'

'Sorry, I didn't mean it like that. Do you want to stay?'

'Yes, thank you.'

She brought two blankets and a pillow into the room, kissed him good night on the cheek, and left him. He stripped to his shirt and lay between the blankets on the old horsehair sofa. For some time he did not sleep but lay looking at the room of shadows about him. Then his eyes closed and he drifted to sleep. He awoke after only a few minutes with his sister-in-law standing by him, her face a white disc, the ends of her fingers upon his nose.

They went slowly into the bedroom and they together climbed beneath the eiderdown and fell against each other. They lay hugging in the dark, arms and legs enfolding, before even they kissed, and when they kissed it was not from passion but from need and friendship. Her mouth was open against his neck, her eyes clenched.

446

'Pull your hair down, please, Millie,' he whispered. 'Like it always was.'

Without word or hurry she took the combs out in a few swift plucks and her long beautiful hair slid down her face and on to her full shoulders. He took a handful and buried his face in its luxury. Their bodies enfolded, they moved against each other. Millie pulled the shoulders of her nightdress away. His hands and then his mouth went to her deep breasts and she was still and silent, before her head lolled against him again and she kissed his hair.

'I'm so lonely,' she said. 'I'm so bloody . . . bereft.'

'I am too,' he said. 'There never seems to be anyone when you need them, does there?'

Sister and brother-in-law made love in the dim room. Then they lay against each other in the dimness. She was weeping softly and he said she must not.

'It's the war,' he said. 'It's all because of the war.'

On the same July night that action was taken against the ships of France in the ports of Britain, the French fleet in harbours at Oran and Mers-El-Kebir, Algeria, was bombarded and virtually destroyed by a British naval force. The great battleships *Bretagne*, *Provence* and *Dunquerque* were sunk or disabled and many submarines, destroyers and other vessels were also destroyed. More than twelve hundred sailors, the allies of only weeks before, died, nine hundred of them in one ship, the *Provence*, which capsized under the gunfire of the British.

'Mr Churchill,' said James, 'was in tears. He came from the cabinet room with tears running down his cheeks. But he was cheered in the Commons. The

Americans believed it was a courageous thing to do, that we had won a great naval engagement.'

Harry, sitting opposite his brother on the lawn, the family arranged in deck chairs, choked over his tea cup. He regarded James angrily. 'It was bloody murder,' he muttered, wiping his mouth with his hand. 'Sheer, inexcusable, bloody murder.'

Their mother, their father and Millie reacted sharply. The brothers fixed each other over the tops of their tea cups. 'Would you repeat that?' asked James. Each word fell like a drop of cold water.

'I think you heard,' said Harry, putting his cup and saucer on the grass. It was another fine blue day, the trees fanning over the garden, the flowers thick in the herbaceous beds and the shining roses on the sunny wall. 'I said it was murder.'

'Who would like some more tea?' suggested Elizabeth as if she had heard nothing. Millie had gone pink. Robert regarded his two sons with apprehensive amusement.

James recited: 'It was a courageous and entirely necessary operation.'

'From where I was,' responded Harry, 'and I was a bit closer than you, it was a lousy, cowardly business. It made me feel dirty – and take it from me, major, I wasn't the only one. Great naval victory! Balls!'

Elizabeth stood shocked. 'I think we ought not to shout so in the garden,' she said firmly. 'The village will think we're quarrelling.'

'I think we are,' commented James looking briefly towards her. He turned on his brother again. 'So you saw a man shot. So what? Men do get shot in wartime. Lots of men.'

Harry rose from the deck chair. The brothers, in their different uniforms, remained facing each other. 'I saw a *friend* shot,' he said. 'Mr Bloody Churchill needed to cry, I can tell you. And, from what I hear, his tears won't cover all the other poor bastards who died.'

'So,' grunted James, 'you would prefer it if those French ships were running along the English Channel bombarding your friends in Portsmouth?' He paused. 'Or even your friends in this village.'

Harry said: 'Just tell our wonderful bloody Prime Minister, if you've got the guts . . .'

James shifted towards him. 'I've never been short of guts, Harry.'

Millie stepped forward. 'James,' she pleaded.

'Be quiet, Millie,' snapped her husband.

'That's right,' sneered Harry. 'Obey the major's orders, Millie.'

At that moment Robert stood up and ponderously moved between the two young men. They were only two yards apart, their eyes full of dislike. Their father, tall and rounded, reached his arms out both ways and gave each one a brief sharp push. It took both by surprise and sent them staggering back. James fell ignominiously over his own deck chair, his khaki legs, socks and brown shoes pointing upwards, and Harry trampled on his cup and saucer, breaking them.

'Be quiet, both of you,' ordered Robert. 'You're spoiling your mother's tea.'

'Ah, it is teatime,' sounded a voice from the gate. The tense little group looked up alarmed and saw the head of Johanes Van Lorn projecting over the top. He pulled back the bolt of the gate with the emphasis of a field gunner and entered the garden urbanely.

'Would you like some tea, Mr Van Lorn?' asked the relieved Elizabeth, as if there might be some doubt. Millie, smiling now, turned and without a word went to replenish the teapot. Elizabeth turned formally. 'I don't know whether you have met everyone. You know my husband, of course.'

Robert gave a heavy, almost Germanic bow. 'Ah, yes. He is the resistance leader,' enthused Mr Van Lorn. He turned to the still glowering brothers. 'And these are your sons. Fighting men.'

'Er . . . yes,' put in Robert carefully.

'Have some cake – please,' suggested Elizabeth, still blessing his intrusion. James and Harry had sunk back sullenly into their chairs.

Harry was about to pick up the final piece of cake from the plate when his mother made her invitation. He withdrew his hand. The Dutchman took the piece and began to eat it, but then abruptly looked concerned. 'Oh, but I have taken the cake,' he said sadly.

'You certainly do,' muttered Robert towards the grinning Elizabeth. Millie returned with the teapot and cups were replenished after a large cup had been filled for Mr Van Lorn.

'Have you any news of your family?' asked Elizabeth.

'They are safe, I hear,' the Dutchman said. 'But we will not meet until the war is over now. I will be here and they are there.'

There came a further noise from the garden gate and they saw that a breathless Mrs Spofforth had arrived and was waving over the top.

'There he is, the old swine!' she exclaimed loudly. 'Scoffing everybody's rations.' She flung back the bolt and strode into the garden, her white legs stiff as stilts. 'Got you, Van Lorn!' she bawled accusingly. 'Caught in the act.'

'Cake,' confirmed the Dutchman. 'It is very good. Everyone is so kind to me.'

'Would you like some tea, Mrs Spofforth?' asked Elizabeth, still appreciative of the diversion. James was making exit eyes at his wife. 'I'm afraid we have no more cake.'

'I'm not surprised,' said Bess's grandmother.

'Please sit down, Mrs Spofforth,' requested Elizabeth.

James stood and said: 'Please take my seat.' He glanced at Millie. 'We'll need to be going soon. I have to get back to London.'

Mrs Spofforth sat down ceremoniously. 'Give our regards to Mr Churchill,' she said. She noted his alarm. 'Don't worry, everybody knows you work for him. Tell him I hope he knows what he's doing. And tell him to watch one or two of his friends, slippery swine. They'd sell us down the river to Hitler, given half a chance.'

'Your granddaughter won herself some eminence,' pointed out James obliquely. 'Capturing a German pilot.'

'Trust her,' sniffed the old lady. She emitted a growl. 'Have you seen her since, going round on that horse? Like Joan of blinking Arc. I swear the horse has its nose in the air as well.'

James said amid the eased smiles, 'We must be off.' He and Millie said goodbye to everyone and shook hesitant hands with his brother. From outside the gate they waved back to those in the garden. For a moment Millie caught Harry's glance. She turned and went quickly behind the hedge.

'You're such a *nice* family,' offered Mrs Spofforth. She turned to Mr Van Lorn and nudged him with an elbow like a spike. '*Real* English people,' she said nodding around generally. She added, 'And, it was nice to see the brothers part such good friends. Wasn't it?'

Millie drove the pony and trap to the station. The late warmth of the summer day lay over the village, the elms scarcely trembled. Rooks sounded like rusty hinges. There had been an air-raid warning half an hour earlier but no enemy aircraft had appeared and now the sky was untroubled. They drove with silence between them, the sound of the pony's steps echoing in the lane. 'Will you be bringing Harry to the station later?' James inquired when they were almost there.

She tried not to look surprised. 'I said I would. His train goes at eight-fifteen.'

'I see.'

'I would have brought you both,' she put in quickly, 'but it wouldn't do to have you engaging in fisticuffs in the trap, would it? The pony isn't used to it.'

'Millie,' he pointed out with heavy patience, 'I would not engage in fisticuffs with a junior officer, even if he is my brother.'

She added nothing. Bowley, the porter, smiled and helped Millie down from the trap. 'Like the old days, seeing a nice little vehicle like this,' he said. 'A lot of people are going back to them now.'

452

He took James's rail warrant and the couple stood on the station waiting for the small local train to Southampton. 'Will you be busy this week?' he inquired eventually. 'Lots to occupy you?'

She nodded. 'I thought of putting in an extra day or perhaps even two at the RAF station,' she said. 'It seems to be worthwhile. I feel I'm doing something even if it's only dishing out refreshments and library books.'

He confided quietly and without looking at her: 'I think the Luftwaffe are going to come at us soon. Like a pack of dogs.'

Millie shrugged. 'Well, we'll just have to see them off like dogs,' she said.

He smiled at her, an occurrence that she noticed. 'That's the spirit,' he said.

'Thanks, James,' she replied.

'Look,' he said quickly, 'I'm sorry if it's difficult just now. Being married to me, I mean. I'm under a lot of pressure.'

She regarded him unsurely. 'That's the reason you stay away?' she asked.

'What else?' he asked. 'You're not worried about anything, are you?'

Firmly she shook her head. 'No, of course not. But . . . it just hasn't been right, lately, that's all. I think you must admit that.'

He sighed and the sigh became lost in the steamy hoot of the small rural engine as it turned on the long bend from the coast and came towards the station. He bent towards her and they kissed. 'It seems I can never *quite* say the right thing, doesn't it,' he observed. 'I'm sorry.'

'I am too,' she said bleakly.

'Sometimes,' he added slowly, 'I think you would have done better to marry my brother.'

At eight the same evening Millie again harnessed Horace to the trap and drove Harry to Binford Halt. For some time they did not talk.

Eventually he said: 'You handle this very well now.'

'There's nothing to it,' she replied quietly. 'I read it all in *The Field* magazine. They've had an instruction course. If there's bombing you are supposed to secure the horse to something solid and stationary, but not a lamp-post.'

Harry said: 'That was terrible this afternoon, James and I. Squaring up to each other like that.'

'It wasn't the first time,' Millie pointed out.

'When we were kids, but not now.' He touched her wrist.

'And, after the other night . . . well, I suppose I felt guilty . . .'

'Don't,' she said tightly. 'Don't be apologetic. There's no need. It was both of us. Are you sorry?'

'No, I'm not.'

'Neither am I. It was something that happened.' She gave the reins a soft tug. 'Come on, Horace,' she said. 'Don't let's miss the train.'

Joanne had parted the curtains and opened two of the casement windows to the close night. London spread out to the limpid skyline, unlit, scarcely murmuring at that early morning hour. James stirred and his hand went to her, touching her slim stomach.

'Have you been awake long?' he asked.

'For a while,' she answered. She did not move towards him, nor he towards her. They lay on their backs, only a pale sheet covering them. 'I was trying to imagine how it will be in New York or Washington again with all the lights.'

They always talked about her leaving like this; obliquely, knowing that it was to come, neither saying nor asking anything definite. Her fingers felt for his hand and lay gently on his knuckles. Almost absently she moved it lower from her belly until he was caressing her between her legs once more.

He turned to her, easing the sheet away from her breasts. From his place beside her he looked sideways at them, outlined in the vague light, small eastern hills, with pinnacles, one near, one a little distance off. Her head turned towards him on the pillow, a pale round of face, her hair dropping across her cheek with the movement. They kissed with quiet passion. She added her tongue, something he thought perhaps English women did not do. His palms were now stroking unhurriedly against her cool breasts, the nipples finely tapered, the skin firm. He moved into a crouch above her, his legs straddling her waist. Her eyes glazed as she gathered him in her hands, cupping him, rubbing him, until his whole lower body throbbed. She coaxed him down between her arched and open thighs. Still on his knees he surveyed her, a slim whiteness in the bed, the hair framing the serious and beautiful face, the eyes closed in anticipation, the neck curved down to her naked shoulders and chest. He leaned to her and, oddly, kissed her on the cheek, like a fond relative. Her eyes opened to slits. 'Will you come into me now, darling,' she asked quietly. 'I want you now.'

He did as she wished, submerging himself into her, feeling her belly bend like a bow towards him as he did so. The luxury, the pleasure of the simple, everyday act engrossed them. They moved together with the trust of lovers who were no longer strangers. James paused and whispered to her asking that she would pause also, to make the enjoyment last, to delay the climax. From the street below came the clink of milk bottles. Soon it would be light.

The sky was clearing to the left of her window, daylight edging across making its own white curtain. After their encounter they lay perspiring, watching it move over the brow of London. 'It's Wednesday,' he said.

'I think I must go home, sometime next month,' said Joanne without emphasis. 'I'm being pressed by my family and my boss. Various matters. He wants me to do some political profiles.'

'August,' he said. 'That's not long.'

'Maybe towards the end.' He felt her shrug. She shifted against him, extending on her side so that her warm, slender length was slotted against his body as he lay on his back. Her legs held his, her hands were cradling his waist, her breasts lay dozing against his arm; her chin touched his shoulder. She said: 'I hear that there's a flying-boat service starting to New York. You get there the same day.'

'A flying boat?' he said surprised.

'It's crazy, isn't it. British Overseas Airways Corporation. Only your country could start an international air route when it's pinned to the floor. I went to see the flying boat the other day, they took me on a trip. She's called the *Clare* and she's beautiful. Inside too. Just like a luxury train.'

James smiled slightly. 'This country does seem to have some strange priorities.'

'It certainly does,' she laughed. 'I read in *The Times* the other day that you're going all out to make *cookies* ... biscuits. Millions and millions. For export. A great cookie drive! Jesus Christ.'

'Have you made inquiries about a sea passage?' he asked.

'Sure. There's a liner sailing from Liverpool for New York at the end of August, or the start of September. The *City of Benares*. She's more or less been reserved for British children being evacuated to the States, but maybe they'll take other passengers too. I figured it would make a good feature for my paper. Travelling with the kids.'

'September,' he said as if announcing a decision. 'At the latest.'

'At the latest,' she replied softly. 'And, James ... I had a thought.'

'I'd like to come,' he answered with a wry laugh. 'But it would be desertion.'

'In more ways than one, I guess,' she confirmed. 'No, I wasn't going to ask you to run away with me. Don't worry. No ... Mrs Beauchamp told me that John Colin's mother had said she would like to send him to the States. I thought of getting somebody in Geneva to ask her if I could take him.'

Nineteen

In the later days of July the Luftwaffe increased greatly its attacks on the English Channel coast, although London and other cities remained relatively unmolested. There was a bombing raid on the Isles of Scilly, the outriders of England, twenty-five miles west of Cornwall in the Atlantic. One islander was killed. Strange occurrences were reported. An American bomber, a Chance Voight 156, was brought down by British anti-aircraft fire, causing mystification. It was wearing the swastika and black crosses of the Nazi air force and had apparently been appropriated by them in France. The whole coastline of Europe, from Narvik in Norway to Bayonne, was now in German hands, plus the British Channel Islands. Along the chalky cliffs of southern England the narrow-eyed defenders of the island watched. From Romney Marsh in Kent a quarter of a million sheep were evacuated to safer pastures inland.

The Luftwaffe sorties in that time were a harbinger of what was to come; the raiders arrived daily, trundling over the coast, bombing seaside towns and shipping in the Channel. Dover and Folkestone were shelled by big guns from the opposite French shore. Binford, wedged in its estuary with the forest around it, saw the battles overhead and out at sea but remained unbothered.

Robert went daily to stand by Donald Petrie at the coast-guard station and, using the heavy binoculars in the observation tower, watched the convoys of coastal shipping sidling along the protective shore. 'Here they come now,' murmured Petrie nodding towards the headland. He looked up anxiously at the July sky, azure-patched with creamy clouds moving on a moderate westerly. Round the headland Robert saw the small ships rolling in the waves, their attendant barrage balloons bobbing above them. They looked like children returning from a birthday party.

When the last of the clutch of ships had rounded the promontory Petrie gave a grunt. 'Here's Jerry,' he muttered. He picked up the telephone. 'Stukas,' he continued as if talking to himself. 'Bastards.' He spoke into the phone. 'Hello, RAF Control. Binford Haven Coastguard. Convoy three miles off-shore, proceeding west, hostile aircraft in vicinity. Attack imminent.' A voice crackled back along the line. 'Right,' nodded Petrie vigorously as if the speaker were there with him. 'You've picked them up already. Yes . . . Stuka, dive bombers. I can see five. No fighter escort as far as I can tell. Right. Over.'

Motionlessly the two men stood and watched the adjacent battle take shape. There was nothing for them to do but witness it. 'The lifeboat's been alerted,' said Petrie flatly. 'They'll probably be needed too. For one side or the other.'

The German planes were staying high, flying in and out of the clouds like predatory birds hesitating to fall on a victim for fear of a trap. They remained cruising in the cumulus while the alarm klaxons from the convoy sounded plaintively on the breeze. On shore the siren echoed from Binford police station. The people were used to it now. They continued whatever they were doing, those indoors peering with mild interest up from open windows and those in the open keeping only a casual eye on the sky.

The Stukas, however, had no intention of moving inland. Having arranged themselves among the clouds they circled, grunting, and then the leader's nose dipped and the deadly plane screamed down in an almost vertical dive pulling out sharply just above the jolting masts of the convoy, its stick of bombs released at the depth of the dive. White trees of water grew abruptly alongside the small ships. The rattle of a pom-pom gun, a violent but impotent chattering, echoed to the watchers on land. Robert looked down and saw that the people who lived around Binford Haven were standing in helpless idleness, some hands in pockets, the women silent in their household aprons, watching the deadly sideshow offshore. Only Brice the policeman was wearing a steel helmet and he sat on his bicycle in the open, squinting from beneath its rim. A second dive bomber now dropped on crooked wings above the convoy, another stick of bombs churned the sea. A third followed and a bulbous redness appeared amidships on one of the coastal craft. Explosions rattled windows on the shore. Another vessel was straddled. They saw it shudder and heel. 'Where's the bloody RAF?' grunted Robert. 'Those ships are helpless. Sticking those silly damned balloons over them and thinking that's enough.'

Petrie was not listening. He was talking to the

lifeboat down the phone. 'Watch out for the buggers,' he called. 'They'll get you as well if they can.'

As he spoke there was a roar over the coastguard post and three Hawker Hurricanes, at roof height, streaked out over the sea. They banked, laid off and waited their chance. The fifth Stuka had just completed its dive, its ponderous rise a contrast to the flamboyance of its screaming descent. 'Once they're down they have trouble getting up again,' commented Petrie. 'They don't look so clever then. See – they'll get that one.'

Two of the Hurricanes curled almost lazily in their flight and fired from their wing machine-guns as the Stuka attempted to clamber into the upper sky. They peeled off and then returned to the staggering German. The burst of fire sounded succinctly over the water. 'Got him!' said Petrie triumphantly but without raising his voice. It was like a conversational remark.

Robert shouted: 'Well done, chap! Damned wonderful! Look, he's on fire!'

The bomber, with a long groan of complaint, tilted on its side and with a funeral plume of smoke issuing from its belly, fell, now silently, striking the sea with a brief white upheaval.

'They're skedaddling,' said Petrie looking through the glasses. 'They've had enough.'

'I'll say,' shouted Robert jubilantly. 'Sent off with a bloody flea in their ear! Hooray! Hooray!' He cheered wildly, like a schoolboy applauding a winning goal. Petrie could not resist a grin and Robert was embarrassed when he saw it. 'Well, it was, wasn't it,' muttered the older man. 'Jolly good show.'

*

Early in the afternoon Millie cycled to Binford Station to catch the local train for Ringwood. The sky had greyed but the air remained warm, the thickness of July lying over everything. Honeysuckle, lolling over the pointed railway fence along the platform, filled her senses. Nettles and mown grass smelled with a different sweetness. There had been a plague of white butterflies in the south – a matter reported in the newspapers – and Bowley, the porter, was circled by two as he sat on the station trolley, wiping his reflecting head with a piece of tissue paper. He had been sorting parcels. A dog from the village briefly surveyed the platform from the booking office door, decided there was nothing to detain him and retreated to the dust of the street.

Bowley, puffing in his waistcoat, came towards her, legs bowed, arms hung out as if to create a cooling current. 'She won't be long, Mrs Lovatt,' he announced. 'Ten minutes adrift today.' He gave his head another wipe. 'They say it's because of the war, but I don't know. After all she only goes up and down this little line, don't she? How can she be late because of the war?' He seemed to be searching for excuses. 'Could be the sort of coal they're having to use now, I suppose.'

He took her ticket and, with care, punched a hole in it. 'Off to do your bit?' he said. 'How often do you go now?'

'Three or four days a week, depending on other things,' Millie told him. 'I hope it's worthwhile.'

'Oh, 'course it is,' he smiled encouragingly. He had new wartime dentures, like windows. 'We can't all have a gun. That's what I say. There's you serving tea and cakes to the airmen and there's me looking after Binford Halt single-handed. We're all helping, I say.' He leaned defensively towards her. 'How is your husband getting along with Winston?'

Millie laughed. 'Well, I know he's in London, but I don't exactly know what he's doing. I never ask. One mustn't, you know.'

'Oh, I know that all right, Mrs Lovatt,' returned the porter. 'Mustn't tittle-tattle, must we. Old Ma Fox is the one. Terrible. She reckons that Lord Haw-Haw has read out the names and addresses of everybody who owns a bit of land or a house in these parts. According to her Hitler's spies have got lists of certain people around here.' He spotted a puff of steam sprouting in the landscape. 'Here she comes now,' he said looking automatically at his watch. 'Eleven minutes today.' He tutted. 'Nice to know you're helping the RAF boys,' he said going for his red and green flags. 'They reckon three of they Hurricanes from Moyles Court shot down eight Germans in the Channel this morning. Ma Fox said people could see them falling in the water like ninepins. Right off The Haven.'

Bowley put her bicycle in the guard's van for her. Millie was the sole passenger to board the train, which was only one carriage. She sat in the compartment and watched the serene green countryside float past, the water-meadows, streams attended by pollarded willows now leafing again, the brilliant buttercups, the voluminous trees. At the next stop, Forest Halt, a man loaded with fishing tackle boarded the train and climbed, huffing, into her compartment. He sat down bulkily and arranged his umbrella, baskets, waders, nets and tackle around him, sitting like some King Neptune. 'Not a single bite today,' he announced. 'Too noisy.'

'Oh, is it?' she said. 'Noise makes a difference, does it?' She saw that his large umbrella was camouflaged like a military object.

'Difference? I'll say it makes a difference. Frightens the wits out of the fish. All these aeroplanes buzzing around. Half of it's unnecessary, you know.'

Millie's annoyance rose quickly. The man forestalled her. 'Fish hate every minute of it,' he announced as if he had asked them.

She regarded him with controlled distaste. 'There's bound to be some noise, isn't there?' she said. 'War tends to be a bit noisy.'

'War? This is *not* war. Just a skirmish, believe me. I want nothing of it. I've retired and retired I stay. I came down here for a bit of peace and some fishing.' He looked at her patronizingly. 'The Germans don't want to beat *us*,' he said as though pointing out something glaringly obvious. 'It's not *our* hides they're after, young lady.'

'Whose hides would it be then?' she inquired coldly.

'Ruskies',' he confided with a great sniff and a withdrawing of the head. 'They want to put down the Ruskies. And, mark my words, that's *our* interest in the long run too. The sooner Russia is wiped out, the sooner the world will be peaceful again. It's nothing to do with this business now. Nothing at all.'

'I hope it is all sorted out soon then,' Millie retorted stiffly. 'So that you can get some peace for your fishing.'

'Please God,' he said fervently. He opened a parcel

464

of sandwiches wrapped in newspaper, thick layers of bread and cheese. It looked to her like a whole family's ration of cheese for the week. He saw her watching. 'The wife doesn't eat cheese,' he said. 'So I take it.'

'It's very good for you,' Millie said tartly. 'Keeps you healthy. For fishing.'

'Oh, you need your health for that,' he confirmed heartily. 'Wet and cold it gets sometimes, believe me. But it's worth every minute. Most peaceful thing in the world, fishing. Now that's something that's really worth fighting for.'

She took her bicycle from the guard's van and cycled from Ringwood to the RAF Fighter Station at Moyles Court. At the gate the sentry waved her through and she arrived outside the operations room in time to see a jubilant young officer, square, round-faced, with a tight top of curly hair, standing back to admire a swastika which he had just fashioned on the squadron scoreboard. The paint was sticky in the sun. It stood at the end of a line of ten others.

'Look at that, then,' he insisted boyishly. 'Bagged my first one this morning. Stuka over the Channel.' He inclined his hand and made an engine noise, then opened both hands like a fan and said: 'Splash!'

'Good for you,' she nodded gently and seriously. He was the same youth who had been playing netball on the day she had first gone to Moyles Court.

'Wait until I tell my mother,' the young man enthused. 'A blinking Stuka!'

Millie began to wheel her bicycle towards the mess and he walked alongside her, hands deep in pockets. 'Still, all drinks on me tonight,' he mused. 'That's going to cost a packet. Fourteen and sixpence a day isn't much if you're going to keep downing Jerries, is it?' He shook his head and guffawed reflectively. She could see he was still trembling. 'My old man did a hole-in-one at his golf club once but it cost him a fortune in drinks. He wished he'd never done it in the end.' He was chattering relentlessly.

His talk, his youthful expression, the way he strolled with a boy's swagger, made her wonder how someone like him could fly a machine in the sky.

'How are you getting on with the amenities?' he asked her suddenly, a rush of a question as if he had to gather all his courage to say it.

Millie smiled: 'Fine, I think,' she answered. 'I haven't heard any complaints.'

'Oh, there won't be,' he said hurriedly. 'None at all.'

She put her bicycle with the squadron bikes under a low corrugated iron roof and walked towards the office where she worked. He trotted after her earnestly. 'Can I ask you something?' he said nervously. 'Please?'

Puzzled, she laughed: 'Yes, of course.'

'Could you tell me your name? I've only heard you called Millie.'

'That's right, it's Millie. Millie Lovatt.'

'I'm called Graham,' he told her still in his boyish way. 'Graham Smith.' He added hurriedly. 'Flying Officer, of course.'

'Of course,' she smiled. She moved towards the door.

'Stop!' he exclaimed. She turned quickly, again surprised.

'Sorry,' he said, his voice dropped. 'I didn't mean to

say it like that. I just meant to say "Stop" in an ordinary voice . . . but that's how it came out. Sorry . . . but can I ask you something else, er . . . Millie?'

'Last question,' she said lightly. 'I've got work to do.'

'I know, but I have to ask you now, before you can go in there. The other chaps will be in there and I won't get a chance, see. It's . . . well, will you come to the pictures with me one night? In Ringwood. Would you?'

She looked with assumed reproof at him. 'Flight-Lieutenant Smith,' she said, 'I am a married woman.'

He looked uncomfortable. 'Yes, well I can see that. Your ring. But I thought you might be on your own sometimes. I thought perhaps your husband was away. A good distance.'

Kindly she said: 'That's all the more reason why I should not go to the pictures with you.'

'In India, is he? Or the Middle East?'

'He's in London. He's at the War Office.'

'Oh God, I might have known. Sorry I asked. It's just they have some smashing flicks in Ringwood. And it's not a bug-house. It's Abbott and Costello this week, until Wednesday anyway. *Hold That Ghost.*'

'I'm sorry,' she said gently. 'Anyhow, you should go to the pictures with someone your own age.'

'I'm nineteen,' he told her. 'I was looking for some-body a bit older. To take me in.'

In those waiting weeks of July and the start of August the Air Ministry, on behalf of the RAF, claimed the destruction of many German raiders who were marauding the southern coasts. In one eight-day period, it was reported, one hundred and forty German planes were shot down and, although the true figure was significantly less, the evidence was strewn across farmland and hillsides. Fleet-footed children were often the first to these aircraft wrecks, eager for pieces of metal, bullets or shreds of parachutes to add to their souvenir collections, and were occasionally discovered with a distressed and embarrassed Luftwaffe pilot in their custody when the panting defence forces eventually arrived.

Sometimes the defence services, and in particular the amateur soldiers of the Home Guard, displayed an eagerness that overcame discipline. Floating down by parachute over the New Forest, Flight-Lieutenant James Nicholson, who had minutes before displayed gallantry which eventually won him the Victoria Cross, was seriously wounded by a shotgun discharged by an excited Home Guard who imagined he was the vanguard of a Nazi paratroop drop.

The Government of occupied Denmark, with a tardy sense of occasion, announced that it was resigning from the League of Nations. With a July budget in Britain Sir Kingsley Wood, the Chancellor, put income tax up to eight and sixpence in the pound, duty was increased on tobacco and beer. Leaflets were showered on the beleaguered island outlining a 'Proposal for Peace' and 'A Last Appeal to Reason' by Adolf Hitler. These too were much prized as souvenirs by children and some were raffled or auctioned for service charities. Winston Churchill sniffed and put the proposals aside. Fearing the worst, the management closed the famous aquarium at

Brighton on the Sussex coast and the fish were sent to be eaten at local hospitals.

The hot summer still lay across England as July became August. At ten o'clock on a close morning Elizabeth walked into Binford and arrived at the shop to find Hob Hobson fixing a cardboard advertisement to one side of his window, a call for Britons to purchase Carter's Little Liver Pills. It said sagely: 'Wartime Living Affects the Liver.'

She smiled through the window and Hob climbed down and came to the door. 'I reckoned it would make a change,' he said rubbing his chin and considering the addition. 'Can't get much display stuff like that now.' The village moved on its placid course about them, sunlight on the street, windows open, flowers in the boxes, old Josh cutting his hedge with all the intensity of a barber. His head bobbed up and down like a man uncertainly taking cover. Hob's shop doorbell tinkled as it always did when there was a touch of breeze. Gates, the gaitered gamekeeper, trudged head down along the pavement with two of his dogs at heel.

From the south came a long sound, a collective cadence none of them had heard before. The village scene became still, eyes turned to the sky; the note increased to a deep and dangerous drone and across the horizon of the roofs appeared a great armada of German planes.

'They've come for us,' muttered Hob. 'This is it, Mrs Lovatt.'

'God help us,' answered Elizabeth staring upwards.

People hurried into their gardens and into the street to gaze at the formations, spread across the sky like the crosses in a cemetery.

'Wonder where they're going,' shouted Gates above the noise. Hob's window began to rattle and he put his hand out to steady the glass.

Children miraculously appeared in the street, congregating excitedly in the open. Elizabeth's first thought was to shout to them to get under cover, but then she saw Alan Stevens, the schoolteacher, appear at the door of his house. He looked up grimly. When he looked down again his face was sad. He saw Elizabeth was watching. 'They're going over,' he said. 'They won't bother with us.'

Tommy Oakes and the Mainprice boys were dancing with excitement in the street. 'Dorniers, sir,' shouted Tommy towards the schoolteacher. 'And that lot's Junkers! Look at them, sir. 'Undreds of them.'

'It's the bees that's going to be the danger,' called Josh Millington across the barricade of his hedge. 'I get worried about the bees.'

The first planes were moderately high, but a second wave moved ponderously in the sky, below the summer clouds, their black and white crosses clear, their engines louder.

'Where's the guns?' demanded Charlie Fox trotting comically sideways down the street, his eyes on the sky. He held a steel helmet above his head, like a man shading his face from the sun or perhaps leading cheers. 'Where's the anti-aircraft guns? Where's our planes?'

'Where's the si-reeeeens,' called his mother loping after him, wiping her hands as if she might be needed. 'What's the use of having si-reeeeens, if they don't let them off? Lot of good that is!'

As if responding, the siren began to sound across

the forest from the police station where PC Brice had belatedly pressed the button. He had waited until the instructions had arrived from the central defence point, as were his orders. The sight of a hundred undoubtedly German bombers could not be acted upon until confirmed by higher authority. It might have been a trick. Now the wail sounded, derisorily faint under the noise of the enemy's engines.

The formations passed leaving bright silence across the village. The birds sounded again, unperturbed. Dogs which had barked, stopped. The children chattered, looking up, waiting for more planes. Alan Stevens came to the school wall. Elizabeth walked across to him.

'You've seen that sort of thing in Spain, I expect,' she said.

'Yes, I'm afraid so. That was like going back in time. My wife died in an air raid.'

'Yes, I was sorry to hear.'

'We don't have an air-raid shelter, even for the children,' he said helplessly. 'This has been designated a "safe" area. I'm supposed to send them home – out in the open – in case of attack.'

'Perhaps it will be finished by the time the August holidays are over,' said Elizabeth. She realized how ambiguous it was. 'I mean, perhaps there won't be as many raids as we think. After all, at the start of the war we thought we'd all be bombed or gassed out of existence in twenty-four hours.'

'I think this time they're serious,' he said surveying the sky, vacant now except for the blue of summer. They could still hear the planes and the sound of gunfire like distant thunder.

A shout came from the village crossroads and Elizabeth turned to see her husband approaching, red-faced, at a respectable trot followed by four of his Home Guards. It was difficult for her to contain the smile. God forbid that he would ever have to confront a stormtrooper. Robert was waving the unit tommy-gun. The others had a rifle and three shotguns between them.

'See the blighters?' Robert demanded furiously as if a personal insult had been perpetrated. 'See them?'

'We could scarcely miss them, dear,' responded Elizabeth.

Her husband appeared hurt. 'No time for jokes, Elizabeth,' he admonished. He glared accusingly at the sky. 'Swine,' he said. 'Flying over here like that. And not a single damned gun fired at them. Where are our defences, I'd like to know?'

'They're firing now,' said Stevens as the explosions grunted in the distance.

'Too late! *Now's* too late,' retorted Robert. 'Pick them off as they cross the coast, I say. They came in just as they pleased. Without a by-your-leave.' He turned to the other men, and then back at Stevens. 'If we could get the punt gun on top of the church perhaps we can get a pot shot at the swine when they come back.' He looked around with wild hope of support.

'The vicar would hardly agree to that,' pointed out Elizabeth mildly. 'Not on the church.'

'Best place,' asserted Robert. 'Catch the blighters by surprise. Always used churches in Flanders. So did the Huns.'

Stevens said nothing but shook his head either in

disagreement or disbelief. Elizabeth added quietly, 'It's not Flanders now, Robert. This is Hampshire and it's nineteen-forty.'

Her husband huffed sulkily. 'That's the bloody trouble,' he said. 'Nobody knows how to fight a war any longer.' He turned to his puzzled followers. 'We'll get up the hill,' he said decisively. 'We'll wait for them. If they come back low enough we might just wing one with a lucky shot.' He turned to Stevens. 'You keep an eye on things here, sergeant,' he suggested. 'We'll handle this.'

He turned and stumped back up the street with his men. The villagers dumbly watched them go. Robert led his volunteers to the summit of the middle hill of the three like sails and there they waited submerged in the gorse for the bombers to return. From the far distance they heard the returning planes. When the raiders did appear they were flying at ten thousand feet. Howling with anger and frustration Robert rose on top of the hillock and fired a single token round of defiance from his pathetic little tommy-gun.

On that morning, 14 August – Eagle Day, so called by Hermann Goering, the fat Marshal of the German Air Force – fleets of bombers began systematic attacks on airfields and other defence installations in the south and south-east of England. Joanne Schorner heard from Washington that a colleague in Berlin had noted Goering's prediction. 'He says that he will eliminate the Royal Air Force in four days, at the most a week,' she said levelly to James.

'I don't think the RAF would agree with that,'

replied James. It was nine o'clock on a warm, grey London evening. The bombers had not come in strength near the capital up to then, apart from one raid when, due to faulty navigation, they dropped high explosives on Cripplegate in the City, bombs intended for oil installations several miles east.

The two sat in St James's Park by the metallic lake. She had waited for him to finish his duties and they walked under the unstirring trees to the lakeside where they sat, a little apart, with few people about and only the plopping sounds of water birds disturbing the park stillness. Behind them a battery of guns had begun their vigil, their noses raised as if smelling the sky, and the balloons were flying at their highest stations, far up in the fading day.

'It's like the eye of the storm here, don't you think?' she suggested. 'In London.'

'Yes,' he agreed. 'It's uncanny. But it will come.'

Joanne said: 'I had our Geneva correspondent contact John Colin's mother.' James quickly looked sideways at her. She continued to study the tin water of the lake. Five flying ducks seamed the water as they landed.

'What did she say?'

'She grabbed the chance,' she replied. 'I was really amazed. I think she's more of a Red Cross lady than a mother. She said she was worried about John Colin being here.'

'As well she might be,' muttered James. 'It sounds as if Mrs Perkins is having an engrossing time. And she has agreed that you take him to the States with you?'

'She has. Her lawyer called me today and I'm going

to see him tomorrow. I'd like to take at least one little boy out of here before it all starts, James.'

'How soon?'

She shrugged and, still not looking at him, she said: 'The sea passage is no good. That ship, the *City of Benares*, is full. They're packing all the young kids they can on board. I think, though, I can get two seats on the flying boat. We would be in New York the next day.'

'I see,' he said. 'And that will be soon.'

'Right,' she confirmed. 'They won't let out the exact date of departure for security reasons, but I guess it will be towards the end of this month or early in September.' She moved her hand and put it around his arm at the elbow, squeezing the khaki sleeve. 'While we're sitting here like this,' she recited so quietly he could hardly hear the words. She continued to study the lake but further away now, and the little green-treed islands at its centre. 'While we're here, James, I just want you to know that I feel very deeply for you. You've made a great difference to my life. There's something I haven't told you but which I'll let you know about in good time. Please don't ask me now.'

James felt his throat tighten. He looked at her soft profile, the hair fluffy on the forehead, the serious expression of thought, the faint colour in the cheek. 'I won't ask you now,' he agreed. 'If that's what you want.'

'Thank you. That's good. I'd like us to remember each other very well.'

Twenty

Engines in the skies sounded through all the following days. The high blue was furrowed with creamy trails and gentle puffs of gunfire. From the ground the trails were remotely beautiful changing form, fading like a visible echo long after the fight was finished, the gunbursts like dandelion clocks. Men working in the southern fields straightened up to watch the deadly manoeuvres overhead, machine-gun sounds filtering down as delicate as light rain. Children squeezed their eyes against the sun, standing in light dresses and open shirts in playgrounds, meadows and streets, to watch. Wives paused to follow a stricken plane falling, then turned away with closed eyes as it exploded on the earth. Every day hundreds of aircraft occupied the sky. Bombs straddled the British airfields; defending fighters took off between the yawning craters. In four weeks the German Air Force lost 1,389 planes and the RAF 792. They called it the Battle of Britain. In London newspaper sellers chalked the day's toll on their placards in the way they proclaimed cricket scores in peacetime.

Evening closed slowly over Binford on 16 August, a gritty sort of evening, for someone had been burning garden rubbish and the smoke had drifted on the light, late breeze over the neighbouring houses. It mingled with the real dusk, lurking among the trees and gardens of the village. Men had come in from their work and were listening to the wireless news sitting at the meal table. Children were called in from play. Windows were shuttered and near-silence fell upon the houses.

At nine-thirty a low-flying Dornier, going home early and anxious to jettison its remaining bombs, dropped a stick of small incendiaries, which burst and flamed in the empty village streets. Three also fell in a clutch on to Josh Millington's cottage and another set the old roof blazing on John Lampard's long white house down by the estuary.

Robert, like a man in a farce, rumbled hurriedly from his bathroom, a huge pre-war towel around his bulging middle, almost falling down the stairs, only a minute after the plane had passed. 'Something's been hit in the village,' he called hoarsely to Elizabeth who was making tea in the kitchen. 'There's a damned great fire somewhere. You can see the glow.' Wadsworth, thinking he was going for a walk, stood up and yawned.

Suddenly white-faced, Elizabeth hurried into the sitting-room, the empty teapot hanging from her hand. She switched off the music coming from the wireless. Grasping his towel with one hand and motioning Elizabeth to turn out the lights, which she was already doing, he padded to the garden door and they both stared out into the deep evening. Above the trees at the foot of their garden a casual orange glow flickered against the dusk. 'Oh, my God,' muttered Elizabeth as a prayer.

Robert turned heavily. They shut the door together

as if to stem marauders. Elizabeth turned on the lights. 'Get Petrie, will you,' said Robert. 'I'll get some clothes on. Then ring the pub, make sure everybody gets out to help.'

'Yes, yes of course,' Elizabeth replied vaguely, forcing herself to steadiness. She dialled the coast-guard station. 'There are two fires,' Petrie told her. 'One is John Lampard's house along the river. The other's nearer you. I've called the brigades from Lymington and Lyndhurst. Tell your husband I'll be at the Lampards' as soon as my relief gets here. He's on his way.'

'What's he say?' shouted Robert from the bedroom as soon as she had finished. She could hear his elephant steps overhead.

'John Lampard's is on fire,' she called up the stairs trying to control her voice. 'Petrie called the brigades. There's another fire in the village but he doesn't know where.'

'Lampard's!' bawled Robert. He appeared at the top of the stairs and shouted it down at her as if she were to blame. 'That'll burn like tinder. The blighters!' He was wearing his voluminous, newly issued Home Guard trousers and was buttoning up his flapping khaki shirt. His face was flushed with fluster. Turning back into the bedroom he called, 'Ring the pub, Elizabeth. Make sure they're doing something.'

'I was just going to,' she called back. Kathy Barratt put her through with surprising efficiency. Elizabeth's right hand which held the earpiece was shaking. Charlie Fox's mother answered the phone, choked with excitement. 'Who?' she managed to say. 'Who is it? Oh, Mrs Lovatt. Josh's house is on fire. They've hit his roof. Everybody's there. Charlie told me I've got to stay here.' She sounded as if she hoped Elizabeth would rescind the order.

Elizabeth said: 'Keep calm, Mrs Fox,' and put the earpiece on its cradle. 'Robert,' she called up the stairs. He appeared, more or less dressed but with his bootlaces undone, at the top of the stairs. 'It's Josh Millington's,' she told him. 'The house is on fire.'

'Help me with my laces, will you?' he pleaded. 'Do the left one.' She tied his left boot while he tied the right. He straightened up and violently buttoned his tunic. 'You'd better stay here, Elizabeth,' he said.

'Certainly not,' she returned firmly. 'What will I do here? I can help, I'm sure. I'll drive for a start. You can't see a thing.'

The dog had to be pushed firmly indoors. They hurried from the house and across the garden. The arc of orange filled the front of the horizon now, clearly outlining the elms and beeches. There was the smell of ash in the air. She caught her breath like a sob as she ran towards the car. She climbed into the driving seat and Robert bundled in beside her with such force that he knocked her sideways. 'Sorry, Elizabeth,' he grunted. 'Hurry up now.'

She had already started the engine and she turned the car noisily on the gravel away from the dark house. The headlights were mere slits but her eyes were accurate and she drove surely through the lanes out on to the main road and down the hill into Binford. From behind they heard a clanging bell and Robert looked over his shoulder to see the wide shape of the Lyndhurst fire engine rolling speedily down the slope.

The village was thronged with people, most of them standing in dumb excitement, their shapes outlined in the light of the flames that waved through the roof of the stone house. Police Constable Brice, some ARP wardens and several Home Guard men were telling the unmoving spectators to keep back. 'Back now, back,' said Brice, then ridiculously: 'There's nothing to see. Nothing to get excited about.' Elizabeth pulled up the car and Robert rushed out, half-tumbling, getting his legs straight and then running towards the blaze. Elizabeth sat helplessly for a moment and then left the car and walked towards the dark crowd of people crowned by the rising flames. The firemen, whose grey engine had pulled past them as they stopped, were pulling out hoses and manhandling their ladders. Her husband's voice joined the others shouting orders to the watchers to stand back.

Without hurry she walked towards the scene. The onlookers had been pushed back to the pavement across the road, most of them women with children in their creased nightclothes, watching the blaze as once they used to watch the village bonfire on Guy Fawkes Night; the same round, wondering faces, fingers and thumbs in mouths, skin glowing orange with the reflection of the flames. The men who had been trying to get some of the Millingtons' belongings from the house now stood back also to make room for the firemen. To her relief she saw that Josh was standing round-backed in the road, tragic and solitary, watching the flames eat his home. His wife, crouched under a blanket, stood a few feet to one side, separate, as if they did not want to discuss the matter. The hoses were pouring water through the gaping roof now and the firemen had scaled the ladders to the upper windows with more hoses. It was plain that not much of the little village house would ever be saved.

Elizabeth moved quietly towards the old gardener and took his elbow in her hand. He did not respond immediately but continued staring aghast at the scene. When he did turn and saw who it was his mouth trembled. 'Oh, Mrs Lovatt,' he whispered. 'All my bees is dead. That smoke killed they all.'

Elizabeth had to reply. She tried to comfort him. 'The pumpkins are all right, though, aren't they, Josh? Your prize pumpkins.'

'Aye,' he nodded solemnly. 'That's a relief at least, Mrs Lovatt. Glass'll be a bit blackened but I'll clean it off tomorrow.'

Elizabeth could hardly prevent herself crying. She did not trust herself to speak. 'Good job t'weren't one of they big bombs,' sighed Josh. 'Blown everything down that would, greenhouse and all. Wouldn't need to dig the garden again after one of those. Do the job for me, wouldn't it?'

She attempted to smile at his joke. Robert came bundling back through the smoke. 'Can't do much here,' he announced. He saw Josh and his wife. 'Oh . . . damned hard luck, Josh,' he said patting the old man's arm. The wife lifted her wax-like head from the blanket and acknowledged the sympathy with a nod. She still did not look towards the flames. 'We'll see that everything is done, don't worry,' Robert told them confidently. He glanced towards Elizabeth. 'What about tonight? We must get you some accommodation.'

''Tis all right, sir,' said the old lady with unexpected

firmness. 'My brother-in-law . . .' she indicated Josh, "is brother, that is. Gone to get his wagon. We'll go over there tonight with them.'

'Good, good,' nodded Robert. He turned quickly to his wife. 'We ought to get over to Lampard's. See what's happening. Peter Dove's just come from there and he says they're all right, nobody hurt, but the house has caught it.' He took her elbow. Josh thrust out his heavy hand and the old lady a thin collection of fingers and both Elizabeth and Robert shook with them.

'Goodnight, Josh,' said Elizabeth as she went towards the car. 'Goodnight, Mrs Millington. You escaped, that's the main thing.'

"'Tis the bees,' Josh called after her. 'That's the trouble of it.'

'All his bees died,' explained Elizabeth as she climbed into the car and Robert clambered in the other side.

'So I believe,' said Robert. 'Blessing in disguise really. Bad enough having a bombing without having a million angry bees zooming around.'

Elizabeth started the car and pulled around the fire engine and the other vehicles in the littered street. Hob Hobson was outside his shop. His wife was throwing buckets of water everywhere. 'Sparks!' he called to them as they went by. 'Can't be too careful about sparks.'

They thought Millie would be at the Lampards because her house was only a brief distance through the trees. The car wriggled down the heavily scented lanes, the cow parsley giving off its odours in the dark, and turned by the river to see the glow reflected in the night water.

They turned into the drive, between the rhodo-dendrons, in time to see the whole blazing roof of the fine house collapse into its inside, like a man's head falling into his body. 'Oh, bloody hell,' muttered Robert. 'What a ghastly sight.'

Elizabeth felt tears streaming unchecked down her cheeks by the time they left the car. Now there was no hurry even, for there was nothing to be done. The Lymington firemen, their fire engine straddling the lawn, were standing back, black with sweat, knowing that they were defeated; they could not save the house.

Millie came through the smoke towards them, wiping her eyes with the back of her hands. Elizabeth offered her a handkerchief. 'You look like a child who's been crying,' she said gently.

'It's just the smoke,' said Millie.

A glowing red and yellow cone now crowned the house, shot with sparks and issuing smoke. The windows burned orange and one by one fell in. The trio walked forward. The heat of the fire came to meet them like an unseen barrier. On the lawn, behind the fire engine, among a few pieces of belongings, the Lampards stood holding hands like castaways.

Robert put his big arm around Joan Lampard and she looked at him briefly before collapsing against his shoulder and sobbing. Millie moved to the other side of her and stroked her bent head. John Lampard, his face fixed, but his mouth trembling turned to Robert and said quietly, 'First the boat, then this, eh, Robert?'

'You've been unlucky, John,' answered Robert inadequately.

There came a deep rushing sound from the house

as if something were trying to get out. It was only a fire noise. The walls burned and peeled.

John Lampard said, slowly, but firmly, 'Three and a half centuries that house has been there. And now it's gone in half an hour.'

During those days, there was hardly an hour when there was not fighting high overhead. Vapour trails curled like tangled wool and the smoke of battle mixed with the August air. Burning planes fell to earth. Sometimes a parachute would appear, like a single, suddenly opening flower.

Three days after the incendiary bombs had dropped on the houses of John Lampard and Josh Millington, the two areas now standing like some used sacrificial sites, a Junkers bomber crashed on open forest ground a mile from Binford, providing an immediate spectacle for the village boys who were playing Germans and English in the bracken nearby.

The Luftwaffe pilot, attempting to belly-land the plane clear of trees, succeeded in striking the only building for miles, a stone barn used for storing winter feed for the wild ponies. The Junkers bounced and rolled over like an acrobat as it slid across the bumpy land. The boys, after the initial amazement, set off in a cavalry charge across the uneven ground, being joined by some village girls who were washing their dolls' clothes in a forest stream.

Elbows and bare knees flying, Tommy Oakes, in his green uniform, led the charge, smacking his thigh like a horseman urging his steed. He was the most agile boy in the district and he reached the edge of the area before the others. The plane was lying peacefully, a wisp of smoke, but nothing more, trickling from its starboard engine, the propeller blade bent as a scimitar.

'Wait! Everybody stop!' shouted Tommy squeakily as the posse of twenty children piled up behind him. He held out his skinny arms.

'Bullets,' said one of the boys pointing, wonder in his voice. 'Look at all them bullets lying about.'

'And there's a German's boot,' whispered another. 'I wouldn't mind 'aving that.'

'That's mine,' said Tommy decisively. 'I saw it first.'

'Why don't we get them?' asked one of the girls impatiently. 'Nobody'll know.'

'Bombs,' announced Tommy darkly. 'Whole bloody thing could blow up. Us with it. Don't you listen to anything they tell you?' He glared at the girl, Kathy Enwright, who was pale and in love with him, although she had never said so.

She regarded him wispily. 'I see. Sorry,' she said.

'We better wait till somebody comes,' said Tommy. He looked closely towards the wrecked plane. 'Don't think there's anybody left in there. Not living.'

They stood in their semicircle, with the girls slightly behind the boys, watching the black-crossed bomber lying like a floored elephant. 'There's a man on the shed roof,' said a small voice from the rear. 'Lying on the roof. I reckon he's dead.'

As one they turned and looked at the boy, Georgie Mainprice, who had come with the news. Short as they were, the winter-feed barn was out of their sight, over a slope towards Binford. ''Ow d'you reckon he's dead?' asked Tommy Oakes.

'He ain't movin',' replied Georgie solemnly. 'I shouted up and then I chucked some stones up at 'im. I 'it 'im on the 'ead wiv one, but 'ee didn't move.'

The gaggle of children wheeled and went riotously down the slope. As soon as they had cleared the ridge they saw the man clearly, on his face, lying like someone putting the tiles right. Tommy was in the van quickly and led the eager charge to the foot of the barn. There they stopped, a little way from the building, where the ground still canted enough to provide them with a gallery. They stood, silent and enthralled, at the sight of the prostrate man in a flying suit.

'Must 'ave fell out of the plane,' said Tommy.

'Wonder 'ee didn't go right through the roof,' put in Gordon Giles, who everybody called Franco. 'That 'ole roof is rotten.'

'Let's get 'im down,' suggested Billy Hobson. He was usually a timid boy and he was enjoying the bravado. Some of the girls were looking at him. 'Get a rope around 'is leg and we can tug 'un down,' he went on. 'I never seen a dead Jerry.'

'Can't,' announced Tommy firmly.

'Who says?'

'I do,' replied Tommy facing him. 'You got to have respect when 'ee's dead, see. And he might be booby-trapped.'

'You think you know every soddin' thing,' blurted Billy, angry at being diminished. 'Just 'cos you wear those cub's togs. You ain't even *in* the cubs.'

Tommy closed with him and the two boys suddenly began to grapple. They rolled down the bank punching blindly, the others shouting, the German on the roof, for a moment and in a moment, forgotten. As they stood up, apart, breathless, flushed and scratched, Kathleen Enwright appeared on the bank above them. Nobody had noticed she had not been with them.

'I brought you the boot, Tommy,' she called as she began to walk down. 'For your souvenirs.'

Tommy flushed with pleasure. 'You shouldn't 'ave,' he said. 'But I'll take it.'

He ignored the grimacing Billy and walked up the slope towards the little girl. She held up the shin-length green flying boot like a prize and handed it to him modestly.

'Thanks, Kath,' he muttered deeply. He took the boot from her. 'That'll look good. I got a German belt already. Franco's seen my German belt.'

Franco nodded confirmation.

'There's something inside,' mentioned Tommy. He turned the boot upside down and shook it firmly. Something like red wadding tipped out on the ground and the children crowded round to look.

'It's a bit of foot,' whispered Kath. 'Look, I can see the toenail.' She began to cry and turned and ran away.

By now Millie had made herself stop counting the planes in. She purposely turned her back on the mess window or the little open door of the room they used as a library, so that she could not see the Hurricanes coming back. The squadron was flying up to ten sorties a day now and almost every day someone failed to return. She resisted counting the engines as they shuddered overhead to come into the runway.

August continued with many cloudless days. Good invasion weather, people said wryly. But the sea remained clear of enemies, the German stayed on his opposite conquered shore, and the only battles were joined in the sky.

Millie was arranging books in the library when the first flight of the morning returned. She had been around the mess and the recreation room picking up volumes left lying about by the young men. Often they were left open, face down on the grass outside the operations room when the pilots were called to take off on the approach of raiders. The titles said much. *The Thirty-Nine Steps, How to Become an Accountant, The Beano Annual, Highways and Byways in The Levant, Gentlemen Prefer Blondes, Great Cricketers of the Twenties* and *Fanny Hill*. The last named had not, she was certain, originated in the station library, but she had found it abandoned on the grass one day and claimed it with a smile. From then on it was borrowed every day. Now, as she took it with the others into the shady library room, she opened it at the page where one of the pilots had left a lemonade straw as a marker. ' "I saw, with wonder and surprise, what? not the plaything of a boy," ' she read aloud, ' "not the weapon of a man, but a maypole!" ' Millie giggled to herself and replaced the straw in the page.

The noise of the fighter engines faltered and one by one died on the tarmac outside; she went to the door now and saw by their jovial demeanour that they had all come back. There was shoulder slapping and banter as with boys changing classrooms at school.

One pilot turned his head and paused as he saw her framed in the door. He turned off from the rest and she could see by his chubby shape that it was Graham. He had taken off his flying helmet and his sweat plastered his hair. With a shock she realized how haggard he was.

'Come for a nice book,' he announced cheerfully. 'Got something adventurous? Biggles or Percy F. Westerman. I could do with a bit of excitement.'

She saw how ironic the joke was. 'See the conquering hero comes,' she recited cheerfully. 'Have a good morning?'

'All right,' he said. 'Survived it anyway.' He began to read along the spines of the books. 'Now let's have a look. Something to keep me out of trouble . . .' He glanced up at her. His eyes were misty and black-rimmed. 'Occupied.'

Millie picked up a book: '*How to Become an Accountant*,' she announced. 'What about that?'

He smiled wryly. 'Don't think I'd finish the course,' he said taking the book from her and touching her fingers as he did so. He sighed. 'Anyway, I'm off the hook,' he said. 'Twenty-four hours of peace and doing nothing. I'd go to the pictures in Ringwood tonight if I had somebody to go with. It's *The Mummy's Terror*, Mummy as in Egyptian, that is. Not mother sort of mummy. I wouldn't mind seeing it but I'm scared to go by myself.'

She regarded him, his shoulders sagging under the flying suit and his weariness, the face turned up hopefully towards her. 'What time does it start?' she asked.

She went home in the late afternoon, let herself in from the sunlit garden and made a cup of tea. It seemed senseless, somehow, sitting there drinking tea as if nothing was happening. Or lending out books when the readers might never return. She wondered what James might say if she told him she was going to the picture palace in a small town with a nineteen-year-old airman. Not that James was likely to ring. He had not done so for three days. By the time he finished at night it was very late, he said, and he did not want to disturb her. And he would not call her at the air station in case, as he said, they thought she had some fussy husband pursuing her.

The telephone sounded. She took her cup with her and went across the room to answer it.

'Hello, Millie.' It was Harry. He sounded throaty.

'Harry, how are you?'

'Fine, thanks. Fed up with waiting for Jerry to come.'

'He's come,' she said. 'He's overhead every day.'

'Yes, of course. I meant the real thing . . . well, you know what I mean.' There was a hesitation. Then he said: 'You're all right, are you?'

'Yes, I'm fine.'

'Good. I just thought I ought to ring.'

Her lips tightened. 'You don't need to feel like that,' she said. 'You mustn't feel so guilty. We've joked about it over the years, but *you* know I've always felt that you were somewhere around. And I've sensed that it was the same for you. If needed.'

She heard him sigh. He said, 'I wish I could get things straight like that in my mind.'

Millie answered: 'It's all I can think of just now.''

'Yes, I see. What are you doing now?'

Surprised at the question she said: 'Well, I was

drinking a cup of tea and then I'm going to get ready to go to the pictures.'

'Oh, really.'

'Yes, I'm going to see *The Mummy's Terror*.'

Three hours later in the small smoky cinema, grandly called the Regal, in Ringwood, she sat beside Graham, holding hands, while the screen was rent with the cries of horrified archaeologists who had disinterred a ghoul three thousand years old. Halfway through the film she felt a touch on her shoulder and turned to find her cheek against his short curly hair. He was asleep and he gently began to snore.

'You missed half the picture,' she said as they were walking towards the bus stop.

'I would do. Was it good?'

'Riveting.'

The people coming from the cinema soon dispersed and they walked along the old black streets of the little town, theirs the only footsteps. The bus stop was in the market place. She was to get the bus to Lyndhurst where she had left her bicycle. He could get another back to the RAF station.

'It's haunted, you know, our billet,' he said. 'Some old dear is supposed to walk around with her head under her arm.'

'Alicia Lisle,' said Millie.

'You knew her?'

'Not personally,' she laughed. She put her arm into his. He patted her hand. 'She lived in Moyles Court centuries ago, and when she was in her seventies she was sentenced to death by Judge Jeffreys at Winchester Assizes. They cut off her head.'

'What for?'

'Harbouring two priests, if I remember.'

'People used to have some rum excuses for killing each other, didn't they?'

The bus was at the stop, its windows blacked out, its engine rumbling. Before it went she kissed him and he said: 'Thanks for coming to the pictures.' She boarded the bus and sat, eyes closed, all the way through the dark forest to Lyndhurst.

James realized how strange it was to be walking along a leafy London suburban road, holding the hand of a small boy, while Joanne strolled smiling on the other side of the child. Trees were ruffled above them, leaves and branches sounding like the sea, sunshine mottled the pavement. They had taken the train to an almost deserted Sunday station and were now walking the warm half a mile to their destination.

'Are the camels and the elephants safe here?' inquired John Colin. 'The Germans won't drop bombs on them?' He looked lugubrious at the thought of a bombed elephant. James smiled.

'They're just fine,' Joanne assured him. 'They must think it's just like a vacation.'

'Will there be a circus again? After the war?' inquired the boy. 'Are the clowns here too?'

They arrived at a high fence, thickly knitted with barbed wire, and James raised his eyebrows. As they cleared the trees and the wayside hedges they saw that the compound within the wire was occupied by a strange congregation of men, trudging men, wearing odd but respectable clothes – coats, waistcoats and some hats; men sitting on the steps of long huts, smoking, grimacing at newspapers. Some just stared into space or gazed through the wire. They looked oddly hopeless as if waiting for a train which in their hearts they knew was unlikely ever to arrive.

'Aliens,' said James as he realized. 'God help us, they've put the poor blighters with the circus animals.'

'No, sir,' came a loud voice through the wire. 'The elephants are right along the street. They don't let us mix up with them.' His voice was accented and his laugh hollow.

Joanne stared at James and then said 'Thank you' to the man. She suddenly asked him: 'Where is your home?'

'Cricklewood, London,' replied the man firmly. His face just fitted an aperture in the wire, like a lugubrious picture in a thin frame. With less conviction he added: 'Before that, Salzburg.' He stepped two paces back from the wire and performed a token but elegant bow. 'I am an enemy alien, madam. I am in prison here because Churchill is afraid of me.' He emitted a nasal laugh, turned and shuffled away. Several other men had stopped to stare at the trio outside the wire. One glared single-eyed through a monocle. As they moved on towards the next gate he shouted: 'Get us out of here, British officer! Get us out!'

'This story gets better,' suggested Joanne slyly. 'I only came to write about the homeless camels.'

'*Don't*,' he pleaded seriously. He shook his head. 'Somebody, somewhere, lacks finesse, I think.' He stared at the men. They seemed to have forgotten him now and had returned to their private despond.

A trumpeting through the trees stopped John Colin;

he hung on to their arms, amazed at first, then with a slow delight drifting over his face. 'That,' confirmed Joanne, 'was the call of the wild.'

The man who came to greet them at the gate was improbably dressed in a ringmaster's red tailed coat and gaiters, but with a mothy and discoloured jersey below. His large stomach expanded the jersey and pushed the curves of the coat aside. 'Ah, I got the message,' he said without formality. 'Want to have a look around, do you? Well, it's not very posh. My name's Nately and I'm in charge here. Most of the time I'm the only one here anyway. All alone with the wild beasts.' He laughed patronizingly and shook hands before he led them into the compound with its assorted huts and larger buildings below the trees. A girl of about seventeen, wearing a blouse and jodhpurs, came out of a stable with a bale of hay swaying on a pitchfork. 'Is this for Rajah?' she asked in a cockney voice.

'Right,' said the man. Despite their presence he paused to watch the girl's rolling buttocks as she went up the yard. 'Here,' he said, as if suddenly remembering his role, 'we have some of the circus animals. Not many, a few camels, the elephants and one old lion, who's just about had it. Mind, there's a few horses, as well, and a lot of the old circus props. The animals get fed up because they haven't got much to do. Most of them won't see this war out.' He saw the girl at the top of the yard. 'Sal,' he called hoarsely, 'get that old saddle on Rajah, will you?'

'Right you are,' she called back. 'Where's the ladder?'

'In the shed. Give him another half a bale to keep

him sweet.' He lowered his face towards John Colin. 'How about a ride on a jumbo?' he suggested. He straightened up. 'I suppose I'd better ask mum and dad,' he added.

He caught Joanne's uncertain glance at James. 'It's quite safe, madam,' he assured. 'Old Rajah's a bit ancient now, the stuffing's coming out of him, but he still remembers carrying the kids around pre-war. While Miss Ashworth is getting him ready perhaps you'd like to see the circus props. They're all in the barn just here.'

Squeakily he opened one side of a pair of double doors and turned on a wan electric light. They stepped into an eerie place, the walls hung with huge painted heads and costumes, holes for the eyes, the mouths laughing widely but without mirth; a whole clown's suit was suspended from a beam as if the performer had finally despaired and committed suicide. The little boy looked entranced but apprehensive. He touched tentatively the frame of a one-wheeled cycle with its saddle ten feet from the ground. Amazingly, the man called Nately quickly picked it away from the wall and without preliminaries mounted it and began to ride it furiously around the centre of the barn. It creaked and squeaked as he pedalled, shouting madly: 'Roll along now! Roll up, ladies and gentlemen. Last performance this year! All the thrills of the big top!'

He ceased just as abruptly as he had begun, jumping lightly to the ground and steadying the cycle with one hand. He whirled it on its wheel and set it against the wall. 'Don't do any harm to keep in trim,' he announced. Joanne and James were laughing but John Colin's eyes were filled with surprised admiration. The man picked up a trumpet and blew down it hideously. Then he balanced a red ball on his head and two others on his fingertips. 'Happy days,' he said.

The girl Sal appeared in the doorway. 'Rajah's ready,' she sniffed. Nately let the balancing balls fall. 'I managed to get it on.'

Apprehensively they went out to the yard again. A dusty-looking elephant was standing apathetically, its trunk swinging like a rope. On its back was a threadbare saddle of what had once been red and gold leather. A ladder had been placed against its flank. 'Well . . .' began Joanne apprehensively.

Nately said hurriedly: 'Perfectly safe, lady. Sal will go with you.'

Joanne looked at James who grimaced. 'You want to ride on the elephant, don't you?' he said to John Colin.

'Of course he does,' broke in Nately. 'What lad wouldn't? Not many of them get a chance nowadays, do they. Right, up we go. You too, sir.'

Feeling foolish James began to climb the ladder to the elephant's high back. He wished fervently that he was not in uniform. He reached the saddle and sat on one of the side-facing seats. He could feel the elephant wobbling beneath him. Breathless with anticipation John Colin followed and then the sheepishly smiling Joanne. The girl Sal came last. Nately removed the ladder. He went to the front of the elephant and taking a ringmaster's whip from inside the door of the barn touched the animal on the mouth. It began to ponder forward.

They went, yard after slow yard, around the

compound and between the buildings. Two other elephants in an enclosure trumpeted as they trundled by but the aged Rajah took no heed.

'You'll be able to smell the camels soon,' announced Nately confidently from below. He was walking with them. 'They niff like billy-o. And kick! One of them kicked my good wife, just a glancing blow, but she's been laid up for five weeks. Hasn't she, Sal?'

'I'll say,' grunted Sal. 'Look out for the trees just here. You've got to duck.'

The camels gathered in a disconsolate group in another enclosure, bunched like a pile of threadbare rugs. 'What are they eating?' asked John Colin.

'Nothing,' answered the girl. 'They do that all the time, just move their jaws around and around. I expect they're just practising.'

Joanne, trying to hide her reaction to this wisdom, looked away and James followed her glance. They were nearing the area of the gate and, after clearing some trees, they came to a high honeycomb fence, against which the hapless aliens were now congregated, clutching on to the wire as prisoners and caged birds always do. The men, mostly middle-aged or elderly, with stomachs, fallen shoulders, domed heads, began to cheer, not derisively but as if they were pleased to see that someone, at least, was enjoying life. One produced a flute and began to play a cheerful jig. The elephant looked around with slow interest, found it was unexciting and plodded on. 'German spies,' announced the girl as if it were another section of the circus quarters. 'They ought to be shot.'

The aliens summoned a last cheer as the huge

trousers of the elephant's backside went around the corner of a building and from view. James climbed down the ladder and helped Joanne and the boy. 'How do you get on with the neighbours?' he asked Nately.

The circus man leaned closer. 'Bastards, aren't they, sir?' he whispered man to man. 'Always moaning. Ought to have them digging trenches, I say. And they've got the nerve to complain about the smell of the camels.'

When they left, John Colin holding a coloured flag which had been the man's parting gesture, Nately locked the rusting gate behind them with an air of finality which suggested that he would not open it again for some years. The girl Sal stood next to him and watched them go. Then they turned and went back towards the buildings round the compound. James glanced at Joanne. 'Have you ever seen anything like that?' he said.

'Not very often,' she agreed. 'War certainly has some unusual aspects.'

'I didn't like that man,' put in John Colin. 'But he was clever on that bike, wasn't he.'

They had no choice but to walk along by the perimeter of the aliens' camp again. A group of men, including the one with the flute, followed them on the other side of the wire, observing them, but in silence. The flute player had ceased his tune and now carried his instrument under his arm like a cane.

'Sir . . . sir . . . Major Lovatt!'

Surprised, they stopped. The perambulating prisoners on the reverse side of the wire halted also. Their heads moved around on their worn necks. A younger man was advancing to the wire. James realized he had seen him somewhere before. The man reached the wire, clutching it. 'Major . . . oh I beg your pardon for this interruption, but I thought you would remember me . . .'

'I do,' said James. 'Yes, Mr . . . Mr Burton, wasn't it? From the estate agents.'

'*Wasn't* it,' emphasized the man. 'Now it is Bormann again. Look where they have put me. In here. Why do they do this to me, major? Can you get me out?'

James looked at Joanne. 'Would you . . . I wondered . . . would you walk back to the station with John Colin? Perhaps I'd better . . .'

Joanne smiled and nodded: 'Sure, we'll wait for you.'

'I won't be very long.' He looked at his watch. 'It's half an hour for the train anyway. I think I ought to try and see this chap.' He said through the wire, 'How do I get in?'

'Easy, easy,' called a toothless alien. 'It's getting out is the trouble!'

'Yes, yes,' said Bormann anxiously, ignoring his fellow-internee. 'Go to the gate, sir. I will ask the commandant. He will allow it, I am sure. For an officer.'

Joanne took the boy's hand and they continued towards the station. John Colin hung back several times to see what James was doing. James, making his way towards the wired gate, waved and Joanne and the boy waved back.

'Your wife and little son are very nice,' said Bormann. They sat at a wooden table under a canvas awning so faded that its stripes were only just discernible. Two collapsible canvas chairs, the unchecked growth of weeds and some rampant poppies around them gave the place a tropical air.

'It looks nice,' said Bormann, 'but it is a bad place. I want to be away from here.' He looked starkly at James. 'First the Nazis,' he complained. 'Now the fucking elephants. They drive me crazy, those fucking elephants, if you will excuse me. Hooting like a mad band. And they *smell*. Those and those ridiculous camels. Never will I forget the smell.' He regarded the Englishman sorrowfully. 'You hear that I have learned to swear in English. All the time it is *fucking* this and *fucking* that. I learn it from the guards here. They say it all the time.'

'What do you do to keep yourself occupied?' asked James.

'Do? Sir, there is nothing to do. I cannot be an estate agent in this place. First they set me writing letters to German people. With another man. We had to write letters to be dropped from aeroplanes.'

'Leaflets,' nodded James. He had always wondered who wrote the leaflets.

'Another British madness. Here you are trapped . . . yes, *trapped*, that is the word, on these few fields with all the sea and the Germans around and it is the *British* who write to the *Germans* telling *them* to surrender. What madness is that?' He stared at the sunshine making geometric patterns on the warped plywood under his feet. 'There was another man to write these leaflets, as you say, also with me. But they took him away because he was no good. I think he really *liked* Hitler. He spelled Adolf A-D-O-L-P-H-E. *Adolphe*. He made it sound like some philosopher.'

'What would you like to do if you were away from here?' asked James.

'Anything.' His enthusiasm shone but then he paused with the patent thought that he had over-committed himself. 'Anything, but not dangerous, you understand, sir. Not spying in Germany or in my own country. I could never be a spy in Vienna anyway because everybody knows me there.'

'What happened to your mother? I remember you telling me about your mother.'

'She is working in the Harrods store. Doing very well, thank you. They did not arrest her because they say she is harmless. But I also am harmless. I am a refugee, not a spy. I would like to work in Harrods.'

James rose to go. He shook Bormann's hand. 'I will see if there's anything that can be done to get you released,' he promised. 'It seems that the whole system is a little odd.' At the gate the man was playing the flute as he went out. 'God Save the King', he played. Bormann called after him hopefully. 'Some of us, the aliens, they sent to the Island of Man. There I hear it is like a holiday. It is very nice. Maybe they could send me there, sir.'

On the evening of 20 August, Winston Churchill was to broadcast one of his stirring speeches on the wireless. That it would be stirring there was no doubt; they always were. Even the dullest mind could not fail to respond to the resonance of voice, the gallant words and phrases of that summer, phrases that were already written deeply into the pages of history.

At RAF Moyles Court, however, on that mellow late daylight hour, the wireless set in the mess and the second set in the stand-by room issued their sound to little but tables and chairs. In the mess the stewards were clearing tables and there was only one man in the stand-by room when Millie entered, a pilot who said little and read deeply all through the periods when he was not flying. He was twenty-five years old and tended to treat the others as the boys they were.

Outside on the grass alongside the airfield young men lounged, like wasps in their yellow Mae West life jackets. They made up the last stand-by flight of the day, for the light was fading. They lay scattered in the warm and settled air, joking, reading, lying and intently studying the now vacant battlefield over their heads, or kicking a saggy football around. Sometimes the ball, punted off course, fell among a group of reclining pilots who shouted protests as people disturbed on a beach might do. They were waiting for the previous operational flight to come back. It had taken off twenty minutes before but the Germans they had been dispatched to intercept had turned back before crossing the coast. It had been a good day for the squadron, for no one, so far, had been lost.

Not for the first time Millie thought how strange the battles were; like performances, kept to certain times with set rules, ceasing with the oncoming of night. The sky would fall quite suddenly quiet then. There were a few times in the hours of darkness when bombers drummed blindly overhead but they were passing enemies and they had not yet begun their bombing of London by night. The British fighter pilots knew they would not be called out in darkness, for there was nothing they could do; the time of the night-fighter was yet to come. So they turned over in the safe luxury of sleep.

She had thought about it on the train, in her house, or riding her bicycle, or when, with the many watchers below, she had traced their conflicts in the sky (she sometimes felt certain that she could recognize individual Hurricanes five thousand feet above her head). On the ground there was often a curious picnic atmosphere. People sat in the open air with their war-time bread sandwiches to squint at the lofty curls of vapour trails; pointing out a slow parachute or a spilling plane. The fliers themselves jovially crowded village inns or lined the bar of their station mess, when they were not sunbathing beside the runway, or facing death among clouds.

The combatants had as little idea as the everyday civilian of the widespread gravity of the battle; of how the shortage of replacements for lost aircraft and lost pilots threatened to defeat them despite their successes and their courage. Nor did it appear to concern them. Only the personal moments did; the German coming to attack and their going to meet him, to turn him back or destroy him, the laughter and the beer afterwards.

They believed, as did the civilians, that these fights in the sky were only the preliminary skirmishes to the real battle, the invasion by ground forces. They were not dismayed by the prospect, for tomorrows did not figure greatly in their thoughts. The evil of each day was quite sufficient.

Churchill was due to broadcast at nine o'clock. Charlie Fox's mother in the Old Crown at Binford had said that it was not Churchill at all who made the speeches but an impersonator. Churchill was too busy. She also said that Lord Haw-Haw, broadcasting that day from Germany, had said that the Lymington clock was fast – and it was. There must be spies everywhere. People grouped around their wireless sets throughout the country awaited Churchill's speech, the large veneered box set altar-like at the centre of many a living-room.

At Moyles Court, however, the young airmen continued to enjoy the evening warmth out of doors as though the speech were nothing to do with them. The returning flight was now circling the airfield before descending. Through the open windows of the stand-by room came the symbolic notes of Big Ben. They took a minute to strike nine o'clock and there were many who devoted that special minute for saying their daily wartime prayer. As the sounds drifted out into the open some of the airmen stood casually and began to wander towards the windows. Millie heard them laughing and smiled at their banter. Three of them began to sing, inconsequentially and softly:

> 'Roll me over,
> In the clover.
> Roll me over, lay me down and
> Do it again.'

They stopped singing and stood dutifully by the open window while the BBC announcer said in his important voice: 'The Prime Minister, the Right Honourable Winston Churchill.'

The first of the Hurricanes came into the runway, flattening out over the darkening pine trees and hovering before landing with an airy curtsy. The other four planes circled like evening crows. Then the station klaxon, the alarm signal, blared across the dim air. Millie's hand went to her mouth and the airmen turned from the open windows and went back to the grass verge where the others now began to stand soundlessly, as if some hidden anthem were being played. She found herself going forward, timidly, almost with a feeling that she might be intruding. 'His undercart's gone,' she heard one of the men say. 'Stand by for some sparks.' The klaxon had ceased and the blue-grey fire engines jolted from their sheds and ran to the side of the runway. A growing sense of anxiety fell across the watchers. They had fallen to an almost religious silence. The only voice to be heard was that of Churchill: 'The great air battle which has been in progress over this island for the past few weeks has recently attained a high intensity . . .' It issued eerily from the open window as one by one the Hurricanes, now little more than silhouettes in the dusk, approached and touched down, taxiing away to the grass verge. Once landed, the pilots climbed out on to the wings or remained in their cockpits, waiting and watching for the last plane. It circled, droning sadly, two hundred feet up. No landing wheels were visible below it. It looked like a legless duck.

'It's Chubby,' Millie heard one of the men say. 'He'll be all right. He's got luck.'

'Chubby?' she asked the young man, touching him on the sleeve with quick concern. 'Which one is that?'

'Him,' responded the airman a little stupidly. 'Up there. Can't get his undercart down . . .'

The youth's companion realized what she had

meant. 'Smith,' he answered. 'It's Graham Smith. He's called Chubby.'

Her body went cold. She said nothing but stood with her eyes on the ground when everyone else was gazing at the sky. Quickly she prayed. Please God, make him get down safely.

'He's trying to lose fuel,' said one of the young men.

'He didn't have much to start with,' said another dropping down on the grass without taking his eyes off the plane. 'He's windy, I expect.'

Millie realized what he meant. That the pilot was *frightened* of coming down; somehow trying to put off the telling moment when he would *have* to do it. The Hurricane droned complainingly as it turned over the ashy light of the field again. From the open window the loud bulldog words of Winston Churchill came across the grass. 'The gratitude of every home in our island, in our Empire, and indeed throughout the world, except in the abodes of the guilty, goes out to the British airmen . . .'

'Shut that row off!' demanded a boy's voice. But no one moved. Their attention remained on the Hurricane.

'He's going to have a go now,' said one of the pilots. 'The old man's talking him down.' Millie looked towards the control tower. 'Come on, Chubby, you can make it,' the pilot said. His companion called shrilly: 'Give Chubby a cheer! Come on, a cheer! Hip-hip . . .'

'Hooray!' they all shouted at once, some waving their flying helmets and gloves in the air. And twice more: 'Hip-hip-hooray.' Then deep silence.

Churchill's voice resounded over them. A young

airman turned, anguished and affronted. 'Shut up!' he shouted at the radio. 'Shut up, will you!' Savagely he rushed towards the window and pulled the wire and the plug from the set.

The fighter made its final turn above the trees and came in on a low path. Every face watched it. Millie could feel the fearful tears choking her eyes. She stared with the others. As soon as the bare underbelly struck the ground a fire began, streaming out like a red, yellow and black flag. She cried out and turned away. Cries went up from the young airmen.

'Oh fucking hell!'

'Oh, what a bastard!'

The plane skidded madly along the runway, slewing first one way, then another, streamers of fire coming from its engine and its wings. Almost opposite the assembled men it made a final slurry and whirled like a roundabout. All the nose was aflame. Ammunition began to explode, small bright bangs, like fireworks. The group on the grass bent their heads. Millie saw that the figure in the cockpit was moving, almost casually it seemed, in the oily smoke. The sliding roof was pushed back and the pilot attempted to rise.

Along the verge ran the fire engines, shuddering to a stop, their crews paying out hoses towards the plane and within moments covering it with foam, huge blobs like a giant's shaving soap. A tongue of fire licked through. Ammunition crackled. Two of the helmeted firemen had reached the side of the aircraft and were clambering on to the wings. They trudged through the white foam and the red flames, pulling down the swaying figure of the pilot, falling with him to the ground where they struggled like three fighting snowmen. The ambulance crew ran forward and disentangled them, rolling the young airman sideways until he was clear of the plane. They laid him out on a stretcher. Then he began to scream.

Millie, hardly able to see through her sobs, ran forward with some of the others. Graham had stopped crying out when they arrived and shouted wildly: 'Not bad, boys! Not too bad!' He did not see her.

She saw how terribly burned he was. His hair was gone and his face was meat-raw. One eye had vanished. They ran away with him and left the woman and stunned pilots standing impotently. Millie turned back towards her library room, still crying deeply into her shaking hands.

The young men turned slowly, and, in an aimless way, began to drift back towards the buildings. Hardly seeming to know what he was doing, the youth who had pulled the plug from the wireless set put it back. They had missed Churchill's speech. An announcer promised that the variety programme 'Garrison Theatre' was to follow shortly.

Millie went back to Binford that evening and, cycling from the station, went first to Robert and Elizabeth's house. Robert was enthusing over Churchill's speech. 'They've just quoted some of it on the news,' he said. 'I wrote it down. Listen . . . this is about the RAF boys: "Never in the field of human conflict has so much been owed by so many to so few." Isn't that grand. Did they have it on at Moyles Court?'

Millie was still trembling. Elizabeth had given her a cup of tea and the china rattled in her hands. 'No,' she answered. 'Something happened and they switched it off.'

Twenty-one

It was not until the first days of September that the Germans turned their attention from the airfields of southern and eastern England and sent the bombers by night and day to London. Berlin had been bombed by the Royal Air Force and revenge was required, revenge that was to cost the Germans dear, for they had fallen for a ploy. If their attacks on the fighter fields had continued even briefly they would have broken the British air resistance. Instead they fell for the bait and sent their bombers to attack civilian London, giving a respite to the aerodromes. To encourage these reverse attacks the RAF continued to bomb Berlin. Sometimes the British Wellington, Whitley and Hampden bombers crossed the Channel while the Dorniers and Heinkels were flying in the other direction.

The first anniversary of the outbreak of the war, 3 September, was marked by a preliminary raid on London. The weather had continued bland into the autumn and the leaves in London were changing colour early because of the long and dry summer. Early on that evening James and Joanne walked to the Queen's Hall for an anniversary concert given by the London Philharmonic Orchestra. It was an evening of patriotism and nostalgia. Chopin's military polonaise was played by Moura Lympany, who was also the soloist in the defiant piano concerto by Edward Grieg. As the moving music of Elgar's Pomp and Circumstance filled the great drum of the hall, so notes of the air-raid sirens filtered over London in the dusk.

Joanne would be leaving the following morning, taking John Colin with her. They had sat close in the crowded auditorium, their shoulders touching, and had given themselves to the moment. Then there sounded the rumbling of guns, distant but distinct, underscoring the music.

Joanne, once, pressed her cheek into his sleeve and he moved his head so that his face touched hers. Afterwards they walked through the empty streets in silence, their hands together, until an air-raid warden appeared like a comic actor as they rounded a vacant corner. He was the same man who had once before approached them in the same street. There was no apparent recognition.

''Evening, sir, madam,' he began like a doorman, his hand going to his helmet in a vestige of a salute. 'There's an alert on, you know, sir.'

'Yes, yes,' said James.

The man pursed his lips. 'They've started on us, I reckon.' He appeared inclined to conversation. 'The blighters are after London,' he continued. 'South London's getting it now, so I got a report. Croydon. Bombed the airport, I understand.'

'Yes,' agreed James impatiently. 'I thought it might be in that direction.'

'I haven't got over the first lot, yet, sir,' added the man with doleful belligerence. 'Went right through it, fourteen to eighteen. Gassed in nineteen-seventeen, 22 April, at seven in the morning. Badly gassed.'

Joanne said: 'That's really terrible. And now you're in another war.'

He stared at her accent. 'Yes, miss. Maybe your country will be coming in to help us soon. Don't want to leave it to the end, like the last time, do you?'

James said: 'I'm sure they won't. We must be off now. We really ought to be under cover.'

'Exactly, sir, exactly,' agreed the warden ponderously saluting again. James returned the salute which pleased the man immensely. His smile dropped, however, when they had walked on. 'It's all right for some,' he grumbled. 'It always is.'

This was their final time together and a feeling of deep sadness and reality surrounded them as they sat in the apartment. James poured the ritual drinks and Joanne went to the gramophone and again put on the record of 'Above the Stars'. The rumblings of the raid on south London sounded distinctly into the room.

'You're not afraid?' he said knowing what the answer would be. 'Of the bombing?'

'I'm afraid of a lot of things,' she replied rising, 'but not of the bombing. Not right now. Is it okay if we watch?'

He smiled seriously and walked towards the heavy curtains but she forestalled him with a hand on his sleeve. 'I'll do it,' she said. 'It appeals to my sense of the dramatic. Just sit. Be the audience.'

He leaned back on the deep settee. She went to each lamp in the room and extinguished it so that they were engulfed in the darkness. The music swelled around them in the void. She moved to the window and easing the cords of the velvet drapes pulled them apart, opening out a wide and amazing vista of distant London under attack.

Flashes lit the horizon, guns trembled and search-lights patterned the roof of the sky. Across the immediate housetops there played a low flickering like that of a gas burner; distant buildings on fire. The explosions were muted and they could hear no planes. All around them was dark and calm, Abt's German music accentuating the remote performance.

'You could almost say it is beautiful,' she said eventually returning and sitting beside him on the couch.

He was conscious of her lovely smell in the dimness. 'I don't know what I shall do without you,' he said.

She leaned against him and he could feel her trembling. 'Or me without you,' she whispered. 'I guess we'll have to learn.'

From one edge of the window to the other the show of lights continued. Twice at its centre there was an eruption, a boiling of pink fire.

'I think it's well that you'll be away from this,' he said. 'Very soon all London will be like it. Fire every-where. We are just sitting waiting.'

She shrugged and stood up, her slender shadow outlined against the window. 'That is not something that would upset me,' she said. 'Somehow I feel it would never touch me. America is certainly going to seem very dull and unreal now. But they won't hear of my staying here. They'll fire me first, so my editor says.' She paused and, still with her back to him, she added: 'And there are other things.'

There was no future for them. James had a

momentary picture of Millie asleep in the deep country. The recording had finished and, thoughtfully, Joanne moved the arm of the gramophone back to the edge and it began to play again. Turning towards him she held out her hand and they walked together into the bedroom. Immediately she pulled away the curtains there so that the same remote drama was opened to them.

'This time,' she said standing beside the bed that had become so familiar to them, 'this last time, I would be glad if you would undress me. I want to stand still, just like this, looking out of the window. I would like you to take my clothes off. Will you do that, please?'

He stood close to her and enfolded her body in his arms, his head dropping haplessly against her luxurious hair. Her sensation filled him. His desire for her brimmed over with regret. They kissed and then he began to take her clothes away. She opened his shirt and rubbed her hands on his chest and then laid her face against it. He could feel each tear as it ran down his skin.

When they were both naked they lay back together on the silk counterpane, faintly luminous in the light of night and the far illuminations. They kissed each other's bodies and then, saying nothing, moved together for the final moments of their time together.

As they lay afterwards, cooling against each other, they could hear the needle of the gramophone bobbing with its patient monotony, for 'Above the Stars' was finished. She left the bed and went into the other room to switch it off, then came back and slid against him. They turned together and looked out of the window from the bed. The guns and the bombing had ceased, although the searchlights still fingered the sky and at the base of the stage there were still low footlights of fire. But the raiders had gone for that night.

'It's finished,' said James.

'Yes,' she said. 'It has.'

Sunday sunlight and the tinny sound of a band filled the single street of Binford. That first Sunday of September, one week before the day Hitler had appointed for his invasion of the British, the Home Guard, the coastguard, the fire brigade, the air-raid wardens, the newly appointed Binford ambulance, the Women's Voluntary Service, the veterans of the British Legion and the boys and girls of the scouts, guides, brownies and cubs, paraded below the hamlet trees, on their way to the church. Throughout the country it had been ordained as a day of prayer, a plea to God for deliverance and for a just victory.

The procession was a little ragged. Ben Bennett's New Forest Arcadians had been hastily and not unsuccessfully transformed into a marching band because the Lyndhurst Salvation Army, the Lymington town band and others were needed for their own church parades, and their services were jealously guarded. Henry Bunigan had offered his efforts with his barrel organ mounted on a wheelbarrow, but Robert, the other members of the parish council and the vicar had decided that this was scarcely in keeping with the proper solemnity of the occasion. Bennett's Arcadians, under Mrs Bennett, her knees marching like vertical pistons, her teeth bared, had, at least, semi-military uniforms, and knew some marches.

The parade went twice around the village, going both up and down the main street, before arriving at the sloping green outside the church. There were few people to witness its modest grandeur, since the inhabitants were either marching in the procession itself or already congregated in the packed church listening for the approaching music through the open sunlit door.

Josh Millington and his wife, however, did stand at the trampled fence before the burned-out house and witnessed the straggling line go by. He had returned to water his melons. The British Legion flag borne by a shiningly medalled veteran, and the Union Jack, carried by a rotund and scarlet-faced boy scout, were dipped in respect. The old pair were unsurprised, having lived in Binford through their lives, to find that there were two odd men out in the procession. Henry Bunigan and his barrel organ ground along behind the ragged lines, the instrument mounted on a wheelbarrow bravely pushed by young Tommy Oakes, in his rebel cub uniform. The boy sweated and the old man hobbled and turned the handle. The sounds of bygone Vienna rolled metallically from the trembling box, causing the few marchers actually in step to lose their rhythm and to turn accusingly towards the outlawed pair behind. Henry waved them on with a defiant hand. 'It's our parade too, you know!' he bellowed over the top of his own cacophony. 'We're allowed to say a bloody prayer like everybody else.' Tommy Oakes put down the barrow momentarily and inserting his fingers in his mouth performed a shrieking whistle of approval. Then he picked up the handles and the strange backmarkers continued after the procession.

Major-General Sound was on the raised triangle of grass outside the church to take the salute. The very act of briskly raising his flattened hand to his cap made him puff out his cheeks. His tight tunic was drawn up like a bag on a string, but at his belt was his service revolver bulging in its chestnut holster. He had borrowed it back for the morning.

Robert stood stiffly, properly, but slightly to the rear of the major-general, the members of his family arranged on the small green hillock behind him. James and Harry were both home for the one day, something which pleased him immensely, both sons stiff in their uniforms below the wide shade of the horse chestnuts.

Elizabeth stood, a trifle self-consciously, at attention beside her husband. She had adopted a less military attitude with her shoes a little apart and her hat at a minor angle, but a sharp army glance from Robert had altered that. Behind her Millie stood with the two sons, with the members of the parish council on one flank and the white boys of the church choir with the vicar on the other.

A Sunday breeze fingered through the already yellowing leaves of the horse chestnuts. The spiky green nuts were thickening and the eyes of the choirboys were on them, for they would soon fall and split into the fat polished conkers and the traditional season would start. Harry glanced up to the sun leafing through the lemon foliage. As he looked down he caught the eye of Millie. They both looked away.

516

Mrs Ben Bennett, extravagantly waving her dance-band baton, since she had no marching cane, now brought the New Forest Arcadians wheeling along in front of the church. They had performed creditably, although the drummer, bereft of his full kit, had beaten a doleful pavan on a single side-drum through-out the march. The ragged procession, the Home Guard with their bristling and ancient American carbines, the ARP wardens, the coastguard, the firemen, the green tweed ladies of the Women's Voluntary Service, and the uniformed children curled in a haphazard crocodile before the saluting major-general. The children stared at him with frank interest, colliding with each other as they did so. Elizabeth realized quietly that this pathetic little piece of patriotism, this hapless show, was the reason that England would survive in the face of power and tyranny.

Her thoughts were interrupted by the rearguard of the procession, a rearguard lagging by more than two hundred yards. The man with the limp and the barrel organ and the lone wolf-cub turned the cottage corner to the church green, the boy stumbling along with the wheelbarrow and the defiant man cranking it hideously. Everyone watched their approach. The Reverend Clifford Pemberton closed his eyes to shut out the sight and hoped that those about might think he was deep in a private preliminary prayer. Bunigan and the boy stopped their march and their music and stood at the tail of the halted procession. 'Everybody's 'ere now,' called the organ man rudely and to no one in particular. 'You can carry on with it now.'

Pemberton had inside doubts about the validity of a

national day of prayer at all. Why were they praying? That their enemies might perish? That Adolf Hitler might be struck by lightning or a plague? Christians were supposed to love their enemies, to pray for sinners, though their sins be at least crimson. They were *supposed* to, weren't they? He felt that a prayer for the reformation of the Nazis offered up at that moment, however, might not be afforded a universal amen. He opted to compromise. He envied those non-conformist churches with notice boards proclaiming: 'God so loved the world that He gave his Only begotten Son to die for Our Sins.' To which there was an additional line which read: 'According to the Scriptures.' It had always seemed to him to be a let-out in case things were not as they appeared. Now gladly he resorted to the same compromise.

'We will say a prayer here, as we stand,' he announced from the small green hill. 'And then we will file into the church for our service.' The children squeezed their eyes tightly, as children do when praying, half thinking that to take even a peep would be invalidating. 'Lord God,' Pemberton prayed loudly. The barrel organ groaned, but it was only Bunigan leaning on the handle. The vicar continued echoingly: 'As we are gathered here in our village today, our home, the place we love, we ask you to protect us from the power of our enemies. We pray for victory against them, that their tyranny and evil may be vanquished.' He had a fleeting thought that somewhere in Germany another man might be saying something on similar lines. They would be trying to pray down each other! To whom would God, providing He was listening at all, give His right ear? At the end of the exhortation he uttered his compromise. 'If it be Thy will,' he added. No one, at least no one in Binford, noticed.

Flushed with hymn singing, the hoary and likeable incantations of the Church of England, words that had mingled with the million sunlit dust particles and had echoed among the secrets of the church roof, the people of Binford went out into the village noon. Robert was pink with patriotism. He hummed: 'I vow to thee my country,' as he waited, behind the ladies, to shake hands with the vicar at the arched door. He ushered his sons before him, proudly, but also to allow himself time, privately, to reach his favourite line: 'The dearest and the best.'

'Good service,' he grunted amiably to the vicar, whose eyes were still doubtful behind his glasses. 'Fine singing, didn't you think? I wish Hitler could have heard it. It might have shown him we mean business.'

The vicar almost replied that the intention had not been so, but he desisted. 'Lovely harvest weather now,' he said instead. 'Have you ever known such a beautiful summer?'

Robert, slightly taken aback by the change to meteorology, said that he could not remember one. He stood aside, with his family, and watched the other villagers troop out, blinking in the light. A distant jangling told everyone that Bunigan was winding his barrel organ under the chestnuts, Tommy Oakes standing ready to wheel the barrow, the pair having slipped out of the choir door. The metallic tune, the 'Blue Danube Waltz', came not unpleasantly from below the bowing trees.

People were issuing heavily from the church now and standing about talking on the green. Mrs Mainprice and her children shyly shook hands with the vicar, who remembered they were leaving: 'Off to America, are we then?' he enthused. 'Splendid! What a wonderful chance for the youngsters.'

Mary looked embarrassed, unsure, almost ready to cry. She shuffled on and then seeing Elizabeth encouraged her brood towards her. 'I still don't know whether it's right,' she sniffed. 'Really, Mrs Lovatt. Looking around at all the people you know. And we're, well . . . their father said it's a good idea. He seems to think it will make us all rich.'

Mary looked at her pleadingly. 'You think it will be all right? Going across the sea and everything, I mean, Mrs Lovatt. I'm worried it won't be safe.'

Bending forward, Elizabeth kissed her on the cheek. 'I'm sure it will be quite all right,' she said. She added a smile: 'Just don't get seasick, that's all.'

Harry, standing alongside his flushed father, saw Bess come out of the church. He had looked for her during the service but had not been able to see her among all the heads. She appeared from the shade holding her grandmother's arm. 'Better service today,' Mrs Spofforth informed the vicar bluntly. 'Not so much Popery. The Pope is Italian, you know, and you know who's side those swine are on.'

The vicar grimaced tightly and gently urged her on her way. Bess glanced towards Harry and he smiled. They walked the few yards towards each other and their hands touched briefly.

'I'm leaving,' she whispered excitedly before he could speak. 'I'm going back to London. My parents have given in. I'm going to work in Whitehall. My father's got me a job with the Ministry of Aircraft Production.'

Harry said he was glad: 'You and Lord Beaverbrook,' he said. 'The war should soon be won.'

'We shall see,' she replied as if she believed it were possible. She leaned towards him. 'You wouldn't like to look after Merlin, would you?' She saw the puzzlement on his face. 'You know, my horse.'

He could see she meant it. 'Merlin?' he echoed. 'How can I keep a horse? I'm in the navy, not the cavalry.'

'I thought perhaps you could keep it at home. Perhaps your mother might . . .' She saw his expression again. 'No, she wouldn't, would she. She doesn't like me and she wouldn't like Merlin. It's bloody mean, I think.'

'Why not leave him with your grandmother?' he suggested testily. 'The old Dutchman could ride him.'

Bess looked shocked. 'Now who's joking,' she said. 'That old fool spends half his time in bed now. With the bedclothes over his head. He's hiding from the Germans.'

'I can't say I blame him,' said Harry.

'Grandmother's getting shot of him as soon as she can. She's got her eye on two evacuees from Gibraltar. Two brothers about forty. A whole lot of them turned up in Southampton.'

'Evacuees from Gibraltar?'

'That's right. They think the Spanish are going to invade them.'

'And they've come *here*. God, I've heard about jumping from the frying pan into the fire.'

She smiled at him. 'I'll write to you if you like. I've been writing to Paul.'

'Who's Paul?'

'My German pilot. He's in prison camp in Devon. I may go down and see him.'

'Wonderful,' breathed Harry. 'Why don't you take him a cake with a pair of wire cutters in it?'

'Don't be jealous,' said Bess smiling. She looked towards Mrs Spofforth. She faced him again. 'I must go now. I'll see you, dear, sometime. Perhaps at the end of the war or something.'

'I'll look forward to it,' he said.

The family were back at the house, standing in the sitting-room, the garden golden through the french windows, as they had done so many times in the former days; Robert, Elizabeth, James and Millie, and Harry arranged a little apart. Wadsworth lolled in the sun, half in, half out of the room. The English ritual of a drink before Sunday lunch, a meeting time, half an hour to be together even if it were only from habit. Then the air-raid siren sounded, undulating, over the forest, the village and the garden. The basset hound moaned as he always did at the noise. 'Drat it,' frowned Elizabeth: 'It always seems to pick the most awkward moments. The joint is just done to a treat.'

'Then I suggest we eat it,' said Robert jovially. 'It's probably someone being trigger-happy. Half the time Jerry turns out to be heading somewhere else.' Finishing his sherry he put the glass on the familiar table. He looked decisive. 'On the other hand, I think I'll just drop down to the post on the quay, I'll only be a couple of minutes.' He turned speculatively towards James and Harry. 'Want to take a look?' he suggested. 'Give you some idea of what we're doing.'

Millie laughed and touched her father-in-law's shoulder fondly. Elizabeth said: 'Just the opportunity for a bit of showing off,' she said. 'Look out, Hitler – Binford is ready.'

'Not at all. Not at all,' answered Robert but without conviction. 'I thought it might give these professionals some idea of what the rest of us have been up to these last couple of months. Show them we haven't just been sitting on our backsides.'

James grinned and said: 'I'm glad you suggested it. The Prime Minister is always asking me about your state of readiness.'

Robert flushed with pleasure. 'Is he?' he said. 'Is he really?'

'Oh, Robert,' admonished Elizabeth.

James said: 'Actually, he is. He used the Binford unit, or at least my reports on it, as a sort of barometer for the Home Guard of the entire country.' He nodded to his father. 'Come on then, dad, let's see what you've got.'

'It might teach us all something,' said Harry finishing his drink. 'At Portsmouth there seems to be some notion that if you cover the whole place with sandbags then the Germans won't notice you.'

Elizabeth said: 'Well, don't be long, please. And no disappearing into the pub afterwards. It's taken me long enough to get this piece of beef and I don't want it ruined.'

They reached the garden and James, turning, called back to Millie: 'Do you want to come, Millie?'

'No, thanks,' she returned. 'I'll help here. I've seen quite enough of the war lately, thank you.'

The men walked across the bright lawn towards the gate. 'What did she mean by that?' asked James. 'She's seen enough of the war lately.'

His father was climbing into the car. 'Official duties,' he explained tapping the car a little shame-facedly. 'And we can't be late for lunch.' He started the engine. 'She meant,' he said, 'that she had a young pilot burned to a frazzle in front of her eyes the other evening. Right there at her feet. His plane made a crash landing and burst into flames. He survived, apparently, but only just. That's what she meant.'

James pursed his lips. 'She didn't mention it,' he said.

'You should try keeping in touch more,' said his father, his eyes on the lane ahead.

He added nothing to it and James said quietly: 'Yes, I suppose I should. God, that must have been terrible for her.' Harry was silent in the back of the car. They went through the village, past the black stump that had been Josh's cottage.

'Look at that. Poor old Josh,' said Robert. 'It touches everybody, this war. It's not just for soldiers like it used to be. My whole ambition in life is to shoot down one of those blighters.'

Harry said: 'I take it you still only have the rifles.'

'Unfortunately yes,' answered his father. 'There's a promise of a Lewis gun, but it hasn't turned up yet. It's a bit frustrating firing at a bloody Heinkel with a sixty-year-old Yankee carbine, I can tell you. They were probably last used against the Indians.'

He turned the car down on to the stony quay at

Binford Haven and came to a bumpy stop alongside the two small warehouses. Harry took in the scene, as familiar as ever, almost unchanged since they had played down here among the boats and ropes when he was a child. The estuary was almost clear of craft now, it was true. They were drawn up on the hards or cosseted in inlets along the riverbank. But the water shone with the same lovely innocence, the banks were green with trees, the gulls hovered noisily and the air tasted faintly of seaweed. He climbed from the car and breathed it. His father was pointing down towards the end of the jetty that ran out into the river.

'There it is, see it,' he said. At the end of the jetty was a sandbagged emplacement topped by some rounded buttons that were the helmeted heads of the Home Guard. Robert, strutting out, led his sons along the wooden pier, the sound of their feet echoing in the silent Sunday air. 'We worked out that it's not uncommon for Jerry to come up the estuary, flying low,' he explained as he puffed. 'They use it as some sort of navigation or to keep their heads down so that the guns can't get at them. I've suggested to higher authority that the army might like to put a field gun of some sort on the bank to let the blighter have it as he comes up the river. You don't need an anti-aircraft gun, a damned anti-tank gun would do the trick.' He turned to James and said wistfully, 'Or one of those nice pom-poms, firing from nil elevation. Since Mr Churchill is interested in our doings, perhaps you might mention that to him the next time you meet for a beer.'

Robert strode on purposefully. 'In the meantime we live in hope that he comes along so low that we can get a pot-shot at him,' he said. 'Some hope.'

They had almost reached the end of the jetty and the sand-bagged emplacement now. 'Halt, who goes there?' called a rural voice.

'Friend,' shouted Robert. The brothers each concealed a grin. 'Commanding officer,' continued Robert. 'With his sons.'

Harry could scarcely contain his smirk, but the old man was completely serious. 'Advance friend . . . sir,' called the sentry uncertainly. His head moved along the parapet of sandbags and he was revealed as Gates, the gamekeeper. 'Nice day, sirs,' he said reverting to his normal working voice.

'Good day for a shoot, eh?' offered James.

'That's what we been 'oping, sir,' said Gates. 'But Jerry ain't shown 'is face yet.' He looked out to sea. 'That's the way he comes,' he announced with the air of a major strategist.

But the German plane came the other way. From the landward side, creeping up on them, the sound of its engines masked by the trees and the rising land. It came in at two hundred feet and dropped a single, neat bomb, released so deliberately and accurately that it might have been dropped by hand.

The aircraft was above them before they knew it, the fluttering shadow of a cross, and then the brief whine and a white explosion on the jetty, blowing the men in all directions.

Harry remembered only that he thought his ears had burst. He rolled over and over, like a tumbler, and sprawled against a pile of tar barrels that had been stacked on the quay for as long as he could remember.

In boyhood they had served as a ship's bridge or a fort. The air was whirling with hot dust, it was choking his throat and filled his eyes when he tried to see what had happened. Like a child sitting up for the first time he managed to get some support from the tar barrels. He pulled himself half upright and began shouting through the debris: 'Dad! Dad! For Christ's sake, dad!'

His voice joined other shouts and the screeching of the gulls in the smoke and dust and he gradually began to discern crouched figures, like a shadowgraph in slow motion. His legs shook so much beneath him that they failed to support him and he fell into a sitting posture again. He felt warm blood running down his face. His hand went to his forehead and he stared down at his red-smeared palm. 'Bastards,' he moaned. 'Rotten bastards.'

Now he managed to stand again. Staggering forward, his legs bowed, he came to the place where the sandbagged emplacement had been. There was a great gap, like a mouthful taken out of one side, with prostrate forms dangling across the parapet. One man, whom he could not recognize, began an idiotic run past him towards the shore end of the quay. 'Doctor's away, I know!' the man howled from the red hole in his black face. 'Gone to Bournemouth! I'll go for the dentist, Mr Lovatt. He's bound to have some bandages and that.'

Harry, shock still vibrating his body, nodded dumbly at the inanity and the man set off shouting and galloping wildly along the jetty. Stumbling a few more paces Harry saw that half the emplacement had fallen into the harbour. There was a body floating placidly face down on the water. Harry looked wildly about. 'Dad?' he asked quietly. 'Dad?'

'He's here, Harry,' came a voice through the haze. He recognized Stevens, the schoolteacher. His coat and shirt had been ripped away, and his exposed chest was raw. 'I think he'll be all right.' He stared at the grotesque Harry. 'Your brother's on the other side of the sandbags.'

'Oh God,' sobbed Harry. 'Oh God, what's all this? Jesus Christ. Jesus . . . Jesus.' Weeping, he went towards his father.

Robert was lying against some of the displaced sandbags, his eyes wide as if in disbelief. A dead seagull lay across his lap. 'Harry, Harry,' he muttered. 'Are you all right, son?'

'Yes, yes, dad, I'm all right.' He moved the seagull's body. He could see that his father's leg was shattered. Stevens crawled forward with a field dressing and began to apply a tourniquet. 'You'll be all right, dad,' gabbled Harry. 'Won't he?' He turned his minstrel face at Stevens.

'I should think so,' said Stevens. His voice was calm but his face was wet and trembling. 'Go and see your brother.'

'Oh . . . right. James.' Harry said it as if he could hardly recall the name. People were running with stretchers along the jetty, coming through the clearing haze, shouting to others behind. Harry hardly glanced at the dead forms hung over the sandbags. He slithered forward on his stomach. Everywhere smelled of cooking. He had an idiotic thought that his mother would be waiting for them with the Sunday joint. Oh, Christ . . . there was James.

His brother was lying on his back, his face thick with dust, his eyes staring through the coating and up accusingly into the Sunday sky. Harry choked. He heard a weak cawing sound coming from his own throat. At that moment two men with a stretcher appeared. Then two more with another. 'Get yourself on to that,' ordered one as they put down the stretcher. 'You're in no fit state to be walking around.' Then he saw James. 'Oh, blimey, look at him,' he said sadly.

They carried them to an ambulance waiting on the quay, another had just arrived. People had come from the houses and were arriving from Binford. Children watched in astonishment. Only the voices of the ambulance men could be heard, although, for a moment, above the silence came the sound of a woman jabbering the Lord's Prayer.

As they bore him on the stretcher Harry looked about him wildly. The shocked eyes stared back. They put him into the ambulance on the opposite side to his father. They carried the third stretcher in and put it on the rack above. Harry knew it was his brother. Then the outside scene was shut away by the closing of the doors. The ambulance turned and jolted along the quay. There was that cooking smell again. A grey-faced civil defence man stood in the back between the stretchers trying not to retch. Harry heard his father begin to sing:

'Rose of England . . .'

The voice rose trembling from below:

'Thou shalt fade not here . . .'

Another coughing pause. 'Dad, dad,' Harry pleaded from his stretcher.

'Come on, Harry,' urged Robert Lovatt. 'Come on lad, sing. And you, James. You can sing. You used to be a good singer. Come on, boys . . .'

> 'Though the sound of battle
> Thunders near . . .'

Harry, tears mingling with the blood on his face, croaked along with the song:

> 'Red shall thy petals be,
> As rich wine untold
> Shed by thy warriors
> Who served thee of old.'

'James,' called his father upwards. 'Come on, James, sing up. You're not trying.'

Twenty-two

By the second week of September London was under heavy air attack through every night and often by day. The acrid smell of the destruction through the hours of darkness mingled with the autumn mists as the people came blinking from the shelters and went to their work and about the other tasks of their day. Life went on in a strangely nonchalant manner. There were queues for the early afternoon cinemas while firemen were still sending water into gutted buildings in Leicester Square. During the deadly month a long-forecast river bus service began on the Thames, its first passengers cruising serenely between the smoking banks of the city.

Philip Benson thought how strange it all was. He picked his way between streets piled with rubble and charred office furniture to find a taxi to Belgravia. And yet perhaps not so strange. The human spirit was entirely adaptable and resilient.

'Caught a packet down here last night, sir,' said the cab driver conversationally. 'Can't get through half the streets. We been lucky so far where I live, but my kids get upset because we 'aven't got any bombs like they've 'ad on Tottenham. It's got to be a bit of a snobbery if you know what I mean, sir.'

Benson went to the house in the crescent and rang

the shining brass bell. The buildings there were intact, curved and uncannily calm in the quiet of the autumn day. The neat, white face of Mrs Beauchamp opened the polished door.

He said kindly, 'I'm Philip Benson. We spoke on the telephone.'

'Yes, sir,' she said. 'Please come in.'

He walked into the tidy room that James had known. 'I hope that you weren't troubled too much,' he said. 'When they came and took Major Lovatt's belongings.'

'No, sir, it was no trouble.' He could see she was restraining herself and she bravely did not cry. 'What a dreadful thing, sir. A good man like that.'

'Yes, he was indeed,' said Benson. 'I've known the family all my life.' He paused. 'Have you had any news of the little boy who went to America?'

Her face cleared. 'Oh yes. John Colin. I had a very nice letter from Miss Schorner, the American lady, only yesterday.' She reached out and picked up a letter from the sideboard. 'He's having a lovely time. And he loved the aeroplane.' She added wistfully, 'Fancy a little tot like that going on an aeroplane. I was worried to death.'

There was something else she wanted to say. He waited and she opened a drawer. 'I'm glad you've come, sir, because I didn't quite know what to do about this. It came yesterday too.' Still hesitant she handed another letter to him. 'Air mail,' she said. 'For Major Lovatt.'

He glanced at the stamps and the Washington postmark. 'Yes, of course. Thank you. I'll be able to take care of this.'

'Good, that's very kind of you,' said Mrs Beauchamp. 'It's a load off my mind. I didn't know what to do . . . I suppose Miss Schorner has been told . . .'

He patted her hand. 'Yes, she has. I attended to that. I must go now. Thank you for all you've done, Mrs Beauchamp.'

She said: 'There was a postcard for Major Lovatt too.' She handed him a black and white picture postcard. It was of the promenade at Douglas, Isle of Man.

Benson thanked her and handed her a visiting card. 'Please telephone me at this number if you have anything that worries you. I shall be in touch with Miss Schorner. I'm sure she will let you know how John Colin is getting on.'

He left her and imagined her sad forehead touching the polished woodwork on the door on the other side as she closed it on him.

He walked along the crescent under the trees. The pub on the corner was open and he went into the saloon bar. Half the room was debris, the ceiling hanging like a white tongue, the walls crumbled. The landlord was polishing glasses. 'Sit yourself down over there, sir,' he invited. 'A nice seat away from the shambles. You're just in time. I was just about to close.' He looked around jovially. 'That's if it's possible to close this place.'

Benson ordered a Scotch and soda. He sat down on the proffered seat. 'When did it happen?' he asked. He did not know whether he should open the letter or simply destroy it. He decided to open it.

'Two nights ago,' said the landlord eyeing the

wreckage. 'Had a full house last night. People came to have a look at the damage. Never had so many in on a Monday.'

The man went to the room behind and Benson, still not completely certain, opened the letter. It read:

Darling James,

We are here! The trip was marvellous. Not a bump all the way. John Colin enjoyed it and he tells me he is really impressed with the US of A!!!

Now I must tell you the thing I could not tell you before. I am to be married on 29 September – next week – here in Washington. It is one of those long-standing engagements. I know I will always love you.

Joanne

He looked at the picture postcard. It said: 'It is good here in the Isle of Man. Thank you kindly. M. Bormann.'

He finished his Scotch. Joanne knew by now. His cable would have reached her. 'Thank you,' he called to the landlord, who appeared still wiping glasses and returned: 'Thank you, sir. Good afternoon.'

A taxi came by and Benson hailed it. He was going to the House of Commons. He left the cab there and walked past Parliament to the centre of Westminster Bridge. Smoke was still drifting up-river from the previous night's fires in the City. St Paul's stood out bravely against the dun sky. Taking the letter and the postcard from his pocket he tore them into small pieces, let them flutter over the bridge and drift down to the flowing Thames.

The war had given ordinary people amazing experiences. Elizabeth could hardly believe that in the first week of October Mary Mainprice was back, dusting around the house as she always had done. She and her three children had been torpedoed in the ocean and had watched the liner *City of Benares* sink from their seats in a lifeboat. They were back in Liverpool two days later, picked up by a Royal Navy destroyer, and a taxi driver, who had refused to charge a fare, had driven them all the way from the northern seaport to their cottage in the New Forest.

Elizabeth left the house for the village. There had been a shower and the trees dripped. Robert, grumbling about his inactivity in hospital, was promised to be home at the end of the week. There were plenty of commanders, he had insisted, who had overcome the loss of a leg. It was nothing in the long run.

Harry had not been home since James's funeral and had since been posted to Rosyth in Scotland, so they would not see so much of him. Millie was still working at the RAF station, every day now. Graham Smith had died. Without telling anyone in Binford, she went to his funeral the day after her husband's.

Binford was not further directly troubled by the war, although a random raider machine-gunned a solitary fisherman who sat under an umbrella up-river from the village. No one knew until the body and the umbrella floated down the estuary. The umbrella was camouflaged and P C Brice was of the opinion that the German pilot might have thought it was a military target. They found the man's creel containing several fine trout. His widow said she did not want them (she said she had eaten all the fish she could ever want) and they were shared between PC Brice and the ambulance men who recovered the body.

Hob Hobson was sweeping the front pavement of damp leaves when Elizabeth arrived at the shop. She saw something odd and walked a few paces along the pavement beyond the window. A large, round emergency water tank had been erected on the green by the Lymington Fire Brigade, much to the surprise and satisfaction of the local ducks. Tommy Oakes, in his cub's uniform, stave held out like the rifle of a sentry, was standing guard over the water tank while the white and brown ducks cruised serenely.

Josh Millington, appearing behind his fence, a tarpaulin draped over what had once been his roof, called a greeting to her. 'Look at that boy,' interrupted Hob Hobson, who had peeped around the corner to see what had interested her. 'That Oakes boy. Been there all the morning. Says he's waiting for the Germans. And he's not really in the wolf-cubs even.'

Elizabeth waved to Josh. He called back: 'Looks like the weather's on the turn now, Mrs Lovatt.' He sniffed the air. 'Still, it's been a beautiful summer, 'asn't it.'

Bibliography

Although *The Dearest and The Best* is a work of fiction, many of the events therein are, of course, based on true happenings in the summer of 1940. I would like to thank all those who have helped me with their memories of that period and also to acknowledge the following books and journals:

Sir Winston Churchill, *The Second World War, Vol. 2: Their Finest Hour*
Angus Calder, *The People's War, Britain 1939–1945*
Norman Longmate, *How We Lived Then*
Margery Allingham, *The Oaken Heart*
E. M. Delafield, *The Provincial Lady in War Time*
Peter Fleming, *Operation Sea Lion*
Tom Harrisson, *Living Through The Blitz*
Roger Parkinson, *Encyclopaedia of Modern War*
E. S. Turner, *The Phoney War – On the Home Front*
James Wedgwood Drawbell, *The Long Year*
Frederick Grossmith, *Dunkirk – A Miracle of Deliverance*
Richard Collier, *1940 The World in Flames*
Robert Goralski, *World War II Almanac 1931–1945*
Chester Wilmot, *The Struggle for Europe*
Laurence Thomson, *1940 Year of Legend, Year of History*
Gordon Beckles, *Dunkirk and After*
A. G. Street, *From Dusk Till Dawn*

Sir John Hammerton (ed.), *War Illustrated, September 1939–October 1940*

Leslie Thomas
Somerton
Somerset
December 1983